Michael Finlayson was born into a Glasgow working-class family. Leaving school aged fifteen, he secured an apprenticeship at British Rail as a mechanical fitter. He moved to Nottingham, followed by Merseyside, pursuing various self-employed roles in the motor industry, road haulage, and finally joinery manufacture. A brief spell in aircraft engineering added to his diversification.

His interests are railways and photography. He has had published articles in various railway magazines over the years.

To my late wife, Laura, who supported me throughout; also Vicky, who continues to do so.

Michael Finlayson

REICHSBURGER RESURGENCE

AUSTIN MACAULEY PUBLISHERS™

LONDON * CAMBRIDGE * NEW YORK * SHARJAH

Copyright © Michael Finlayson 2024

The right of Michael Finlayson to be identified as author of this work has been asserted by the author in accordance with sections 77 and 78 of the Copyright, Designs and Patents Act 1988.

All rights reserved. No part of this publication may be reproduced, stored in a retrieval system, or transmitted in any form or by any means, electronic, mechanical, photocopying, recording, or otherwise, without the prior permission of the publishers.

Any person who commits any unauthorised act in relation to this publication may be liable to criminal prosecution and civil claims for damages.

This is a work of fiction. Names, characters, businesses, places, events, locales, and incidents are either the products of the author's imagination or used in a fictitious manner. Any resemblance to actual persons, living or dead, or actual events is purely coincidental.

A CIP catalogue record for this title is available from the British Library.

ISBN 9781035827510 (Paperback)
ISBN 9781035827534 (ePub e-book)
ISBN 9781035827527 (Audiobook)

www.austinmacauley.co.uk

First Published 2024
Austin Macauley Publishers Ltd®
1 Canada Square
Canary Wharf
London
E14 5AA

Chapter One

Friday, 30 September 2022, was a day Robert John Cameron would never forget, for quite innocently he was drawn into events which served to change his whole life; the sequence of these events commenced the previous weekend, which neither he nor most of the population had any knowledge of. From 17.00 hours on this day, he could not have envisaged the series of events he was about to encounter.

It all began when he closed the factory gates of the old family business for the final time. A few hours earlier, he had summoned the remnants of his staff to attend a meeting in the works canteen, although the employees were already aware of the company operating under the control of the Official Receiver, they were optimistic about the survival of the firm; however, the assemblage were not fully prepared for what was to come.

Robert John Cameron, to most people who knew him, presented under normal circumstances an imposing figure, still in his early thirties and standing over 6ft 3in tall, fairly handsome some would say with a well-toned physique, a neat and business like hairstyle adorned his full head of dark brown hair, which showed the odd trace of red in places confirming his Celtic heritage.

He combined his natural good looks with an impeccable dress sense, he was overall, a man of good nature and attitude who was respected by most who knew him. However, the sad and forlorn looking figure of Robert Cameron standing on a makeshift rostrum hastily assembled from canteen tables draped in green baize, in front of him a podium which had previously been solely for use of the union works convenor. Robert stood, shoulders crouched and looking downward to avert his eyes from the gathering.

Staring at the announcement, he was disconcerted at the thought of what needed to be said and worse still, the fact he had the unpleasant task of uttering the statement readily prepared on the papers in front of him. Robert was flanked immediately to his right by the works manager, Pat McConachie aged 55 who had been with the company since leaving school in 1970 and had worked up to this position due to his dedication to the firm, next to him works convenor, James Morton 58, again joined the firm from school as an apprentice at 15 years old, he had worked up to being the union representative of 30 years with the firm.

To his immediate left personnel manager, Brian Nelson 42, was a recent replacement and had only been with the company around 5 years, next to him Marian Evans, Robert's personal secretary; Marion 58, was due for retirement in two years and was the longest serving staff member on the podium and had been Robert Cameron Senior's secretary prior to his health issues, which forced his son to fill the role of CEO.

All the above were seated as Robert summoned up the courage to commence proceedings and nodded to Pat who rose from his seat and called the meeting to order, the general chatter of the workforce quickly drew to an eerie silence. 'Ladies and gentlemen, I give you Mr Robert Cameron,' announced Pat McConachie.

'Thank you, ladies and gentlemen, colleagues and friends.'

Robert hesitated momentarily then raised his head slightly and continued. 'I am afraid I have the unpleasant task of announcing that following the Official Receiver's efforts to find a solution to the firm's financial situation and several attempts to gain new business, we have been unsuccessful to date.'

Robert gripped the sides of the rostrum so tightly that the whites of his knuckles could plainly be seen, he began to perspire, his voice now trembling slightly, he continued.

'The Official Receiver has informed me of his intention to close the company at five o'clock this evening.'

The assembled workforce gasped with shock, cries of bewilderment, disgust and outrage bellowed out amongst other more expletive comments from all corners of the room. Pat stood up and called the meeting to order once again. Robert composed himself as best he could whilst the noise subsided, his voice quivering, he continued.

'I very much regret the Receiver's ultimatum issued today.' Another short hesitation followed before he continued.

'My management team and I together with your continued support have endeavoured to the best of our ability to prevent this disastrous situation, which I'm sure you're all already aware of; however, the announcement by the government in line with the proposed carbon neutral policy has driven the last nail into the coffin.

'Mining in the UK has now become a dirty word as the handful of mines remaining are also hanging on by a thread as coal fired power stations and the like are being decommissioned and either mothballed or demolished with haste. There is currently little or no demand for our specialist field of mining engineering and therefore, our position within this once vibrant industry is no longer viable.'

Once again, he hesitated, taking a handkerchief from his jacket pocket, he wiped his brow and continued.

'Words cannot describe how saddened I am, we have all tried every avenue to avert this closure, I have personally pleaded with the environment minister, highlighting the soaring energy costs recently imposed as a direct result of the invasion of Ukraine that this dependence on external supplies and renewables is far from ideal.'

'I have shown the department figures proving the move to from coal to biomass fuel increases our carbon footprint once the costs of transportation, re-planting and nurturing forests for decades is factored in, all I'm sorry to say was in vain. Coal is to be removed from the UK's power generation schemes as soon as is practically possible.'

He continued after a sip of water.

'I personally feel this decision will be a momentous folly for which all of us, by that I mean the whole country, will suffer the consequences.'

The room gave a rousing round of applause. Robert continued.

'Words cannot describe how saddened I am, saddened knowing the obvious consequences this decision will have on each and every one of you and your families, I can only sympathise with you and wish you good luck for the future, whatever it may hold.'

'For myself, I am the last of four generations of Cameron's placed in control of the family firm by my father some twelve years ago due to his ailing health with aspirations of continued growth and success for the company, I have failed him and I am sorry to say I have failed you,' said Robert remorsefully.

The assembly challenged in disagreement and following a few comments directed mainly at the government, the assembled workforce applauded Robert and sang, "For he's a jolly good fellow"! Robert Cameron was regarded as an extremely fair employer whom the employees knew had worked incessantly to rescue the firm.

James Morton, the works convenor rose and beckoned Robert to sit down, he could see he was emotionally drained as traces of tears were visible running down his cheeks, which he had tried in vain to combat. Marian Evans rose from her seat and asked Pat McConachie to take over.

She took Robert by the left arm and ushered him off the podium to prevent the assembly noting his woebegone appearance, she asked him to walk with her to the office and join her in a strong cup of coffee, he agreed and they walked together slowly along the corridor, Marian still guiding him by the arm.

Fortunately, only a few people noticed Robert's departure as they were too engrossed talking between themselves. Pat took the opportunity to instruct Brian Nelson to continue the meeting. Brian took to the rostrum and began detailing the redundancy packages and answering any questions posed by the anxious staff, he then concluded the meeting in Robert's absence.

"Robert Cameron and Sons. Specialist Mining Equipment Engineers Limited". Originally founded over one hundred years ago by Robert's great, great grandfather and throughout the family history, the first son had been christened Robert. Originally a Scottish based concern, however the firm was relocated in the Bristol area early in the 20th century to compete favourably with the vast number of collieries in the Midlands and South Wales opening at the time.

The company had been remarkably successful until the mid-1970s when the long National Coal Board strikes forced a scaling down of operations. This situation had detrimental effects on Robert's father who had taken control of the company as CEO following his father's death.

Robert Senior was 52 years old at the time and his son and heir had reached the tender age of seven years old. Sadly, Robert Senior took seriously ill and could no longer continue, therefore by 2015 Robert, then aged only 25 succeeded his father as CEO and tasked with rebuilding the company, which had been suffering from recessions and downturn of business in general.

Sadly, the company never really recovered from the problems going back to the 1970s and the workforce had depleted from several hundred in the early 20th century to a mere 60 currently, even attempts at diversification failed to produce meaningful results.

Only several fruitful export orders had served to keep the company afloat over the past five or so years as the zero-carbon emissions ruling took effect year on year. Now sadly, time had run out for "Robert Cameron and Sons. Specialist Mining Equipment Engineers Limited".

Pat McConachie dismissed the workforce early, announcing there was to be a farewell party, more of a wake really, to be held in what had long been regarded as the works local public house "The Ship Inn" and that all were welcome. However, most of the group were despondent at the news and reneged the offer, the couple of dozen or so who attended were provided with a buffet and all drinks were courtesy of Mr Cameron.

The hour of five o'clock was fast approaching; Marian had brought Robert round to almost his normal self. Robert, Marian, Brian and Pat all shook hands and the men exchanged a kiss or two with Marian in the office before heading towards the main gate, the receivers who had wisely kept largely out of sight until now, emerged from one of the other offices and followed discretely behind.

Once all were outside, Robert stood back and viewed the works complex for a few moments in silence then walked forward and locked the gates for the final time. He then hesitantly handed the bunch of keys to one of the receivers, giving him a wry look as he did so, there was no response in way of a gesture from him, only a simple statement.

'Thank you, Mr Cameron. Please attend our office on Tuesday at ten o'clock sharp, goodbye.'

He and his associates then walked away.

Robert and his colleagues headed towards "The Ship Inn". The evening sky, a little dull for the time of year did little to alleviate the depression felt by all of them as they strolled along. On entering the public house, James Morton who had left earlier with the general workforce called out.

'Mr Cameron's here, everyone.'

The overall chatter subsided as he made his way over to the bar, most of the crowd had separated to form small groups around the room, they all rose and again gave a rousing rendition of "for he's a jolly good fellow". Robert was seen to be moved yet again by the sight and sound of the men and women all standing glasses swaying from side to side in the air.

He knew he had been regarded as more than just an employer by many as was his father before him. The singing ended and an exceptionally large malt whisky was presented to him by Pat, in a glass of a most elegant crystal design, which was engraved with:

To Robert

from all at

Cameron's Mining Equipment

Reading the inscription and admiring the exquisite glass, he said, 'Thank you all very much indeed, I shall treasure it always and thank you all for joining me this evening, I'm very sorry the circumstances cannot be—'

He was interrupted by Pat.

'Enough of that speech for one day Robert, we're here to enjoy a final fling together, so sit yourself down and drink up.'

Robert heeded the latter part of Pat's advice, held out his glass and said aloud, 'Cheers everyone.'

Then proceeded to swallow its contents in one. The assembled crowd were delighted and gave a rapturous cheer, he then announced to all in the room that the bar was a free bar, another resounding cheer was heard. The party continued beyond closing time for an hour or so, most of the group had said their farewells to Robert and each other over the last hour and parted company just after midnight, leaving Robert with his closest colleagues to end the night together.

The publican had been lenient in allowing extra time to the group, many of whom he had known for many years, nevertheless he was obliged to call. 'Time gentlemen, please.'

Following exchange of handshakes, embraces and a few kisses, the final farewells were said. Pat was last to leave and whilst giving Robert a long and firm handshake, said, 'Keep in touch boss. Listen, I know how you must be feeling, you probably want to be on your own, so I've ordered a taxi for you, it'll be here soon. I'll wait with you till it arrives.'

Robert smiled and replied, 'I'll be okay Pat, we'll have that drink sometime and I'll call you, yeah.'

Pat made some small talk in the interim to cheer up his old friend, colleague, and indeed one-time employer. He suggested, 'Robert, listen, when you feel like it why don't we get together down at the Sports and Social club again. We could get back into the martial arts training, I for one need to tone-up some.'

'We'll see, Pat,' Robert replied despondently. Pat continued.

'Well, if not, what about the shooting gallery, you could get a few more trophies. Be honest Robert, you were good, eh.'

'Yeah, at one time Pat, I'll see. Promise, I'll give you a call, just give me a week or two, Bud.'

'Okay mate, you take care,' Pat replied as the two taxis duly arrived, the pair shook hands firmly once again then pulled themselves together in an act of true friendship before Pat boarded his cab.

Robert's final words to Pat were, 'Au-revoir my friend.'

Pat waived his arm as he could no longer speak due to the emotion taking hold. Robert asked the driver of his taxi to hold on whilst he said goodbye to the landlord and settled his account. The landlord wished him the best of luck, adding, 'Safe journey home, Mr Cameron.'

Robert thanked him for all the years of doing business together, shook his hand then boarded the taxi. The driver asked, 'Where to, Sir?'

Robert had little or no intention of heading for home. Although he had put on a brave face throughout the evening, he felt melancholy and the prospect of returning to an empty house would be little comfort. He and his wife of eight years, Diane had divorced three years earlier due to an "Irretrievable Breakdown of the Marriage".

Or so the Decree Absolute stated. Diane was unable or unwilling to tolerate the effects of Robert's business problems on her lavish lifestyle. When the recession and the other problems began to bite, Robert had sustained the company for some time, liquidating personal assets he had either inherited or purchased himself.

The loss of their spacious and elegant home which a small four-bedroom detached house replaced was the final blow for Diane; six weeks later, she walked out on him.

Although Robert had drank several malt whisky's whilst in the "Ship Inn", he was far from inebriated, he instructed the taxi driver to take him to a lively nightclub in the city centre, he simply needed to be among people enjoying themselves as he'd had enough of this endless depressing day.

He knew drink was not an answer to any problem but on this occasion, he felt it would help take his mind out of the ever-present torment he was currently suffering. The driver suggested the ANTEX club in Park St, this sounded ideal, so thanked the driver saying, 'That will do nicely, thanks.'

The ANTEX was only a few miles away, the taxi arrived at the entrance around 00.30hrs. Robert hoped he'd managed to compose himself enough to gain entry. He stood upright and walked towards the main door with barely a swagger. Upon arrival, the door attendant halted him saying, 'Excuse me Sir, what's that you're carrying?'

'Oh this,' Robert said as he held up the crystal glass. He continued. 'This is a presentation from my good friends and colleagues at work.'

The door attendant read the inscription and replied, 'A leaving present, Sir?' Robert smirked slightly, shook his head and replied, 'You could say that.'

The door attendant allowed him to enter, he paid the entrance fee and headed for the bar. A few more malts would certainly not solve anything other than ensuring he would at least get some sleep if nothing else. Once inside the club which was found to be full of energetic youngsters dancing the night away to the loud music, Robert purchased two double malts dispensed into his own glass and looked for a quiet corner where he sat alone with only his thoughts.

He began to realise for the first time in his life he felt completely alone, until now he always had his work, the business and the struggle to survive kept the mind focussed. As time passed sipping away at the malt whisky, his thoughts sadly turned to the loneliness of his new lifestyle, he was fast descending into the depths of depression and he could sense this happening.

He would need more malt whisky to enable him to fully relax and so further top-ups were supplied and consumed, until now he had managed to avoid any conversations apart from ordering the refills, just prior to 2 a.m. a club official noted Robert was slumped in the seat, barely awake and politely advised him he should head home and would he like a taxi; he agreed as he realised he was pretty well inebriated and left the ANTEX club with a visible stagger soon after.

The club was close to the Bristol Marina and for some inexplicable reason, Robert's thoughts had turned to his lifelong ambition of owning a luxury yacht, this now of course seemed utterly unachievable. He began to recall how he had already disposed of a fine sea-going cruiser and replaced it with a small cabin cruiser barely seaworthy in his strive to preserve the ailing company, all sadly to no avail. The taxi arrived around 02.20 a.m. and Robert instructed the driver to head for the marina.

The driver said, 'Cor mate, you've supped a few tonight ain't ya.'

Robert replied, 'Not enough, not nearly enough, my friend.' He continued. 'Do you know anywhere that's still open; I'll pay no problem.'

Suddenly getting a second wind. The driver replied, 'In your condition mate no way, they wouldn't let you in.' he added. 'Tell you what though mate, you ain't a copper is ya?'

Robert laughed and waived his arms in an action showing the negative. 'Okay I'll believe ya, I've a bottle of whisky here if yer' interested, twenty quid and it's yours.'

Robert forced himself to answer although his speech was notably slurred by now. He knew it was not a clever idea but cared little about the consequences. He needed more whisky to nullify the traumas of the day.

'Yeah sure, just take me to the marina,' he said, falling back into the seat as the taxi pulled away.

Arriving at the marina, he paid the driver the fare and the twenty quid requested, plus a handsome gratuity. On noticing his passenger's struggle to alight, the driver got out and assisted him.

'Are you sure you're alright Sir, is this really where you want to be?' he asked.

'Yes, just help me out and sit me on that bench over there if you would please, I'll be fine in a moment,' replied Robert.

'Whatever you say, mate.' The driver helped him in his request. 'Thank you very much driver, most appreciated.'

The driver bid Robert goodnight and told him to take care around the water's edge. Robert raised his empty glass in one hand and the full bottle in the other rather than try to speak. Around ten minutes later, he composed himself enough to make his way along one of the jetties towards his own small cabin-cruiser, which was berthed there.

His legs unsteady, he staggered in the general direction, still clutching the crystal glass in his right hand, the bottle was now precariously jostling about in his jacket pocket. He had a little difficulty in negotiating the floating jetty, his unbalanced steps causing it to rise and fall more than was usual.

Robert was oblivious to all this, he only wished to look at the yachts and cruisers as he headed towards his own somewhere amid the vast array of masts bobbing back and forth gently in the calm waters of the marina. The waters were glistening with reflections from the quayside lights and the moonlight from an almost clear night sky.

Slowly he continued, reading the names of the various craft and stopping momentarily to admire the larger vessels. The night security guard on his patrol had noticed Robert's presence and more so his wavering condition as he staggered along, he proceeded swiftly towards him calling out.

'Excuse me Sir, excuse me!'

On closing, in he recognised the figure and called out.
'Good evening, Mr Cameron, I'm afraid I didn't recognise you at first.'
'Hello Mark, yes it's me, sorry to trouble you.' Robert paused as he felt a little nauseous. 'Just having a look around before I try to locate my own vessel.' His speech notably hampered by his alcohol intake.

'No trouble Mr Cameron, let me help you to your boat,' offered Mark. 'I'm fine, I'm fine Mark, just point me in the right direction and I'll be fine,' insisted Robert, followed by some senseless ramblings. 'I want to look at the dream boats Mark, I once had a really nice boat, much, much nicer than the one I have now you know, Mark.'

Mark interrupted. 'Yes, Mr Cameron, I remember you did but you shouldn't be on the jetty, you're in no condition to be wandering along here, what if you were to fall in?'

'I told you I'm fine,' Robert replied a little curtly.

'I'm sorry Sir, I'll have to get you to either your boat or the quayside, you cannot wander along the jetties in your condition, so which is it to be?' Mark said firmly. No answer was forthcoming, so he reiterated. 'Well Sir, the boat or the quay, which is it to be?'

'The quay! I want to look at the dream boats, I told you,' Robert said, sounding a little agitated at the thought of being ordered about. Mark raised Robert's left arm and placed it over his shoulder to assist him. The pair then headed for the quayside, Robert persisted in his mumbling about the fact he only had a small boat now and that he would never be able to fulfil his ambition.

Mark continued attempting to console him as they headed for a bench. Both Mark and Robert sat down together and Mark implored him to stay there for his own safety. Robert raised his glass he was still carrying in his right hand and answered.

'Fine Mark, whatever you say.'

'I'll have to go about my duties now Mr Cameron, stay put for your own sake please, will you?' Pleaded Mark.

'Yes, yes course I will. I know, stay here; I know.' Robert answered fed-up with the intimidation, he waved at Mark to go. Mark shook his head and walked away to continue his rounds.

Robert sat motionless for almost thirty minutes just staring at the various craft. He then began to feel the night chill and became uncomfortable, he decided to seek out his boat and retire to bed. His eyes were heavy from fatigue as he looked around just to check if Mark was still lurking about. He was not eager to receive yet another chastisement.

He rose and made his way down the jetty heading for his boat, his even more unsteady progress showed the ill-effects of the whisky he had consumed. Turning into one of the bays off the main jetty by which he felt sure his boat was berthed, he felt somehow relieved at the imminent prospect of getting some well-deserved sleep and a little night-cap!

Halfway down, he caught sight of the most magnificent super yacht he had ever seen, berthed in the adjacent bay. He was stopped in his tracks by its sheer size and sleek design, his eyes fixated upon the vessel. The dream boat he had spoken of so many times was right in front of him. It's design, an absolute masterpiece, he began to look her over at a distance from stern to bow and her hull shimmering from the reflecting waters rippling along the hull was a delightful sight.

Several moments passed and Robert had shaken off the feeling of fatigue but somehow doubted his eyesight, he raised his left hand and rubbed both eyes using thumb and forefinger, opened them and she was still there.

He decided to have a closer look, turning about face he started along the jetty his pace, accelerated by his spirited efforts to reach the craft of his dreams, several times he almost toppled over in his haste but somehow regained co-ordination between mind and body to continue.

Rounding the bays, he headed down the short distance towards the dreamboat, part way along he slowed to a halt as if in awe of the majesty the craft enthused upon him, slowly he closed in on the stern, studying the majestic lines from a different viewpoint, his eyes lowered and focussed upon the stern where sign written in Italic style and surrounded by ornate scrolls and lining the vessel's name KATRIANA.

The letters were embellished in gold leaf and shaded black. He spoke the name softly to himself and thought, 'A beautiful name for a beautiful lady.'

After a few moments, he moved off towards the bow looking the craft up and down, he paused just ahead of the bow for a while then turned back, as he approached the stern, he came adjacent to a boarding point in the handrail, he paused aside it, glanced around wondering whether to board her and have a look on deck.

He decided no harm would be done just looking her over for a few minutes whilst no one was around, he released the catch and stepped aboard, closing it behind him. Once aboard he could fully appreciate his surroundings, the luxury appointments were calling out to be admired. The gold plate cabin door handles, gold plate deck lamps, the cabin windows either side of the double entrance doors etched with an anchor and life-belt design, the windows in the doors themselves etched with a heraldic crest, the same crest he found he was standing aside, which was designed into the highly polished parquet tiling on the deck.

Robert decided to walk along the port side towards the bow, he moved silently forward unsure if anyone was aboard. All the windows had their curtains or blinds drawn preventing him from seeing inside, he realised this was only to be expected but thought jovially that it was dammed inconvenient of the owner!

He walked the full length of the vessel on both sides returning to the bow looking down at the water below, turning about he saw the impressive view afforded by the front bulkhead of the KATRIANA. He moved towards the bulkhead and climbed the narrow stairway on the starboard side, at the top he found a small deck area leading to another bulkhead, which he presumed to be the bridge.

He climbed another narrow stairway and reached a large deck area surrounded by handrails apart from yet another bulkhead, he climbed the last stairway and viewed the KATRIANA from her highest point, and he was captivated.

In front of him was a built-in seating area with a central table, he decided to take a seat for a few moments. Sitting down in the centre of the aft bench, he placed his crystal glass in one of the recesses formed into the table for this very purpose. In fact, he noted several recesses; he then realised they formed place settings, he chuckled to himself.

Would you believe it?

Robert removed the bottle of whisky from his pocket, still in one piece considering the events of the past hour or so. He poured himself a generous portion of the amber liquid. Upon tasting it even though he was in a bibulous condition, he could perceive it was not a malt but an inferior brand of the blended variety.

He chewed on the contents for a moment, swilling it round his mouth then swallowed it hard, his liver rejected the inferior substance as it travelled down causing him to shudder for a few moments, this however did not discourage him, replenishing his glass and continuing!

Soon after, Robert rested both forearms on the table and lowered his chin onto them, he gazed ahead, pondering the thoughts of sailing the KATRIANA. His vision of the open sea ahead, he at the helm.

It was all too much for him to believe, he began to tire, overcome with a mixture of despondency, excitement and the copious amount of alcohol he slowly slumped down from the table to the seat, taking with him accidently the open bottle, which toppled over spilling until the amber liquid settled at a level.

Half asleep, he felt his left leg getting wet and realised the bottle was draining over him, standing it upright, he refitted the bottle top then placed it on the deck out of harm's way. He noticed several old newspapers and magazines in a rack and attempted to clean the mess.

Robert then folded several into a roll to form a pillow. With semi-unconscious comfort seeking movements, he managed to lay along the bench with one leg drooped over the edge reaching the deck. The events of the day and the effects of the enormous amount of alcohol he had consumed had indeed taken their toll, at last he was at peace with the torments of the day laid to rest at least for the meantime.

***

A couple of hours later around 05.00 a.m. Saturday, October 1st the tranquillity of the marina was disturbed by the arrival of a chauffeur driven limousine entering the quay at speed. The passenger did not await the chauffeur to open his door as would be his duty, for as the vehicle slowed quickly to a halt, the rear near-side door swung open and the imposing figure of a tall man in his mid-50s emerged, clutching a briefcase in his right hand.

He was dressed in black trousers, white dinner jacket, white shirt and black bowtie, his hair a shade of dark silver grey was short and well groomed. Looking over the roof towards the chauffeur who had now alighted from the vehicle, he called to him briskly.

'Follow me Marcel, bring the baggage quickly!' Marcel replied, 'Oui, Monsieur at once.'

Marcel opened the boot, removed two matching suitcases and a hold-all style bag, leaving the boot open, he hurried towards his employer with a suitcase in each hand and the hold-all bag draped over his right shoulder, his employer had already started quickly along the main jetty.

A few minutes later, another limousine arrived, this time the chauffeur stepped out and walked around the car to the nearside rear door, as he did so the off-side door also opened out and a tall well-built man in his early 30s stepped out immediately closing the door behind him, he walked around the rear of the car to join the chauffeur glancing around the quayside as he moved.

Stepping just behind the rear nearside door, he nodded to the chauffeur to open the door. As the door opened, a young lady in her early to mid-20s elegantly eased herself out of the limousine, looked up at the chauffeur and said, 'Merci Paul, will you attend to the baggage s'il vous plait.'

Paul replied, 'Of course, Mademoiselle.' As he closed the door behind her. The tall man gestured to the lady with his left arm raised to shoulder height, his whole hand outstretched with fingers tight and straight in the direction of the main jetty and announcing.

'Your father has already arrived Mademoiselle, this way please.' She replied simply, 'Merci.'

Both headed along the main jetty. Back on the quayside, Paul signalled to a further two large vehicles as they were arriving to draw up aside him. The first a large saloon car in standard dark navy had the words "ROYAL NAVY" on the front doors, the second vehicle in similar colour but unmarked was a sizeable crew-cab style van.

The occupants of the two vehicles immediately alighted and were busy bustling and organising each other and the array of various baggage and crates, etc. In their mid, a smartly dressed man of average height and build also in his mid-50s and dressed in a naval uniform seemed to be issuing instructions.

Within a few minutes, all concerned were heading along the jetty with two of the group members utilising one of the harbour trolleys loaded with the contents of both vehicles.

The young lady in contrast to her father's pace was walking elegantly along, clutching a small handbag in her left hand, a fine silk wrap covering her otherwise bare shoulders was partially obscuring her full-length slim fitting pure white evening dress, which sported an abundance of sequence and featured a side split on her left side just above knee height only.

It was through necessity rather than choice she showed no sign of haste, following close behind was the tall man. As they reached the KATRIANA which by now was in a blaze of illumination, the tall man boarded and assisted the young lady over the steps and down onto the rear deck, holding her right hand gently.

'Merci beaucoup.' She thanked him politely. 'Mademoiselle,' the tall man replied and took a short bow.

She acknowledged him then turned and entered the double entrance doors, walking through to the cabin.

'Bonjour, Papa!'

She exclaimed excitedly, obviously incredibly pleased to see him. Holding her arms outright, she moved towards him. Her father was stooped over a large central table studying charts and papers, he turned around and opened his arms, hugged, and kissed his daughter on both cheeks saying.

'Ah! Bonjour, my precious,' he announced with equal delight. He stepped back and looked at his daughter.

'You look exquisite my dear, have I spoiled your weekend plans? I am sorry, please forgive me.'

'Nonsense papa, the company was so dull in any case. I was relieved when André telephoned, gave me an excuse to get away. Talking of getting away, where are we headed in such a hurry? It won't be Nassau now, I'm sure,' she quizzed.

'Ah, just like your dear mother, so perceptive. Now get some sleep, we shall be underway very shortly.'

Her father answered, averting the subject whilst turning to start up the vessel's engines.

'Alright papa, I do feel a little tired,' she replied. They kissed on the cheeks once more.

'It will be daylight soon, my dear,' said her father, she smiled and blew him a kiss then turned and headed for her cabin.

Her father resumed his position over the table, meanwhile outside, the men from the two vehicles had arrived at the yacht with the array of baggage, several crates and cases, the smartly dressed man in naval uniform was first to board.

'Good evening, Captain,' said the tall man who had escorted the daughter, he saluted the captain as he boarded.

'Good evening, Carl, I take it Monsieur Larousse and his daughter are aboard,' inquired the captain.

'Yes Sir, a few moments ago,' Carl confirmed.

'Thank you, Carl, we must make haste,' said the captain as he entered the entrance doors. Carl remained stood at his position on the aft deck, observing the movements of the crew members now arriving with the assorted items unloaded from the vehicles. The captain walked through to join Monsieur Larousse.

'Good evening, Sir,' addressed the captain with a salute.

'Ah, Captain, I think you will find it's morning, my friend,' replied Larousse with a little wry humour in his voice.

'I do believe you are correct, Sir.'

Checking his wristwatch, he announced, 'It is 05.15 hrs precisely, Sir.'

'How soon can we be underway, André?' asked Larousse with a hint of impatience in the tone.

'Once everything is aboard Sir, the crew are loading the equipment now.'

'Very well André, once we are safely out of the harbour, please re-join me.

I have prepared our course for we must make haste,' said Larousse in a tensed tone.

The captain saluted and went about his preparations for departure. On the jetty, the remainder of the baggage and equipment had now been loaded aboard and stowed away. The captain issued the order to release the mooring lines. Two crew members swiftly executed the command and called out.

'Lines cleared.'

The captain slowly opened the throttle levers and steered the KATRIANA gently away from the jetty and headed for the harbour mouth. Only Paul, the daughter's chauffer and the drivers of the other two vehicles plus another brought along to take charge of Larousse's limousine was left to look on as the majestic craft eased effortlessly out of the marina and along the river Avon.

Soon the dawn sky broke just brightening up what appeared to be dawn of a promising lovely day, as the KATRIANA soon reached the open waters of the River Severn estuary as the sun cast its brilliance over the port side of the luxury craft, she glowed a pastel shade of yellowish orange from the sun's rays.

The powerful engines were opened as the craft swiftly gained speed along the North Devon coastline and headed for the Atlantic.

André remembered Larousse's request to join him below began to ponder the urgency of their departure for it had been many years since Larousse had plotted a course and handed it to him without any consultation. He thought back to how they had met, he knew he was regarded as one of his closest and most trusted friends for their alliance had been nurtured since pre-school days when André's family were transferred from France to England only a few weeks prior to the Nazi occupation.

Over the years, his father (Phillipe André Deveraux) had told him the story of how the family had been spirited away to England and "why" many times as a child.

Following the invasion of Poland by the Nazi's on 3 September 1939, French Naval Intelligence acted quickly to ensure key personnel were positioned in various Allied nations and André's grandfather (Louis Gaston Deveraux) was a naval Lieutenant who showed great promise within the intelligence division, he was offered transportation to England for duties within the British Admiralty in Whitehall, London.

He agreed provided his immediate family of wife, Camille and 14-month-old son, Phillipe André accompanied him. This he was advised had already been consented. Therefore, in March 1940 his family moved to England settling in the small village of Bishop's Waltham some twelve miles from the naval base at Portsmouth.

Given a week to settle in, he reported to the Admiralty in Whitehall, London where he was introduced to his commanding officer, Honorary Commodore, Frederic Yves Larousse. Frederic Larousse's honorary role bestowed upon him as he had immediately volunteered at the outbreak of war to serve once again in the French Navy, which was truly a grand gesture as he was the owner of a global commercial shipping line at the time.

The Larousse family had a tradition of sending their sons into the French Navy to instil in them the various attributes and skills required prior to entering the family's global shipping enterprise. It was here the two family's friendship grew as Frederic Larousse had already settled from France several months earlier coincidently close-by.

His wife Yvonne had also a young son (Claude François), who grew up with Phillipe through the war years and remained close friends and became colleagues. Both their fathers proved an invaluable asset to the Royal Navy Intelligence sector and assisted primarily with any covert operations planned by the SOE (Special Operations Executive.) Under their commanding officer; Rear Admiral John Godfrey.

Larousse had wisely relocated his shipping business concern enmasse from France to Monaco in advance of, as he saw it inevitable war given German Chancellor Adolf Hitler's rise to power and the doctrine, he was decreeing becoming intense and blatantly clear his quest for German dominance would march on.

Frederic Larousse had been vocal to French defence ministers of future conflict looking certain in his view. The French Navy in particular, took great heed as Frederic Larousse was a very influential character hence the secondment to England and the Royal Navy posting in the intelligence division following his request to re-enlist.

Here he had selected André's grandfather Louis Gaston Deveraux as his second in command on reading his French naval records to date. Throughout the Second World War their two boys Claude and Phillipe were boarded at a private school together followed by the naval College in Portsmouth.

Both fathers Frederic-Yves Larousse and Louis Gaston Deveraux knew the training provided by these institutions would mould their sons into naval officers, which in later years would assist them in both merchant and civilian life once their training and service concluded.

With a little "pulling of strings" and "a word in the right ears" so to speak. The two young men therefore served their final years with the Royal Navy also in the intelligence division.

André felt a little uneasy as he went below to join Larousse. He walked into the large cabin, François Larousse was sitting behind the table with an array of maps and charts spread out in front of him. As he entered, André announced.

'You wished to see me, Sir.' André refusing to withdraw formalities whilst on duty.

'Ah, André, close the door and join me, please. We have much to discuss.' Larousse continued whilst André carried out his request.

'Firstly. Here is the course I have prepared. Please study it and verify the details.'

André was inwardly pleased; his position had not been completely overlooked. He suspected that although both had relinquished their positions within the Royal Navy some years ago that Larousse had remained available if required. He knew François had maintained contact with old colleagues in the department since taking control of the family business upon his father's retirement due to ill-health.

Softly spoken, Larousse continued.

'André. I have been requested in a roundabout sort of way by our old department to investigate a delicate matter on their behalf. The details of which I will familiarise you with later. But firstly, I wish you to call the crew together for a meeting preferably when my daughter's asleep tonight. She must know nothing of this.'

André nodded in agreement. Larousse continued with some minor details and concluded the short meeting admitting he needed some sleep and requested to be awakened at 13.00 hrs.

André replied, 'I shall see to it, Sir. Shall I wake Mademoiselle Larousse also?'

'No André, she's had a tiresome few days. Leave her be.' he replied thoughtfully, adding. 'Ensure lunch is prepared please, André.' He then bid the captain good morning.

***

The steward awoke Monsieur Larousse at the prescribed hour, advising him his lunch was ready. He thanked the steward, rose out of the bed and showered before dressing far more casually than he had arrived on board. He walked through to the dining table where a fresh salad had been prepared with a choice of cold meats and various cheeses.

A large jug of fresh orange juice and a coffee pot were placed in the centre of the table. No sooner had he started his lunch, his daughter entered the cabin.

'Bonjour, Papa!' She announced, sounding bright. 'Ah! Bonjour, my dear. Did you sleep well?'

'Oh yes papa, the sea air you know always makes me sleep.' Her father laughed slightly then called out. 'Gerrard!'

The steward entered.

'Prepare some lunch for my daughter please, Gerrard,' he requested. 'Of course, Monsieur Larousse.'

'Only a light salad please, Gerrard,' instructed his daughter. 'Very well Mademoiselle, I shall bring it through shortly.'

Larousse and his daughter spent some time idly chatting whilst they both ate their lunch. She advised her father she was taking a shower and inquired if the weather was fine enough to sunbathe. He replied.

'My dear. I could not say for sure. I have not ventured on deck as yet. Though it may be a little chilly I suspect, we are not in the south of France now you know.'

She smiled and replied, 'Never mind. I shall ask André to have the windbreaker fitted if it's too chilly.' She turned to leave, paused momentarily by the door and turned, asking.

'Where are we headed now, papa?' she said, expecting a change of plan as usual!

Her father stood up and turning slightly away, said softly, 'Kinshasa.'

'Oh! Africa! How wonderful, papa!' She exclaimed excitedly as she had not visited Kinshasa before.

Larousse turned back and walked over to his daughter, holding her arms gently, he said, 'It is only a business meeting, my dear. I want you to stay with Carl in Matadi, we are unable to take the vessel through to Kinshasa. I have someone collecting me and some crew members when we dock. I should only be gone two or three days.'

'Oh papa!' His daughter said, sounding disheartened.

'You know I don't like Carl that much. He's so boring. Can't do this. Can't do that. Can't go there.'

Her father interrupted. 'My dear. It's for your own good. Carl is here to protect you. Please do as I ask,' he said in a dominant tone.

'Can't I go ashore at all whilst I'm there?' She whined.

'I would rather you stayed on board. We may have to move on quickly. You will have plenty of opportunity to shop when we get to Nassau. I promise.'

Perturbed by her father's request, she began a scowling protestation. 'Why take me all the way to Africa if I can't even get off the boat, I would rather have gone straight home!'

'Very well, my dear. I shall evaluate the situation when we dock. However, I must insist you stay with Carl, no matter what. Agreed?'

She placed her arms around her father's neck and kissed him on the cheeks. 'Merci papa!' she said with a broad smile knowing a maybe, could well turn into a yes. Her father shook his head in the knowledge his daughter had just got another one over on him.

'Go and have your shower.'

His daughter bounced away along the passageway, delighted at the change of heart.

Half an hour or so later, Larousse's daughter returned wearing an all-black swimsuit under a full-length silk robe. She was carrying a book in her left hand and a glass of mineral water with ice and a slice of lemon in her right. She walked out onto the rear deck. Carl was still sitting there, holding a coffee on his knee. He placed the coffee on the table, stood up and greeted her.

'Good afternoon, Mademoiselle.'

'Bonjour, Carl!' she said brightly. 'It's a lovely day. Why don't you take that suit off and enjoy the sun?'

'No thanks, Mademoiselle. I prefer to stay in the shade.'

'You should let yourself go occasionally Carl, nothing's going to happen out here and you can relax. Go on, why don't you join me in a spot of sunbathing? It's a long trip.'

'Sorry Mademoiselle. I am not the sunbathing type, thanks all the same for the offer.' He nodded and returned to his coffee.

She walked over to the stairways leading up to the top deck and ascended the flights of stairs nimbly, as she approached the table area, she noticed an unusual glass in one of the table recesses. Wondering where it had come from, she stepped over to examine it. In doing so, she saw the still figure of a man lying face down on the deck under the table.

She screamed out and simultaneously dropped both the book and the glass of mineral water with the shock. The glass bounced as it hit the deck spraying most of its contents over the still figure as she turned and ran for the stairway. Before descending, Carl had scaled the stairways and was now on the top deck. She grasped Carl around the waist as he stepped forward.

'What's wrong, Mademoiselle?' he asked impatiently.

Her speech was hindered by her trauma. She pointed to the table and somehow managed to utter the words.

'A man! There's a man under the table. I think he's dead!' She cried remorsefully.

Her father and André, hearing the commotion had also rushed to ascertain the cause. Larousse climbing the stairways first, took hold of his daughter from Carl.

'What's wrong, my dear?' he asked as he comforted her in his arms. 'There's a man under the table, papa. I think he's dead.' She sobbed.

Carl immediately reached under his jacket and produced a small automatic pistol from his shoulder holster. He walked cautiously over to the table where the man awoken by either the scream, the bang of the glass hitting the deck or the drenching with mineral water or a combination of them all was attempting to struggle to his feet.

Larousse passed his daughter to André and walked the few short steps to join Carl. He shouted out. 'Who the bloody hell are you?'

The man pushed the stack of crumpled newspapers aside. His eyes somehow noticing the date on a copy of the Financial Times, Friday, September 30th. He quickly realised his position and pondered a few moments over the apology he would need to offer.

Deciding to rise to his feet first, he found his progress hindered by the table top as he knocked his head in the process. He managed to slide out and on to the bench seat. In a loud monotone, Carl demanded, 'Who are you?'

Larousse stepped forward to join Carl. 'Who the hell are you?' Larousse demanded of the stranger again, quickening the tone.

The man turning his head around as he slid up through the gap, caught sight immediately of an incredibly beautiful young lady, who whilst clasping her face in her hands, had permitted her robe to be blown open in the breeze to reveal her shapely figure.

She was a vision from heaven, he thought at first although his eyes were not focussing correctly yet, as he looked her up and down with his eyes only. He soon realised she was distressed by the way she reached over to hold on to the older man beside her.

'What's wrong?' He looked around. 'Who are you people? Where am I?' he asked.

'Never you mind. Who are you?' Came a demanding voice.

He looked around to his left to see two men and immediately slumped down again at the sight of the gun barrel pointing at him.

Larousse reiterated in a slow, demanding, calculated tone. 'I said. Who-the-hell-are-you?' His words lengthened and more pronounced.

'Put the gun away, Carl,' Larousse said quickly, noting the fear on the stranger's face combined with the rough condition of his appearance.

'Get out of there. Come on, get up, man. What are you doing on my yacht? Who are you? Answer me, man!' Larousse was becoming impatient.

The stranger, whilst sheltering below the table, said hesitantly. 'Cameron. My name's Robert Cameron.'

Chapter Two

The sequence of events whereby Robert John Cameron was discovered aboard the luxury yacht KATRIANA began on the previous Saturday morning, that of 24 September 2022. These events, just like Robert's situation commenced quite innocently with François Larousse, a major shipping line owner and industrialist with world-wide connections whilst on a business visit to Portugal was none the wiser regarding what he was heading into.

He and his personal crew aboard his superyacht at least had some formal training in such matters but at this date, even he had no knowledge of the impending dangers he and the others were about to encounter over the next two weeks.

On that bright Saturday morning just prior to noon, François Larousse was eagerly awaiting the arrival of his daughter at Lisbon airport. She had agreed to spend a month or two on board the yacht with him. She recalled the feeling of excitement she felt when her father called from Lisbon earlier in the week, inviting both her mother and her to accompany him on a trip to the Bahamas. His only condition being that Carl must accompany them or whomever decided to come.

Her mother questioned the purpose of the journey and once establishing the trip was in the main for business reasons, declined the offer. By now, she had become a little tired of pompous dinner meetings and the idle chit-chat which inevitably precluded any form of enjoyment for her.

The daughter pleaded with her mother to join them saying that it was only for a month or so and that in any case neither of them had seen him for two months, all to no avail, her mother's decision was decisive.

With only a slight feeling of discontent, Larousse's daughter instructed the château staff to make the flight arrangements for Carl, her personal bodyguard and herself for Lisbon early on the forthcoming Saturday, whilst she, meanwhile, packed her own choice of clothing and accessories, a task she would not leave to others, she was decidedly selective about her wardrobe and the manner in which her wardrobe was packed.

Around 05.00 a.m. on the 24th a bright sunny Saturday morning at the Larousse château on the outskirts of Marseille positioned high on the hilltops with a magnificent view of the coastline to the east of Marseille towards St Tropez, his daughter was awoken by the maid after a restless night, she had been over excited about the forthcoming trip, not so much the flight from Marseille with only Carl for company but the journey to the Bahamas, she was looking forward to it immensely, except for Carl tagging along, who would no doubt turn the journey into a tedious nightmare.

She emerged from her bedroom in a cool, capped sleeve, printed chiffon dress, the skirt section of which had several layers of flowing material, the bodice snugly fitting her superb figure, the neckline of which was tailored to a point which merely afforded a glimpse of cleavage.

She descended the staircase carrying a small red handbag and a simple lightweight plain white jacket featuring no lapels draped over her arm, her deportment impeccable.

She entered the small dining room used by the family when there were no guests staying at the château and sat opposite Carl, who had awaited her arrival before commencing his breakfast of coffee and croissants, she declined the croissants settling for toast and marmalade followed by coffee. The conversation was indeed dull as she fully anticipated, this would indeed be a tedious trip she surmised.

Once breakfast was over, Carl assisted Pascal the chauffeur to load the baggage into the limousine, on completion he advised Mademoiselle Larousse they were ready to depart, she thanked him and said she was going to say au'revoir to her mama before leaving.

Their journey to the airport and thence to Lisbon was uneventful, for Carl was the silent type who only spoke when spoken to and then only sententious, this situation was intolerable to Larousse's daughter who was naturally vivacious, in her eyes he was a downright bore.

She tried several times throughout the journey to make pleasant conversation with him, asking had he ever visited the Bahamas before. Had he been to Lisbon? Had he ever had sex yet? Anything to alleviate the boredom. However, she realised it was as hopeless as usual and left him be, deciding to read the paperback book she had purchased in the airport lounge prior to boarding.

Lisbon was hot and humid as François Larousse and Marcel, his personal chauffeur who accompanied him throughout his travels waited in the arrivals lounge of the airport for his daughter's flight to touch down and disembark. With minimum formalities, she appeared, passing through the customs barrier, Carl following immediately behind. Her father quickly walked towards her, arms outstretched, calling.

'My dear! Over here, my dear!'

She was overjoyed at seeing her father awaiting her in person, this was indeed a good sign, for it was the norm for her to be met by Marcel or another of her father's entourage. Nevertheless, she maintained her imperturbability and walked gracefully towards him, clasping his hands and kissing him on both cheeks.

'Bonjour, Papa! How lovely to see you here, I expected Marcel or someone.'

'Ah, my precious, I haven't seen you for almost two months, I couldn't wait any longer!'

'Oh, papa! I've missed you terrible!' she said, combining a frown with genuine excitement.

'Well, my dear, you have me all to yourself for a month or so, perhaps longer, we'll see. I only have a little business to attend to in Nassau, we'll spend some time together once I've finished.' He kissed her again and gave her a huge hug before welcoming Carl.

'Ah, Carl, good morning, I trust you are well?' Larousse asked as he offered his hand.

'Yes, thank you Sir, I'm very well,' Carl said as he shook Larousse's hand.

'Come,' her father said as he placed his arm around her shoulder, guiding her to the car.

'Tell me, how is your mama, why wouldn't she come? Couldn't you persuade her, my dear?'

'I tried papa but you know what mama thinks about business meetings.'

'Yes. Strange though, she used to adore travelling,' Larousse said, sounding a little disconcerted.

'I know papa but she is content around the chateau. She seldom entertains now, you know?'

'I'll see if I can return to Marseille after our trip, I must confess my dear, I'm a little worried about your mama.'

'Oh, she'd love you to papa, she misses you as much as I do, we should all spend more time together, don't you agree?'

'Yes, my precious, you're quite right, right as usual.'

They walked together, his arm around her shoulder, her arm around his waist and both their thoughts on the same person.

Marcel and Carl pushed the baggage trolleys to the car and loaded them into the adequate space provided in the boot of the limousine. Carl sat aside Marcel in the front seat, leaving Larousse and his daughter in the rear. Larousse informed them that lunch had been organised for their return to the hotel and that they would be staying for a few nights before setting sail for the Bahamas. His daughter was delighted, she adored Portugal.

'Are we staying at the "Avenida Palace", papa?' She asked. 'Yes, my dear, if you find that suitable?'

'Oh yes papa, it's wonderful, do we have the same suite as before?'

'Of course, my dear, Ribeiro seen to it. You even have the same room.'

'How is Ribeiro?'

'He is just fine, always the perfect gentleman, he has changed little since you were here last. How long ago was that my dear, can you remember?'

'Papa!' she said curtly. 'When I was eighteen! I had my birthday party there. Remember! Mama was there too, we had a fabulous time, surely you remember.'

'Ah! Of course, how foolish of me to forget. Your old papa, he's getting forgetful in his old age.'

'Nonsense, papa,' she said, reaching around to kiss him on the cheek. 'Never mind, Ribeiro is looking forward to seeing you again, he remembers you well.'

Both Larousse and his daughter talked incessantly through the five mile or so journey from the airport, which took almost thirty minutes in the heavy traffic of Lisbon. Upon arriving at the hotel entrance, the Commissionaire stepped out to open the limousine door.

'Bonjour, Monsieur Larousse, Mademoiselle Larousse,' he said, saluting. 'Ah, good afternoon, Jorge,' said Larousse who alighted from the car first, then assisting his daughter.

'Bonjour,' she said simply as she headed into the hotel foyer. Ribeiro was waiting to welcome them as they entered.

Ribeiro was a man in his late forties, dressed in black braided trousers, white shirt and a black jacket and tie sporting the hotel logo, his height around five foot eight inches, his hair jet black with a few early grey tones in places yet groomed to perfection as was his moustache. He was an extremely pleasant individual, perfectly suited for his position of hotel director.

'Mademoiselle Larousse, bon retour parmi nous!' he said, welcoming her back in French, as he clicked his heels and reached for her hand to kiss it.

'Mademoiselle, you look delightful if I may say,' Ribeiro added.

'Merci Ribeiro, you have not changed in the slightest since my last visit,' she said plausibly.

'Merci mademoiselle, that was several years ago, perhaps a little older, a little greyer, wouldn't you agree, yes?' He smiled.

'Please, follow me. I shall escort you both to your suite personally.'

'Merci,' she replied graciously as she took Ribeiro's arm.

'Monsieur. Mademoiselle, would you prefer lunch in your suite or the dining room?'

'Oh, papa the dining room please, I love looking down on the street below.'

'The dining room please, Ribeiro,' said Larousse as if he had little choice in the decision making.

'Ribeiro, is the view still the same, is it still as busy?' She asked with intrigue.

'Oui, mademoiselle. I shall arrange a window table for you.'

'Merci Ribeiro. I have treasured that view since my last visit. It's so beautiful, I love to see the hustle and bustle of a busy city with all the people and the glorious mix of colours in the streets, there's always so much going on. You know what I like to do, I like to lock on to one person and follow their movements through the crowd and it's quite fascinating.'

'Sadly, Mademoiselle I never seem to have the time for such pleasures,' said Ribeiro humorously as he opened the doors to the suite.

After freshening herself up, she joined her father who escorted her to the dining room, everything was as she'd remembered. The "Avenida Palace Hotel" being one of Lisbon's finest, furnished in the classic old style with marble bathrooms, it personified luxury. She recalled her eighteenth birthday celebrations as if they were yesterday and how everyone enjoyed themselves, especially her mama.

With lunch over, she suggested a stroll around the city, her father declined which she knew beforehand he would, she knew he despised shopping expeditions; however, she was determined to see some of Lisbon this trip. It was agreed for Carl to accompany her around Lisbon for the afternoon while her father made some arrangements regarding their trip.

Unperturbed, she dragged Carl around Lisbon for several hours, combining shopping with sightseeing and stopping for coffee here and ice cream there. She wanted to buy a small present for her parents. She chose, for her Papa gold cuff-links, for her mama, a beautiful, jewelled brooch, which she had gift wrapped and forwarded. Later the same evening around 20.00 hrs, they were enjoying a cabaret in the hotel when a waiter came over to Larousse.

'A telephone call for you, Monsieur Larousse. A Monsieur Charles Saunders, calling from Jersey.'

'Charles! Charles Saunders. What the devil can he be calling me here for, I wonder?' He thanked the waiter and excused himself from the table. As he headed for the lobby, his daughter looked sceptically on. She remembered the name Saunders and what it meant.

Walking to the telephone, Larousse speculated what Charles could be calling him about, he had not seen or heard of him for over ten years. More intriguing, was how did he know his whereabouts?

'Hello, François Larousse speaking,' he said, appearing undaunted.

'Hello! François, this is Charles Saunders, remember me?' Came a nervous sounding voice.

Larousse answered jovially.

'Ah, Charles, yes of course I remember you, Charles. How nice to hear from you, it has been a long time, my friend, I trust you are well.' Larousse was curious, though reluctant to ask outright the reason for his call.

'Are you still living in Jersey?' Larousse inquired after a short lull.

'Yes François, fifteen years this year.' He paused awkwardly again. There was a silence which seemed to last far longer than it actually did.

'Something wrong, Charles?' Larousse asked candidly. 'Kathleen and your daughter, how are they?'

'They're fine honestly. How did you know I was here?' Larousse inquired. Knowing he could have no knowledge of his whereabouts.

'I telephoned Claire-Louise, I hope you don't mind.'

He sounded tormented. Larousse sensing something was troubling him, decided to be blunt and ask outright his reason for calling as nothing seemed to be forthcoming.

'What can I do for you, Charles?'

'I'm afraid it's a rather delicate matter François, something I dare not discuss on the telephone.'

'Charles my friend, are you in some sort of bother?' Larousse was by now feeling genuinely concerned.

'François, I must see you! It's imperative! I must talk to you! Please.'

'What's this all about Charles, I'm in Lisbon presently and sailing for Nassau in a couple of days. What can be so imperative, eh?'

'No! No, you can't! François. We have been good friends for a long time, please trust me, you have your yacht there, Claire-Louise told me, sail here, to Jersey! As soon as you can, it's vitally important!'

Larousse had by now had a little time to cogitate what could be the basis of this sudden predicament.

'Has this anything to do with the department by any vague chance? If so Charles, then I'm afraid I'm not interested.'

'No! Please François. I need to speak to you, this matter is of grave concern to you, that's all I can say for the present.' He sounded extremely tense. Larousse thought for a moment. Something serious was obviously bothering his old friend and colleague.

'Very well Charles but you had better not be wasting my time. I do have a few business matters to attend to here first, shall we say I'll leave Monday around mid-day, I shall be with you about 19.00 hrs on Wednesday and will that suffice?'

'Yes François, thank you. I shall meet you at the marina in St Helier at Seven p.m.'

'Very well, until Wednesday then, Charles. Au'revoir.'

Larousse rested the receiver down slowly, his mind concentrating on what possible purpose this unannounced meeting could hold. Returning to the cabaret, he informed his party there had been a change in itinerary and that they would be leaving on Monday initially for Jersey, before heading for the Bahamas.

His daughter was not amused, for she had unpacked several of her outfits, expecting to stay in Lisbon at least a few days, needless to say, she made her feelings known to her father who upon advising her of the circumstances changed her tone somewhat.

The following day Sunday 25th was indeed frenzied for Larousse as he concluded most of his business in Lisbon barring a number of clients which were closed for the weekend. His daughter on the other hand spent a very relaxing day shopping, followed by sunbathing in the late afternoon.

The evening was a quiet affair, his daughter on her travels had booked a show at the Campo Pequento theatre and persuaded her father to join her and of course, Carl.

The following morning Monday, September 26th following breakfast his daughter decided to shop yet again whilst she still had the opportunity. Her father first having to conclude the remaining business at hand, which could not be done over the weekend.

Following a final meal at the Avenida Palace Hotel, the party collected their belongings and made their way to the marina, setting sail for Jersey just before 18.00 hrs.

The superyacht KATRIANA capable of 50+ knots was not pushed to the limit and simply cruised calmly north-east towards the Channel Islands. Larousse confided in André and Carl the purpose of the visit informing Carl that Charles Saunders was an old colleague, André, of course, already knew him.

When they approached at St Helier around 18.30 hrs on the evening of Wednesday September 28th, Charles was observed waiting on the quayside pacing up and down, anxiously wiping his brow with a handkerchief and lifting his white trilby on and off his head and fanning his face with the brim. Larousse spotted him from a distance through his binoculars.

'My God André, I feel something decidedly unpleasant awaits us. He's pacing about like a cat on a hot tin roof,' Larousse said, sounding disturbed.

'Perhaps it's more serious than you think, François,' replied André.

'We shall soon see André; we shall soon see. Charles was never one of strong character, you know that but he is flapping more so than usual,' commented Larousse.

André steered the KATRIANA into the jetty, Charles had scurried down to meet them. He was standing on the jetty, fidgeting, and perspiring in an uncontrollable frenzy. As Larousse stepped out onto the aft deck to disembark, Charles welcomed him saying.

'Oh François, I'm so glad you could come. I have something especially important to tell you, something that concerns you, something I'm sure you know nothing about!'

'Alright Charles, alright, calm yourself man, all in good time.' Larousse pulled him to one side and whispered quietly in his ear.

'My daughter is aboard; I don't wish her to know there's trouble of some kind or other. Please pull yourself together, there's a good chap.'

'Yes, yes, of course, sorry old boy, I'm just so nervous about this whole thing. Listen François, I've made a booking for eight at the Longueville Manor in St Saviour, will that be adequate?'

'The Longueville Manor! You'll be spoiling my crew, Charles; they may want to stay,' Larousse said flippantly to quell his anguish a little.

'Actually, four will be sufficient, Charles, many thanks.'

'It's the least I could do,' Charles answered graciously.

'Come Charles, I have a surprise for you!' Larousse turned him round to face the yacht.

'My dear! Come and meet Charles.'

'I'm coming, papa,' She answered brightly as she put the finishing touches to her hair, which had been blown about somewhat.

'Ah, there you are, my dear,' he said as she walked out on to the aft deck. 'Well Charles, what do you think of my daughter now that she's all grown up? Isn't she beautiful?'

'Papa, please! You're embarrassing Mr Saunders and I both.'

'Nonsense my dear, Charles hasn't seen you for over ten years, do you remember him?'

'Of course, I do papa but only as Mr Saunders, I was far too young then to call him by his first name. How nice to see you again, Mr Saunders.'

'No more Mr Saunders my dear, call me Charles, please. You look delightful, you have grown into a most beautiful young woman but then you were beautiful as a child, I remember.' He kissed her on both cheeks as he announced.

'Welcome to Jersey.' He then assisted her on to the jetty. 'Merci, Charles.' She giggled from embarrassment.

The group set off for the hotel in two taxis. Whilst the booking formalities were being attended to, Larousse made it clear no discussions were to be made in front of his daughter, as far as she was concerned it was simply an urgent business meeting.

He suggested they talk sometime after midnight, assuming his daughter had retired. Charles insisted that their talks must be in private. Larousse agreed. Charles meanwhile hastily arranged for his wife and daughter to join them at the hotel later for dinner, the unexpected arrival of Larousse's daughter thwarted his plans somewhat, his theory being, to provide Larousse's daughter with some female company and perhaps distract her from the purpose of the meeting.

Around 20.30 hrs, Larousse and his company were sitting in the dining room awaiting the arrival of the two ladies before ordering their meals, his daughter was remarking on how long it had been since she had seen Jacqueline and how she remembered them playing together on the once frequent visits to the Saunders home when they lived in Hampshire.

Charles rose to meet his wife and daughter in the foyer as they arrived and took them through to the dining room. Once the introductions had been made, the meals were ordered and the evening passed pleasantly by in loquacious conversation without a hint of the impending disclosures.

The ladies had spent most of the evening talking with each other about their times together when the girls at the time were young and how it had been almost fifteen years ago when Larousse moved his family close to Marseille, which put an end to the once frequent visits to each other's homes.

One of them suggested the ladies should visit a nightspot in St Helier and leave the menfolk to their boring business talk, Larousse and Charles were delighted at the suggestion, persuading them under some duress to allow Carl and André to tag along.

Once the party had left for St Helier, Charles called for the manager asking him to show them to the room he had requested. They were led to a fairly large sumptuously decorated oak panelled study where refreshments had been provided in advance to avoid disturbance.

The manager bid them good evening and assured them they would not be disturbed. Larousse settled himself into a high-backed leather Chesterfield chair after pouring both of them a large measure of malt whisky from the selection of drinks provided.

'Now then, Charles. We can get down to business. What in heaven's name is all the flap about? And why all the secrecy?'

'François, I'm in a rather difficult situation which is going to take some explanation, I have brought you in on this against the department's strictest orders.' Charles was immediately interrupted.

'I told you not to bother me with the department, Charles! I have no wish to involve myself further in their operations. Do I make myself clear!' Retorted Larousse angrily.

'François, you don't understand my friend, it's because you are my friend that I'm putting my career on the line for you, please listen.'

'For me!' said Larousse raising his voice. 'You're right Charles, I don't understand! What can anything the department's involved in have to do with me?' Larousse was unsettled slightly.

'François, this situation has been monitored by the department for eighteen months. It involves co-operation between the British and French government's, an unofficial delegation from the DOC, the Diamond Mining Consortium, SIBEKA'S, Dè Beers, plus the port authorities at Bristol, Marseille, Le' Havre, Rotterdam, Hamburg and several others, also the world's diamond producer's association, to name but a few.' Charles gave Larousse a moment to think and hopefully to calm down a little.

'Charles, I'm sorry, I don't see what any of this has to do with me, where do I fit into this puzzle?' Larousse was indeed confused.

'François, I must trust you on this, I'm taking an awful risk, my friend. My career, perhaps my life depends on our friendship and the trust we have always had of each other,' Charles said pensively.

Larousse was utterly bewildered, he pondered over the memory he had of them working together for the department and some of the undercover assignments they had carried out, assignments which could only be achieved through trust, he knew they had a mutual trust of each other, a trust that many people never experienced.

'Charles, the one thing neither of us have to worry about is our trust in each other, whatever this problem is I'm certain we can solve it between us but please just tell me directly what this is all about, I'm too old in the tooth for guessing games,' said Larousse as he settled back into his chair in an effort to ease the tense atmosphere in the room.

'Yes, you're right François, enough beating about the bush, the fact of the matter is,' Charles sighed and took a deep breath. 'There's an extensive diamond smuggling operation coming out of the Democratic Republic of the Congo and heading into Europe. The value of diamonds has plummeted in the last year or two and SIBEKA'S in particular have seen massive losses in more or less the same period.'

Larousse was even more confused with this revelation, he swung himself around in his seat and raising both his voice and his arms, he screeched.

'What's this all got to do with me, Charles? The one thing I don't deal in, is diamonds, in fact I've never had anything to do with the bloody things other than buy them as jewellery!'

'Yes, we know that François, nonetheless our surveillance teams have made positive identifications of the transportation used. I'm afraid to say François, it's one of your vessels.'

'What!' Screeched Larousse. 'Are you trying to say I'm involved in a smuggling operation, Charles? Or is it the bloody department who's saying so?' Larousse was infuriated at the intimation.

'No, no. Of course not François, I am not suggesting anything of the kind, neither is the department. They however have a different view; they are only interested in the fact that it is one of your ships that's involved. You know their methods François, that's why I asked you to come here, to Jersey, so we could discuss the matter in private. I've known and respected you long enough to know you're not involved; you must believe me when I say that.'

Charles looked sympathetically at Larousse as if sensing the torment he must be feeling. Larousse considered the disclosure for a moment in silence and realised he had no choice, he had to get involved to clear his name at the very least.

'Thank you for that Charles, I appreciate your discretion. Tell me, who's in charge of this operation?'

'You don't know him François, he joined us about five years ago. Rear Admiral, Jeremy Bartholomew-Smythe. Don't be deceived by the name François, he's a pragmatic individual who will stop at nothing to get results, strictly speaking we would not normally deal with this sort of situation, however when it was discovered one of your vessels had consistently been involved, we were given orders to investigate the matter further. You having been associated with the department, you understand.'

'Yes, yes of course, I see. So, when can I meet this Bartholomew-Smythe?'

'Oh no François that's quite impossible, I can't let them know I've talked to you about this, I'll be court-martialled or worse, I'm only telling you all this because of our friendship.' Charles was uneasy over François's request.

'As I see it Charles, there's no other way. I can't be expected to take on a smuggling ring single handed. Surely you must see that?'

'But François, the department won't look at it that way, I'll be dismissed for sure!'

Charles was overwrought, he took a packet of cigarettes from his jacket pocket, fumbled with the contents until he withdrew one, lit it and began pacing up and down the study. Larousse thought in silence for a while watching Charles perspire and smoke the cigarette as if it were his last.

'Charles, I understand how you must feel and I appreciate your good intentions but I'm afraid we have no option, I may have a business empire at my disposal but they're not an army, I couldn't consider involving them in something as potentially dangerous as this.'

'But François, I hoped you could do something discreet, made it look like you found out yourself, by accident, you know!'

'I'm sorry Charles, if this has been going on as long as you say it is, I'm afraid it's past that stage. I must put a stop to this now and I'm going to need both yours and the department's help. We'll go and see this Bartholomew-Smythe tomorrow. Don't worry,' he said reassuringly. 'I'll straighten everything out with him, I still have friends in high places you know.'

Larousse asked Charles to furnish him with whatever information he had in readiness for the meeting with Bartholomew-Smythe the next day. They spent a couple of hours discussing details of the Departments findings that Charles was aware of to date. He concluded by mentioning the fact that something had occurred a month or so ago close to Bristol but he had no more details at present, although he was certain there was a significance.

Larousse pondered for a short while on the information Charles had given him, knowing it to be incomplete by his own admission that he had been privy to only part of the investigation. He decided to continue with his plans to meet with Bartholomew-Smythe, in the hope he would disclose more details of the Bristol affair, if not, he would make his own enquiries. Before retiring, Larousse made flight arrangements to London for Charles, Marcel and himself.

The next morning Thursday 29th over breakfast, Larousse disclosed to his party that they may be further delayed in their Nassau trip as he had to go to London, followed by Bristol perhaps for a few days. He instructed André to proceed to Bristol with the yacht and await his arrival perhaps on Friday. He apologised for the delay saying that it was merely an urgent business matter which required his immediate attention.

His daughter was rather annoyed over the recent developments protesting that she joined him to go to the Bahamas, not Jersey and Bristol and God knows where else in between, she then remarked on now knowing why her mother declined the trip.

Larousse tried to alleviate her discontent by informing her he would arrange for Graham Foster, head of his British staff to organise his chauffeur to meet them at the marina and take them to the Mercure Hotel, saying he would request him to bring his wife and family along to keep her company. She did not look impressed with the proposition and told him in no uncertain terms "not to bother".

Breakfast over, Larousse instructed Marcel to make appropriate car hire arrangements at Heathrow, then he, Charles and Marcel took a taxi to the airport and boarded the flight for London. Charles looked apprehensive, his thoughts of how Bartholomew-Smythe would react to an unannounced confrontation with François Larousse were indeed un-nerving.

Larousse's daughter asked André to stay in Jersey until Friday so she could see more of Jacqueline. He regretfully had to decline her request, stating although her father had arranged to meet them on Friday, his plans were at present flexible and that he may proceed to Bristol earlier than expected. She realised there was no point in arguing and asked what time they were leaving.

She said her goodbyes over the telephone to Jacqueline and promised they would get together again soon, then began to pack her wardrobe once again, this time a little less thoughtfully. In the process, she opened the small jeweller's gift box containing the gold cufflinks and looked at them, with a tear in her eye she snapped the lid closed and threw them to the back of her suitcase in a mix of temper and despair.

The flight touched down at Heathrow on time, Marcel hurried off to collect the hire car and returned to the arrivals lounge to collect Larousse and Charles and they made their way through London to Whitehall and the department's Headquarters at the Admiralty.

Larousse instructed Marcel to book the party into the Dorchester Hotel in Park Lane and if he had not heard from him by 18.00 hrs to consider himself off duty and take in a show or something in the West End. Marcel drew up outside the Admiralty building, Charles began inferring that perhaps they should telephone first, Larousse dismissed the suggestion unequivocally. On entering, the Admiralty soon after mid-day the security officer at the desk saluted Charles saying.

'Good afternoon, Lieutenant Saunders, I hadn't expected to see you this week Sir, I was advised you were on leave.'

'That's quite correct Jenkins, however I'm here with Monsieur François Larousse to see Rear Admiral Bartholomew-Smythe on a matter of great urgency.'

Jenkins looked through the large leather-bound appointments book laid open on the desk before him, he looked at the two men facing him and then double checked with the computer details, then casting his glance up to Charles said.

'I'm very sorry Sir, there's no entry in the Rear Admiral's appointments today for either yourself or Monsieur Larousse. In any case Sir, Monsieur Larousse will require security clearance before I can allow him to proceed.'

Charles already perplexed at the thought of confronting Bartholomew-Smythe unannounced and against his explicit orders not to divulge any details of Operation Windcutter to anyone outside the department, especially François Larousse. He himself began to undergo a small anxiety attack, slapping his hand on the desk, he shouted.

'Damn it man! I said it was urgent.'

Before he could say anything else, Jenkins whilst maintaining his calm replied firmly.

'I am very sorry Sir. You will have to make an appointment through the proper channels, the Rear Admiral is extremely busy.'

Larousse who until now had stood back from the desk, walked up to it, saying.

'Tell me, Jenkins, is it?' he asked although he knew. 'That is correct, Sir.'

'If the Rear Admiral is busy, where can we find Admiral Lawrence Salisbury?'

Jenkins looked shocked. Charles turned to Larousse, saying.

'François! You can't be serious, Admiral Salisbury, it's like getting an appointment with God himself!'

Jenkins meanwhile had overcome the shock of the stranger's request told Larousse directly, that it would be impossible to see Admiral Salisbury without official documentation.

Larousse giving a frustrated look directed both at Charles and Jenkins, said. 'What time is it?' Then looked up at the wall clock in preference to his wristwatch.

'Come Charles, we'll go on to the Dominion Club, we'll find the Admiral there and I have no time to waste on all this security nonsense!'

Jenkins was astonished that Larousse could know the whereabouts of the Admiral, he ran round from behind the desk to catch them before they left, shouting out.

'But Sir! Sir! You can't go there; you won't be allowed in!' Jenkins gripped Larousse's arm to restrain them from leaving.

Larousse swung round swiftly and looked him in the eye.

'I strongly suggest you remove your hand, young man,' he said authoritatively. He reached into his jacket pocket and produced a card wallet, flipping through it, he stopped at his membership card for the "Dominion Club" which had his Naval Rank of Commodore printed upon it.

Jenkins jumped to attention on reading the details and saluting, said. 'I'm very sorry Sir! I had no idea.'

'At ease, Jenkins, you're not to blame. Am I correct in assuming the Admiral will be at the club?'

'Yes Sir! Shall I contact the Rear Admiral and advise him you wish to see him, Sir!'

'No need, Jenkins. I shall speak with the Admiral first, he and I are old friends.'

They saluted each other and with that Larousse and Charles caught a taxi to the club.

On entering the club, the door person took their names, Larousse signing Charles in as a guest, asked where Admiral Salisbury could be found, the doorperson confirmed the Admiral would at this time of day be in the "Ark Royal Lounge".

Larousse went firstly to the gentlemen's rest rooms to adjust his tie and groom his hair in readiness to meet the Admiral. Charles was too nervous to even think of his presentation. Larousse once satisfied with his appearance, walked confidently out into the main hallway.

'Come Charles, let's get this over with,' he said boldly.

Both walked along to the "Ark Royal Lounge" where they found the Admiral sitting in one corner of the room with only a copy of The Times newspaper for immediate company. Unaware of his visitors, he continued to read on, there were several other club members sitting around the lounge quite content to simply read their newspapers, the only sound which could be heard was the tick-tock of an oak grandfather clock in far corner.

'Ah, Admiral Salisbury. Good afternoon, Sir,' Larousse said, saluting him. 'Yes, yes, what is it? Can't you see I'm busy,' he said, sounding as ruffled as the newspaper he was folding up. Looking up at the two visitors, his initial intimation of annoyance changed quickly to an expression of delight.

'François! My dear boy, how delightful to see you.'

The Admiral rose from his chair and returned his salute, looking at Charles for a moment, he said. 'It's Saunders, isn't it?'

Charles saluted. 'Sir. Yes Sir,' he replied nervously.

The Admiral looked back at Larousse, offering him his hand saying.

'I deduce from your unexpected arrival, François. You're here concerning this Operation Windcutter.' He announced directly then sat himself down again.

'Are you familiar with the operation, Admiral?' Larousse asked inquisitively and somewhat astonished with his manner.

'Oh, I pop in every now and then to see if any progress has been made. I'm officially retired now, though I do like a bit of intrigue to keep me on my toes, you understand,' he said in a flippant tone.

'Then you must be aware the department is targeting both myself and my shipping interests?' Replied Larousse, somewhat disconcerted at the Admiral's seeming disinterest in his plight.

'Oh yes, dear boy! Take a seat both of you, I'll order some port, then we can have a good old chat. Oh, I am sorry, have you two chaps had lunch yet? I surmise you haven't. I'll tell you what, we'll go through to the dining room, you chaps can have a spot of lunch while we talk, it should be quiet in there at present; something to do with the new chef, I presume,' he added as an afterthought as he tapped the side of his nose.

Larousse and Charles raised an eyebrow, each wondering what was in store for them.

'Come along you two, follow me!'

Larousse and Charles were astounded at the Admiral's equability. Admiral Salisbury was remarkably composed, showing no sign of tension which Larousse had expected with his sudden appearance.

The Admiral, now in his mid-seventies was still as alert as he had always been, showing little sign of his true age, springing up from his chair he walked sprightly through to the dining room, talking casually to François about his family asking in particular over the health of Claude François; François's father.

They sat down to lunch, neither François nor Charles in any mood to eat. Admiral Salisbury began the discussion by raising his glass of port saying. 'To you, François! And may your troubles soon be over. Now let's get down to the matter in hand.' He took a sip from his glass and placed it on the table. 'François, there appears to be several connections between your shipping division and this business of diamond smuggling out of the Democratic Republic of the Congo. The people concerned in the investigation came across several instances where one of your freighters was involved.'

'Your ship African Envoy IV was in Hamburg eighteen months ago when a young computer whizz of some sort on a university work experience posting at the berth offices organising your vessels' cargo was crushed by a container. Then at the dock in Rotterdam twelve months ago when a docker was again fatally injured whilst unloading her cargo, then several months later she was in Marseille where a foreman in charge of the unloading went missing, he's never, yet been found, at least not to our knowledge.'

'Similar tragic and unsolved, so called, "accidents" have happened at Le' Havre a few months back and the most recent up the road there in Avonmouth Dock's Bristol of all places! This accident, I say accident for that is what it was meant to look like, occurred strangely enough outside the Dock's complex, the following day to the driver of a heavy goods vehicle who was contracted to deliver part of the African Envoy's cargo. This incident I'm afraid was particularly nasty and the only one I have been familiarised totally with to date.'

'But Admiral, what has this got to do with me directly?' asked Larousse as he pondered on the facts.

'It was from this incident our department became involved, you are attached and all that, you know what the "powers that be" are, François. I shall give you the full details in a copy of the report later, suffice to say they're not happy there's a connection between your shipping line and this smuggling matter.'

Larousse was speechless, all he could say was for the Admiral to continue.

The Admiral continued familiarising Larousse with a few more details when the figure of an extremely tall though slightly built man entered, carrying a portfolio under his right arm. Marching in military fashion, though in civilian clothes, his pounding steps alerted Charles who knew them well. Charles jumped to attention, saluting the gentleman.

'Rear Admiral. Sir!' Charles exclaimed pusillanimously.

On confronting the threesome, the Rear Admiral, his face white with anger and his piercing eyes casting an invisible wrath upon the proceedings, gave an overzealous salute to the Admiral, saying. 'Good afternoon! Admiral Salisbury. Sir! Might I enquire, what is going on here? Sir!'

Admiral Salisbury glanced at him casually and replied. 'Jenkins on the ball, is he? I believe you and my old friend François have never met. François, let me introduce you. Commodore François Larousse, this is Rear Admiral, Jeremy Bartholomew-Smythe.'

Larousse stood up and saluted. 'Jeremy. François was one of our old colleagues who was with us until the nineties.'

Charles remained at attention and saluting until the Admiral noticed him and said.

'Put your arm down, man.'

'Mr Larousse.' Smythe said hastily and deliberately omitting both his naval rank and his normal "Monsieur Larousse" greeting.

'Rear Admiral, how nice to meet you after all this time. I feel you almost know me already. You have me at a disadvantage,' Larousse said with a touch of cynicism in his voice.

Smythe turned away from Larousse to face Charles. 'Saunders, I require an explanation, you have totally ignored my explicit orders on this matter. I want a full report on my desk first thing tomorrow. After that consider yourself suspended until further notice!'

Smythe was incensed more so at the Admiral being present in their discussions, he turned on him next. 'Admiral Salisbury. Sir. I am astonished at your presence here. I have no alternative other than to report this matter to my commanding officer, Admiral Stevens!'

'Saying, what? Exactly!' The Admiral asked calmly.

'Sir. My orders have been countermanded.' The Admiral interrupted him. 'By me? I think not Smythe, we are merely old colleagues having a chat in a Members Club, is that not so François,' suggested the Admiral.

Larousse was simply not quick enough off the mark, Smythe blasted.

'Sir! I protest, I see no other reason for this Larousse chap to be here other than our investigation. It's blatantly obvious to me Saunders is responsible for leaking information to forewarn him of our involvement. I! If you recall Sir, I vetoed Saunders' inclusion to the team, primarily! Because of his long-term association with the target.'

Admiral Salisbury stood up, staring into the cold piercing eyes of Smythe, he said.

'And it was I! Rear Admiral, who insisted together with Admiral Stevens he be included. I had a long serious chat with Admiral Stevens before you knew anything whatsoever about Operation Windcutter. It was decided then to involve Saunders from the outset. We knew that Saunders would contact his old friend, François here, at some stage or other.'

The Admiral turned to Charles and Larousse, holding his right hand out towards them, he continued.

'Their trust in each other would force him to contact François at some time. I must admit Saunders, you took a week or so longer than I had anticipated, good show my man.'

Smythe's expression of rage had now become an expression of bewilderment. His head turning from side to side, his eyes blinking repeatedly, the actions of him raising his arms momentarily as if intent on doing something, then not bothering indicated a man who was by now, totally confused.

'But Admiral. Sir, I don't understand?' Smythe uttered in bewilderment. 'You will. Don't worry Smythe, you will,' said the Admiral humorously.

Larousse who had been remarkably composed throughout, soon began to realise that he'd been set-up. He stood up and offered Admiral Salisbury his hand, saying.

'Admiral Salisbury. Sir. I congratulate you and Admiral Stevens on your Machiavellian methods.'

The Admiral shook his hand firmly and continued to do so for a while before explaining to Rear Admiral Smythe the significance of Larousse's statement, for he could see Smythe was still at a loss as to what was going on.

Looking directly at Larousse, the Admiral began.

'You see Jeremy, the plan was to involve François from the beginning, however both Admiral Stevens and I knew François would turn down a direct request from the department, regardless of the reason. Therefore, we devised this charade to lure him into the plot voluntarily.'

'We also knew that you would instruct your staff to regard the matter as "Top Secret". Therefore, placing Saunders with you, knowing his close allegiance to François would eventually draw him in. Am I making myself clear so far?'

Both Smythe and Saunders answered, 'yes' to the question, though their expressions were more of disbelief. Larousse on the other hand wore the expression of a duped man, though he bore no malice.

Smythe, still uncertain over the involvement of Larousse and determined to regain his authority commented.

'Sir. I still fail to understand why you have gone to all the trouble bringing this Larousse chap into the operation. I would have preferred to have continued as we were. In any case Sir, he was one our prime targets.'

'Of course, he was Smythe. That's why Saunders forewarned him, that's why he's here now and that's what we wanted. You're a good officer Smythe, however you're a little too obstinate at times, so much so, you fail to see an advantage staring you between the eyes. If anyone can pull this off, Operation Windcutter, that is, then François Larousse can. Both Admiral Stevens and I know full well that François would never get involved in such dealings and we place our trust in him implicitly.'

The Admiral swung round and asked Larousse directly.

'François, will you assist us on Operation Windcutter? We will naturally provide you with anything you may require. The choice is yours.'

There were a few moments silence while Larousse contemplated the question.

'Admiral Salisbury Sir, I see I have little choice in the matter; therefore I agree,' Larousse said, a touch dismayed.

'Excellent! Excellent François. I must apologise for our methods, dear boy, when need's must, you know when need's must.' The Admiral smiled then added. 'Oh Smythe, I'm countermanding your orders once again, I'm afraid.'

'Sir?' Smythe looked bemused.

'Saunders, dispense with the Rear Admiral's request for a report and consider yourself off suspension, there's a good chap.'

Saunders was relieved to be discharged, for up till now he knew he could have faced a court-martial.

'Come gentlemen, we shall proceed to the Admiralty, I wish to furnish François with full details of Operation Windcutter for which Jeremy I shall require your full co-operation.'

'Sir. Of course, Sir,' Rear Admiral Bartholomew-Smythe replied knowing he also had precious little choice in the matter.

The four men returned to the Admiralty where Larousse was led to one of the Operations Rooms by the Rear Admiral, Charles following close behind. Once within the spacious room, Larousse immediately observed the series of nasty and graphic photographs appertaining to the so called "accident victims" showing the extent of their fatal injuries and where possible the way the incidents occurred, together with the reports and documentation relating to their cause of death.

Thorough background information, including their employment record, family history, previous convictions, if any, known associations with undesirables and any other matters thought to be of interest to the investigation had all neatly been collated.

Larousse began by saying.

'Rear Admiral, I must congratulate you on your work so far, these reports make remarkably interesting reading. In all but one, it would appear the victims had never been in any trouble with the authorities, just ordinary men with ordinary jobs, yet they all suffered a tragic death.'

'Not quite! Monsieur Larousse.'

Larousse turned to the sound of a stranger's voice. At the doorway stood the rather short, stocky figure of a man who looked to be similar ages with Larousse, dressed in a plain grey suit.

'Admiral Stevens. I'm in command of this little shebang. I'm so pleased to meet you at last, Commodore Larousse. Glad to have you on the team. Back to the fold, so to speak.'

Larousse ignored the equivoque.

'Delighted to make your acquaintance, Admiral Stevens. Sir.' The two shook hands firmly. Admiral Stevens continued.

'As I was saying. Not quite. We have one chap who miraculously survived a horrendous road traffic collision in his articulated lorry, he was carrying a consignment of oranges from Avonmouth Docks brought in on your vessel African Envoy IV.'

'He's currently in Bristol Royal Infirmary recuperating from his ordeal, been in a coma for some time but is now recovering, poor fellow. He's under police protection, might I add. I thought perhaps we could visit him sometime tomorrow; the Doctors have consented to our request providing we keep it brief as possible.'

Larousse was intrigued.

'What has a truck driver, who's suffered a road traffic accident have to do with all of this, Admiral?' he asked curiously.

'Oh, it was no ordinary accident, the poor chap was forced head-on into a bridge support and the police have confirmed this. At one point, they questioned the driver of another truck some twenty miles into the next county. A patrol stopped him after spotting severe damage to the vehicle's near-side.'

'Unfortunately, at that time those officers had no knowledge of the previous incident and simply booked him and instructed him to leave the road at the next exit and have the vehicle recovered. Needless to say, it was found burnt out and abandoned when the matter came to light.'

Admiral Stevens continued disclosing the details of the operation to Larousse. Once he was familiarised, Larousse began to offer several scenarios which he thought could assist in clearing his shipping division of any involvement, the simplest method being the withdrawal of his vessel from operating out of Matadi.

This suggestion was met with looks of disapproval. Larousse, who knew by now he had never been implicated personally by the department, had obviously opted for the simplest solution.

Admiral Stevens rose from his seat, walked over to the large screen monitor and selected a large-scale map, upon the map were markers where incidents had occurred at various European Ports, several more than Larousse had been familiarised with at present. He continued.

'The Admiralty has been requested to pursue this matter jointly with the police to a successful conclusion, including apprehending the culprits responsible, tracing the whereabouts of the missing diamonds and discovering the purpose behind this massive operation.'

Larousse looked over at the Admiral.

'I take it you wish me to fully investigate the matter rather than simply clear my position?'

The Admiral smiled, saying.

'We shall assist you all the way. We want you to go to Kinshasa where the African Envoy's cargo was organised at an agency. Go there and see what you can find out from them, we need someone who's known to them, we daren't send in a stranger at this stage, it could jeopardise the whole operation!'

Larousse intervened.

'Admiral Sir. I haven't been to Kinshasa since I set up the initial shipping contracts, that was over twelve years ago.'

'That should make no difference, you will simply be seen as a businessman inspecting your operations first-hand. As a coincidence the vessel is loading there at this moment, that gives a credible reason, don't you agree?'

'Perhaps but it's not my way, those in charge there will know that.'

'I believe you have a daughter, perhaps she could travel along with you?' Larousse's tone changed suddenly.

'Admiral, my daughter will not be involved in this, I won't hear of it, I shall send her back to Marseille as soon as I return to the yacht!'

The mention of his daughter made Larousse shudder for a moment. He asked. 'Admiral Sir, do you know the name of the chap killed in Hamburg by any chance?'

The Admiral talked over him, saying.

'I take it from that, your daughter is with your party at present Commodore, just think for a moment, you have the perfect cover, a businessman travelling with his daughter, she needn't get involved in anything dangerous, she'll simply give credulity to your presence. Say you're on a sight-seeing trip with your daughter and thought you would combine business with pleasure.'

Larousse could see the obvious benefit, although he thought the whole affair too dangerous to involve his daughter, he informed them he would consider the option. Larousse reiterated the question to Admiral Stevens.

'Sir, I must ask, do you know the name of the chap killed in Hamburg?'

The Admiral glanced through the documentation, saying he could not see the actual file but would investigate it if it was important. Larousse said he was unsure however, something was bothering him, why would that file be missing. The Admiral agreed to make relevant enquiries in the meantime. Larousse added. 'Admiral, I'm afraid my concerns are raised somewhat over this missing file. The fact of the matter is my daughter was dating a young German student a couple of years or so ago. I only met him once, nice young boy. Oh, what was his name it's oh, let me think, it'll come to me in a moment.

'Anyway he was a student in electronics or something like that, it may have been computers I can't quite remember. Dieter! That was his name, Dieter, Dieter. No, I can't yet recall his surname but I do recall my daughter being devastated hearing of his death in some accident or other, I'm sure that was around eighteen months ago, I was in Australia at the time. I do hope none of this is related to this investigation.'

'I see no obvious connection however as I say we shall make the relevant enquires as a matter of urgency,' added Admiral Stevens.

They continued discussions until late that evening involving suggested strategies and further scenarios. Once they had collated all the relative information and Larousse had satisfied himself as to how he would undertake the mission, the evening was concluded by making the arrangements to meet in Bristol the following day to interview the truck driver if possible.

Larousse and Charles then returned to the Dorchester very late on Thursday evening in order to get some rest, this however proved impossible for Larousse, his mind was too alert contemplating the pros and cons of the operation.

The following morning Friday 30th after breakfast, Larousse returned to the Admiralty to meet with Admiral Stevens. The Admiral having planned for them to travel down to the naval base at Bristol in order to organise equipment and assign a couple of men to assist in the operation. Rear Admiral Bartholomew-Smythe had instructed his staff to make further enquiries throughout other maritime towns and cities in Europe and Africa for any similarly linked events.

Marcel drove Larousse and Admiral Stevens to Bristol whilst the Rear Admiral and Charles were driven in an Admiralty car. Saunders received constant chastisement from his superior the whole length of the journey, he was to say the least relieved when the car drew up outside the Mercure Hotel in Bristol where Larousse had arranged a luncheon before the hospital visit.

Over lunch, Admiral Stevens received further information over the telephone. He returned to the table and informed them he had received some very disturbing reports from the Foreign Office, which connected the series of events emanating from The Democratic Republic of the Congo to similar events from South Africa, furthermore the largest diamond consortium, De Beer's had reluctantly reported yet further losses in their output also.

François Larousse was astounded at what he took to be an insinuation his shipping division was involved in wholesale smuggling, albeit without his knowledge.

The Admiral calmed him down by saying they had no information relating to his company's involvement in the South African affair. However, he continued.

'His Majesty's government, the European Commission, The United States, SIBEKA'S, De Beer's and several others, I could go on, are all extremely worried over this diamond business, it appears to be far greater than first imagined, furthermore all parties are no longer solely concerned over the value of the missing stocks, rather their whereabouts and their purpose.

'Diamonds are not simply of monetary value alone, their use in weapons technology and such is becoming widespread. We must both find the source and the end user before something nasty develops.'

Admiral Stevens commented further that the whole operation was now beginning to sound far too complex to expect Larousse to handle it alone and that perhaps they should re-evaluate the operation.

Larousse insisted that he should be allowed to continue with the plans as agreed, having spent the time studying the reports and making arrangements.

The Admiral agreed in principle, saying.

'Providing if things get too hot, you must pull out, take no unnecessary risks.'

Larousse consented to the Admiral's wishes. Adding had they found out anything about the Hamburg incident.

'Oh, yes. Sorry should have mentioned this earlier. It appears the file on this has been misplaced or lost along the line somewhere, it's currently deemed a clerical error and the relevant authorities in Hamburg are looking into it at our request. Do you think it important, François?' The Admiral replied.

'Missing files are always important Admiral, the file is either lost or purposely removed, the question is which.'

'Well Commodore, as I say the authorities are looking into it and we will keep you informed as soon as we receive any further information.'

With that overshadowing the proceedings and leaving Larousse suspicious, they finished lunch and headed for the Hospital.

***

Upon arriving at the private room guarded by two police officers, they showed their credentials and advised they had a meeting arranged with the doctor to question the patient. The doctor was summoned and duly explained her patient was very weak following his ordeal and they had five minutes at best. She took them into the room and introduced them both to the driver, saying.

'These gentlemen need to ask you a few questions to do with your accident, is that okay with you?' The driver nodded in agreement and the doctor left the room.

Upon interviewing the truck driver who was barely able to speak, so severe were his injuries, Larousse learned that he had had a scuffle on the dock berth with three of the loaders and somewhat surprisingly, one of the office staff. The driver detailed how they caught him filling a carrier bag with a few oranges from a pallet awaiting to be loaded onto his truck.

The dockers, he explained, were so incensed they dragged him into the warehouse and set about him, beating him up quite viciously. He had reported the matter to the British Transport Police (BTP) on the dock at the time, then went to get cleaned up and decided to return to his vehicle and await loading when the next shift came on.

At this point, Larousse asked.

'Again Admiral, have we any information about this incident? I don't recall seeing it on any of the reports. Another missing file perhaps?'

The Admiral whilst thumbing through his portfolio answered that he didn't recall any mention of this in the police reports; only that of the road traffic incident. He instructed one of the constables on guard to contact his commanding officer to make enquiries to the BTP and report back any findings. The officer left the room and radioed the message to his station.

The truck driver continued to detail how his accident occurred.

'The truck was loaded by about one o'clock in the morning, I didn't feel like taking it out mate, I can tell you, I was bruised from bloody head to toe, those bastards gave me a good going over for a few bloody oranges! I mean, Christ, all the drivers pinch a bit of fruit and that from their loads, its common practice, it goes with the job.

'It's a perk, for the kids, you know what I mean. Anyway, I was driving north on the A38 heading for Gossington Truck Stop at a steady forty, forty-five miles an hour, it was a quiet night, maybe because it was raining heavy, I don't know, anyway there wasn't much traffic about but there was this truck following me more or less all the way from the dock gates, that's nothing unusual normally but then he began to overtake me, very close to my off-side.'

'I just thought he was tired or something, not concentrating and that, I pulled on the air horns to warn him off, he didn't take a blind bit of notice, in fact he got even closer, then, I felt him hit me quite deliberately. I swung to the left to avoid him when he closed in again and rammed me, I was bloody scared mate I'll tell you.'

'Anyway, I had nowhere left to go, there was a steep embankment, then I see the bloody bridge abutments loom up in front of me, I knew he intended forcing me into it, I didn't know why, only that was what the bastard intended to do. I couldn't do anything, so I just let go the bloody wheel and jumped into the bunk bed area behind the seats. It was all over in a flash, I don't remember anything else until I woke up in here, I've been in a coma for a few weeks, so they tell me.'

At that point, the doctor returned, advising their time was up. The driver with all the strength he could muster, lifted his left arm and gripped Larousse's hand. He continued.

'Look, I don't know why they did it but please! Get those bastards for me, make them pay for this! Please! Promise me you'll try; I've got a wife and three kids. Please,' he asked emotionally as his eyes filled with tears and he began to cry uncontrollably.

The doctor checked the patient's pulse then said he'd had enough for one day and requested they leave. The Admiral told the driver that they were not sure, yet, why he was attacked or forced off the road. But he would be looked after and they with the police would pursue the matter vigorously.

As the group were leaving the room, Larousse turned back to look at the sorry state of the man laid out in the bed.

'One moment, doctor,' he said, then walked back to the bedside.

'Listen, here's my card. If there's anything you need, anything at all, you can contact my office through this. I'll arrange to ensure your family are provided for whilst you're incapacitated, now you rest assured and don't worry about them, alright?'

The driver looked at Larousse and his eyes filled again until tears trickled down his face. 'You're a real gentleman pal, I'll repay every penny.'

'There's no need, you just get yourself better and back to your family, okay.' The driver continued to thank Larousse as he was escorted out by the doctor.

They waited outside the drivers' room, discussing his chronicle of events whilst waiting for a reply from the police.

Within half an hour of waiting at approximately 16.30 hrs, a woman in her late thirties walked briskly towards them dressed very smartly in a beige suit, the skirt of which came to slightly above the knee and wearing a white blouse under the jacket. She looked very confident and attractive with it, the two constables saluted her as she approached, both saying.

'Good afternoon, ma'am.'

Taking her warrant card from her handbag, she introduced herself. 'Admiral Stevens,' she said with a general glance towards them. 'Ma'am,' replied the Admiral with a short bow of the head.

'I'm Detective Chief Inspector Angela Pearce, Avon and Somerset Police CID. I think you gentlemen had better accompany me to the station. I have some information which I think will interest you.'

Following a little light-hearted humour regarding her comment which bordered on them being arrested, they joined her in her request. Once in the police station, she disclosed the fact that the young officer from the BTP Dock's Division who had been dispatched to attend to the matter of the assault on the driver, had met with a fatal accident on the Dock's involving a fork-lift truck, seemingly, shortly after taking statements, unfortunately he never regained consciousness.

She apologised for the fact that the two incidents had not been regarded as related in any of their investigations as the truck driver, due to him being in a coma, had not until now mentioned there had been a squabble on the dock earlier that same day, however she had now instructed two of her officers to urgently liaise with the BTP on this matter.

Larousse requested that they make discreet enquires and resist from questioning the dockers' involved on anything other than the police officer's fatal accident, explaining that he did not wish to arouse their attention towards the Admiralty's investigations until he reported his own position. He asked if he could speak with his Admiralty colleagues alone for a moment.

Agreed, he continued. Larousse asked the Admiral if he had any objections to the local police knowing the extent of their involvement, after a short pause it was deemed best to advise the police the reason for their interest as they would no doubt find information out that they may need as the investigation proceeded.

The DCI was brought back to the meeting and briefed on the objective; Larousse continued.

'This operation is obviously extremely well planned, whomever is controlling it has placed their people in strategic locations throughout Africa, Europe and God knows where else. Just think for a moment about the organisation these people, whoever they are, wherever they are, have at their control.'

'Their collecting diamonds from various sources throughout Africa, transporting them, sometimes, hundreds maybe thousands of miles to port's like Kinshasa and Matadi, which we know about. From there, they travel to any number of destinations where there are members of this syndicate placed ideally to locate and retrieve the diamonds. From which point, we know nothing as yet.'

He paused for a moment, no one ventured to comment on what had been said. He continued.

'DCI Pearce, gentlemen. This whole operation is a lesson in logistics unsurpassed at present by any industry standard. We must tread very gently until we know exactly what we're dealing with.'

The DCI agreed to contain their investigations to "Regarding the person or persons responsible for the death of the Transport Police constable and the attempted murder of the truck driver".

The Admiral thanked her and bid her good afternoon.

Larousse invited Admiral Stevens, Rear Admiral Bartholomew-Smythe and Charles Saunders to return with him to the "Mercure Hotel" to continue discussions and make necessary arrangements for equipping him for his trip to Kinshasa. Their discussions continued through the afternoon, the Admiral making several telephone calls to various naval depot's arranging the procurement of certain supplies and hardware.

Larousse contacted André on board the KATRIANA and instructed him to take several crew members with him by car to Bristol naval base at "HMS Flying Fox" and report to the commanding officer for instructions.

His daughter had left a message at the hotel reception that she would be attending a garden party throughout the day with the Foster's. Adding that she was not very happy with the situation. From there, they would be going on to the theatre and finally a casino where it was hoped by all he would join them later.

Larousse reneged the offer and grateful his daughter was unaware of any of the disturbing issues. He continued to finalise his plans with the Admiral, agreeing reluctantly to have his daughter accompany him, although in the event she became under threat from any source, he would get her out before continuing any further.

After dinner, Admiral Stevens and Rear Admiral Bartholomew-Smythe wished him the "best of luck" and departed for London.

Charles stayed with Larousse throughout the remainder of the evening, both enjoying a leisurely drink in the hotel lounge into the early hours, Larousse mentioning the fact that he would now have to tell his daughter they were not going to Nassau for the third time, something he was not looking forward to, especially with the mood she would be in when she returned.

He had decided to stay in the lounge until she arrived, however shortly before three in the morning, Larousse received a telephone call from the Admiralty informing him to make immediate departure for Kinshasa as the African Envoy's itinerary had been reported changed.

They advised him his captain on the KATRIANA had been informed and both he and two naval officers plus the equipment requested was at this moment heading to Bristol naval base by helicopter for immediate transfer by vehicle to join the KATRIANA.

Larousse quickly arranged with André to make a telephone call to the casino to contact his daughter and advise her to meet them at the marina as soon as possible.

From now on, it would be a race against time. He had to reach Kinshasa before the ship sailed in a week. He also could not consider arriving by air, the smugglers would no doubt know he was in the habit of travelling normally by sea. Time was against him, he had to move fast, there was only one thing for it.

The KATRIANA had to set sail as soon as possible.

Chapter Three

The first day of the weekend, Saturday, 1 October 2022, when the signs of autumn were in abundance and the only sounds normally heard in the early hours throughout the countryside were those associated with the customary call or two from the various forms of nocturnal wildlife.

However, it was not the foxes or owls which abruptly interrupted the serenity at 03.15 hrs, it was the first and slightly irregular ring from a telephone. The device continued to ring out impatiently, calculatedly, each double bar being superseded by the same monotonous pause before repeating itself only to pause yet repeatedly.

The reaction from the nocturnal creatures in the immediate vicinity was much more expeditious than their human counterparts housed within the protective walls of Hadlowe House, in Surrey, the country seat of Sir Roger Clarendon, a high-ranking defence minister with His Majesty's government.

The early hours of that Saturday morning had now reached 03.18 hrs before any sign of activity was noted from within the household. Perhaps not so surprising for only one telephone rang out from a total of seven similar devices positioned strategically throughout the spacious Edwardian establishment.

Clarendon's almost suspended consciousness was finally disturbed by the penetrating sound reverberating throughout the building. He awakened partially and with only the moonlight to assist, he struggled to focus his attention on the switch operating the bedside lamp.

Depressing the button firmly, a combination of the click and the illumination disturbed his wife who drowsily enquired as to the time. He glanced at the combined radio, alarm, calendar on the bedside cabinet.

'Three eighteen in the bloody morning!' He snapped at the seeming injustice of the situation. 'That is what time it is, my dear. This had better be bloody important and not some damn fool's prank that's all I can say.'

He mumbled in a low tone as he raised his shoulders from the pillow. His wife turned over to her front then snatched the pillow from his side of the bed and placed it over her head whilst also mumbling some disdainful remark or other.

Clarendon having noticed the date on the panel of the time piece recalled mention had been made at the office the previous day of tomorrow being of non-importance from a security point of view. Swinging his legs out from under the duvet, he sat bolt upright and rubbed his face and eyes before proceeding.

He then reached under his now singular pillow and retrieved a single key which he kept hold of whilst stepping into his slippers awkwardly. He semi-hopped to the bedroom door still attempting to fit his right heel into the now crushed back of his slipper.

He removed his dressing gown from behind the bedroom door, slipping into it as he headed downstairs still mumbling to himself. It was now a choice between a prank and the fact that something just had to happen whilst he was standing in for the minister.

The telephone was still ringing relentlessly as he descended the wide balustrade stairway leading down to the spacious hall, upon reaching the foot of the stairs his butler appeared from a doorway at the rear of the hall, also in night attire.

'It appears to be your direct line from the Ministry, Sir.'

'Yes, Albert and at three twenty in the bloody morning. You go back to bed, Albert; I'll see to it.'

Albert thanked him and retired back to his room.

Clarendon inserted the key into the escutcheon of the oak panelled door and quickly turned the levers to unlock, he opened the door to his study and with force of habit he removed the key. He proceeded towards his desk, without any great haste, whereupon there were two telephones. He lifted the receiver on the farther of the two.

'Clarendon speaking,' he said in a dull monotone.

'Minister, this is Station Commander, Group Captain Tewkesbury at Portsmouth.'

'Yes, Tewkesbury, what's the problem?'

Clarendon asked curtly as he yawned then rubbed his eyes in an effort to bring himself around. The rubbing subsided as he realised the nature of the call.

Tewkesbury was detailing an event in an agreed code form, which he grasped immediately.

His left hand clenched across his cheeks as he squeezed softly, then they began slipping ever downward as his fingers slowly lowered and his clenched palm slid towards his chin. The colour in his rosy, red cheeks visibly drained from him, his spine was tingling.

He stretched the cable of the handset around the desk and headed for the sanctity of the mahogany 'Captains' chair whereupon he slowly eased himself down into the luscious leather upholstery. The conversation had finished but it hadn't quite penetrated.

'Say again,' asked Clarendon in a bemused tone. 'Am I hearing you correctly? This isn't some damn prank, is it?'

Clarendon was obviously extremely perturbed by the message he just received. Tewkesbury began paraphrasing the previous statement.

'Listen Tewkesbury, enough of this nonsense, I'm standing in for the minister, this code is totally irrelevant over this secure line, come to the point man.'

'Are you sure, Sir?'

'Of course, I'm sure! Get on with it, man!'

'Very well Sir, if, you're sure,' Tewkesbury continued.

'Sir. Two eagles down, one returning to base, all three were conveying full compliment.' He paused, then continued as Clarendon had not said anything.

'Sir. Three of our F35 Lightning fighter jets tagged DT534, DH536 and DA619 for the exercise have been involved in an incident which has resulted in two of them, 534 and 619 being destroyed. I'm afraid both crews are down also.'

'Good God, man! Are you serious? Give me the details quickly Tewkesbury, I'll have to make some calls,' said Clarendon as he reached for the brandy decanter on the drinks table to his right. He poured himself a generous measure as the details unfolded.

'It's rather patchy Sir, the aircrew of DH536 are traumatised by the incident and are being talked back to base but we have reason to believe one of our own F35's DT534 opened fire firstly upon DA619 then on DH536, which took evasive action and deployed countermeasures. DT534 self-destructed soon after.'

'Well, who destroyed D? Well, whatever 534 was it? Was it the third aircraft?' Interjected Clarendon, still confused.

'Absolutely not Sir, 534 simply blew herself up, we followed the whole scenario on screen, my chaps down here are totally bewildered as to why or how this could possibly have happened. The F35s were conducting a routine low-level night flying mission over the Atlantic, they were carrying out manoeuvres against a dummy target when suddenly 534 fired upon 619 then 536, then within an instant, 534 also disappeared from the screen. The pilot in DH536 took immediate avoidance action and carried out missile avoidance drill utilising his complement of flares until he was sure there was no further danger.'

Clarendon took a large swallow from the brandy glass, then interrupted. 'And where and when exactly did this happen?'

'Over the Atlantic, one hundred miles southwest of the Isles of Scilly at precisely 03.00 hrs.'

'There were no other aircraft in the vicinity who could have been involved?'

'Absolutely not Sir. In any case, the pilot in DH536 witnessed the whole event and we ourselves saw it take place on our radar screens. I'm afraid it doesn't look too good, Sir,' concluded Tewkesbury.

'No, quite right, it doesn't,' replied Clarendon, somewhat disconcerted at the thought. He concluded the conversation by ordering an enquiry and a media ban, he then requested Tewkesbury to ensure he be kept fully informed of developments. After a dozen or so further calls and almost half a decanter of brandy, he retired back to bed in the opinion a weapons system malfunction had befallen DT534. He never slept, however, so decided to head for the office.

Tewkesbury, as ordered, immediately initiated a full inquiry as to the cause of the F35 incident. The Royal Navy ordered the Frigate; HMS Somerset to divert from patrol duties in the area to help in the search for any survivors or wreckage. At that same moment, DH536 touched down rather gingerly at RNAS Yeovilton, where the pilot attended an immediate de-briefing and received medical attention to counteract the effects of shock.

By lunch time, the Royal Navy Fleet Air Arm investigation branch was in full control of the situation and the implemented media silence ensured a thorough investigation without interruption. In fact, the incident had taken place so far out at sea there were no witnesses other than the surviving F35 crew and those at Yeovilton.

Of course, the crew of the Navy Frigate knew sketchy details but nothing more. Matters were proceeding reasonably well until a message was received at

Ministry Headquarters at 15.00 hrs precisely twelve hours after the F35 incident. It read:

We believe two of your F35 aircraft were destroyed twelve hours ago. To deny would only worsen the situation. Your country was chosen as our first target purely at random and this is simply the beginning. We will avenge!

The MOD immediately began to trace the source of the message. Within the hour, investigations led to a small parcels' carrier and courier service adjacent to Heathrow airport. The MOD front desk receptionist well trained in observation recalled in detail the motorcyclist delivering the message as a single letter and the name of the company was noticed from the vinyl sticker attached to his helmet, which he had carried in his left hand. The receptionist also remembered asking if he required a signature, he had replied that it was not necessary.

MOD personnel and police officers swooped on the small parcels' outlet, demanding to know the origin of the sender. Staff there, although shocked by the mass attendance of military and police personnel, made a thorough investigation of all documentation and could find no details of any package or otherwise destined for the MOD offices.

Within the first five minutes, demand was made by police to contact all ten motor-cycle delivery personnel and order them back to base, as they returned each was taken into a room and interviewed, all ten denied any knowledge of being in or near MOD HQ at any time that day.

The Managing Director realised there may be good reason for the silence, for as company policy, No driver or courier may collect or deliver goods of any kind unless authorised. He decided to offer his staff an amnesty considering the circumstances, which in truth he was unaware of, though obviously realised they were extremely serious. Once he had made his announcement, one young man aged about seventeen to eighteen stepped cautiously forward. Hesitantly, he announced.

'I, I, I've been to the MOD today,' he said it nervously, quietly, his head bowed as if in shame.

He was led off to a room and re-interviewed. It transpired that having completed a delivery of a package to a firm of city solicitors, a man rushed out behind him, seemingly as if he'd meant to catch him before he left. The young man then repeated the request made.

Pop this letter into the MOD offices in Whitehall just before three p.m. would you? There's a good chap, it's very urgent and critically time sensitive, it must reach there just a few minutes before 3pm, if you must wait outside for a few minutes then do so, okay, would you do that for me? Here you go, fifty quid in it for you if you'll drop it off. Please don't let me down, will you. It's very important and urgent.

The young man said he'd agreed and carried out the deed.

The police demanded the money be surrendered to carry out forensic tests and were also quick to point out that there could have been a bomb or anything in the package. The young man replied.

'I might be stupid to have risked my job but I'm not a complete idiot. The man had bandaged hands, he said he'd just been scalded in the kitchen and that's why he's in a hurry. He held the letter out in the open and placed it in the envelope then sealed it right in front of me, so I saw no harm, it was a quick fifty notes, that's all.'

The questioning continued until the authorities were satisfied the courier had no further evidence to offer. The MOD officials returned to the office still none the wiser as to where the letter had come from.

Before the day was through, tests by forensic scientists had been carried out on the money, the letter, the envelope and the courier together with his motorcycle. The firm of solicitors where the letter had been collected had also been investigated, every possible check had been carried out, the only results of which were the scientists had narrowed it down to the type of paper used, the fact that it was a rather poor photocopy of a laser printed page rather than an original piece of typed or printed matter and strangely the only fingerprints to be found were that of the courier and those who had handled it since delivery. In other words, a dead end.

The message however bore other connotations, the three words at the end "We will avenge" deeply disturbed all concerned. Who? Why? They would have to wait until he, they, whoever contacted them. 'It would not be long,' thought Clarendon, 'as he studied the simple piece of paper.' His assumption soon proved to be correct.

***

Slightly earlier than the arrival of the courier at the Admiralty around 14.30 p.m. back on board the KATRIANA, Larousse leaned forward placing his hands on the rear of the seat and glaring at the stranger, he said conceitedly. 'Ah!

So, we have a name at last! Now for the second question. What are you doing on my yacht, Cameron?' Larousse demanded.

Robert looked at the stranger peering down at him, in an attempt to diffuse the situation, he replied jovially. 'I'm sorry, I apologise. Honestly. Look, I came aboard last night, just to have a look around your yacht, it looked magnificent!'

Larousse contemplated his answer in silence.

Robert meanwhile was slowly coming round and in the process, he realised the most terrific hangover was developing. His head began to pound inside. He could feel a swaying feeling throughout his body. Holding his head in both hands, he muttered. 'Oh god, my head.'

'Never mind your bloody head man, just get on with it!' Larousse intervened impatiently.

Robert, not quite "compos mentis" to his surroundings yet, thought it wise to leave while the going was good, looking at the stranger, he said. 'Look I've caused you enough bother, I'll be on my way, I apologise once again.' Robert attempted to rise from below the table. 'I'll have to—'

Interrupting whatever Robert was about to say next, Larousse began to enlighten Robert to his plight. 'Ah, my dear Mr Cameron, you'll have some difficulty in being on your way to anywhere!' Larousse raised his voice in a sardonic tone and culminating in a crescendo, he enlightened him. 'We have been at sea! For some seven to eight hours!'

'What? You are joking! You must be joking?' Replied Robert, clearly perplexed at the revelation. Regaining some co-ordination, he began to scramble out from under the table. Looking around the moment his head rose above the table top, all he could see was the horizon surrounding him. Holding his head in his hands, he exclaimed.

'My god! Where are we? Where are you headed? I don't believe this, is this some kind of prank? Where are we headed? Please!' he asked in a worried tone. 'Our destination is of no consequence to you, Cameron. I shall decide what's to be done with you when we dock!' Larousse said dismissively. 'Search him Carl, then put him below until I decide what's to be done with him.'

Robert moved quickly under the table towards Larousse, raising his arm and pointing directly at his face, he said demonstratively. 'Now you wait just one minute!'

He was immediately prevented from getting any closer as Carl held him back by the shoulder and raised the pistol once again.

'Don't try anything, Cameron!' Carl said in a callous manner.

'Try anything! Try what, for god's sake! What's with the bloody gun? Who are you people, have you all gone completely mad!'

Robert was rapidly becoming apprehensive over the series of events of the last few minutes.

'Papa, please!' shouted Larousse's daughter, who had witnessed the rough treatment administered to the stranger was clearly concerned over what was actually happening. She continued.

'You can see the man is obviously distressed, why are you treating him so harshly? He's told you why he came aboard, why can't you believe him, it's obvious to me he's telling the truth.'

Larousse walked over to his daughter. 'My dear, this does not concern you. I need to know more before I can begin to believe his story.'

'What do you mean? This does not concern me. Of course, it does, you're behaving intolerably, papa! The poor man's trembling, look what you've done to him!' She screeched at her father.

Larousse looked back at Robert and as his daughter had said, he'd broke into a sweat and was physically trembling.

Robert was unable to control his condition, for he was unsure if it was due to the events of the last few moments or the results of his heavy drinking the night before. However, he was grateful the young lady had intervened to moderate the situation.

Larousse took his daughter to one side, speaking softly, he said. 'I'm sorry my dear if this upsets you but I must be careful, I need to be sure. Please understand.'

'I don't understand why you're being so harsh towards him, there's bloody Carl pointing that gun at him for a start!'

'He's only doing his job, my dear and less of the profanities please.' His daughter gave a growl and sat down quickly on the opposite side of the table to the commotion. Larousse turned and waved his hand at Carl, saying. 'Put the gun away Carl, my daughter is right, he poses no threat to us for the moment.'

Carl reluctantly replaced his pistol back in his shoulder holster and fastened his jacket.

'Mr Cameron, would you mind being searched. If you are telling the truth, I can see no reason for your refusal, eh.'

Robert looked at Larousse and his daughter momentarily, the young lady nodded at him to comply with the request. Robert thought it was possibly better than being forced at gunpoint and agreed.

Carl carried out the search. He removed his wallet, passport, pen and a sealed envelope, leaving him with some small change, a bunch of keys and a handkerchief. He passed the item's over to Larousse.

Larousse, glancing quickly through them held the passport up. 'Planning a trip abroad, were you? Take him below Carl, put him in one of the cabins for now until I find out some more about our Mr Cameron here,' Larousse lowered his voice to a whisper and continued. 'And lock it, I shall talk with him later.'

'Papa!' His daughter protested.

'No, my dear! People in England do not carry their passport around, there's more to this than he's admitting to. I must insist you leave this to me,' Larousse said, sounding earnest.

Robert attempted to explain but Larousse simply waved his hand to Carl, gesturing him to take Robert below. Robert was bustled down the steps, both Carl and André leading him to a cabin. He continued to protest. 'This is a god damn nightmare! I'll see to it you're all charged with assault! Kidnap! Something! Mark my words.'

Carl grabbed Robert's arm. 'Shut up and move, you tiresome little man!' He said in a menacing tone.

Robert could see no reason to resist any longer, no one was listening to anything he had to say, he shrugged his arm from Carl's grip, saying. 'Alright! Alright, no need for the rough stuff, you overgrown baboon.'

Larousse's daughter looking down as Robert was physically manhandled, grinned at the comment turning her head away to avoid detection. Robert was led to a cabin with André reassuring him he would be fine if he was telling the truth. On entering the cabin, Robert asked if he could have some black coffee, as he felt dreadful. André replied.

'I'll see what I can do. But no tricks, mind.'

'Tricks! Why are you all so bloody paranoid? You don't have to worry about me playing any tricks, it's that bloody gangster and his lap dog you should be wary of!'

'Enough, I'll see to your coffee shortly, just calm down,' replied André, again trying to quell the situation. Carl however, on hearing the remark about the "lap dog" was about to strike him, André stopping him by simply calling his name.

'How can I calm down, I'm being locked up against my will, stuck out here in the bloody high seas. I don't know where I am, don't know where I'm going, don't know what's going on. Jesus! Calm down you say, you must be bloody joking!'

Robert looked at André, hoping for some enlightenment.

'Don't worry, Monsieur Larousse is no gangster, he's merely being cautious.'

Robert looked again at André inquisitively on hearing the name Larousse but was unable to place it.

On deck, Larousse's daughter was trying to reason with her father.

'Papa, I have never seen you act like this before, what is going on? Are you in trouble? Please, please tell me, I want to help if I can.'

'My dear, I am in no trouble, I simply don't like the way this is going. I assure you; nothing will happen to Mr Cameron if he's telling the truth. But I need to verify his story, I must question him further a little later, please understand, I have no wish to harm him.'

'I should think not papa, please, no more violence, I beg of you, the poor man's petrified, can't you, see?'

'Yes, my dear, you are right, violence will get us nowhere, I shall see to it he's treated with a little more courtesy. Now why don't you continue your sunbathing whilst I attend to our guest. I'll have Gerrard bring you another drink and clean up this mess, what do you say?'

'Very well papa but call me when you are questioning him, I want to hear what he has to say.'

'If you insist my—'

His daughter interrupted him. 'Yes, I do insist, papa!'

'Very well I shall see to it, now go on.'

Larousse headed down into the cabin, he called for André and Gerrard. He instructed Gerrard to attend to his daughter and tidy the broken glass. André informed him the stranger would like a coffee.

'Gerrard, when you have finished, have some food and coffee prepared for Mr Cameron, he must be feeling hungry having been out there all that time. I need to make some inquiries meanwhile.'

'Yes, Sir, I shall see to it at once.'

'Now André, close the door, we must discuss this awkward situation. My daughter feel's Cameron is telling the truth, what is your opinion of his story?'

'I am of a mind to believe him also, he's come aboard with nothing, bar personal possessions.'

Larousse interrupted.

'But André, the passport! People don't walk around in England carrying their passport! Do they?'

André thought for a moment.

'We haven't ascertained his reason for having his passport on him yet, there may be a simple explanation.'

'Yes, I know André but first, we must find out if he's telling the truth up to now. I want you to contact our British H.Q. Ask them to do a check on this Robert John Cameron, see if what details they give us match up to what we have here, we'll go on from there.'

'Yes Sir, straight away.'

'Ask Carl to join me please.'

'Of course, Sir.' Carl entered the cabin a few minutes later. 'You wished to see me Sir.'

'Ah, yes Carl, come in and close the door behind you. Take a seat.'

'Thank you, Sir.'

'Now Carl, shortly I will be interrogating our guest, however, I want no more rough stuff, you understand?'

'Sir?'

'My daughter is bewildered over what is going on, I don't want her worried, he poses no threat to us at present, so let us be civilised towards him, yes!'

'Yes, Sir, I understand.'

Just then Larousse's daughter knocked and entered.

'I am disgusted with you, all of you, you are treating that poor Mr Cameron like a common criminal, Gerrard's told me you have him locked in one of the cabins! This whole thing's getting out of hand. It's obvious to me he's telling the truth, he must have been drinking last night, he's even brought his own glass!'

'Glass! What glass?' Larousse asked inquisitively.

'His glass is on the table he was lying under. If you had cared to look in the first place—' her father interrupted.

'Carl, go up and fetch this glass, bring it here.'

'I saw no glass, my dear,' he commented.

'No! Well, you wouldn't, would you. You were all too busy pushing the poor man about!'

'My dear, you don't understand.'

'No! I don't, I've already said. What in heaven's name is going on, papa? Why is he locked up? Where can he go? What can he do? This is making no sense, no sense at all!' His daughter broke into tears, clearly tormented by the recent series of events.

Larousse stood up, walked over and held his daughter, she placed her head over his right shoulder and her arms around him, her tears began to trickle off her cheeks and onto her father's shirt.

Carl re-entered the cabin, coughing slightly to alert them of his presence. Larousse reassured his daughter that he would release the stranger once he had clarification of his identity from England.

'The glass Sir, it was where your daughter described along with this half empty bottle of whisky laying on the deck.'

Leaving hold of his daughter, he reached out. 'Let me see.' Carl passed them over.

'A fine piece of crystal, I see,' he said, admiring it as he read the inscription aloud.

To Robert. From all at Cameron's Mining Equipment.

'Well, now were getting somewhere, at least his name is on it or at least the name he's using.'

'Papa!' His daughter shouted angrily. 'Why on earth would he have a glass with someone else's name on it? You're impossible! I'm going to my cabin.' His daughter protested. Arguments continued for some time with Larousse's daughter getting increasingly indignant with the situation.

'I think it's time our Mr Cameron joined us. My dear, it's best you leave us for a while, you're understandably upset.'

'Don't patronise me papa, I'm not leaving now, I'm not allowing you and Carl to bully that poor man anymore!'

'My dear.'

'No, papa!' She shouted defiantly. Larousse succumbed to his daughter's tempestuous outburst, saying.

'Very well my dear but I warn you now, you may find it distasteful if I find out he's lying.'

'I'm staying, papa!'

'May I suggest you cover yourself up before our Mr Cameron arrives my dear.' Larousse quickly smiled then continued.

'Carl, fetch Cameron here please.'

'Yes, Sir.'

His daughter opened a cupboard and reached for a silk gown.

Robert had heard much of the shouting which had taken place, so when Carl opened the door announcing. 'Monsieur Larousse wishes to see you.'

Robert replied. 'At least, the young lady has an open mind on the matter.'

'Don't push your luck, Cameron!' said Carl menacingly.

Robert smirked as he pushed past Carl and headed out. As he entered the lounge cabin, he saw Larousse, his daughter and André seated around the large table.

'Ah, Mr Cameron please be seated.'

'You've changed your tune. I must confess for the better if you take my meaning,' Robert said with some contempt.

'Don't be facetious, Mr Cameron. I merely wish to verify your identity and your explanation of how you come to be here that is all.'

Robert added, 'I would like to thank you though for the food and drink, much appreciated.'

Larousse continued after a short silence and a nod of approval. 'Now, firstly, you are Robert Cameron, is that correct?'

'No. Robert John Cameron, to be precise.'

'Very well, now why are you here?'

'I told you, I got drunk last night, I came aboard, I obviously fell asleep. How many more times, there's no other way to tell you, I don't remember anything after that.'

'Well, let's start at the beginning, shall we? Why did you get so drunk? Surely you remember that much or perhaps you're in the habit of getting so drunk you can't remember, eh.'

'That's none of your business!'

'Oh but it is! I need to believe you before I can help you.'

'I'm not prepared to discuss my private life in this kangaroo court!'

'Mr Cameron, be reasonable, if your story checks out, I can assist in your return to England.'

'And if it doesn't?' Robert said inquisitively.

'If what you say is true, then we need not discuss that matter any further.' Larousse looked directly at Robert; the short silence was broken by his daughter.

'Please Mr Cameron, I beg of you, help yourself,' she said emotionally.

Robert looked at the four faces surrounding him, he still had no idea what he was mixed up in, although at the back of his mind, the name Larousse meant something but he knew not what yet.

He decided, probably the best policy was to inform them fully of the circumstances surrounding his discovery.

'Look, I'll tell you what you need to know and I assure you it will check out. But first, I could do with a drink, I've a terrible hangover and the only cure I know is "the hair of the dog", as they say.'

Larousse smiled, then shouted for Gerrard. 'Yes, Sir,' he said on entering.

'Ah, Gerrard, a drink for our guest please. What shall it be?'

'Malt Whisky please if you have any?'

Larousse interjected. 'Malt Whisky! What's wrong with this bottle you brought aboard, eh?'

Robert had to think for a moment. 'Ah, of course, I remember. I was in a taxi and wanted to go to another club but the driver advised me I would be refused entry, so he offered me a bottle of whisky for £20.00 I didn't notice it was of a blended variety until I opened it on the top deck. But at the time it was better than nothing.'

Larousse laughed a little and spoke. 'Gerrard bring us all a drink; I feel we may need it.'

'Yes, Sir, I shall attend to it at once.'

Larousse looked contented with himself, the fact that at least the stranger was willing to talk, was indeed an improvement.

'I take it then; it was malt whisky you were drinking last night, Mr Cameron.' Larousse remarked sagaciously.

Robert sighed. 'Yes, I'm afraid so. Rather too much of it, I regret to say.'

Robert looked around him again at the four inquisitive faces awaiting his account of the previous night's events. He felt inwardly embarrassed at the thought of disclosing the fact his company had gone to the wall the previous day.

Although on reflection, considering all that had occurred since his discovery and the fact he still had little knowledge of what he was involved in, he concluded that honesty would be the best policy.

He was just about to commence when Gerrard entered with a silver tray, placing it on the table. There were two crystal decanters, one containing whisky, the other vodka, a soda syphon, a jug of orange juice and five glasses, all containing a few ice cubes each.

'Mademoiselle, would you care for a drink?'

'Oui Gerrard. Vodka and orange. Merci.'

'Mr Cameron.' Gerrard looked at him as he lifted the whisky decanter. 'Yes, please Gerrard, may I call you Gerrard?'

'Of course, Sir, whisky and soda, Sir?'

'No, Gerrard. Neat please and you can dispose of that ice for a start!' Robert said amusingly.

'Shall I dry the glass also, Sir?' Gerrard inquired knowledgeably. 'Now, there's a man who knows where I'm coming from. Thank you!'

Gerrard emptied out the ice and dried the glass using the glass towel he had draped over his arm; he then poured a generous measure of the malt whisky into the glass. Robert looked pleased as he took the glass from Gerrard, holding it up to his nose, he inhaled the strong aroma.

'Ah, the amber nectar. You should never serve it with anything other than a glass or better still another one, if it's offered!' He said in a jocular tone.

Larousse's daughter laughed a little at the bare faced cheek of the stranger. Taking the glass, Robert swallowed over half of its contents, saying. 'That's better, I'll feel much better already and it's like, medicinal if you understand me?'

'Do you always drink whisky neat, Mr Cameron?' asked Larousse's daughter curiously.

'Malt whisky mademoiselle, only malt whisky and always neat,' replied Robert then finished off the contents of his glass.

'It's small wonder you get inebriated, Mr Cameron!' Larousse's daughter said discerningly.

'Not necessarily, mademoiselle. Although last night, I had my reasons.'

Gerrard had again poured drinks for all except Carl and replenished Robert's glass. Larousse then dismissed him.

Robert held his hand out saying. 'Before you leave Gerrard, can you confirm this is from the Dalmore distillery?'

Robert felt sure it was a Dalmore however, the decanter obviously showed no details. Gerrard replied. 'You are indeed correct, Mr Cameron; it is a Dalmore 30-year-old from the 2022 release.'

Larousse was astounded, he had not given Robert much credit so far but he could not fault his knowledge of malts.

'Wow, from the 2022 release, this must be at least £4000.00 a bottle surely?' said Robert knowledgeably. Larousse added.

'No doubt, so please enjoy it as we have to move on.'

'Enjoy it! I will savour it, Monsieur Larousse. Thank you so much.' Larousse nodded.

Robert noticing that Carl had no drink said. 'What about you mate, aren't you joining us in a drink?'

Before Carl could answer, Larousse intervened. 'Carl does not drink, Mr Cameron.'

Robert looked at Larousse's daughter and commented. 'He's the life and soul of a party, don't you think?' His eyes casting an exaggerated glance over at Carl.

Larousse's daughter held her hand up to cover the smirk on her face. Carl glared at Robert with contempt.

'Now Mr Cameron, no need for sarcasm, Carl is always on duty so let's get down to business.'

Robert's expression changed markedly. 'Monsieur Larousse, you have "hit the nail on the head" there.' Larousse and company looked bewildered.

'Business, ah good old business, that's where all this started.' Robert had suddenly changed his previously jovial tone to one of depression.

'What's wrong, Mr Cameron?' asked Larousse's daughter.

Larousse noting the change in Robert decided to start the formal interrogation.

'On your possession, you had these item's. Passport, wallet containing three hundred and eighty pounds and some credit cards, also a sealed envelope unmarked other than your name, which I have not yet opened. Now firstly, why the passport?'

'I collected it from my office safe before leaving yesterday.'

'Planning on leaving the country, were you?'

'No. But I had no plans to return to the office.'

'Ah, so you have left the company you work for, is that it and that's the reason for your celebration.'

Larousse was about to disclose the fact they had discovered the glass earlier but thought better of it.

'In a manner of speaking, yes. If you let me explain, I assure you all will become clear.'

'Very well, carry on.' Larousse sat back, making himself comfortable. Robert reached out for the decanter, looking at Larousse.

'May I?' He said.

'Help yourself but don't get drunk on us again, Mr Cameron. Please!'

Robert smiled, replenished his glass and began his tale. 'Yesterday morning when I arrived at the factory—'

Robert began to disclose the facts surrounding his appearance aboard the KATRIANA. Whilst he was talking, a crew member knocked on the cabin door asking to see the captain. Carl informed André he was requested; André left the cabin for several minutes. Returning, he handed Larousse a folded piece of paper, saying.

'A message for you Sir.' Larousse glanced briefly at the details, re-folded it and placed it on the table.

'Thank you, André. I shall attend to it shortly,' he said heedlessly.

Robert's story continued for another fifteen minutes or so. He concluded by saying. 'If you need more proof just open the sealed envelope, it contains the documents handed to me by the Official Receiver.'

Larousse reached for the envelope and opened it, pulled out the papers and unfolded them. It became immediately apparent to him that the documents were indeed the Official Receiver's copies given to Robert as he had explained, the stamped date on them confirmed their authenticity.

'Furthermore, Monsieur Larousse if you send someone up top, they should find a crystal glass which was presented to me last night, which as I told you also bears my name. It's probably under the table. God, I hope it's not broken!'

'Mr Cameron, I have your glass here.' Larousse reached down for the glass by his side.

'There you are, still in one piece as you can see.' Larousse passed the glass over from his seat to Robert. He quickly inspected it, saying.

'It is beautiful, don't you think. They must have known long ago there was no hope for the company, I must have been oblivious to all of it for some time. I had made some good friends over the years, you know.' Robert began to ramble until Larousse interjected.

'Yes Mr Cameron, your friends and colleagues must think quite a lot of you, it's obviously a commissioned piece.'

'I thought so, they never said though.' Robert realising what Larousse had just said, looked over at him and said. 'You mean you believe me; you actually believe me now?'

'Yes Mr Cameron, I have enough proof to believe what you say is the truth. I have also had word back from England which substantiates your story and more important, your identity.'

Larousse lifted the paper André had brought in earlier, waved it at Robert, and then replaced it on the table without showing its contents.

'Thank god for that, you had me quite worried for a while.'

'I apologise for our treatment of you earlier.' Larousse was interrupted. 'And so, you should papa! I knew Mr Cameron was telling the truth from the outset.'

Larousse's daughter stood up and walked round to Robert, holding his arm gently, she said.

'Would you like to get cleaned up, Mr Cameron? Gerrard will provide you with some clean clothes and shaving equipment, you look terrible!'

'Yes, please Mademoiselle, thank you.'

Larousse caught sight of a glint in his daughters' eye, he had seen this glint once before some years ago. He dismissed his thoughts as quick as they arrived. 'Come Mr Cameron, enough of the inquisition.' Larousse's daughter lifted his arm.

'Follow me,' she said. Robert was pleased to leave, especially in the company of the beautiful young lady, in fact he looked at her differently now, now that the tension of the last hour or so had disseminated. Walking down the corridor, he said.

'Thank you very much mademoiselle, I don't think I could have got through this without your support, I heard you and your father arguing before. I'm so sorry for the trouble I've caused.' Robert looked into her eyes.

'Mr Cameron don't be deceived, if I thought for one moment you were lying, you would see a different side to me. I guarantee it.'

Robert cast his glance away and said. 'Thanks anyway, for what it's worth.' Larousse's daughter called to Gerrard and instructed him to attend to Robert's requests. Robert took a step turned around and reached out for her arm, she turned back quickly and Robert was staring into her eyes. 'I mean it, thank you, I am grateful.'

She pulled her arm away, saying, 'So, you have said, Mr Cameron.' In a chilled tone. She turned and headed quickly along the passage, she glanced back at the last moment, Robert was still standing there, their eyes locked as looked at him momentarily then dashed out of sight.

Gerrard looked at Robert. 'You'll get nowhere there Sir, she's her father's daughter through and through.'

'I don't know about that Gerrard, she is beautiful though, worth the effort, wouldn't you say?'

'Perhaps Sir but heed my advice and steer clear, please, it's for your own good.'

'How many times have I heard that since I've been here?' Robert said callously.

'Well, I've warned you Sir, you don't know what you're in for.'

'We'll see Gerrard, by the way, what's her name?'

'I think the young lady is the one to tell you that, it's not my place to say. This way, Sir,' Gerrard answered brusquely.

Robert said nothing and followed him. He was escorted back to the same cabin as before.

'Don't worry Sir the door shan't be locked this time, you are free to go anywhere on this deck or above but not below, you understand?'

'Yes Gerrard, thank you.'

'I have laid out some clothes for you on the bunk, there is a shower through there, where you will find a personal bag containing shaving equipment, shampoo, soap and such. It's all new and unused, you'll have nothing to fear. Shall there be anything else, Sir?' Gerrard inquired.

'No thanks Gerrard, that's fine, I could do with a shower I'll tell you.'

'Yes, Sir,' agreed Gerrard willingly.

'Shall I call you at seven for dinner Mr Cameron, that is, if you're still in the cabin?'

'For dinner, yes but I shall probably be up top taking the air. After all, I've been cooped up in here enough today.'

'Of course, Sir,' Gerrard said and left.

Larousse and André were now sitting out on the aft deck, his daughter had gone up top to commence her long overdue spell of sunbathing and Carl had gone below. Larousse was discussing what to do with Cameron when they docked at Matadi.

'We'll have to get him to the airport and sent off on the first available flight heading towards England, we can't afford to have him hanging around André, he's caused enough trouble as it is. I shall instruct Carl to escort him to the airport and ensure he board's the flight. Once he's away I can rest easy.' Larousse sounded disconcerted.

'You do believe his story, don't you?' asked André, inquisitively. 'Well yes? I see no reason to doubt it.' Larousse hesitated.

'Unless he's an impostor?' André looked at Larousse in astonishment. 'You don't think he's!' Larousse interrupted.

'I don't know what to think André. Remember both our grandfather's giving us the account of Philippe Roulet and Monique Rabier prior to our enlistment and how they had led them to believe they were dedicated resistance fighters since the start of the war.'

'They were even brought over to England to discuss plans at S.O.E. headquarters. Yet it was not discovered until 1943 that they were also working for the Nazi's and if you recall André, the circumstances surrounding their arrival was very similar to that of this man, Cameron.'

'Yes, my god you're right, François! Sorry, Sir.' André had forgotten himself with Larousse's disclosure of this possible parallel.

'No matter André. This is no time for formalities, we have been close friends too long to worry over that. It's probably nothing, I'm living in the past. You know, old habits die hard. We'll just have to be vigilant until he's off on that plane.'

'Yes Sir, I'll instruct the crew to watch his every move.'

'Have them do so discretely, we don't want him to suspect we doubt him, especially now he feels we trust him. No, perhaps that's too strong, believe him, is more appropriate, eh.'

'Of course, Sir.' André paused for a moment, then looking at Larousse he said in a soft though inquisitive manner.

'This mission François, it's that important then?'

'Yes, my friend, it is. We may not be back in 1943 plying across the English Channel like our grandfather's, although I must warn you, it may be just as dangerous if not more so! I shall give you the full details at the meeting tonight.'

'Very well Sir.' André rose and went about his duties, a feeling of apprehension developing within him he had not sensed for many years.

Robert had by now been showered, shaved and changed into something more casual than the suit he had been wearing, he walked down the passage from his cabin and onto the aft deck and Larousse was sitting there looking out to sea as if he had not a care in the world. Robert walked over to him.

'May I join you?' he asked.

'Of course, Mr Cameron, please take a seat.'

'I've been wondering?' Robert said cautiously. 'Yes, what about?' asked Larousse flippantly.

'The name Larousse. Your name, it, it's in the back of my mind somewhere but I just can't place it. If you don't mind me asking what exactly it is you do.'

Larousse thought for a moment and decided no harm would be done by enlightening him.

'I do little Mr Cameron, I am merely the figurehead of our organisation. Carrying on the old family business, you might say. Oh, I do apologise Mr Cameron that remark was in poor taste considering your circumstances,' Larousse added, sounding sincere.

'Apologies accepted, please continue,' Robert replied, shrugging off the insult.

'Mainly our prime concern is shipping, my family have always had a passion for the sea. Our other interests include locating raw materials, processing and distribution of the same, engineering, construction, among other things too numerous to mention. Has that enlightened you any, Mr Cameron?'

'No, not yet but I'm working on it, I know your name from somewhere. I wonder have we done business with you in the past.'

'It's possible, I'm afraid I can't say for sure, my board of directors take care of those details.' Larousse sounded disinterested.

Robert took the hint, realising he was getting nowhere, he asked. 'You don't mind if I have a look around, do you?'

'Be my guest Mr Cameron, after all that's why you came aboard in the first place, isn't it?' Added Larousse sarcastically.

'That's true. Thanks.' Robert replied as he stood up and walked over to the steps leading to the top deck. He climbed the steps and walked past the table he was discovered under several hours earlier, as he passed it by to descend the steps at the bulkhead to the lower flat deck, he saw Larousse's daughter sunbathing below.

He looked at her for a good two or three minutes. She was unaware of his presence, her eyes closed beneath the sunglasses she was wearing. Robert could feel the adrenaline pumping through him, he had become quite aroused at the sight of the beautiful young lady laid out below him, clad in only a swimsuit, the silk robe she had worn previously now discarded to one side.

Her auburn hair flowing out and around her shoulders was billowing gently in the sea breeze, her slim and already well-tanned body glistening from the sun's rays on the lotion she had applied to her skin. Robert was captivated but he realised he was in a different league, there was little possibility of the daughter of a rich and powerful man ever having anything to do with him, especially now.

Rather than be caught glaring, Robert decided to put those thoughts out of his mind and return to reality, however he did wish to talk with her, she seemed to be the most approachable of them all.

'So, this is where it all began then!' He said, loud enough for her to hear. She turned onto her side and looked up behind her, shading her eyes with her left arm slightly.

Pardon? she said simply and in a strong French accent.

'I said, this is where it all started. Under this table, you know!' Robert reiterated with a little embellishment.

'Oui. Yes, yes, it is,' she said a little surprised.

'How long have you been standing there?' She asked.

'Oh, I've only just come up.'

'Robert began to smirk at the statement he just made,' thinking to himself. If only she knew the truth.

'May I join you, mademoiselle?' he asked politely.

'If you wish,' she replied, sounding a touch discontented.

'You don't mind me calling you mademoiselle, do you?' He said as he descended the steps.

'No, why?'

'It's just that I've worked out the name Larousse is French, you have spoken in French and you even have a French accent sometimes.' Robert walked over and sat down a few feet away from her, continuing he said. 'In any case, I don't know your name anyway. Do I?'

She smiled at him and said, 'Katriana.'

'Katriana?' Robert said, looking slightly bemused for a moment. 'Katriana! But of course, that's where I've heard it before, it's the name of this fabulous yacht!'

'Yes Mr Cameron, that's correct. Papa named her after me,' Katriana said delightedly.

'Do you know what I thought when I saw the name on the stern last night?' Robert asked, holding his composure as best he could.

'No, what?' Katriana rolled over on to her front, moving closer to him, her elbow's holding her up revealing her enchanting cleavage, she said. 'Well, are you going to tell me or not?'

Robert, averting his eyes from the superb cleavage on display, he looked directly into hers, with an engaging smile, he said.

'Last night when I saw the name KATRIANA on the stern, my first thoughts were a beautiful name for a beautiful lady.'

'Oh, how charming Mr Cameron, I could believe you're a romantic at heart,' she said speculatively and smiling amiably.

'I've had my moments.'

'Had! What do you mean Mr Cameron, surely your life's not that dull?' She asked curiously.

'Robert, please call me Robert, if you don't mind?'

'No not in the least. Robert.' She giggled.

'May I call you Katriana, it's such a beautiful name?'

'Of course, you may. It is my name after all.' She smiled at him. 'It's so nice to talk to someone as charming as you, most of papa's friends and colleagues are so disagreeable, especially Carl, you made me laugh before when you made that comment about him to papa. But be careful with him, he can be dangerous.'

'Never mind him, tell me about you, are you French or English?'

'I was born in England but mama and papa are both French, my grandparents settled in England just prior to the war I believe. Something to do with Grand-Pere's work. Mama insisted I attend finishing school in France and we have more or less stayed there since.'

'Where is your mother now?'

'Oh, she's at our château just outside Marseille.' She paused slightly. 'I miss her an awful lot, we're more like best friends rather than mother and daughter. Papa is wonderful but he's always so busy. Mama and I don't get chance to see him much, that's why I'm here now.' She paused again.

'Listen Robert, papa is not a bad man, he's concerned about something and he's acting irrationally, I don't know what it is but it is definitely worrying him, please try to understand. He'll see to it you get back home safely; I promise.'

Robert smiled and looked at Katriana. 'Yes, I believe he will. Although he has no need, after all it's my own fault I'm here in the first place. The amber nectar, you know.'

'That's true, you've no one else to blame, bar yourself!' she said, sporting a cheeky smile. Robert laughed at her remark.

Robert and Katriana continued talking for quite some time. Talking about each other and their lives in general, until Gerrard informed them dinner would be ready in thirty minutes.

'I must go and change Robert, please excuse me.'

'Of course, I'll go and freshen up myself, I have enjoyed our little tête-à-tête, Katriana.'

'Oh Robert, you'll be speaking French next,' she said jovially.

Both then walked together to their respective cabins. Robert wondering what could happen next, his life was in a turmoil. He considered his present situation bleak to say the least, almost broke with little chance of ever getting back further up the ladder, so to speak. Then his thoughts turned to the gorgeous lady he had just spent a pleasurable hour or two with.

Young, beautiful, rich. These were the immediate positives, he could see the negatives far outweighed them as he was; broke, her father despised him, he knew he was a bit older but unsure by how many years. All these set against the obvious simple standard male desires would be no match, however he thought there was a spark of mutual interest which gave him some solace as he changed for dinner.

His heart was pounding as were other feelings which were physically showing an interest, which he hoped he could contain at bay in the company of her father soon.

At seven o'clock precisely a gong sounded calling all present to dinner. Robert was particularly enthusiastic in reaching the dining room, hopeful of sitting next to Katriana. His good fortune or haste paid dividends for as he entered, Katriana was already seated and called him over saying. 'Robert, please come and join me.' She offered him a chair next to her.

He made no effort to conceal his delight at her invitation. Larousse, André and Carl followed Robert in and took their seats.

'Ah, good evening, Mr Cameron, I trust we find you in good spirit?' Larousse asked.

'Indeed, Monsieur Larousse, I've spent a delightful time this afternoon chatting with Katriana, she's full of surprises.'

'Ah my dear, so you've been entertaining our guest, I take it you have informed him of our destination?'

'No papa, Robert never asked me, did you Robert?'

'No, I don't believe I did, as a matter of interest, where are we headed?'

'Matadi, Mr Cameron.'

'Matadi. That's in Africa, Old Zaire if I'm not mistaken.'

'That's correct, Mr Cameron. You don't seem too concerned.'

'To be quite honest, I'm not. I could do with a break. Will you be staying there long? I would like the opportunity to repay your hospitality, perhaps dinner somewhere one night.'

Robert looked at Katriana, her expression looked agreeable as she smiled at him.

'Ah. That suggestion I'm afraid Mr Cameron is quite out of the question. I have already made appropriate arrangements for your return to England as soon as we arrive,' Larousse said casually.

The looks of astonishment on both Robert and Katriana's face needed no explanation.

'Papa! You can't send Robert back the moment we arrive, we've had a wonderful afternoon chatting on deck, I was going to ask him to join us while we were there, at least until we head for Nassau. Please papa!' She pleaded.

'I'm sorry, my dear. However, as I have said, Mr Cameron will be escorted to the airport and placed aboard the first flight out of Matadi. I don't wish to discuss the matter any further.'

Robert looked menacingly at Larousse, the tension round the dining table intensified.

'You may not wish to discuss the matter any further Monsieur Larousse, though I'm afraid you have no choice. You see, the main problem with your plan is that I can't fly or to be honest, I won't fly. I have a phobia about flying and that's the truth.'

'Anyhow, once we dock, I shall make my own arrangements and be out of your way as soon as I can, it's plainly obvious you still mistrust me despite everything "checking out" as you call it!' Robert stood up and placed his napkin on the table. 'I've suddenly lost my appetite, please excuse me,' Robert said despondently, as he left the table.

Katriana, clearly outraged at her father's callous attitude stood up also, throwing her napkin down onto the table in a melodramatic and gauche manner, looked sternly at her father saying.

'Papa, you are behaving like a bloody imbecile! I'm going to my cabin and staying there until you come to your senses. Mama would be affronted if she could see you treating anyone the way you're treating Robert!' she said, sounding exasperated.

'My dear, please try to understand, the situation is exceptionally difficult at the moment. I've told you all I can for the time being. Mr Cameron must be sent back to England as soon as we arrive in order for me to ensure no further disruption from him.'

'Disruption! There's only you who's causing any disruption, papa. Robert is a genuine person, I've spoken with him all afternoon, he's kind and good hearted, humorous, he's a gentleman in fact, more so than you three sitting there, I'm so disgusted with you all!

'In fact, the arrangements you've made for Robert shan't go to waste, I shall return to Marseille and stay with mama! I'll be in my cabin, call me when you come to your senses!' She retorted furiously.

Katriana stormed out of the cabin and walked swiftly down the corridor. Larousse looked at André and shook his head.

'This situation is becoming intolerable, André. My daughter thinks I'm going mad, I'm sure of it.'

'She's understandably upset, Sir.'

'Yes but I need to convince her that it's for the best without disclosing any details of our mission. Her presence assists us in being looked upon as merely visitors going about our normal business.'

Larousse looked worried. He continued to discuss what to do about Robert with André and Carl for some time.

Katriana, while storming off down to the cabins, had her emotions playing havoc within her mind, she stopped at Robert's cabin and she knew she had to make excuses for her father's behaviour but that was not her only reason for being there, she knocked on Robert's door.

'Yes, who's there?' Robert answered in a terse tone. 'It's me,' she said, sounding a little emotional.

Robert jumped up and opened the door, Katriana was standing there sobbing, the tears trickling down her pretty face, carrying lines of mascara which they had softened.

'My god! What's happened? Are you alright?' Robert felt so sorry for the trouble he had caused as he looked at Katriana and realised, he was to blame for her state.

'May I come in, please?' She whimpered.

'Yes, yes, of course. Come in, sit down and tell me what's wrong.' Robert was agitated as he led Katriana over to a chair.

'It's papa, I don't understand him anymore, he's behaving like a madman, there's no getting through to him, something's going on and he's keeping it from me, I don't know what to do. I've told him I'm going back to stay with mama as soon as we get to Kinshasa.'

Robert passed her his handkerchief; she thanked him and wiped her eyes briefly.

'I can't bear to be with him while he's acting like this.'

Katriana broke down, the tears flooding from her eyes. She rose from the chair and threw her arms around Robert's neck.

'I'm sorry, I'm sorry, Robert. Papa has treated you dreadfully, you don't deserve it,' she mumbled through her crying.

'It's alright, it'll be alright, it's not your father's fault, Katriana it's mine. I should never have come aboard, if I hadn't, none of this would have happened,' Robert replied, sounding vexed.

'No, maybe not. But then I would never have met you, would I?'

Katriana raised her head off Robert's shoulders and gazed deeply into his eyes, she caressed the side of his head with her right hand.

'You're such a nice person Robert, I'm sorry but I can't help the way I feel about you. I don't know anything about you and I don't know what's happening to me but I don't want you to go, not yet, not until—oh, I'm sorry, I'm so confused. Please Robert.' She pulled Robert close to her and hugged him.

Robert was perplexed at her disclosure. He couldn't believe what he had heard, his backbone tingled with excitement. Swallowing hard, he said. 'But Katriana, you hardly know me, do you?'

'Well, enough to know what type of person you are, Robert. Someone I'd like to get to know better if you'll let me. If you're interested that is?' she said sincerely.

Robert was dumbfounded. He released her grip slightly and looked into her eyes, they were tearful but not tears of sadness alone, in there were tears of joy also.

She continued. 'Robert, as I've said, I've told papa I'm going to stay with mama. I want you to come with me, please say you will, please Robert.' There was a silence as Robert took in the magnitude of the moment.

Katriana continued. 'My mama will treat you much kinder than you have been up to now, I know this for a fact. Please Robert, say you'll come to meet my mama.'

Robert whilst still attempting to overcome the shock, put his arms around her and drew her to him, they gazed into each other's eyes for a moment then both their lips met and they kissed a long and passionate kiss lasting several minutes.

Robert raised his right hand and placing his forefinger under her chin, he released her from his lips and in a soft whisper like voice, he said, 'I was right.'

'Right about what, Robert?' She asked breathlessly, looking into his eyes and longing for the kissing to continue.

'A beautiful name for a beautiful lady, remember?'

'Oh Robert, kiss me again, please.'

Katriana pulled him to her, they kissed and caressed each other for some time until a knock was heard on the cabin door and they automatically jumped apart. Katriana sat down quickly, running her hands through her hair in an attempt to make it look presentable.

'Yes, who is it?' Robert shouted.

'Gerrard Sir, Monsieur Larousse wishes to see you.'

'Tell him I'll be along in a moment.'

'Very well, Sir.'

Giving Gerrard a few moments to clear the corridor, Robert asked Katriana to stay in his cabin whilst he saw her father, assuring her that everything would work out alright. Katriana stood up and held Robert's hands.

'You haven't answered my question yet, Robert,' she said apprehensively.

'What question?' Robert replied, sounding puzzled.

'Will you come with me to meet my mama?'

Robert kissed her gently and said. 'Of course, I'll come with you, now that I've found you, you won't get rid of me so easily. The only thing is, I was telling the truth about my phobia.'

She embraced him saying. 'No matter, we'll take one of papa's ships out of Matadi, papa will see to it, I promise. Talking about papa, you had better go and see him but don't let him push you around,' she said, wagging her finger.

'Oh, don't worry about me, I can take care of myself. I'll be back soon.' He kissed her again and left to join Larousse. As he knocked on his door, he stepped in.

'Ah, Mr Cameron, thank you for joining me, please take a seat. We have been discussing our little dilemma and I think we have found a solution.'

Robert gave Larousse a look of disregard, saying. 'I have plans of my own Monsieur Larousse, as soon as we dock, I shall make my own arrangements and be out of your way as soon as possible.'

'Mr Cameron, please hear me out. I'm trying to help you.'

'Don't be deceitful Monsieur Larousse, you merely wish to get rid of me. Well that you will but it will be by my own efforts.' Robert sounded earnest.

'Mr Cameron, I have gone to a great deal of trouble over you. You have caused me enough inconvenience already; I must insist that you return to England by my means. Arrangements have already been made! I bid you good evening!' Larousse was exasperated. Robert however had no intention of following his demands, he stood up, hands on the table and whilst glaring a look of contempt, he said loudly.

'Now just you listen to me, I've had just about as much as I intend to take from you!'

Carl stood up quickly. Robert straightened his stance immediately and pointed at him in no uncertain manner.

'And you can sit down before you start something you'll regret!' Robert said irascibly.

Larousse signalled to Carl to be seated. Robert placed his hands back on the table.

'I will not be ordered about by you or anyone else, is that understood!' He glared at Larousse.

'What is it about my presence here that frightens you so much? The captain says you're no gangster so just what the hell are you?' He queried.

Larousse maintained his composure. 'I regret to say Mr Cameron, you have no choice in the matter and you will do as I say,' Larousse said assertively, avoiding answering Robert's question.

'You can go to hell!' Robert replied defiantly.

Just then Katriana entered the cabin. 'I could hear you both at the other end of the yacht, what's going on now?'

'I'm sorry Katriana, it's your father. He's got it all arranged for me to be bundled off back to England as soon as we dock, well he's got another thing coming, I can tell you!'

Larousse looked at his daughter, the traces of mascara still on her face. 'My dear, you've been crying. You see what you've done Cameron, my daughter's upset over this!'

He gave Robert a look of despise.

'It's not Robert who's upset me papa, it's you!'

'But, my dear.'

'Don't bother papa, no more lies, I can't stand it anymore, as soon as we get to Matadi I'm going to stay with mama and Robert's coming with me, we'll get one of your ships to take us and he'll be out of your way for good then. Will that satisfy you?' She remonstrated.

Larousse was speechless. That glint he saw was indeed the same one he had seen some years ago when his daughter met the young German electronics student, Dieter Schäfer at University. Larousse recalled how happy his daughter was with Dieter in the two years they were together.

Dieter sadly died eighteen months ago in a horrific accident and Katriana was just about getting over her loss. The glint in her eye said it all, it looked to Larousse his daughter saw Cameron as more than a stranger. 'Things will now be more difficult than ever,' he thought. He also realised giving the seriousness of Operation Windcutter, he would need to concentrate on that and hope his daughter would see sense quickly.

Katriana disturbed her father's thoughts, shouting.

'Come Robert, let's go out on deck, the air's fresher out there.'

Robert shook his head at Larousse as he turned to join Katriana. She reached out for his hand, clasping it, she glared at her father, saying. 'Don't bother to ask. You wouldn't understand!'

The looks of astonishment on the faces of Larousse, André and Carl said it all.

'My god André, what do we do now?' said Larousse looking disconcerted;

André just shook his head in disbelief.

Robert and Katriana left and went out on the aft deck where they sat talking about how they would travel to Marseille and how she was sure her mother would take to Robert far better than her father had. Robert however was still puzzled at the sheer determination of her father to ship him back the moment they arrived. He asked Katriana if she had any inclination as to why he was so determined, she could not give any plausible interpretation of her father's behaviour towards him.

The chill of the evening began to penetrate them both as they sat outside, she suggested they retire to her cabin and avoid any further deliberation until the morning. Both sat in her cabin until the early hours getting to know each other better. Gerrard soon provided them both with a substantial selection of food knowing both had reneged dinner at the table and would obviously be feeling somewhat hungry by now.

Robert and Katriana both enjoyed picking at the selection with the occasional break from eating to continue chatting and a kiss or two or three as the evening progressed into the night.

Robert decided around three o'clock in the morning of Sunday, October 2nd to retire to his own cabin, saying he felt somewhat exhausted after the day's events. In truth, he thought it wiser to withdraw before his passion was aroused to explosion level, the consequences of which he daren't contemplate.

Katriana lay on her bed wide awake for some time, her constant thoughts of Robert inhibiting her from her physical need for any sleep. By the time she was overcome with fatigue, she had decided in her mind, she was indeed falling for Robert, she only hoped and prayed that he felt the same.

***

Over three thousand miles away, some five hours later at exactly 08.00 hrs (03.00 hrs Eastern Standard Time) the Americans suffered a similar fate although this time there were a few survivors. Three naval personnel had bailed out into the sea in the nick of time. The initial report arrived on the desk of the Navy's Chief of Staff as he entered his office in the Pentagon at 05.00 hrs (EST), it read like a nightmare.

"At 03.00 hrs whilst carrying out specified duties over the Atlantic, Apache helicopter TG111 opened fire, releasing a barrage of air-to-air missiles directed at and destroying Chinook KK99 plus compliment, no survivors. Reports confirm Apache then trained missiles upon itself and crashed into the ocean, 3/6 survivors".

The Pentagon went into immediate action to ascertain the cause with the same vigour as the British Ministry of Defence had done the previous day, malfunction was the only viable answer until they too received a message, again at 15.00 hrs., their time, with the same connotation as that of the message sent to the MOD in London.

We believe two of your aircraft were destroyed twelve hours ago, to deny would only worsen the situation. Your country was chosen purely at random and this is simply the beginning. We will avenge!

At this point, the MOD had not made public its situation, nor had it informed anyone outside its confines, bar for the families of the aircraft crews who had been killed in the incident. They were respectfully asked not to divulge any information until the inquiry had been concluded.

The families were promised a full military funeral and offered counselling and support. The Americans however played it a little differently, the Pentagon released an open memo to all divisions with a compliment of Apache helicopters stating:

"Immediate action. All Apache helicopters to be grounded for investigations into electrical malfunction and missile guidance system checks. Details to follow".

A more detailed dispatch was forwarded to all Commanding Officers regarding the investigations to be carried out. It was from this communiqué which also arrived at all NATO divisions and in particular those units placed in the former Yugoslavia that the news filtered through to MOD headquarters.

The MOD immediately contacted the Pentagon to verify the details, upon doing so their desire that the whole thing had been a single terrorist act now had to be re-thought. This was now a serious global situation, far more serious than initially imagined.

Chapter Four

Returning to early Saturday morning, October 1st at the Bristol Headquarters of the Avon and Somerset Police, DCI Pearce had been presented with files of four individuals from the group of dockers the British Transport Police had interviewed at the time of the constable's death.

The details revealed the fact that three out of the four had served prison sentences at some time over the past ten to fifteen years for various crimes involving violence, theft, burglary and the likes. However, a common connection existed, in that all four had been involved in political protests at some time or other.

The most notable features of the reports were pointed out to DCI Pearce by Detective Sergeant, Frank Tomlinson.

'Ma'am, it appears the three who served prison sentences have served their time with at least one of the others, whether they met then, which is the most likely explanation or not, I think we should investigate it further. They appear to be working together at present, ma'am and not only on the docks.'

'Why do you say that, Frank?' The DCI Inquired.

'There is a file here on a Mr David Matthey, the fork-lift driver responsible for the fatal injuries to the BTP constable. He was arrested in Germany two years ago over the petrol bombing of a refuge for foreigners in a "Reichsbürgersbewegung" protest. He was released after the statements of two apparent bystanders, both English tourists supposedly on holiday, swore he'd not been involved in the protest and guess what?'

The DCI looked at him, then impatiently said.

'Two things, Frank! One, what is a "Reichsbürgersbewegung" and two; what do I have to guess?'

The DS explained that the "Reichsbürgersbewegung" was translated as the "Reich Citizens Movement", a group dedicated to restoring Germany to that of the German Reich in preference to the present Federal Republic of Germany.

The DCI snapped.

'Come on Frank, what's the second thing!'

'Ma'am, the two witnesses were none other than Mark Blanford and Jason Allen, the two guys he currently works with on the docks!'

The DCI who had been fidgeting with her pen throughout the Sergeant's report, threw it down, saying.

'Now we're getting somewhere! The fourth man, anything on him?'

'Yes ma'am, plenty. James Stein, the dock's berth manager! His real name is Jürgen Steinbacher! Born twenty-eighth of August 1983 in Wiedenbruck, a town lying between Dortmund and Hannover, he's been on the files of most European forces for "political activism!" Most recently, an incident in Hamburg, two years ago, involving again, the "Reichsbürger" movement. There's an instruction ma'am, to inform Special Branch of any interest in him.'

The DCI sat perusing the files for a few minutes whilst biting gently on her left thumb nail, which among other things helped her concentrate.

'Nothing on any of them in the last two years, Frank?'

'No ma'am, not even a parking ticket.'

'Owen!' DCI Pearce shouted through from her office.

Almost immediately, Detective Inspector Owen Griffiths arrived at the door. 'Yes, ma'am?'

'Close the door Owen, take a seat. Now listen, both of you. The death of that transport constable on the docks, at the end of last month was initially deemed as "accidental death". I, however, believe the incident relates to the attempted murder of our truck driver in the early hours of the following morning on the A38 trunk road.' She picked up her pen and began tapping it against her desk, then after a short nibble at the capped end, she continued.

'I'll give you the full picture. This whole thing seemingly revolves around an alleged diamond smuggling operation emanating from Africa, The Congo, to be precise. As you know, I attended a meeting at the Royal Infirmary yesterday, involving some high-ranking officials, one of them, a Frenchman, a Monsieur, François Larousse, from whose shipping line the vessel African Envoy IV, regularly docks at Avonmouth.'

'The others were naval officers direct from the Admiralty itself. Regarding these two incidents, there appears to be far more to it than we first thought, unfortunately however, I have been instructed to concentrate our inquiries to the matter of the BTP constable's death and the truck drivers attempted murder only, as this Larousse chap is sailing out to Matadi and from there overland on to Kinshasa at this very moment. The top brass doesn't wish us to spook his smuggling investigation, at least for the time being. Understand?'

The two officers nodded and replied in agreement. Still clutching her pen, she stood up and walked over to the window, biting the end of her pen again, for a moment before saying.

'Owen, drop whatever you're doing, get search warrants arranged for these four addresses, get a team together and go through them with a fine-tooth comb!'

'What are we looking for, ma'am?'

'Anything linking any of them with the constable's death or anything to do with political affiliation or even an African connection. If we produce something else, all well and good but restrict any questioning to those inquiries that means no mention of smuggling whatsoever, understand.' They both understood.

She took the few steps back to her desk and picked up the phone, whilst dialling an internal number, she instructed DS Tomlinson.

'Right, Frank! Whilst I organise a warrant to search the berth at the Dock's, you organise a few wooden tops ("uniformed officers") and a couple of vans, we'll get down to Avonmouth Dock's and bring the four of them in. I'm regarding the BTP constable's death as a murder inquiry now. I'm of the opinion the constable found something out when he questioned them and they silenced him for it, I'm sure of it. His notebook is missing and that concerns me, I mean really concerns me. What was in it to cause his death, that's the question we need answering!'

'What about Special Branch, ma'am?' DI Owen asked to serve as a reminder.

'Later, let's see if we have something first.'

Within the hour at around 13.00 hrs., two police cars and four police vans entered the docks at speed and headed for the berth where the suspects all worked together. Once at the berth, the vehicles diverged some to the office and some to the warehouse and associated outbuildings.

DCI Pearce instructed her driver to proceed immediately to the berth offices, accompanied by two detective constables, while DS Tomlinson and three officers headed for the warehouse. The vans complimented with the wooden tops took strategic positions as instructed.

She glanced around the office quickly noting the faces behind the desks, none of them were of James Stein the berths' supervisor. Removing her warrant card from her handbag and holding it up, she demanded, 'James Stein, where is he?'

One of the clerks, whilst looking confused, spoke out after a short silence. 'He went home sick, yesterday. Sorry, can I help you?'

'Sick! I'll give him sick. What about Matthey, Blanford and Allen?' She hastily inquired.

'Blanford?' The clerk hesitated.

'He didn't turn in this morning but the other two are here, down on the berth, probably at the warehouse. What's going on?'

'Never you mind, it's Stein and the others we're after. Come on, let's get down to the warehouse!' She cried out.

She turned and left the office and with a feminine style dash of a few fast paces followed by a few steps then repeated by further several fast paces, she headed to the awaiting car, the two officers in tow until one of them passed her and jumped into the driver's seat.

'Over there!' she said as she pointed out the warehouse about two hundred yards in the distance.

The officer started the car and skidded away on the wet surface towards the direction pointed out to him, as he passed close by several containers placed alongside the outside wall of the warehouse the figure of a man rushed through between two of them unaware of the approaching car, he was being pursued by DS Tomlinson and the two uniformed officers, there was no hope of avoiding him.

Within a split second, he was mowed down by the police car, his body somersaulting over the bonnet and smashing the windscreen before rolling off the rear of the car and into a pool of rainwater. Once the car had slid to a halt, three doors flew open simultaneously.

With total disregard to feminine decorum, DCI Angela Pearce swung her left leg out swiftly causing her knee length skirt, already five or so inches above her knee from her quick entry to the car moments before, to rise abruptly and display her stocking top, suspender belt and a glimpse of her panties in the process to DS Tomlinson, who had by this time caught up to the unfortunate victim.

'What are you gawping at, Sergeant? Have you never seen a pair of stockings before?' She screamed at him. DCI Pearce was quite an attractive lady and dressed accordingly.

'Yes ma'am, sorry ma'am,' Frank embarrassingly replied. She continued. 'What happened Frank? Who is it?'

'Jason Allen, ma'am. As soon as he seen us, he took off, we all pursued him, you know the rest.'

The driver of the car had gone immediately to the victim's attention. 'Well! How is he?' She asked.

'It looks bad ma'am, sorry.'

'Well, call in for an ambulance! For Christ's sake! What's the matter with everyone today!' She remonstrated. 'What about Matthey? Have we got him at least?'

'I'm not sure ma'am, when Allen ran off, I—' Pearce intervened. 'Don't bother Frank, they've got him, look.'

Tomlinson turned to see two officers struggling towards them restraining Matthey between them, their uniforms showing evidence of a struggle probably on the warehouse floor judging by the dust on them. Detective Constable Quinn placed Jason Allen into the recovery position, he was still unconscious.

'Right, Matthey! You're nicked, old son!' Before she could read him his rights, he spat in her face.

'Bitch!' He cried out.

As she wiped the saliva from her face, she asked.

'Did you have a struggle, boys? You weren't too rough on him, were you?'

'No, ma'am. Only enough force to restrain him from resisting arrest.'

'That's good.' she said, as she quickly raised the right side of her skirt, then with a powerful thrust, she buried her right knee into his groin. Collapsing from the excruciating pain, Matthey dropped quickly to the ground, she pulled his head back by the hair, saying. 'Do you want to try that again?'

He hadn't the breath to reply, though his bright blue eyes looked decidedly menacing.

'Read him his rights and get him back to the station, I'll deal with him later.' The DCI went to the car, opened the boot and removed a first-aid kit. She opened several hygienic wipes and cleaned her face thoroughly of any traces of saliva deposited on her by Matthey.

Soon the ambulance arrived, the crew checked on the patient informing DCI Pearce and the others it was touch and go, they put Allen on a stretcher and loaded him into the ambulance.

'Gashani! You go with them, keep an eye on him, I don't want him getting away after all this, I'll arrange for your relief at change of shift,' she shouted, instructing one of the Uniformed Constables, a young Asian lady in her very early twenties, she didn't look too keen on the prospect by the way she reluctantly answered.

'Yes, ma'am.'

'Right Frank, we've made a right balls-up of this, out of four targets, we've only managed to get two and one of them might not last the day. It's that Stein or Steinbacher we need to talk to, I'll lay any money, he's the ringleader. When you get back to the station, you better inform Special Branch and alert the airports, ferry ports, the usual, you know what to do. I'm going to get a team down here to search this berth and the offices, there's got to be something here.'

Noticing Frank was still there a moment or so later, she shouted. 'Go on Frank, move!' In an attempt to motivate him into action.

The immediate panic over, she walked over to the car and called in the details of the incident to the station, requesting they send extra officers to conduct a search of the dock.

By almost 21.00 hrs., that evening, Bristol Police had produced nothing of significance from the searches on the suspect's homes or of the dock office and warehouse. Angela Pearce decided to stop for the day and start afresh in the morning.

'Okay everyone, that's it for today, seal up the place.'

She posted two constables each, to guard the dock office and the warehouse. 'Right Frank, it's back here for you tomorrow after the briefing, I'm going to town on Matthey first thing. I'll have given him long enough to stew by then.'

'Yes, ma'am.'

'Have you heard how Allen's doing?'

'Last I heard, he was stable, ma'am.'

'Good, there's a chance we'll be able to interview him also.'

'Yes ma'am, it might be a few days though.'

'That's okay, we've got a few days left before that Larousse chap reaches Kinshasa. I want something concrete to give them before then. I'll see you in the morning, Frank. I've had it for tonight.'

'Goodnight, ma'am,' Frank said as Angela Pearce picked herself up from the chair she had been balancing rather than sitting on in the small warehouse cabin whilst she checked through warehouse copies of the ships "Bills of Laden" for any significant similarities. Though enough was enough. She shouted out.

'Frank get me another chair here by tomorrow, this thing is all lopsided and damned uncomfortable.'

'I'll see to it, ma'am. Goodnight,' he replied, accompanied by a yawn which Pearce noticed.

'You had better get a good sleep tonight, Frank, you'll have to be on top form in the morning.'

'Yes, ma'am,' replied Frank, a little embarrassed.

***

Seven o'clock the following morning, that of Sunday October 2nd, Angela Pearce held her briefing at the station, instructing the officers on the case to continue searching until they found something. She then instructed Detective Sergeant, Robert Lynton-Reece to accompany her in the interview with David Matthey.

The custody officer ushered Matthey out from the cell and into an interview room, he posted a constable outside, awaiting the arrival of the DCI. Shortly before eight, the DCI and DS Lynton-Reece entered the interview room.

On entering, Angela Pearce took a long look at Matthey as he sat slovenly behind the desk. She could not begin to contemplate what lurked within this man's somewhat Neanderthal body. Ugly, was too benevolent a compromise for his outward appearance.

'This individual was so grotesque, she contemplated presenting him to science as the missing link in the evolutionary chain,' she thought inwardly. In addition to his outward and readily visible repulsion, she was soon to find out his mental condition matched the packaging.

To be more accurate, he was indeed a plebeian individual who had little regard for anything or anyone, perhaps if possible, even less so for himself. Matthey had been stripped of the clothes he wore at work the previous day and possibly a fortnight or more, before he was placed in the cell overnight and was sitting in an all-in-one paper suit provided to him following the forensic tests undertaken on him overnight.

He had a blanket around his shoulders for a little warmth. Such was his lack of personal hygiene, he had already turned the air in the small interview room malodorous. Angela Pearce opened the door to the corridor and requested the constable to fetch an air freshener.

'God above Matthey, when was the last time you bathed?' she said as she screwed her face up in disgust.

'Fuck all to do with you. Bitch,' he replied, unruffled.

She looked him over again. She knew his clothing consisted of a pair of tight-fitting denim jeans with the knees torn across, a T-shirt with risqué slogans printed back and front and a pair of training shoes, soiled underpants and socks all of which had seen better days, all of which certainly hadn't seen a wash in well over a week or perhaps longer, she could sense there would be a problem interviewing this unsavoury character.

Switching on the recorder, she announced. 'Detective Chief Inspector Pearce and Detective Sergeant Lynton-Reece, conducting an interview with David Matthey at 08.30 hrs on Sunday, 2 October 2022. The suspect has been informed of his rights and has refused the services of a solicitor offered to him.'

At this point, Matthey shouted directly into the recording device. 'Don't need a poxy solicitor! I ain't done nuffing av'e I!'

'If you haven't done anything David, why resist arrest?' asked the DCI.

'I didn't, they just came at me, didn't they! Your fucking lot.' He was interrupted.

'That's not how the officer's see it, David.'

'I don't fucking doubt that the bastards have well sorted their stories out, ain't they? You and them both ya' bitch. Fucking copper's, ye'r all the fucking same.' He riposted.

Just then, the air freshener was delivered and DCI Pearce liberally sprayed it around the small, contained room.

'What's your game? That poxy thing stinks,' Matthey complained. 'Not half as much as you do, David,' replied the DCI.

'Who said, you could fucking call me David, only my fucking friends can call me David and I don't fucking like you, bitch! And I don't fucking like him either.'

'Well, that's something you shall just have to get used to, because you're liable to be here for some time.'

'You can't hold me ya' bitch! A've done now't.'

'Well for a start we've got; resisting arrest. Assault on a police officer. GBH. Conspiracy. Attempted murder. Possibly murder itself. Do you wish me to continue?' said DCI Pearce after spelling out the catalogue of probable charges which could be brought to bear upon him.

'Ah told you misses bloody copper, a've done now't!' he answered casually as he sat back, stretching his legs out from under him.

'What about your friends, Stein and Blanford, they've left you and Jason to face the music, that's if Jason makes it of course, if not, you're on your own. Your other two so-called friends are doubtless out of the country by now, I don't suppose they told you they were going, eh?'

'Ah, don't know what you're on about, you've nuff'in on me, bitch and you know it.'

'Tell me, Mr Matthey,' she said cautiously, avoiding another barrage of abuse from using his forename. 'When you and your friends beat up the truck driver the other week, why did you do it? What purpose did it serve?'

'He asked for it,' Matthey said quickly, before realising he'd done so. 'Which one of you followed him and ran him off the road later that evening?'

Matthey covered his mistake well. 'Yeah, we smacked him about a bit, he was nicking stuff, wasn't he but that's all we did. Don't know now't about nobody following him.'

'A few oranges! Surely that doesn't call for the beating you and your so-called friends gave him.'

'Ah, told you he deserved it!'

The DCI continued to question Matthey until lunch, though she freely admitted to DS Tomlinson afterward, they were getting nowhere.

Matthey, though not terribly bright was a hardened criminal with a long history of violence and an intense hatred for the police and authority in general. The one thing that puzzled Angela Pearce was the fact that Matthey had not been involved in anything illegal over the past two years.

For a man whose second home was prison, this sudden change in his lifestyle had to be due to something they were overlooking at present. She knew once she found out what it was they would be on the right track. They sent Matthey back to the cell and had some lunch before proceeding down to the docks in the hope the on-going search had made some discoveries.

On entering the Avonmouth Docks berth warehouse around 14.00 p.m. hrs., Angela Pearce whose temper was rising due to the inability of finding any evidence, sat down at the desk to continue checking the papers she left the previous night. On realising the chair, she had previously complained about to DS Tomlinson had not been changed, she picked it up.

The construction was of welded lightweight, square metal sectioned legs with a moulded plastic, all in one, back and seat. She stepped out of the cabin and in temper slued the chair behind her back and with a powerful thrust, she swung it forward and hurtled it towards the wall some fifteen or so feet away in the general direction of DS Tomlinson, remonstrating.

'Frank! I told you to get another chair in here! For Christ's sake, do I have to do everything myself.'

Frank Tomlinson realised he was in for one of those days. Although the chair would not have hit him, he side-stepped it just in case, his eyes then followed its flight as it crashed against a concrete stanchion abutting the wall and watched the chair as it dropped to the floor.

Something caught Frank's eye on its decent, he walked over to the chair to examine it, three out of the four hollow section legs had plastic ferules fitted at the base of the tubular legs, the fourth was missing and from within, a secluded semi-glittering object had been dislodged and rolled out a few inches ahead next to the dislodged ferrule.

'Ma'am! Quick! Look at this!' Frank shouted in amazement.

Angela Pearce gave her customary feminine dash over the fifteen or so feet to join him.

'It's a diamond, Frank! It's a bloody diamond!' She exclaimed joyously. 'Frank, bag it up along with the chair and get them back to the station, forensics will want a look at those. And get forensics' down here to search this cabin also.'

Here at last was the evidence they needed. She immediately ordered the search for the two missing suspects, Stein and Blanford to be intensified.

***

Jürgen Steinbacher, alias James Stein, some weeks ago following the BTP Docks Division interviewing all the Docks' berth staff regarding the truck driver's beating had returned home as normal after his shift finished at the docks and immediately began packing his essentials and making necessary arrangements.

Steinbacher, a German by birth had always been obsessed with the history of Adolf Hitler and the Third Reich. In his younger days as a student studying in Hamburg was very impressionable. He attended rallies and demonstrations organised throughout Germany, from one of which he was recruited into a "Reichsbürger" group after several attempts to contact their leaders.

Once contact was made, it was hardly surprising he was accepted as a member considering he was extremely intelligent and showed without any doubt his allegiance to the groups cause. Year after year passed and Steinbacher became a prominent figure amongst the group's hierarchy and a trusted member.

The "Reichsbürger" movement to Steinbacher was the answer to all his nationalistic dreams, he could see the day when Germany was once again a Reich and not a Federal Republic.

As the intervening years progressed, Steinbacher became privy to many grandiose plans for overthrowing the present government but this current plan which he was directly involved in showed great promise and was undoubtedly destined to succeed.

He knew many influential individuals within the movement from aristocrats to politicians, military personnel and Polizei figures most in senior positions who were actively recruiting all manner of like-minded nationalistic Germans with the will to overthrow the present government and others should they stand in their way.

Therefore, following the altercation on the dock, he concluded his time here in Bristol was limited, things were getting too close for comfort due to police investigating two issues, firstly the truck driver's assault followed by the death of the BTP police constable. He knew the time had now come to move on. He made contact through secure channels to his associates in Germany who detailed an exit strategy for his urgent withdrawal.

At this time luckily for him, he was totally unaware of any further investigations by the Bristol Docks Transport Police, however when a number of BTP officers returned on the morning of Wednesday September 28th to conduct follow-up interviews on the Accidental Death of the BTP Police Constable, he instinctively knew the time was right.

Therefore, he activated the exit strategy and chose Friday 30th September the day to make good his escape. The previous day, he feigned an illness and advised he would not be in work on the Friday thus giving him good reason to be missing.

Steinbacher rose early that Friday morning and was double checking his apartment ensuring he had left nothing to incriminate him, he felt confident to make his way to the station and get underway. During this inspection, the doorbell rang at the front door of his Housing Association ground floor flat. This was a bad sign, why would anyone be calling as normally he would be in work.

He moved slowly over towards the bedroom window where he had a strategically positioned mirror, angled specifically to view the area around his entrance. Without need to move his curtains, he could identify anyone without their knowledge of his watchful eye.

Below was Mark Blanford, impatiently ringing the bell once again and holding it for at least half a minute. Steinbacher swore to himself 'Shit,' then quickly undone his shirt and removed it as he headed into the bathroom.

He placed the plug in the sink and opened the hot tap, he dashed back to the bedroom and secluded his almost fully packed suitcase under the bed. Moving back to the bathroom he shut off the water, doused his hair and applied a little shampoo, rubbing it in as he went towards the front door and shouting.

'I'm coming! Hang on a minute, can't you!'

Opening the door, he gave a feigned look of surprise to Mark Blanford who was obviously paranoid over the police returning to the docks.

'Jim! You've got to help me. I saw your car wasn't at work, so I've come straight back here!'

Steinbacher grabbed Blanford by the lapel of his heavy donkey jacket and dragged him inside.

'Shut-up you fool, do you want the whole estate to hear you? What's wrong with you?'

Blanford spluttered out as fast as he could.

'You've got to get me out of here! Out of the country! The police are on to us, I know it,' he said, fumbling his hands together, clasping them and squeezing with nervous energy.

'Don't be stupid, they've got nothing on any of us, you handled it extremely well. I'd have given you a bloody Oscar for that performance the other day. Listen, they're only re-checking details with it being one of their own.'

'I'm telling you Jim; they know! They know he was murdered because they found marks on his wrists where we held him. That copper who interviewed me told me they're possibly considering it a murder inquiry!'

Blanford was by now trembling. Steinbacher calmly turned away, saying.

'Go and pour both of us a drink Mark, it'll help you calm down while I go and finish washing, we'll talk about it when I get dressed, alright?'

'Yeah, okay but you've got to help me, promise!'

'Of course, I'll think of something, don't worry, I'll be through in a minute, the drinks are in the cabinet through there.'

'Thanks Jim, you're a real pal,' Blanford said with relief.

Steinbacher returned to the bathroom, he realised Blanford was in no condition to be questioned further by the police, he was in essence a weak man, he could not endure a full interrogation, this Steinbacher was sure of. In any case, he couldn't risk his interrogation in view of what he could tell them.

In the few minutes, it took to finish washing "again" and dressing, he decided the only thing to do was take him along, in any case he was adept in other ways and he'd proved himself to be loyal to the cause and he had become a true and good friend in the time they were together.

He returned to the sitting room dressed casually though smart. He noted Mark was still pacing the room. Picking up his drink, he announced his plan.

'Right Mark, it looks like you and I are going on a little trip abroad!' Blanford's face lit up with relief. 'Oh, thanks Jim, I knew I could trust you,' he said appreciatively.

'We're in this together Mark, for the good of the cause. There's no point in our staying around now, I think you're right, the heats on to us. I will advise we are closing the operation here forthwith. There is nothing left at the docks to incriminate us, is there Mark?' He questioned.

Mark looked a little concerned.

'Well, is there? I don't think we'll have the opportunity to return now, so let's hope it's clean, eh!'

'Yes, erm' I mean no. No, I don't think so, Jim. Where will we go, Jim?'

'Mark, you don't look convincing. Just tell me you destroyed the crates as directed that is the only weakness as I see it, if they find out about the smuggling method, we are both in the shit, do you understand me. Do you?' he asked sternly.

'Yes, I'm sure they are all destroyed, honest. Jim, please tell me where are we going?'

'To the Fatherland, of course!' Steinbacher announced loudly as he clicked his heels and gave a Nazi Party salute in earnest.

Blanford immediately jumped to attention and returned the salute, saying. 'The Fatherland!'

Both finished the contents of their glasses and smashed them against the fireplace. Steinbacher raised his hand, placing it upon Blanford's shoulder, he said.

'We must make ready quickly, Mark. Go home and pack. No more than one average size suitcase, we don't want to be burdened down with baggage. Dispose of any communication devices, they can be traced. Only take essential items and don't forget your passport and papers, we must move fast.'

'I'll contact section HQ on the way and advise them the both of us are withdrawing immediately. I have a contact number to ring once we reach Koln. Now, go and be back here within the hour, we'll have to make the night ferry from Harwich. I don't intend to risk the airports.'

Blanford looked very uneasy, he quietly asked. 'You will wait, won't you Jim?'

'One hour, that's all. If you're not back by then, you're on your own. Understand?' Steinbacher replied definitively.

Blanford agreed and hurriedly left. Steinbacher could see him scurry across the grassed play area, constantly looking over his shoulder. In a way, he felt sorry for him but this was not his reason for taking him along. He had to get him away from the police whilst he himself made his escape.

Steinbacher returned to finish packing, the task took no longer than five or ten minutes, he then sat down in front of an old oak dressing table he'd bought second-hand, as were most of his possessions, he'd always realised he may have to "cut and run" someday and now the time had come.

Reaching into one of the drawers, he removed several items of clothing and a cosmetics box, then pulling the drawer out completely he upturned it and manipulated the base gently until the lower half slid out, though somewhat too easily for his liking, considering he thought he'd made it tamper proof.

Quickly he checked the contents revealing a passport and an enlarged photograph of the face within, plus numerous documents, papers and several other photographs. Satisfied the contents were complete, he refitted the empty drawer bottom.

He remained disturbed regarding the ease of access; he knew it should have felt much more secure. Perhaps it was just the timber shrinking due to the warmth of the room, he hoped it was only that as he replaced the drawer with the non-required contents into the dresser.

Placing the enlarged passport photograph under one of the mirrors clips, he studied it for a short while, recollecting the last time he'd had cause to use it, just on, three years ago. As he studied it, the memories came flooding back.

He was at home in Hamburg when a friend from the "Reichsbürger" group knocked and advised him to attend a meeting at what was Hamburg HQ for the time being.

He presented himself at the appointed hour and was ushered through the large double doors into a study where the walls were draped in Nazi banners and a large painting of Adolf Hitler took pride of place above the carved marble fireplace.

You could almost be forgiven for thinking you had been transported back seventy or so years to the time of the Second World War, such were the theatricals of the Nazi Party then, as now. As no doubt, they would always be. Steinbacher was announced by a fellow group member, in uniform.

'Herr General! Lieutenant Steinbacher.' Jürgen Steinbacher marched in and gave the Nazi salute.

'Jurgen! Kommen Sie, sich hinsetzen.'

'Ja wohl, Herr General.'

Steinbacher did as he was ordered and took a seat in front of the General's desk.

'Now Jürgen, we will conduct this meeting in English, you may need the practice,' the General said in a heavy German accent.

'Yes Sir, of course. May I ask for what purpose?' Inquired Steinbacher. 'We want you to go to England Jürgen, on an operation of great importance to the "Reichsbürger" movement.'

'May I ask, why me? General.'

'We can think of no better officer to handle such an undertaking. I will give it to you straight, Jürgen. The movement have selected you because of your knowledge of England and the fact you speak the language perfectly. This we feel, along with your qualifications will enable you to take the position we have arranged for you at the Port of Avonmouth Docks near Bristol, the position is of berth manager.'

'Cargo handling! Sir, surely.' Steinbacher began to protest though he was cut short by the General, a man not renowned for his patience.

'Herr Lieutenant!' He shouted, slipping back into German momentarily.

Standing up from his desk, he took hold of his walking stick, an aid he had not been without since injuries received from the German Polizei in a previous protest march. He made his way over the short few feet to the window, looking out to the gardens whilst Steinbacher remained silent, he continued.

'Many people loyal to the "Reichsbürger" movement have worked extremely hard over the last three years Jürgen. They have devised and already began implementing an operation of extreme complexity to assist us in bringing about the "Fourth Reich" far sooner than predicted. For this, we require funding, immense funding! You Jürgen, are being offered the opportunity. No! Privileged, to become part of history in the making. Tell me now! Are you interested or not?'

'Of course, General!' Steinbacher answered without hesitation and in English.

The General swung round on his good leg and with a broad smile, he said. 'Then I shall detail your orders Herr Hauptsturmführer. (Captain)'

'Herr Hauptsturmführer? General!'

'Of course, Jürgen! Now you are head of the British Section of this operation you will require the proper authority, we at HQ have already sanctioned your promotion, the fact that you have jumped rank shows how much faith we have in you.'

Steinbacher was stunned at the notification, he himself slipping into German in gratitude to thank the General for his faith in him and ensuring he would do his utmost to ensure the successful outcome of the operation.

The General continued with the briefing, the outcome of which, Steinbacher was given a completely new identity and contacts had placed him in a position ideally suited to the task he was instructed to perform on behalf of the "Reichsbürger" and ultimately the Fourth Reich.

Once established, he would be given full instructions and assistance as required. Throughout, Steinbacher recalled being more and more dumbfounded at the extent of the operation itself and the depth of his own responsibilities.

Just then the telephone rang curtailing his reminiscence, Steinbacher answered it saying, 'James Stein speaking.'

'It's Mark. Jim, I've been thinking, what about Jason and David, shouldn't we take them with us too, they might talk!'

'Don't worry about them Mark, they don't know enough to trouble us, they were good enough for what we wanted here and for throwing the odd petrol bomb or two, anyway we don't all want to be away from work tomorrow, do we? In any case, I don't think our superiors would be impressed if we brought them back to the Fatherland with us, especially Matthey! Eh?' He said, rejecting the suggestion and laughing a little.

'If you're sure, Jim.'

'Yes, I'm sure. Now stop wasting time and get yourself back here,' he demanded and put the phone down.

In a way, he was glad Dave had rung, for he had not, yet attempted to disguise himself as the man in the photograph.

By the time Blanford arrived back, Steinbacher had transformed himself into a man of at least twenty or so years older, so much so, that Blanford got a shock when Steinbacher opened the door to let him in, at first thinking the police had beaten them to it, he was ready to turn and run until Steinbacher said.

'Good. You don't recognise me then?'

Blanford couldn't believe his eyes, he stood gaping at him, his mouth wide open.

'Come in, you imbecile! Are you all set?'

'Yes Jim, all ready. My god! You look so different.'

'Never mind that, from now on, no more Jim or James Stein, I'm now Gerhard Farbmacher. A Sales Engineer from Bremen. You understand, Mark?'

'Yes Jim, sorry Gerhard!' Blanford replied clumsily.

'Practice it, Mark and for god's sake, don't get it wrong again.'

The two men left, carrying a suitcase apiece. They walked to the main road and hailed a taxi rather than take Steinbacher's car, which could be traced. Steinbacher told the driver to head for the Guildhall, from where it was only a short walk along Victoria Street to Bristol Temple Meads Station where they boarded a London Paddington bound express before which Steinbacher telephoned his section HQ to advise immediate withdrawal.

Once in London at around 18.00 hrs., they took the Circle Underground line to Liverpool Street Station, from there the Harwich International train which gave them a little time at Harwich International station before the ferry sailed at 23.00 hrs., allowing Steinbacher to survey the surroundings for any sign of police on the alert.

The two men left boarding the ferry, Stenna Britannica until the last minute, as they passed through Custom's, Blanford needed to summon all his composure to remain calm, Steinbacher now posing as Farbmacher on the other hand had no difficulty in presenting himself to the Border Control officer who simply waved him onward after checking his impeccable credentials.

They were off and, on their way but Steinbacher could not or would not relax until they had disembarked and passed through both the Dutch and German Customs. This still several hours ahead.

On Saturday, October 1st before Angela Pearce and her officers arrived at Avonmouth Docks, the overnight ferry docked at Hook of Holland. Steinbacher and Blanford had made it to the comparative safety of Europe, Steinbacher commented to Blanford.

'At least, we're off that godforsaken little bloody island!' Blanford laughed a little too loudly for Steinbacher.

'Shut up, you fool! We're not home and dry yet, don't attract attention.'

Steinbacher told Blanford to stay close, though not to show they were travelling together. Both then boarded another train which would take them straight through to Koln (Cologne). Both alighted in just under four hours from the fast express train at Koln.

Blanford kept pace with Steinbacher along the underpass until they were outside the station building. Neither was aware of the fact both Matthey and Allen had been arrested around the same time as they travelled to Koln.

'Right Mark, I need a drink, then I'll make that phone call, look there's a bar over there, that'll do, come on,' he said enthusiastically.

Steinbacher ordered two beers, the bartender took two glasses from the shelf and holding them both in the one hand placed one under the tap, Steinbacher immediately halted him.

'Nein mein Herr! Zwei gross glass bitte,' he asked him to change them for larger ones, adding that there was barely a mouthful in those.

The bartender did not look too pleased with the comment though exchanged them for "Stein's".

Steinbacher asked if there was a telephone, the bartender simply pointed to the rear of the long narrow room then handed him the beers and marked them down on a beermat with two simple strokes.

Steinbacher took a long drink from the Stein and placed it down on the bar, wiping the froth off his lips with his sleeve he turned to Blanford, saying. 'It's good to be home. I'll make that call now.'

Once the call was answered, he spoke softly in his native language and in a coded phrase, he said. 'Anglo African delegation arrived at Koln Station.'

'One moment please,' came the reply.

A few moments of silence passed before someone asked. 'Identify yourself please.'

Using his alias, Steinbacher replied. 'Gerhard Farbmacher.'

Another few moments elapsed before the reply. 'What is your location and situation, Herr Farbmacher?'

Steinbacher detailed his whereabouts and informed them he had Blanford with him, the voice at the other end instructed both of them to be outside the Cathedral's main entrance at 16.00 hrs on Sunday 2nd where they would be met. He confirmed and returned to his drink, informing Blanford of the situation.

They returned to the station and deposited their suitcases in the left luggage, then spent the rest of the time wandering round Koln, with Steinbacher giving Blanford the guided tour taking in lunch along the way. They found suitable accommodation for the night in a rather non-salubrious part of town, so returned to collect their luggage before settling down for the night.

***

As arranged, the following day, Sunday 2nd October, Steinbacher and Blanford were being met outside Koln Cathedral at 14.00 hrs., precisely.

'Guten Tag, Herr Farbmacher, Herr Blanford,' the stranger said as he approached, shaking hands with them. 'We will speak in English as we walk, less people to overhear us, yes?'

'Yes, of course and you are?' asked Steinbacher, still posing as the alias Farbmacher.

'My name is Axel Oefner, I am General Friedrich Stoltz's personal assistant, I recognised you Herr Farbmacher from your photograph, I am impressed. Please follow me.'

Axel Oefner was a fit looking 52-year-old though you would easily assume him to be in his early to mid-forties given his physique. He was a no-nonsense type of man, straight to the point and very matter of fact in his language.

The three men walked briskly away from the Cathedral across the paved plateau surrounding the impressive double towered Gothic structure, weaving between the several busking bands and solo performers who were playing music of differing styles.

Among—them, pavement artists were creating quite large chalk drawings of varied subjects, all of whom were plying locals and tourists alike for gratuities.

Axel Oefner continued to walk briskly along, paying no heed to their presence and headed towards the road which followed the course of the river Rhine for some distance. The area was very busy with locals and tourists alike and the traffic was as bad as a weekday.

Once clear of the roads, they found themselves on a grassed area and footpath alongside the Rhine. Oefner gestured them to join him on one of the pleasure boats which plied the river day and night ferrying tourists, only this time there were no tourists on this boat.

The closed sign was removed from the entrance to the floating landing stage as they approached and replaced as they passed through. Oefner remained silent until the vessel had taken up its position in the traffic flow of the river. As the vessel passed beneath the wide overhead railway bridge north of the railway station, he told Blanford to go below and have a drink while he had a matter to discuss with Steinbacher alone. Blanford did as he was bid judging the request as simply a senior officer being briefed.

Steinbacher listened as Oefner in native German disclosed the fact General Stoltz was most displeased with the recent events which had taken place, resulting in the abandonment of the Anglo-African operation which until now had been running smoothly and that he was particularly worried about the murder of police constable Cameron, knowing the authorities would investigate the matter further until satisfied, this he feared could jeopardise the whole operation.

Steinbacher refused to comment, saying he would give the General a full report when he met with him.

Oefner continued to subject Steinbacher to a torrent of abuse over the management of his section and demanding a full explanation before meeting with the General. Steinbacher refused to comply with his demands, advising he had no authority over him and that what he had to report would be done so to General Stoltz personally.

Oefner, a trifle upset shouted instructions to the wheelhouse to pull over to a small jetty on the far side of the river. As it docked, he led the two of them off ahead of him and directed them towards a car, advising them they would be taken to a safe house for the night and collected early the following morning. From there, they would be taken to the General's secure retreat where he would meet with them.

He also confirmed they had advised Kinshasa of the closure of the Anglo-African route immediately and alternative arrangements had been made for re-direction of supplies at great expense. Blanford having overheard some of the conversation remarked on the efficiency of the operation overall. The reply being.

'German efficiency is second to none, something you British fail to understand!' said Oefner.

Steinbacher gripped Branford's arm with the intention of curtailing the conversation, the action of which Blanford understood perfectly.

Little more was said before arriving at the safe house, Oefner simply advised them to stay indoors and make themselves comfortable and make use of whatever was available. He bid them goodnight, reminding them to be ready for 06.00 hrs prompt, as they had a full day ahead of them tomorrow. Steinbacher and Blanford both thanked him, saying they would be ready and waiting.

Blanford took himself to his room with a bottle of brandy and a glass he found in a cupboard. He sat on the bed staring at his suitcase and considering his position. Pouring out almost quarter of the bottle into the glass, he took a large gulp and swallowed it, shuddering slightly as it hit the back of his throat.

He focussed again on the suitcase, whatever happened he was not to let it out of his sight for one moment. That suitcase contained his future. He had plans of his own now he was out of England. He took another swallow to help him think. Half a bottle later, he decided he'd go along with Stein or Steinbacher or even Farbmacher or whoever he pretended to be for a while longer, he didn't know for sure what his real name was, even now.

Then, when he was ready, Steinbacher and the "Reichsbürger" movement could get on with whatever they wished, he'd almost killed for them; that was the ultimate sacrifice, the highest price he was prepared to pay and he'd already paid it. Blanford finished the bottle off and slumped back in the bed, one eye on his suitcase, at least for a while.

Steinbacher, by comparison, had no intention of allowing alcohol to cloud his judgement, he spent the night on his bed staring out the window at the changing sky, a night without sleep. He had far too much to think about. Would he be given a new position after such an unpropitious result with the Anglo-African arrangement?

Would he be sent abroad to co-ordinate matters there, he doubted so. Everything had been moving smoothly elsewhere as far as he knew. Could he remain in his native Germany, certainly not under his own name, nor that of the alias Farbmacher? A new identity would be in order.

He pondered over these thoughts and the fact his old friend, the General was disappointed in him as he watched the night sky give way to dawn. Sleep mattered not for the time being, his future was at stake but he felt confident the group would do its utmost to assist.

This he was sure of. The only thing he was sure of. The group protected its members above all else. He was a member, he'd be safe, and they would ensure his safety. Steinbacher rested his eyes, satisfied he would be in good hands come the meeting with his old friend, General Stoltz later that day.

***

When DCI Pearce returned to police headquarters at 08.00 a.m. on Monday October 3rd Special Branch and the Admiralty had been informed of the recent developments and she was at this moment receiving a dressing down from both parties in her office.

Special Branch claiming they should have been informed immediately any interest was sought in Jürgen Steinbacher, alias James Stein as requested in his file. Followed by Rear Admiral Bartholomew-Smythe for alerting them at this stage of their investigation, possibly causing the investigation to be terminated forthwith.

Angela Pearce, unaffected by the bombardment of criticism defiantly replied. 'Gentlemen, you have your job to do and I have mine. I am conducting both a murder inquiry into the murder of Constable Bruce Cameron of the British Transport Police and the attempted murder of our truck driver by most probably the self-same people you have an interest in.'

'Perhaps had you the foresight to inform us here from the beginning of your little secret investigations that officer would still be alive today and the truck driver, well we all know what state he's in, eh!'

The DCI had a quiet word with DI Owen who scurried off. Bartholomew-Smythe stood up, then in his usual aloof manner, he began.

'DCI Pearce. Gentlemen. It is fair to assume that the cover of the Admiralties operation is blown. Special Branch had only a distant interest in the subject, whereas we, at the Admiralty were conducting sensitive investigations into a major diamond smuggling network with a view to firstly, putting a stop to it!'

'And secondly, ascertaining the reason behind it! However now, we shall never know for sure whether diamonds had been smuggled into England or for what purpose. Thanks to you, DCI Pearce!'

He turned to leave, saying quietly to the Special Branch officers that he would contact the party involved (Larousse) and advise him to suspend any further action.

As he concluded his bombastic outburst directed solely at DCI Pearce, DI Owen returned and handed the DCI an evidence bag, she opened the bag and dropped the diamond they had found at the dock's warehouse onto the desk, Bartholomew-Smythe noticed the uncut stone bounce a little as it hit the desktop.

'My god! Is that what I think it is?' He inquired. Angela Pearce, in a certain supercilious manner, replied.

'Yes! It is! Rear Admiral. We located it whilst searching the dock warehouse, whilst! Might I add, we were conducting our murder and attempted murder investigations!' She replied with a smug look.

'So, we have proof at last. They were undoubtedly bringing diamonds in. Now all we must find out is where they were going to and why?' Bartholomew-Smythe and the Special Branch officers resumed their seats around the desk.

'Have you gathered any other information from your investigation which may be of use to us, Chief Inspector Pearce?' Requested the Rear Admiral, still a little stunned.

'We've covered the files on all four suspects, repeatedly, we've concluded there's a definite connection involving some "Reichsbürger" organisation. All four suspects have been involved with the "Reichsbürger" movement for some years, at least, it seems until two years ago, since then there has been nothing on any of them, we feel sure they have been acting under orders on this smuggling caper of yours since then. Finding that diamond gave us the proof they were involved.'

'I think we should have a talk to this chap you have in custody, perhaps he will be willing to tell us something now?'

Angela Pearce laughed aloud at the Rear Admiral's suggestion.

'You can have a talk if you wish Sir but I'm afraid he's the type who'll say nothing, even if it means him doing a long stretch for his silence. To put it bluntly Sir, Matthey abhors authority.'

Immediately, the Rear Admiral queried the statement.

'If that's the case, then why has he been associated with an organised "Reichsbürger" campaign and been able to stay out of trouble for the past two years? No, I don't agree with your precis, I think Matthey has at last found a sort of leadership he feels comfortable with, the fact he is able to carry out acts of violence and organised crime simply encourage him to obey their commands.'

DCI Pearce thought for a moment then agreed there could be something in the Rear Admiral's hypothesis.

The Special Branch officer suggested holding Matthey on the "Suspicion of Terrorism Act", which would allow them more time to investigate the matter further without Matthey being able to alert anyone to the fact they were no longer conducting murder and attempted murder inquiries alone.

All parties decided this would be the best course of action and began collating their information and planning where the investigations should continue from here.

***

As the British MOD and American Department of Defence continued their investigations in earnest, yet another incident occurred this time over the East Siberian Sea on Monday 3rd October, only twenty-five miles off the New Siberian Islands, the target this time, the Russians.

Two MIG fighters destroyed each other at exactly 03.00 hrs their time and again at 15.00 hrs the same message was delivered in the same manner in Moscow as the previous two. By now, all three governments were gravely concerned; however, only the UK and US agreed to pull their resources in a determined effort to locate the terrorist source.

The Russians had their own beliefs that the Ukrainians carried out the attack on them due to the ongoing conflict between the two countries and were following this hypothesis adding the attacks on both the UK and USA were the work of the Ukrainians to undermine the Russian advantage.

They believed the Ukrainians were attempting to bring the NATO alliance into the current "Special Military Operation" as they deemed the conflict to challenge Mother Russia.

Amid all this international frenzied activity, an emergency meeting was called for all NATO member countries for the following day, Tuesday October 4th. Until then the searching, probing, questioning and thorough investigation work would continue. It was agreed that all training and non-essential manoeuvres would be suspended meantime.

The air defence policies across the whole of the western world was effectively on stand-down. Essential missions were carried out without a complement of weaponry loaded aboard any aircraft. The risk factor was of course immense but there was no choice until something could be done to prevent any further incidents.

***

The Rear Admiral returned to London and arrived at Whitehall about 08.00 hrs On Tuesday 4th October and presented his report to Admiral Stevens, upon reading the details it was agreed by 09.00 hrs to inform Larousse of developments via the captain of a supply Frigate lying off the West African coast. The KATRIANA it had been agreed needed to be re-fuelled enroute rather than putting into a port should any unforeseen change of plans arise.

As Admiral Stevens listened to Bartholomew-Smythe detail the events in full, he suddenly realised where he had heard the name Cameron before.

'Jeremy!' He Interrupted.

'Yes Sir, sorry Sir, am I going too fast?'

'No! Don't be stupid, man. The name of that BTP constable, the one who was allegedly murdered, what did you say it was?'

Bartholomew-Smythe whilst flicking through his portfolio said.

'Cameron, I think, Sir? Yes, PC Bruce Cameron. Why, what's the significance, Sir?'

'None! I hope. Jeremy, you see the thing is, shortly after Commodore Larousse set sail, we received an inquiry from his captain, Deveraux, I think, to check on a Robert John Cameron, who had been found on board the yacht around lunch time yesterday, apparently a little worse for wear from an over-indulgence of alcohol the previous evening or so he claims. I didn't mention it to you at the time, there seemed to be no point but now the names cropped up again, I'm not so sure it's as simple as it seems.'

'You don't think he's involved, do you Sir?' asked Smythe.

'Good god man! I sincerely hope not. Though the thought has suddenly occurred to me he could possibly be related to this constable Cameron.' Admiral Stevens paused for a moment, then added.

'The thing is Jeremy, if he is connected in some way or other, how did he find out about Larousse?'

Bartholomew-Smythe fidgeted with his portfolio, whilst remarking.

'We must make direct contact Sir, at least to verify if there's a connection or not.'

'I agree Jeremy, do what's necessary, find out first if there is a family connection between them before informing Larousse but remember, restrict it to this Cameron situation only, the other details will be passed on to the Frigate in code as usual.'

'Yes, Sir, at once.'

Bartholomew-Smythe carried out the Admiral's request before going along to the communications room where he instructed the operator to contact Larousse direct.

Didier Lagross, one on the yachts' crew was manning the communications room aboard the KATRIANA as the call came in around 10.00 hrs Contacting André Deveraux, he informed him a Mr Smythe from your Bristol office wishes to speak privately with Monsieur Larousse. André found Larousse out on the aft deck; he walked quickly over saying nervously.

'François, Rear Admiral Bartholomew-Smythe is on the radio, something must be wrong, they said they would only contact us direct if there was a problem.'

'Well André, we won't know what it is unless I answer it, will we?' Larousse said indifferently as he headed to the nearest handset.

'François Larousse speaking, what can I do for you?'

'Are you free to talk, Monsieur Larousse?'

'Yes, perfectly.'

'What is your position, Larousse?' Smythe enquired. 'I have just completed refuelling and about to cast off.'

'No, not yet Larousse. Can you still board the refuelling vessel? It's vitally important. I need you to receive a message via the secure channels,' instructed Smythe.

Larousse could tell something was disturbing him and agreed to re-embark the Frigate. The lines were re-tensioned and the ladder dropped. Larousse made his way to the ships' communications room. The operator passed the headset to Larousse.

'Ah Commodore, I have just been informed by Admiral Stevens you have an uninvited guest aboard, is that so?'

'Yes. What's the problem?' Larousse replied.

'This chap's name is Robert John Cameron,' came the reply. 'Yes, what of it? You've already verified those details.'

'So, I believe. The fact of the matter is, do you recall the current investigation of a police constable who suffered a fatal accident with a forklift truck on Avonmouth docks.'

'Yes of course, where's this leading?'

'His name was Bruce Cameron. He just happens to be Robert John Cameron's brother!'

There was long silence.

'Are you still there? Larousse! Hello!'

'Yes, yes, I'm here. I don't believe this; how did you find this out?'

'Admiral Stevens remembered your request to have your uninvited guest checked out, so when I mentioned the constable's name in my report, he thought it too much of a coincidence. Now listen, we don't know if he's involved or whether it is just simply a coincidence but we thought we better advise you immediately.'

'Yes, Rear Admiral, I understand, thank you. I'll keep you informed, goodbye.'

Larousse walked out of the communications room, visibly stunned by the news. He thanked the Frigate's Captain and Communication room staff and returned to the KATRIANA. As the lines were cast off and the yacht pulled away, Larousse entered the bridge.

André, noticing the look of shock on François's face, went over to enquire. 'Here François, take a seat. I take it, its trouble?'

'I don't really know, André,' said Larousse, holding his head. 'Maybe, maybe not. It's that bloody Cameron again, the man's been nothing but a thorn in my side since we found him. That young police officer who was killed on the docks, remember I told you about him?'

'Yes?' André answered somewhat mystified.

'Well. He was only Robert John bloody Cameron's brother! As if I don't have enough to deal with. You don't think he found out what we're up to and this drunk business is all a pretence, do you?'

'Perish the thought François, you mean he could be here for reasons of vengeance?'

'Well, it's possible, isn't it! There's only one way to tackle this André, I'll get my daughter to find out, she can be discreet when needs must.'

'I'm not so sure that's a good idea, François,' André knowledgeably replied. Larousse took little notice of the comment and went to find his daughter. She was sitting on the lounge cabin, talking with Robert.

'Ah, there you are, I don't know what you two find to talk about for all this time, as long as you're enjoying yourselves.' Larousse tried to sound unperturbed.

'My dear, could I have word; I won't keep her long Robert, I promise.'

Katriana jumped up from the seat and with a spring in her step, she ran over to her father and followed him down and into his cabin.

'Yes, papa what is it?'

'Close the door, my dear,' he said firmly.

'Oh no, not again papa, what's wrong now? As if I didn't know, it's Robert again, am I right?'

'Well. Yes, it is my dear, there's something I want you to find out for me, if you will?'

'What, papa?' she said curtly. Larousse held her in a comforting fatherly way, continuing.

'Find out about his family, you know mother, father, brothers, sisters and that.'

'I know what a family is, papa and anyway, I already know all about Robert's family, that's one of the things we find to talk about, for your information.'

Larousse hesitated before continuing. 'Well, my dear, has he any family?'

'Yes! Of course, he has papa, though he's only just lost his younger brother recently in a horrible accident, he was a policeman in Bristol. It's so sad, you know, he was almost the same age me. All Robert will tell me is that he died on duty, he said it's too awful to tell me the details.'

'Then there's his mother and father; they're still alive, though his father is rather ill, he has no other brothers or sisters and he has no children if that's what you're asking. Why do you want to know, anyway?'

'Oh, just double checking, my dear.'

'Yes, I'm sure you are! Well, the next time you want to know about Robert papa, ask him!' She protested as she slammed the door behind her.

Larousse chased after her, shouting for her to stop and listen for a moment. She turned about and faced him, raising her voice, she demanded, 'Papa! Why can't you just give it a rest! I'm sick to death of your interference between Robert and I, do you hear me! Just leave us alone!'

The shouting had alerted Robert who had come to see what was wrong now. 'What have I done now, Monsieur Larousse? At least I assume the shouting match is over me.'

Katriana gripped Robert's arm and began pulling him along the corridor, saying. 'Never mind Robert, it's only papa prying again, he simply refuses to leave us alone, now it's your family he wants to know about.'

'There's no problem there, sweetheart, I've nothing to hide.'

Robert turned around and noticed Larousse standing in the corridor with his arm placed against the wall and his head resting against it, it was obvious to him that he was looking somewhat perturbed, he halted his passage along the corridor with Katriana still tugging at his arm.

'Hang on, sweetheart,' Robert said as he held Katriana close around the shoulders.

'Monsieur Larousse, let's get this over and done with, what is it you want to know now?'

Larousse took a few moments to decide to tell Robert about his brother, feeling if he didn't already know, he would find out sooner or later in any case. It was obvious to him Robert had no knowledge of the events leading up to his brother's death. If he did, he was a damn good actor, he concluded.

'Robert, I think we better go to the lounge and pour ourselves some of that malt whisky, there's something I have to tell you, it's rather unpleasant I'm afraid.'

Katriana was first to speak. 'Papa! What is it?'

'I think it's best Robert and I discuss this alone, my dear.'

'Oh no, papa! I'm coming too!'

'I would rather you didn't, my dear.'

'I'm coming, papa!' Larousse raised his eyebrows and sighed a heavy sigh. 'Very well my dear but remember, I did warn you it would be unpleasant.'

Robert sensed this was going to be difficult and pleaded with Katriana to stay in her cabin; however, she was so determined no one could change her mind.

The three of them went to the lounge. Larousse himself, poured them all a drink then sat down facing Katriana and Robert who were sitting close together, Katriana holding Robert's hand in her lap.

'Robert, I'm deeply sorry, I have some grave news for you, I'm afraid.'

Robert was clearly puzzled, he asked. 'What do you mean, grave news? I don't understand. Is it my father?' Larousse hesitated, then took a large mouthful from his glass of malt.

'Robert, it's about your brother.'

'My brother! My brother is dead, how can you have anything to do with him.'

'Yes, I know he is. Look, please listen, the fact of the matter is you were told, officially at the time and quite rightly so, that it was due to an accident on the docks, is that correct?'

'Yes, he was.' Robert had to stop before describing the incident with Katriana present, he continued.

'Sorry, Bruce, that was my brother's name, suffered fatal injuries at Avonmouth Docks a few weeks ago whilst on duty, where's this leading, Monsieur Larousse?'

'The police now have reason to believe it was no accident, I'm afraid. After further investigations, the police are now classing the incident as murder.'

'Murder! What do you mean, the police said it was an accident! Why have they re-opened the case anyway? How come you know about any of this in the first place?' Robert was mortified by the announcement. He simply couldn't believe what he'd just heard.

'I'm sorry Robert, I told you it would be unpleasant.'

Robert fought back the tears forming behind his eyes, composing himself best he could, he asked somewhat erratically.

'How do you know about this? How long have you known? Why has nobody told me about this until now? God almighty, this is unbelievable!' Robert jumped up and began pacing the floor.

Katriana having overcome her initial shock, interrupted him.

'Oh Robert, papa! This is terrible! Papa, who's responsible for this? Robert, I'm so sorry, this is awful.' She held him tight, tears forming on her pretty face.

Robert was still incensed with the disclosure. 'Yes! Who's responsible for this? Do you know?'

'No, not at present but they are re-investigating the matter fully back in Bristol, I can assure you. I'll keep you informed if I hear anything. I promise.'

'Thank you for that Monsieur Larousse but there's one thing I don't quite understand.'

'What's that?' asked Larousse.

'How have you come to find this out? Is the alleged murder of my brother connected to your trip to Kinshasa?'

'Yes, I'm afraid so. It was the attempted murder of a truck driver which prompted my old department to investigate this organisation, it was then we found out about your brother's death, although I must tell you I only found out he was your brother less than ten minutes ago as we were departing the Frigate and that's the truth, Robert.'

Robert sat down again next to Katriana and took hold of her hand.

'So, if you're investigating something which is directly responsible for my brother's death, I want to help, I want to put these people behind bars where they belong!'

Larousse waved his hand at Robert.

'I'm sorry, Robert but that's quite out of the question, I cannot allow you to get involved with my plans. No, you and Katriana will go on to Marseille as soon as we dock, as arranged,' he said emphatically.

Robert jumped to his feet again.

'I told you before Monsieur Larousse, I will not be dictated to! If you won't allow me to help you, then I will have to do it alone!' He shouted in a frenzied rage.

'Don't be so bloody stupid, Robert! You don't know what you're up against, these people are hardened criminals, fanatics even, you wouldn't stand a chance alone.'

Katriana stood up and held Robert close.

'Please darling, listen to papa, it's too dangerous for you to get involved, you're only one man, he's right, you wouldn't stand a chance. Please darling, I don't want to lose you. Please,' she pleaded with Robert to no avail.

'I'm sorry Katriana, I love you very, very much but this is family, it's something I must do, with or without your father. Excuse me please, I need to be alone for a moment. I'm sorry.'

Robert quickly left the lounge and headed for his cabin. Katriana began to cry as she sat down beside her father.

'Oh papa, I love him so much and I love you papa, I don't want to lose any one of you, please papa, don't go to Kinshasa, take me home please, it's too dangerous, let the authorities deal with it, please papa, please,' she implored.

Larousse held his daughter close, her head bobbing against his chest from her sobbing.

'I'm sorry, my precious but I have no choice, I have to clear the family name and it's a matter of honour.'

Katriana sat upright, protesting, she said. 'Robert's family is important to him, yet you deny him any involvement but it's alright for you to go blazing in! What if you get killed in the process! What good will that do the family name! Tell me that!'

'I'm sorry my dear, there's no other way.' Larousse kissed his daughter on the forehead and left the cabin.

The tension aboard the luxury yacht was now almost at breaking point. What could possibly happen next was the question.

Chapter Five

The weather had taken a turn for the worse yet again in Bristol on the Tuesday morning of October 4th as Angela Pearce was to realise when she opened the curtains and looked out of her bedroom window at seven o'clock in the morning. The rain was lashing down from the heavens and the sky looked decidedly stormy.

The gutters along both sides of the road flowed like two small streams carrying pieces of debris, litter, discarded cigarette packs and such on its passage. The drains themselves inadequate to cope with the downpour caused a turbulence to the surface motion of the rushing water momentarily as it passed swiftly over rather than down the overflowing grids.

She straightened her curtains and took herself off into the shower, already in a state of depression as the thought of re-interviewing the unsavoury character David Matthey came to mind. This in addition to the fact the investigation was getting nowhere, apart from uncovering a rough diamond, which was of more importance to the other parties than to her.

The sight of the weather conditions that morning did little to improve matters. She was indeed discontented. Having showered under a piping hot power shower spray, she turned the temperature dial down until she could bear the cold no more.

She had to do this to wake herself up, it was not the act of someone caring for their skin, ensuring the pores were closed after a hot treatment; no, this was merely an attempt to motivate herself for she'd slept little that night concentrating on the investigation. She found the solitude therapeutic to her work.

In fact, she was happy to be alone, totally alone. There had been men of course, several men to date but none she felt enough for to form a long-term relationship, she wouldn't allow her career to be jeopardised by their involvement. The men she'd been with till now tended to be too dogmatic and demanding. Angela Pearce would lead her life her way, her career, the job, that was what she lived for at present.

Stepping out from the shower cubicle, she patted herself down with a towel and adorned a dressing gown also made of towelling in order to soak up the remainder, she then wrapped another dry towel around her hair whilst she went along to the kitchen, put the kettle on and fumbled around in the fridge looking for something for breakfast, finding nothing amongst the limited choice on offer that she fancied. Angela Pearce did little shopping due to the long hours she put in at the station. In the end, she settled for a bowl of cereal and a pot of tea.

She sat munching her way monotonously through her breakfast, obviously eating it more from necessity rather than pleasure, then the telephone rang. Annoyed at the imposition at such an early hour, she pushed her bowl aside and went to answer it.

'Hello, who's calling?' she said as if she didn't know with despondency in her voice.

'DCI Pearce, this is DS Lynton-Reece at the station.'

'Yes Sergeant, what's the problem?'

'Not a problem ma'am, the hospital has just informed us your suspect, Jason Allen, has regained consciousness, the doctor has given us permission to speak to him briefly, he's still rather poorly.'

'Thank you, Sergeant, will you contact DS Tomlinson and ask him to meet me at the hospital as soon as possible. Oh and tell him to bring the evidence bag also.'

'Yes, ma'am.'

Angela Pearce dashed back upstairs to her bedroom and dressed, dried and tied her hair. When she came down again, she took a few quick mouthfuls of the well soaked cereal and gulped her tea down before rushing out to her car. She started it up and drove off as if in hot pursuit, all the time she was thinking about how to handle Jason Allen and hoping he would prove less difficult than his associate David Matthey and if so, this could prove to be a turning point in their investigation. She was pleased he'd pulled through.

Arriving at the hospital, she was met by DS Tomlinson outside Allen's room which had been arranged was adjacent to the truck drivers for ease of security. The doctor in charge of Allen spoke with her briefly, pointing out, that Allen was still very weak from his ordeal and asking her to consider his condition and not to overtax him for the present.

DCI Pearce assured her she would tread carefully. He was for the moment, perhaps her prime lead. The doctor left them to their interview and went about her duties.

Both Angela Pearce and Frank Tomlinson went into the room quietly and stood on the left side of the bed for a few moments. Jason Allen was lying there with drips, tubes and electrodes attached in various places, his left leg and arm raised off the bed in plaster, his head bandaged and his neck in a support. They looked at each other on seeing his condition, without words it was obvious they both felt some pity for him.

Angela Pearce was first to speak, in a soft voice, she said. 'Jason, can you hear me?' Jason opened his eyes slowly.

'Jason, I'm DCI Pearce and this is DS Tomlinson from Avon and Somerset Police. Is it alright if we ask you a few questions?'

With a very weak voice, Jason answered. 'I've got nothing to say.' Angela Pearce pulled up a seat beside the bed.

'Jason, listen to me. Your so-called friends Stein and Blanford have skipped the country for sure, leaving you and David Matthey on your own to face charges including conspiracy, attempted murder and possibly murder. All I want to know for the moment Jason is; where do you think Stein and Blanford might go, can you tell me that?'

'Where's David? Have you got him?' Allen asked painfully, slowly and avoiding answering DCI Pearce's question.

'Yes, Jason he's in custody.'

'Then what do you need me for, won't he talk? If he won't talk then neither will I, you're wasting your time.'

'Look Jason, we know you were involved in the smuggling of diamonds and we know you're also involved with the "Reichsbürger" movement, tell me, are the two connected?' Angela Pearce knew perhaps she shouldn't have mentioned the diamonds as yet but she had and that was that. It was out now.

'What diamonds? What's the "Reichsbürger" movement? What are you talking about? I don't know anything about any of that!'

'Listen Jason, there's no good denying it, we found an uncut diamond at the berth cabin, it fell out of the chair leg, was that where you stored them or was one of your so-called friends on the make for themselves?'

That statement by Angela Pearce certainly upset Allen, he attempted to raise himself up from the bed.

'I don't believe you! You're trying to trick me into saying something I'll live to regret. I'm saying nothing.' He settled himself back down with the look of excruciating pain written in his expression.

'Jason, believe me it's no trick, here's the diamond to prove it!' DCI Pearce took the diamond from her colleague who had collected it from the evidence room at the station. She held the diamond up still sealed in the evidence bag for him to see.

Jason looked at it for several moments, then with an enraged tone, he said. 'Cheating bastard! That was Blanford's cabin, Mark Blanford. How many more did you find?'

'This was the only one Jason, if there were any more, he must have taken them along with him, this one fell out of a chair leg after the chair was knocked, the ferrule at the bottom had already been disturbed, we assume they were stored in the hollow leg. Tell me, do you think Blanford was responsible?'

'Yes! Of course, he was, that was his cabin.'

'Well Jason, with friends like that, perhaps you feel a little differently now?'

'Oh no! I'm saying nothing, when I get out of here, I'll see to him by my own means.'

Angela Pearce looked at Frank Tomlinson, then as if by telepathy, he said. 'There's something you're forgetting Jason, when you get out of here, you'll be going to jail along with your friend David and for an exceedingly long time. Neither of you will be in any position to get to Blanford and on top of that, once the inmates find out you are both Nazi's, I doubt if either of you will survive to carry out your sentence.'

'Nazi's! Where did you get that from?' Allen asked.

'Oh, we know all about your little smuggling racket and your "Reichsbürger" affiliation Jason but it's Stein and Blanford we really want, what do you say, will you help us?'

Allen lay again in silence for a moment, concentrating his thoughts. Whilst all was quiet, the doctor entered the room to check his patient was not being over exerted. Angela Pearce made an issue of rising from her seat and walking over to the window to raise her voice in reply if the doctor asked her anything. Hoping she would.

'Jason, how are you doing, are you alright?' said the doctor. He nodded then said. 'Yes, thanks.'

'You're not pushing him too hard are you, he's still very weak.' Added the doctor, directing her question to the DCI.

Angela Pearce showed no sign of elation as she answered her question, saying. 'No Doctor Abrahamson, we're being very gentle with him, isn't that so Jason?'

Jason's eyes showed a slight sign of alarm which luckily only DS Tomlinson and the DCI noticed.

Doctor Abrahamson made a few checks on Jason, then said. 'Five more minutes that's all, he needs to rest.'

'Yes, doctor we understand, thank you,' answered DCI Pearce.

The doctor left the room, as the door closed behind her, Frank Tomlinson made the obvious comment.

'Well Jason, there's a lady who wouldn't be too pleased to hear you're a Nazi, I'm sure. With a name like Abrahamson, she must be Jewish or at least married to someone who is.'

'You wouldn't tell her that would you, I'm no Nazi. Really, I'm not, I was only in it for the money and a bit of a thrill, that's all.'

DCI Pearce walked back over to the bed.

'There are not too many thrills in a prison cell, are there Jason and you can't exactly spend your money there either, take my point. You're going to go down for a very long stretch, although, if you help us, we could help you!'

'What do you mean, help me?' Jason asked.

'I can't promise you anything Jason, only that I'll do my best to lighten your sentence, put in a good word, you understand? But only if you help us.'

Jason thought for a few moments, soon realising he hadn't the stomach for prison and the sudden realisation of another far worse aversion, he said, 'Okay, look, I'll do a deal with you.'

DCI Pearce stopped him and read Allen his rights before allowing him to continue.

'The thing is, I know a lot more about what's going on than they thought I did, I kept my ear to the ground, did a bit of snooping, you know, no doubt you've checked my record, so you'll know what I'm capable of, eh? Anyway, I found out what their planning. You quite obviously have no idea what's going on and I'm the only one who can tell you, even David Matthey doesn't know what I know, so you'd be wasting your time with him.'

'And what's that, Jason?' The DCI said with a tone of indifference.

'Oh no! It's not that easy. I want assurance that any charges against me are dropped. And! I want a new identity, protection and the works! In addition, I want to be moved out of the country and quickly, understand! Well, that's what supergrasses get, isn't it?'

Angela Pearce laughed aloud.

'Supergrass! Is that what you think you are Jason, don't make me laugh!'

Jason, with great determination, managed to raise himself up from the bed only a few inches or so, staring into Angela Pearce's eyes with a cold calculated response, he said.

'Laugh! You won't have time to laugh once they start again, I'll tell you that for nothing.'

Frank Tomlinson couldn't help himself, he had to ask. 'Once who starts?'

Jason Allen thought it was his turn to laugh a little and in doing so, felt worse for it, holding his stomach with his good hand, he eased himself back down, answering DS Tomlinson in the process.

'The "Reichsbürgersbewegung" mate! They're planning the Fourth Reich, that's what the bloody diamonds are for! To fund it, you idiots. Find it funny now, eh?'

DCI Pearce and DS Tomlinson were clearly shocked by the statement. 'What do you mean they're planning the Fourth Reich?' The DCI's previous tone of indifference changing to that of intrigue.

'That's all I'm saying until I get my deal, once you've sorted that out, I'll tell you what I know and nothing until then.'

'Jason, I can't promise you anything like a deal, that's out of my hands but the people who can need something more than just a simple statement, do you understand.'

Jason interrupted. 'No deal! No squeal! I mean it.'

Just then the doctor returned. 'Your five minutes are up sorry,' she said as she entered.

'Fine, Doctor but we'll need to speak to him again. Our inquiries have taken on a new meaning.'

'It will have to be tomorrow Detective Chief Inspector, he'll be sedated for some time, I'm sure you understand.'

'Yes, Doctor whatever you say.'

'Tomorrow then, about ten but not for too long, he's in a very weak state.'

'I understand Doctor, thank you.' DCI Pearce turned back to Jason.

'Look Jason, I'll see what I can do but you better be on the level for your sake.'

'I've no worries on that score, you just get it sorted out. I'll be waiting. But you had better make it quick.'

'You have whatever it is you know to tell us by the time we return, we need evidence, proof, something tangible, okay.'

DCI Pearce and DS Tomlinson returned to the police station and began informing the relative departments of Allen's disclosure and demands, commencing with the Admiralty.

Upon the Admiralty being advised of Allen's statement, Rear Admiral Bartholomew-Smythe arranged for a car to take him to Bristol directly. Angela Pearce and her officers were still busy informing the various interested parties who had all been calling back, emailing or video conferencing with her department since the announcement, also she was attempting to secure some sort of deal for Allen in the process.

She was talking to the Home Office when Bartholomew-Smythe entered. DS Tomlinson noticed the Rear Admiral being led along the corridor to the investigation room.

'Good afternoon, Rear Admiral, please take a seat.'

'It's DCI Pearce I need to speak to, Detective Sergeant,' he commented abruptly.

'I'm sorry Sir, she's on the phone at the moment.'

'Well tell her I'm here, damn you man!' He yelled.

Frank Tomlinson was unaffected by his outburst, replying casually, he said. 'To the Home Office. Sir.'

Bartholomew-Smythe swallowed hard, then said. 'In that case, perhaps you can tell me what's going on?'

'Best coming from the boss, Sir. She won't be long, I'm sure.'

'Oh, very well, if you insist,' the Rear Admiral replied then reluctantly sat in the seat Frank Tomlinson had offered, drumming his fingers on his portfolio which he'd placed on his lap.

'Would you care for a coffee, Sir?' asked Frank. 'Have you any tea? I prefer tea, if you don't mind.'

'Yes of course Sir, I'll see to it.'

Frank Tomlinson returned a minute or two later with a plastic carton of vending machine tea.

'There we are Sir, a nice cup of rosy lee, that's what you Londoner's call it, am I right?' said Frank in his West Country accent.

Bartholomew-Smythe looked disgustingly into the cup, saying. 'I'm not one of your so-called Londoner's old boy, I only happen to be deployed there. Have you no proper tea in this place?'

'Only in the canteen Sir, it's not much better mind, if you wish to go along there I'll show you the way.'

The Rear Admiral shook his head.

'No need Detective Sergeant, I suppose I'll make do.'

Frank Tomlinson smirked behind his back as he returned to his desk. Five or so minutes later, DCI Pearce opened her office door, still unaware of the Rear Admiral's arrival, she shouted out.

'Listen, the Home Secretary may be calling me soon, make sure you find me when she does.'

'Ma'am, Rear Admiral Bartholomew-Smythe is waiting to see you,' announced DS Tomlinson.

'Oh, good morning, Rear Admiral,' she said, then noticing the clock was after one, she corrected her statement. 'Sorry, good afternoon, Sir, it's been one of those days, you know?'

'Quite,' he replied, still feeling disgruntled.

She showed him into her office, sitting him opposite her across the desk, she began.

'Rear admiral, this investigation is becoming bizarre, this "Reichsbürger" connection appears to have a far greater significance than simply a diamond smuggling operation. This chap we have in the hospital, Jason Allen, he's talking of anarchy, his own phrase being The Fourth Reich. God, if he's telling the truth we could be in for World War Three! If we're not careful.'

Smythe laughed aloud.

'Pure exaggeration, I can assure you Chief Inspector, the man's backed into a corner, he's trying anything, take my advice. We amongst other NATO members have been monitoring that sort of scenario since the last war, there's no possibility of a Fourth Reich, at least not in the foreseeable future. In fact, we have had reason to review that situation quite recently, I can assure you they're of no more a threat now as they've been since the war ended.'

Angela Pearce leaned over her desk and challenging his comment, she retorted.

'I seem to recall a statement to that effect was made after the First World War!'

Bartholomew-Smythe rebuffed her quickly, saying.

'Yes, that's quite correct, however with the technology available today there's very little possibility of any major threat developing undetected, in any case there's no Adolf Hitler, no Fuhrer; holding rallies up and down Germany in support of a Fourth Reich, is there?'

Angela Pearce began to nibble the end of her pen again, thinking for a moment before replying.

'Rear Admiral, there's little point in conjecture at this time, I think we should do whatever we can to extract any information Jason Allen has before we make any decisions or take any action on the matter.'

'Yes, I quite agree but surely Detective Chief Inspector, you don't seriously think he has much to offer, he's simply a pawn in their operation whose feeling betrayed by being left behind along with this Matthey character to suffer the consequences of their joint actions.'

The two of them continued to debate the matter at length for a full half hour when a call came through from the Home Secretary. Angela Pearce took the call with the Rear Admiral present and the phone on speaker.

'Good afternoon, Home Secretary, DCI Pearce speaking.'

'This story of yours Chief Inspector, do you think it has any substance?'

'I can't say for sure, Ma'am, he won't talk until he gets immunity from you. He also demands the usual protection and wants to leave the country as soon as possible.'

'There's no possibility of immunity for this chap or anything else unless he forwards some information voluntarily, showing at least the scope of the situation, something tangible, do I make myself clear?'

'Yes of course, Ma'am, though I'm not sure if he'll give us anything without his demands being met, he's a pretty cool character considering.'

'Well, that's his outlook, do what you can. Let me know if anything develops.'

'Thank you, Home Secretary, I'll be in touch.' The DCI replaced the receiver.

Bartholomew-Smythe sat with a smug expression whilst rolling his tongue around inside his mouth before remarking.

'I take it the Home Secretary is not impressed by your man Allen either.'

'Perhaps not, Rear Admiral but then we haven't given her much to go on, yet. She wants something from Allen before she'll consider anything. Standard procedure, as I'm sure you know.'

'And you still think he's got something to give, do you?' Replied Bartholomew-Smythe.

'I don't know for sure but I'll tell you this for nothing, I'm damn well going to find out! Time for another visit to the hospital, I think.' The DCI had forgotten the doctor's advice regarding her patient's sedation.

'Care to accompany me, Rear Admiral,' she offered.

'Yes of course Chief Inspector, this story I've got to hear for myself.' He laughed a little at the thought before following Angela Pearce out of her office.

'Frank! Get the car, we're going back to the hospital,' she called. 'Yes, ma'am.'

Arriving at the ward, DCI Pearce explained to the Staff Sister, they had to speak with Allen again, the matter was most urgent. The Sister said he was heavily sedated and she would have to clear it with Doctor Abrahamson first. She contacted the doctor to attend the ward, whilst she was on her way Angela Pearce pointed out to Bartholomew-Smythe that the doctor was more than likely Jewish and that she had no knowledge Allen was involved with the "Reichsbürger" movement, she asked him to avoid mentioning the fact if possible. He agreed to be discreet.

A few moments later, Doctor Abrahamson arrived.

'Oh, hello Doctor, sorry to be a bother but we urgently need to speak with Jason Allen again, it's a matter of vital importance to our investigation. Just a few moments are all we need right now,' she added, realising the previous advice.

'Detective Chief Inspector Pearce, Mr Allen is very weak and under heavy sedation, I told you to come back tomorrow, he's in no state to be questioned.'

Bartholomew-Smythe in his usual pompous manner, interjected.

'Now look here Doctor, I am Rear Admiral Bartholomew-Smythe of His Majesty's Royal Navy, this is a matter of national security, we insist on speaking to Allen right away!'

The doctor did not rise to the intimidation.

'Rear Admiral is it, well you could be Admiral of the Fleet for all it matters, the patient is under sedation and will be for some time and talking to him will get you nowhere for the time being. May I suggest you call back tomorrow morning as arranged? Ten o'clock. Good day to you both.'

'Really! This is preposterous, I shall speak to your superiors!'

'If you wish, you'll find them in the admin department. Now, I have things to attend to, I trust I shall see you both tomorrow. Good day to you again,' she said bluntly and left.

'Well, really! The audacity of the woman!' Smythe exclaimed for all to hear.

Angela Pearce and Frank Tomlinson did all they could to restrain themselves from laughing aloud when suddenly Bartholomew-Smythe commented aloud.

'I've a jolly good mind to tell you what type of man your patient is!'

Angela Pearce was livid, she turned on Bartholomew-Smythe with an enraged tone.

'Rear Admiral! I warn you now! Don't overstep your mark on this.'

'My dear young lady, I'm afraid you're forgetting your position.'

'My position is quite clear, Rear Admiral. I oversee this investigation and if you say or do anything to jeopardise it in any way I promise you, you'll regret it!'

'Oh, very well, have it your own way but I better not be wasting my time here.'

Angela Pearce had calmed down some from a moment ago, she decided she'd get the Rear Admiral out of the way for the time being, suggesting he should find himself some accommodation for the night and meet her at the station at 09.00 a.m. the following morning. He agreed and offered a limp apology for his outburst, she accepted and offered him a lift to a hotel of his choice.

He chose the Mercure. And why not, it was on expenses.

***

Early the same morning whilst maintaining a status of high alert, the various NATO members gathered in great haste for their conference in Brussels. Remarkably, the media had been kept uninformed of the events to date and the conference itself was played down simply as a strategy conference.

It was inevitable however that television coverage of so many defence officials arriving for a hastily arranged conference would stir up interest in media circles. The journalists clamoured for more information as the various vehicles drew up outside the Conference Centre, they were unfortunate as all the delegates issued a "no comment" statement.

By 11.00 hrs, the meeting was in full swing though getting nowhere fast. The investigations carried out throughout the previous fortnight had revealed absolutely nothing, no evidence, no reason, no answers and perhaps consoling, no further incidents.

As the committee inside the building deliberated over the following four hours or so, their consensus was that someone somewhere had developed a system capable of intercepting and controlling aircraft missile systems of differing characteristics. They couldn't say how, they couldn't say who and they certainly had little idea why.

The phrase "We will avenge" written at the end of each message obviously meant retribution for some deed against them in the past but who. It was obvious, they whoever they were had to be found and found fast and eliminated before the whole defence Strategy of the western world was undermined.

The weather in Brussels at the time was atrocious throughout the day, torrential rain kept most people indoors, most people that is apart from the group of fifty or so journalists who were denied entry to the Conference Centre whilst the delegates continued their discussions.

Amid the inhospitable weather, a rather strange event was about to take place. From behind the ranks of waiting journalists, all of whom seeking whatever cover the surrounding foliage and outbuildings offered though each and every one still eager to be at the front line to question the committee as it closed for the day, a rather odd noise appeared to be drawing nearer, the noise was difficult to ascertain amid the thrashing sound of the rain as it pelted the fast-running shallow watercourse which had formed on the sloping driveway.

The sound became more distinctive as it neared, it was a buzz like sound and it was now becoming obvious that it was closing in fast.

Security was alerted and together with the ranks of journalists, they turned to witness a small radio-controlled drone approaching the Conference Centre at speed whilst following an erratic flight path. The security personnel took immediate and decisive action, without hesitation they began opening fire upon the diminutive craft as it swayed from side to side and up and down to avoid being shot down.

Unarmed security personnel began ushering the crowd away from the area, their prime concern was of course for the safety of all personnel, journalists included, in and around the conference building.

A barrage of fire was maintained against all odds of hitting such a small moving object as it came ever closer to the conference building. The delegates had quickly been advised of the circumstances and anxiously, the conference room awaited the outcome.

Upon the drones' final approach, one of the large reflective windows in the conference hall was shattered by a charge dispensed from the drone itself, showering splintered glass both downward and inward, the delegates inside scrambled for cover, some below the seats, others taking refuge beneath the long crescent shaped tiered tabling, others running out into the corridor.

The security staff maintained their assault, realising the craft was now being purposely directed towards the now shattered window. Panic was rife as journalists scattered throughout the grounds for their scoop of a lifetime, the security personnel had little or no control of the situation, the armed officers continued their assault on the diminutive craft and in the process, destroyed several more windows in the conference hall to no avail and the drone entered the building.

In everyone's mind by this time was the obvious thought that the drone was a radio-controlled explosive device and not some childish prank, someone was out to kill the NATO Security Council and this would seem to be as good a method as any.

As the delegates clamoured for cover, the drone circled within the large hall for a moment before hovering over the chairman's table. With no immediate explosion and only the sound of the drone itself disturbing the peace, a few brave faces took the opportunity to see for themselves exactly what the hell was happening.

They hadn't long to wait, within ten seconds of hovering above the chairman's table, two small doors slowly swung open from beneath the drone, those who stood watching seemed mesmerised as to what could happen next, again the action of dropping some explosive device was foremost in their minds. However, they were to be surprised.

For as they looked upon the innocent drone calmly hovering some twenty feet or so above, a simple package was released and dropped. Some of the delegates took refuge again but for others, it was as though they had to see the whole scenario through, they had to know the reason behind such an elaborate set-up, they the brave, the foolish, call them what you will watched the decent of the tumbling package until the second it hit the chairman's desk, as a natural reaction each and every one of them closed their eyes and cowered down in expectation of impending disaster.

Suddenly it was all over, an anti-climax, nothing. Before they could re-focus, the drone had flown out of the building and away still being trailed by gunfire from the ground. The operator whomever he or she was, was putting on a show all the way, tumbling and looping the loop and various other acrobatic actions before disappearing into oblivion.

Back in the conference hall, the package was still lying on the desk. It measured merely the size of a matchbox. The chairperson called for the building to be evacuated before ordering the bomb disposal team to investigate.

Clarendon himself had been attending the meeting together with his opposite numbers from the USA and France, etc. Russia was of course persona-non-gratis as it is not a member of NATO. Clarendon dusted himself down as he filed through between the various delegates to reach them, speaking softly to the American said.

'Notice the time?'

The American looked at his watch.

'Just past three o'clock. Why?' He replied. Clarendon interjected.

'Another 03.00 hrs or 15.00 hrs message it seems.' This timing now becoming rather disconcerting to all.

As the clean-up commenced and the delegates began to leave, the journalists clamoured for information. The military maintained a shroud of silence regarding the package and simply brushed the incident off as a prank by an outsider to disrupt the conference.

The press was not convinced and following several arrests, the security staff cleared the area entirely of unwanted visitors. It would not be long to wait before finding out the truth within the mysterious package. Meanwhile, the delegates took the time to compose themselves before arranging time and place for any further discussions.

The conference hall was now obviously out of commission as anyone with a long-range microphone would be able to hear details of the conversation within.

It was therefore decided to re-locate and re-schedule but not before finding out what was contained in the mystery package.

One hour later, the bomb disposal team having ascertained there was nothing sinister about the package decided to open it, enclosed within a few sheets of old newspaper wrapped in an opaque plastic bag was a miniature flash drive.

The flash drive was inspected thoroughly before being taken to a soundproofed room within the complex. With nerves somewhat on edge, the drive was loaded into a stand-alone computer for fear of a virus affecting the servers, then the message played, this was the message the NATO Security Council heard.

United Kingdom: October 1st. United States: October 2nd. Russia: October 3rd. It is now the French who will suffer the wrath of our retribution. Nothing will stop us. 03.00 hrs tomorrow October 5th. We will avenge!

Following frenzied discussions, the French defence minister immediately contacted his headquarters and ordered the immediate stand down of all military aircraft and the disarmament of all missiles within his jurisdiction. He knew France was now indefensible by air. If there was to be a large-scale attack, it would take hours to re-compliment but under the circumstances, there was no choice.

The long wait until 03.00 hrs on October 5th had begun. Many of the NATO delegates had in the meantime began to move back to their respective countries though several selected personnel from each nation's delegation travelled from the main complex in the city to a NATO base on the French-Belgian border.

Gone were the comforts afforded by the luxurious offices of Brussels, now only moulded plastic chairs and steel framed dining tables used by the foot soldiers was all there was to offer. The base was on red alert and security was tight.

Reports were arriving by the hour from various intelligence agencies throughout the world all digging deep for information, most of them were negative, others a little encouraging but none concrete. The tension in the base grew ever more as midnight came and passed.

Computers spluttered out a myriad of useless information as details and scenarios were programmed in and the results fed out. The heads of the defence world were in a state of controlled panic as the definitive hour arrived, they confidently questioned the ability of the terrorists, knowing that not one military aircraft carrying armaments was in operation either in France or elsewhere in the NATO field of operation. The tension was palpable.

***

Meanwhile in Germany, Steinbacher and Matthey were being taken by a circuitous route to meet with General Friedrich Stoltz at his family's beloved mountainous retreat, located west of Walchensee in Bavaria. After ascending steadily from München, the car turned off the main road and headed towards the small town of Kochel, passing through the town itself, the driver continued for a further few miles then turned into a gateway clearly marked "Eigenes" (Private.) The gates to the long tree-lined winding driveway were opened automatically once the driver had spoken into a security entrance unit. The car proceeded along the drive to a manned gate where it was stopped for clearance by security staff. Once accepted, the driver carried on up to the imposing south facing typically Bavarian facade where another guard checked the occupants and allowed them to proceed to the bottom of the wide stone stairway to alight.

Steinbacher shook Blanford's hand as a gesture, saying.

'We've made it Dave, we'll be looked after now, don't you worry.'

True, they had safely reached the residence of General Stoltz, set high in the hills, the gardens of which were surrounded by a perimeter wall beyond which lay a lightly wooded area giving ample cover from prying eyes. The location lay somewhere between Kochel and Walchensee with panoramic views of the mountains and Lake Walchensee itself.

The building was in the Fachwerkbau style that was typical in Bavaria. It's exposed wooden beam framework being filled with wood mesh and plaster, it looked magnificent. Even Steinbacher was impressed by its appointment. Blanford seemed disinterested in such matters, he merely wished to conclude the arrangements and leave.

On alighting from the car, Oefner ushered them in through the main door which was closed behind them and guided them towards another pair of large oak doors, which were this time guarded outside by two men in full Nazi uniform holding machine guns at the ready. Steinbacher was unperturbed by the sight, in fact quite the reverse, he felt his adrenaline pumping through his body at the spectacle.

Blanford, on the other hand having had no personal experience of Nazi officialdom or theatricals, bar for the odd arm band at group meetings was showing obvious signs of apprehension.

Oefner signalled to the guards to open the doors, they did so together to reveal the archetypally dressed Nazi Party room, with full red banners sporting the Swastika emblem central in a white circle. The banners, ten in total, were draped from ceiling to floor around the walls of the room and the inevitable profiled picture of their Fuhrer, Adolf Hitler in pride of place as usual.

'Please gentlemen, take a seat the General will be with you shortly,' Oefner said, then turned military fashion and left the room.

Blanford was noticeably perspiring with anxiety as he took in his surroundings, summoning up courage, he said to Steinbacher.

'Jesus Jim, this place gives me the creeps, it's like being up in front of the Gestapo, are you sure were going to be alright?'

'Stop fretting Mark, General Stoltz will have arrangements in place, don't worry. I know him well.'

Blanford spent the next ten minutes or so agonising and jostling about uncomfortably in his chair, pondering the outcome of the forthcoming meeting with the unknown General Stoltz.

Steinbacher remaining calm throughout, confident. He walked over to the large French window and looked out towards the gardens, which ran down to the lake.

'This country of mine is beautiful, don't you think? Eh, Mark!'

Blanford sat slightly trembling at the knee, unable to answer bar for the nod of his head, such was the anxiety he felt. Steinbacher couldn't understand his tremulous agitation. Hadn't he assured him often enough, there was no cause for consternation.

Then the sound of several footsteps marching military fashion towards them could be heard on the polished wooden flooring in the hall. Steinbacher hurried over to the desk.

'Stand up, Mark!' He said in a low voice though authoritative.

Blanford was transfixed, he sat through the motion of the double doors being opened and the two guards entering, calling.

'Achtung!'

Fifty-one-year-old General Friedrich Stoltz marched in first, showing his characteristic limp followed closely behind by Axel Oefner, both in full uniform.

The General placed his walking stick on the desk and stood behind it and stared at Blanford, who was still trembling from anxiety.

Oefner knowing Blanford was unable to converse in German, said, 'Stand up! Herr Blanford. You do not wish to offend the General, do you?'

Blanford shook his head and with significant effort, he managed to rise to his feet, his knees trembling slightly more from the terror he felt within. General Stoltz cast his gaze over to Steinbacher who gave an immediate Nazi salute.

'Friedrich, my old friend!' Steinbacher announced as he clicked his heels. General Stoltz returned his salute, shouting aloud. 'Herr General bitte.'

Demanding his rank be respected.

Steinbacher was stunned, this was his old friend and colleague and he could not understand the harsh manner he adopted towards him. He replied, 'Herr General.' As he took the salute again.

'Herr Hauptsturmführer,' the General authoritatively replied.

The General then sat down, Oefner remained standing aside the desk. Steinbacher and Blanford attempted to sit down when Oefner shouted aloud.

'You will remain standing! Until the General orders you otherwise!'

'Friedrich, what's this all about?' asked Steinbacher.

'Silence!'

'You will speak only when spoken to. Understand?' shouted Oefner.

'What's going on, General?' asked Steinbacher, sounding uneasy. 'Jürgen. I am very sorry to say, we are most displeased with your efforts over the past few weeks. You have caused the "Reichsbürger" great concern over the way you have handled your section. You may have destroyed the operation completely for all we know.'

'Herr General! I was not to blame. My men caught a driver snooping through the crates and frightened him off, he may have found the orange crates containing the diamonds in the corner posts, we had no choice other than to frighten him off, things got out of hand, he fought back Herr General, he had to be silenced but by this time, the Transport Police at the docks had become involved, we had no choice other than to eliminate the driver and the policeman.'

'Sir, after the police constable took the driver's statement he began snooping also, he found some of the diamonds we had stored for dispatch, we had to kill him, there was no other way. Herr General, please believe me, we took every measure to make it look like an accident.'

The General stood up, lifted his walking stick and slammed it down on the desk. 'Then why did the police return and question you all again? And why are you running to us for help? Eh! Tell me that!'

'I don't know Herr General; they must have found out something else.'

'Yes! That's self-evident! No doubt they have but only through your incompetence and the stupidity of your subordinates!'

Just then, there was knocking on the door, which stopped the General continuing his chastisement. Oefner called for them to enter. Two men in civilian dress entered, carrying both Steinbacher and Blanford's luggage. They placed the suitcases on the large desk and opened them, it was obvious they had already been searched through.

'What is the meaning of this, Herr General?' Demanded Steinbacher. 'I protest!' he added.

'Silence!' shouted Oefner.

Steinbacher made a move towards the desk, as he did so, he heard the clicking of the two guns held by the guards behind him, he decided to refrain from continuing and returned to attention.

One of the men who had brought in the suitcases was talking to the General very quietly for a few moments then stood aside. The General dismissed the two guards and resumed his position behind the desk.

'Tell me Herr Hauptsturmführer, would you say we took care of you whilst you were in England?'

'Ja wohl! Herr General,' answered Steinbacher with certainty.

'Did you receive adequate reimbursement for your efforts, would you say?'

'Of course, Herr General.'

'Were you reluctant to divide your reimbursements among your fellow comrades as ordered?'

Steinbacher stood firmly.

'Nein! Herr General. The disbursements were divided according to your instructions.'

The General walked around the desk and had a quiet word with Oefner. Continuing, he asked.

'Was there at any time whilst you were forwarding the merchandise you felt perhaps a little of this may not be missed and perhaps put some aside for your retirement so to speak?' The General asked sarcastically.

'Nein! Herr General, I take that as an insult to an officer of the "Reichsbürgersbewegung"!' Riposted Steinbacher vehemently.

'Then, for what reason Herr Hauptsturmführer, can you give me that these several diamonds I hold in my hand were found among your luggage?'

Steinbacher was visibly stupefied and remained speechless for a moment. Contemplating how or why the diamonds had been found, he could only surmise they had been planted on him by anyone whom he had had contact with over the last two days.

Mark Blanford was the first and obvious choice, though he felt that after working so close for so long, he could trust him implicitly. Next was Oefner, who he knew not. Could he have planted them to cause friction between the General and himself or indeed the driver of the car who loaded the suitcases or either of the two men who had recently entered? His mind was in turmoil, he soon realised he had no answer, to tell the truth was his only course.

'Herr General, I have no knowledge of those diamonds among my luggage, I am a loyal officer and would not stoop to theft from the "Reichsbürgersbewegung".'

'Then how do you explain their presence, Jürgen?'

'I'm afraid I'm unable to Herr General, someone must have put them there.'

'You, Blanford! Did you put them there? Tell me the truth!' The General quizzed.

Blanford could not speak; he had stood in terror for the last few minutes, afraid to move.

'Answer me, you idiot! Did you put them there?' The General demanded. 'I, I, I know nothing about them,' Blanford said, stuttering his reply.

'I put it to you that you are a liar! Tell me the truth and I'll spare your miserable life.'

'I, I've never seen them before, honest, I'm not an officer but I'm just as loyal to the "Reichsbürger" movement, please believe me, please General,' he said as the sweat trickled down his face, his body trembling. His treachery had been found out. The moment had arrived he'd been dreading.

'You are a disgrace to the "Reichsbürgersbewegung"! A common thief! The diamonds were found in your baggage and not 'Herr Hauptsturmführer Steinbacher's, as you are aware!'

'General, please forgive me. An indiscretion, a mistake. I have been foolish; it won't happen again, I can assure you,' Blanford said as he stepped forward about to kneel and beg forgiveness. He saw no compassion so decided another tack may be more beneficial.

'General Stoltz, Sir. Be fair, you stole them first, I only stole a few, my whole life has gone up in smoke now, I have nothing and I just wanted some insurance that's all, Sir.'

This outburst only served to intensify the situation and infuriate the General even more. The General looked Mark Blanford in the eye and simply said.

'Schweinhund.' He nodded to Oefner who drew a silencer fitted small calibre pistol from his shoulder holster and shot Blanford without hesitation in the right knee from behind. Blanford stumbled in a heap to the floor, holding his badly gashed knee in his hands and screaming in agony. Whilst he was rolling around the floor, Steinbacher looked at the General with his mouth agape but said nothing.

The General continued as if nothing had happened, detailing to Steinbacher they had obviously monitored the output from The DRC to Bristol and from Bristol to Germany and found discrepancies on several instances. They had assumed until now the losses were inevitable over the period and the distances travelled, although he pointed out only one other route had suffered similar irregularities and they would now investigate the matter fully.

Steinbacher whilst still at attention asked.

'What about Blanford, Herr General? He's in need of medical attention.'

'He's a disgrace to the "Reichsbürger" movement, Herr Hauptsturmführer!

Medical attention is too good for him, a common thief! He will be made an example of!'

Blanford, still rolling around the floor, somehow understood the General's meaning.

'Please General, I'm sorry Sir. Please,' he pleaded.

Before he could plead anymore, the General nodded to Oefner. Oefner deliberately took his time in removing his pistol from its holster again and slowly aiming it at Blanford's head, the aim, central, between the eyes. An execution.

Steinbacher could no longer stand back and watch a cold-blooded execution take place. Blanford was calling out.

'Jim! Jim! Please help me! I'm sorry. God almighty, help me. Please!' Steinbacher swung out at Oefner's arm, knocking the pistol out of his hand, he followed it to the floor and picked it up. Just then the double doors flew open and the two guards entered, machine guns at the ready.

Steinbacher had reached the General and with the pistol to his head, he demanded aloud. 'Put your guns down! And kick them over here.'

The General nodded for them to comply. While the guards were laying down their weapons, Steinbacher called out.

'Dave, grab those guns.' Blanford struggled over to reach the two weapons, he picked one up and pointed it directly at Oefner who shouted.

'Please! Herr Blanford, I was only obeying orders.'

Steinbacher called out. 'No Dave! You'll alert the guards, just cover him. You two! Over here, beside him.' He called to the two guards who moved slowly over to join Oefner.

Steinbacher with the pistol still trained on General Stoltz commented calmly. 'Herr General, this is not how I see the Fourth Reich behaving in its infancy. There is only one disgrace to the "Reichsbürger" in here and that is you. I will not have you murder a man in cold blood, no matter what he's done.'

General Stoltz intervened. 'Jürgen, you are mistaken, put down the gun, we'll talk this over.'

'There's no mistake, Herr General and nothing to talk over, both Blanford and I are getting out of here and right now.'

'You won't get past the front doors Jürgen, don't be a fool like your friend there, put down the gun.'

Steinbacher moved slowly around towards the General. 'We will if you do as you're told, otherwise I'll shoot you myself.'

'Herr Hauptsturmführer! You will be court-martialled for your actions; I'll see to it personally,' General Stoltz replied in an effort to regain his authority.

'Herr General, it's time you realised something. The war was over seventy odd years ago, I joined the group because I believed in the cause but people like you destroy the fabric of the group by actions such as this, I will not allow the "Reichsbürger" to be controlled by men like you!'

Steinbacher told Blanford to keep them all covered. Meanwhile, he tore the wiring from the table lamp and tied the General and Oefner back-to-back on two chairs, he then ripped down two of the Nazi emblem drapes and stared at them momentarily, a feeling of deep sorrow came over him, he knew he would never be part of the movement ever again, he would be an outcast, a hunted man. But there was no going back now, a change of heart would only lead to his own execution.

He laid the two banners along the floor and instructed the two guards and the two other men, each to lay down back-to-back and roll over until it fully surrounded them both.

'Herr General, call the gate and inform them we are leaving alone and don't try to be a hero, I'm not afraid to use this,' Steinbacher said as he pointed the pistol at the General's head.

'You are a fool Jürgen, how far do you think you will get, we have people everywhere, you will be hunted down and punished severely for your actions this day, I promise you!'

'Save your breath, General and make that call now.'

Although the guards outside had not been alerted to any sign of trouble, one guard who was patrolling had noticed through the window, a drape falling to the floor and had decided to take a closer look, as he peered cautiously through the bottom panes he could see the General and Oefner bound together, being unarmed himself, he thought for a few moments on what action he was to take.

Stoltz had trained his personnel to deal effectively with any situation but emphasising above all that attention should not be drawn if possible, to his home. Quickly, he decided on his method and moved slowly away from the window and over to the car which Steinbacher and Blanford had arrived in, reaching into his pocket he produced a Swiss Army style knife and checking no one was watching from the General's room, he lay down aside the car and proceeded to partially cut through the flexible reinforced rubber brake hoses leading to the front wheels, once accomplished he retreated to the gate house where upon his arrival, the telephone rang.

The guard answered it and simply replied, 'Ja Wohl, Herr General.'

The guard explained to his colleague what he had seen and what he had done to foil their escape, his colleague replying that the General had informed him his two guests were leaving unaccompanied and to allow them to pass through.

They decided between them to take no action as they would be armed, the result of which may lead to a shooting match and alert the authorities to one of the few safe "Reichsbürger" locations, this was paramount to the General's instructions.

The guard had done as he was trained, he allowed the escape to continue knowing that in any case the car's brakes would fail within a few miles or so, especially in the mountainous terrain surrounding the retreat.

Steinbacher meanwhile had ripped out the telephone cable and tore off some curtain cord and bound the two guards and the two other men together, he then tore some off another of the drapes, ripped and rolled it to form gags plus a bandage for Blanford, he tied one gag to each man leaving the General until last, saying.

'I'm sorry it's come to this Freidrich, I always admired you and I just wanted you to know that. Please don't waste your time trying to find us, you know my talent for disguise.'

'Jürgen! I beg of you to reconsider, think of the "Reichsbürgersbewegung"! This is your last chance, Herr Hauptsturmführer.'

'The "Reichsbürger" movement is over for me, Herr General; I will not be party to butchery.'

Steinbacher placed the gag over the General's mouth whilst he attempted to protest, then he turned to help Blanford bandage his knee and lifted him up to his feet.

'Come on Dave, let's get you some attention.' He took both guards' guns and removed the magazines and placed them in his pocket. He then supported Blanford with one arm whilst he carried the pistol in the other, cautiously he opened the doors into the hall, all was clear.

'Right Mark, we'll get you out of here.'

'What about the diamonds, Jim?'

'Yes, what about them Herr General, I think you owe them to us for what you've done, don't you?'

The General shook his head frantically but to no avail, Steinbacher swept them from the desk and placed them in his pocket. Blanford approached Oefner, whose eyes wide open and menacing before had changed to those filled with fear. Blanford struck him across the face with the butt of the rifle hard enough to ensure a gash appeared.

'I'll remember you for this,' he said, pointing to his knee with the rifle butt. He continued. 'And you'll remember me every-time you look in a mirror, you shit!' He said, pounding him with another blow.

'Come on, Mark! That's enough,' demanded Steinbacher as he checked the hall was still clear, he returned and assisted Blanford out and into the car.

'Once we're past the gate, we'll be alright Mark, I'm sorry about your knee.'

'Oh, that's alright Jim, at least I'm still alive, thanks for sticking up for me in there, after what I did, you know.'

'It was a bloody stupid thing to do Mark, I trusted you.'

'I know, I'm sorry Jim, honest. Call it temptation, eh?' Blanford said with conviction.

As they approached the gate, Steinbacher had the pistol concealed under his jacket in case of any trouble, his apprehension was relieved as the barrier was opened and the guard smiled and saluted as he drove past.

'We've made it, Jim! Thank God for that,' Blanford said, relieved at the situation.

'Yes but we have to get some distance between us before they find the General and the others.'

'Where are we going to go, Jim?'

'I'm not sure, Mark. The hospital's too dangerous, too many questions, we'll have to find someone to see to your knee.'

Although Branford's injury was indeed painful, with the events of the past few minutes, he hadn't quite noticed the severity of the pain until Steinbacher mentioned it.

'Jesus, Jim! This is killing me; I really need to go to a hospital.'

'Sorry Dave, we'll have to find someone who won't ask questions. There's someone I think may help us in München, an old friend of mine.'

'How long's that going to take, Jim? I've lost a lot of blood and I'm feeling a bit queasy, to be honest.'

Blanford reached down and clasped his knee, Steinbacher glanced over at him and could see the pain and anguish written upon his grey looking face, he swallowed hard, his thoughts turning to whether there would be time to reach München and whether his old friend would still be living there in any event.

Blanford bowed his head slightly and in a soft voice, he uttered. 'I'm sorry about this Jim, it's all my fault.'

'Never mind all that now, just shut-up and rest for the time being. Don't forget to release that tourniquet every ten or so minutes, okay!'

Steinbacher was driving the car hard to make good time, he was only a few miles away from the General and his accomplices when he approached a hairpin bend on a steep descent, braking hard to negotiate the turn, the brake pedal suddenly dropped to the floor!

'Shit, Dave!' he exclaimed loudly as he stamped repeatedly on the brake pedal.

'We've no bloody brakes! Jesus Christ!' He yelled as he swung into the bend at speed. Blanford was hanging onto the handle in the roof above the door with one hand and the dashboard with the other, his face changing from a shade of grey to almost white with trepidation.

Steinbacher managed to steer the car safely round the first hairpin, though bumpily as it left the tarmac momentarily, the car continued to gain speed as it descended the steep gradient towards the next hairpin. Steinbacher was pulling frantically on the handbrake with negligible effect, as they rapidly gained on the approaching bend, Steinbacher shouted out.

'For Christ's sake, Mark jump, it's our only chance!'

Both front doors flew open simultaneously and the two occupants made their move to escape, as the car careered forward, Steinbacher launched himself out and rolled over and over several times on the road, as he looked ahead he saw Blanford whose attempted escape was foiled by the open door striking a tree, the effect of which caused the door to be thrown back and the glass smash as it hit Blanford in the face.

Steinbacher could only look on as the car crashed through the barrier fencing, which offered little resistance to the momentum of the speeding vehicle. Steinbacher could but follow its progress as it went over the edge, he watched as the rear end of the car plummeted over and disappeared down the mountain.

There was nothing he could do, he told himself repeatedly as he tried to come to terms with what had happened. Blanford, he realised, had been slower to react, due to the pain and the inability to move quickly from the nature of his injury. He simply hadn't the strength to move swiftly enough.

Steinbacher pulled himself up and limped over to view the precipice at the edge of the road, he observed the car continuing to tumble and crash down through the trees and boulders, bouncing and spinning over and over on its rapid decent to finally to rest on the rocks a few hundred meters below.

He was thinking about how to get to Blanford in case he was still alive when the car suddenly exploded, he knew there was nothing he could do now. Taking a few moments to compose himself and re-think his plans, he dusted himself down and began hobbling back along the road, he checked himself over, apart from a slightly sprained ankle and a few bumps and bruises, he was in good shape considering.

He took stock of the situation and decided to return to Kochel, which was the closest town, thinking that even if the General and his accomplices had been released, they wouldn't think of looking so close to home for the time being, if at all.

Limping slowly back along the road towards the town, he rounded the first hairpin he had managed to negotiate and continued up the hill, as he climbed the steep gradient, he noticed the sunlight sparkling off something on the road ahead, it was in several places ahead of him, small lines of liquid or something, he hurried his progress towards the glistening substance, hoping he was wrong about what he was thinking.

Upon reaching the first source, he stooped down and rubbed it with his fingers, it was an almost clear thin oily liquid, he touched the liquid with his tongue.

'Bastards! Bastards! Bastards!' he exclaimed at the top of his voice. He knew now that it had been no accident, the brakes had been sabotaged.

'I'll get you for this General, you fucking bastard! You see if I don't!' He shouted aloud.

There was no one to hear him.

Steinbacher was so incensed by the discovery, he decided he had to do something in retaliation for the attempt on his own life and to avenge his friend Blanford who had suffered at the hands of the General. That was a revelation, he realised he actually cared for Blanford and what had happened to him, he had been a friend to him, a true friend. The first he'd had in a long time and now he was gone.

Hearing a car approaching, he took cover among the trees, as the car drew closer he could see General Stoltz in the rear seat with Oefner both of them now in civilian clothes. He hurried best he could through the trees back towards the scene of the crash, as he approached he saw the three occupants of the car alight and look down over the edge to the twisted burning remains of the car below.

The General turned to one of the men with him, the guard who had cut the brake hoses and congratulated him heartily on a job well done, implying there would be no further trouble from those two traitors anymore. The three men returned towards the car amid laughter and a certain amount of patronising.

Steinbacher looked on in silence, saying softly. 'Laugh while you still can, you bastard. You're next!'

The General turned back towards his car, saying, 'We must report this terrible accident at once. Pass me the telephone, Oefner.'

Oefner, still holding his wounds, reached into the superbly maintained black 1970s Mercedes Benz 450 SEL and handed the General the handset, which was of a fully installed version.

Upon connection with the emergency services, the General gave an Oscar winning performance in detailing the "accident" to the Polizei. He then told

Oefner to make himself scarce for fear the Polizei would wish to know the circumstances surrounding his injuries.

Oefner took to the woods, saying he would head back on foot. Stoltz thought a few moments then instructed the driver to also return as the Polizei may find their stories do not match and he was not prepared to take the risk. He added that he would take the car back himself.

Steinbacher listened intently to the conversation, particularly noting the General's willingness to remain at the scene until the Polizei arrived. A short time later two Polizei vehicles arrived, the officer in charge began questioning Herr Stoltz as to what he had seen.

His description of events leading up to the fatal accident was pure fabrication, the story detailing how the car had passed him at a terrific speed a few kilometres back and that he had lost sight of them in the series of hairpins until they saw smoke rising from the valley below and then saw the damaged fence.

The officer asked if he could confirm how many were in the car. 'Two, two men. Most definitely,' came the reply.

He was thanked for his co-operation and informed him he may be needed further and to give his details and a statement to one of the other officers.

The officer in charge began radioing for assistance to recover the vehicle and the occupants. Once organised, he took some time inspecting the immediate impact area around the fence. On noting broken glass, he called to one of the others to assist.

'Look at this, there's glass around the base of this tree and the tyre tracks are almost half a meter to the left.'

The other officer could see no immediate significance, simply answering. 'Yes Inspector, Sir.'

The Inspector stepped back a few paces and walked along the tyre track, acting out a scenario.

'Just visualise you're in a car that's travelling out of control and about to plunge over the edge, what would you do?'

'I don't know, Sir,' replied the other officer. 'Jump! You would jump, yes!'

'Yes Sir, I suppose I would, seems sensible.'

'Yes and I'm betting our two occupants tried to but did any of them make it? The driver perhaps!'

'Sir! I don't understand?'

'If you look closely at this tree, there's traces of paint and glass on the bark at just the height to correspond with the impact of a car door, I think this poor sod just left it too late. The driver! I think was more successful and if I'm right, where is he now?'

There was a silence as the Inspector walked off towards the wood. Stoltz having overheard the Inspector became alarmed at the prospect, knowing if it were true, it would be Steinbacher who had escaped as it was he who was driving.

'Inspector,' Stoltz called out. 'Ya wohl, Herr Stoltz.'

'Forgive me please, I overheard your theory, I don't see how anyone could have survived, we were only moments behind, if someone had got out in time, we would have helped him or her surely.'

'Not necessarily Herr Stoltz, trauma affects people in many ways, in this case he or she may be so shocked they just took off into the woods, we'll mount a search once we establish if there are one or two bodies in the wreckage. You are sure there were two in the car and only two.'

'Yes of course, I'm sure.'

'You were sure it was two men before and now you are it's him or her, why? You also said "we" twice and not "I", additionally you used the word "they". Is there something I should know, Herr Stoltz?'

Stoltz realised his error and tried to recover.

'It looked like two men to me but I only got a glance as the car sped past, sorry I don't know why I thought it was two men initially. It's the shock, I'm not thinking straight, that's all.'

'Well, we'll know shortly, the rescue helicopter has been requested, there's no way down there by road, I'm afraid.'

Steinbacher who had remained within earshot of the proceedings and a safe distance from Oefner's passage through the woods began cursing and abusing the Inspector under his breath, realising full well he would now be sought out relentlessly by the General and his kind, that is, unless he could get to them before they had time to inform the other sections.

He began to think of a plan as the helicopter arrived and lowered one of the crew down to the wreckage, he realised the General would be unlikely to remain at the house for long after finding he was at large, it would prove to be too easy a target. His only choice was to attempt to conceal himself in the boot of the General's car and let him lead the way.

Whilst all eyes were focussed on the rescue attempt, Steinbacher slowly and quietly made his move towards the car, his sprained ankle causing him some discomfort as he walked. Once behind the car, he pressed the release button on the boot-lid, the click of the lock opening was easily drowned out by the noise of the helicopter, he opened the boot and climbed in, closing it to almost shut once inside.

He found a travel blanket and used it to muffle the sound of the boot locking mechanism, which also prevented the lock from fully closing. He could hold the boot lid down utilising the metal strengthening framework on the underside. He was sure a vehicle of this age would not feature a warning light showing an "open boot lid" and he was indeed correct.

Several moments passed as he listened to the conversations through the small gap he had left to watch what he could of the rescue operation when a radio message came through from the rescue team.

'Only one body near the car, no sign of anyone else.'

'Any identification?' asked the inspector.

A few moments later, the reply came.

'Mark Blanford. English and Sir, it appears he's been shot in the knee and not too long ago by the looks of it.'

'Shot! Are you sure?'

'Looks very much like it to me Sir, hard to be sure, he's badly burnt but the injury to the knee appears to be from a bullet. The knee has been bandaged with a red and black cotton type material of some kind.'

'See if you can find anything else.'

'Sir, I'm looking through the glove compartment, the car appears to be a hire car from Koln, hired to a Herr Jürgen, Ste Jürgen Ste. I'm sorry Sir, the papers are burnt, I can't make anymore out.'

'No matter, note down the registration, we'll check with the hire company.' The Inspector turned back to the General.

'Seems there's more to this than first thought, could you recognise them again, especially the driver, do you think?'

'I'm sorry Inspector, we, I mean I, only got a glimpse, they were moving too fast.'

'I see. First its two men, then it's we or I, I think we need a formal statement, Herr Stolz.'

'What about the other man, would you like me to help you search the woods?'

'No thank you, we have trained men to carry out that sort of thing, it's too dangerous without the proper equipment.'

'As you wish Inspector, you know where to find me.'

'Herr Stoltz, I just advised you we need a statement, please take a seat in my car and an officer will be with you shortly.'

The Inspector bid him good-day and returned to the rescue mission. Stolz sat awaiting the statement to be taken down, pondering what to say. He was indeed flustered; he was indeed worried. Once the formalities were over, he was allowed to leave the scene. He was now a good two hours behind schedule.

General Stoltz returned to his car and turning it around on the narrow road, he drove off in the opposite direction. Steinbacher could hear his phone conversation from the boot, he was gravely concerned regarding his disappearance, the General advising they would have to pull out of the house at once, saying.

'There's only one safe place until he's dealt with. "The base". I'll get Oefner to make the necessary arrangements once we get back, quickly, there's no time to lose and he could be there already. We must be vigilant.'

'Ya wohl, Herr General,' came the reply.

'A touch of inspiration from Oefner, I must say. Booking the car in Steinbacher's name, he'll be their prime suspect now,' the General added.

As the car drew up outside the house, the General instructed the guards to initiate closure procedures and pack important papers and equipment for transportation and storage, immediately! He then instructed a driver to carry on to the rear of the house whilst he collected the contents of the safe and other valuables and then to find Oefner in the woods if possible whilst he made the necessary arrangements.

Steinbacher remained pensively in the boot, hoping against all odds they wouldn't open it upon their return to the car. He had the pistol at the ready and would use it on the General and Oefner first if indeed either showed up.

The General was first to return to the car, throwing his briefcase in the rear seat ahead of him, Oefner by this time had been picked up and followed several minutes later.

'Well Axel, I have made the arrangements in your absence?'

'Der Gut, Herr General.'

'We must await Herr Schnorr to commence his shift at the marshalling yard on Friday.'

'Three days! Did you advise them of our urgency?'

'Of course, Axel, there's nothing they can do until then. The fool is on holiday!'

'Incompetent fools, they are jeopardising the whole operation,' shouted Oefner. Stoltz simply replied.

'We must lie low. We should drive into Murnau; no one will find us there between now and then.'

The driver acknowledged the General's request to head for Murnau and sped off down to the gatehouse and passed through it, leaving the guards to close down the operation at the house.

Steinbacher lay quietly in the boot as they proceeded cautiously towards Murnau, all the time contemplating how to deal with General Stoltz and Axel Oefner!

***

Chapter Six

Later in the evening of Tuesday October 4th Jürgen Steinbacher had, fortunately for him, almost completed the most horrendous car journey he had ever made. His body was racked throughout with pain, in part due to the confines of the car's boot space, which afforded him little movement thus causing his legs to cramp on numerous occasions, also the addition of the constant jolting he'd received from the undulating road surface throughout the journey.

On top of this, it was paramount he kept silent even after the occasional moments when his whole body was thrown upward only to crash down a second or so later. Before too long, he could hear the general traffic noise increase around him, Steinbacher knew it would not be long before his nightmare journey was over.

Upon arrival in Murnau, he gave the General and his two accomplices several minutes to clear the area, which he'd overheard them mention among other matters enroute would be a hotel's underground parking area. 'This was, indeed,' he thought, 'fortunate for there would be less chance of a passer-by noticing his alighting.'

Awaiting a suitable silence, he cautiously listened for the sound of footsteps or other vehicles, he allowed the faint sound of what was obviously a woman in stiletto heels to diminish before attempting to release the lock mechanism. Once free, he raised the boot lid slightly and glanced around the hotel's underground garage area, hoping no one was present.

Satisfied all was clear, he alighted as quickly as possible given the feelings of cramp he was still experiencing thanks to the doubled-up position he had maintained for so long and the sprained ankle. Before leaving the area, he crawled underneath the vehicle and disconnected some wiring to disable it.

He would keep a vigil on this vehicle as the General was bound to return to it. He was already formulating a plan in the meantime.

***

With zero hour fast approaching on Wednesday October 5th at the hastily arranged NATO base on the French Belgian border, it was a testing time for all concerned as the clock swept innocently past 03.00 hrs. The room fell into silence as the control staff personnel manned the bank of telephones and monitors, each minute seemed like an hour in the eerie silence.

Before long, the mood lightened as the silence was maintained on the communications front. 03.00 hrs had passed without incident it seemed. Clarendon however remembered it was 03.18 hrs before he was informed of the F35 situation, he hastened those in the room to keep calm a little while longer.

The French, Ministry of Armed Forces Minister was continually receiving direct reports from his various bases around the world who had been instructed to report on any incidents taking place at the prescribed hour, all reports had been negative so far.

At 03.20 hrs, he confidently called the meeting to order and began to announce that all was seemingly in order with the French Armed Forces, all bases world-wide had reported in and all reports were negative. He began his conclusion.

'In other words, my friends it appears our terrorist's plot has failed this time. However, the problem remains whereby we cannot render the air Defence of France or any other NATO member to be dictated and controlled by terrorist actions such as this.'

He was about to continue when he was handed a slip of paper by an aide. Whilst reading it, he placed his hand in his jacket pocket, removed a handkerchief and wiped his brow.

'Gentlemen, Ladies. I have just received a communique from our "Marine nationale" in Paris. It reads as follows:

"At 03.00 hrs our time, the Destroyer De Gaulle in company with other vessels carrying out manoeuvres in the waters of Polynesia suffered attack by torpedo from one of our own submarines engaged in the exercise. The destroyer has been severely crippled and is listing dangerously to starboard as I speak. There has been much loss of life".

That is all I have at present.'

He stepped down from the podium in a visible state of shock.

Understandably, the delegation was struck dumb at the news. They had perhaps with hindsight foolishly thought the terrorists whoever they were could only control aircraft movements and not those of a submarine in the depths of the ocean. The defence of Europe and the western world was now totally undermined it seemed, who knows what these people were capable of or what indeed they were after.

Retribution yes but for what and for why. Could it be the Russians intent on waging a wider war against the NATO alliance due to the support offered to Ukraine and the crippling sanctions applied to Russia since the invasion of Ukraine back in February? It was all conjecture with no hard facts to base any assumptions on. The search must continue until evidence was found but how long do they have, that was the worry for all.

Whilst the French licked their wounds, the various governments issued immediate notices to curtail all military manoeuvres and training sessions using live targets until the situation was under control. The western world was now indefensible against outside attack.

The situation was critical but only the Heads of government knew the exact position, the general public knew nothing and it was to remain that way. The media were presented with a feasible fairy tale regarding the Brussels event and the truth would remain classified whilst investigations continued.

The selected delegation decided there was no reason to remain together at the French Belgian border base, it was thought wiser to return to their respective countries and continue the hunt for the terrorists responsible. Resources would be combined throughout all NATO members and all information meticulously examined, any rejections after thorough investigation would be referred to another section for further analysis until it was beyond doubt, the information was indeed invalid.

This would be the biggest and most exhaustive test of Western defence policy the world had ever seen and at the present time, they had absolutely nothing whatsoever to go on.

***

Later that same morning, Wednesday 5th Rear Admiral Bartholomew-Smythe was awaiting the arrival of DCI Pearce at Bristol Police Station. He was particularly anxious to get the interview with Jason Allen over with and return to the Admiralty, he was still of the opinion Allen had little or nothing to offer.

Angela Pearce entered and bid everyone good morning; the Rear Admiral impatient as ever suggested they make their way to the hospital as soon as possible. DCI Pearce replied.

'The doctor said ten o'clock, Rear Admiral and ten o'clock it shall be, in any case I have other work to do besides.'

Smythe by now realised there was no use in antagonising the DCI, he simply took a seat and waited as patiently as he could. About nine thirty, DCI Pearce and DS Tomlinson advised the Rear Admiral they were leaving for the hospital. The three discussed how best to handle the situation, considering they had nothing yet to offer Allen by way of a "deal".

Arriving at Allen's room, Doctor Abrahamson advised them they could have fifteen minutes, no more. DCI Pearce complained that they needed more time as the interview was deemed as a matter of national security. The doctor reconsidered for a moment and agreed they could continue a little while longer, so long as her patient was able to cope. Any sign of fatigue and she would insist they left. All parties in agreement, the three entered the room.

'Good morning, Jason, how do you feel this morning?' asked the DCI. Allen opened his eyes and replied, 'I'll live.'

'Well Jason, have you had time to decide on what you want to do?'

'I told you yesterday, I'll tell you all I know once I get what I want.'

'Jason, the thing is, I've contacted the Home Secretary and she's the only one who could offer you immunity if he decides it's appropriate. However, he's not prepared at this stage to offer you anything unless you show us something tangible, do you understand?'

Allen looked straight ahead and remained quiet for a few moments, then replied. 'I also told you this yesterday. No deal, no squeal. Do you! Understand?'

'Look, Allen!' Smythe interjected. 'I for one don't believe one word of what you've told us already. Unless you produce something quickly, I shall have no alternative other than to advise the Home Secretary to dismiss your request forthwith, I have no intention of wasting any more time. Do I make myself clear?'

Allen turned to look at the Rear Admiral. 'Go to hell, you pompous bastard! Who the hell do you think you are anyway?' He retorted angrily.

DCI Pearce interrupted. 'Jason, there's no use holding back, if you have any information to give us, please do so for your own sake. I can't help you unless you help yourself first. And I oversee this investigation. Not him.' She scowled, looking towards Smythe.

Allen settled back and thought for several moments before resigning himself to the fact he had to forward something, otherwise there would be no hope of any deal.

'Okay, I'll tell you a little of what I know and how and where I found it out, that should be enough to convince you I'm telling the truth. But no more until I get my deal. Right!'

'Fine Jason, we'll make a start with that and if it's worth it, I'll put it to the Home Secretary again, as I say, if it's worth it.'

'Oh! It's worth it, I can assure you,' he replied.

There was a short silence before Allen began disclosing several details about his involvement with James Stein. 'First of all, James Stein is really Jürgen Steinbacher, a German National and a "Reichsbürgersbewegung" officer.'

Jason was immediately interrupted by Smythe.

'We know about Steinbacher! If that's the best you can do, you may as well forget about a deal.'

'Look! Unless you shut your pompous fucking trap, I won't bother to tell you anything.'

Angela Pearce demanded the Rear Admiral allowed Allen to continue without further interruption. Once a semblance of order returned to the proceedings, Allen continued.

'Okay, so you know his real name but did you know he was also known as Gerhard Farbmacher and that he disguised himself when using that alias?' There was a silence from his audience.

'Obviously not, it would seem,' Allen said sarcastically before continuing. 'Anyway, the reason I know what I do is easy, it's because I broke into Stein's flat and found papers and photos describing some of their plans. You'll be amazed by what they're planning. I'll tell you but that's for later, once I've got my deal signed. For now, I'll tell you a little more about Stein and about the smuggling operation and how and more importantly why it's necessary to the "Reichsbürger" movement.'

Allen described how he had located a hidden compartment within Steinbacher's dressing table and had seen papers detailing the extent of the operation, its progress to date and the estimated date of completion together with the false papers and a photograph of Steinbacher as Gerhard Farbmacher. He informed them he knew a contact number in Koln (Cologne), which Steinbacher should contact in the event of trouble. He also mentioned the fact he had broken into Steinbacher's several times after then to keep abreast of the developments, for his own sake.

Once his statement was complete, DCI Pearce, Smythe and Tomlinson left the room for a few moments to discuss the matter, the Rear Admiral protested there was no evidence to back-up his story and that he had told them nothing about what the "Reichsbürger" movement were planning.

Between them, they agreed the Home Secretary would be unlikely to grant any immunity on the information given to date and that they should attempt to find out at least what the "Reichsbürger" movement were up to.

Returning to Allen's bedside, DCI Pearce advised him they were grateful for the information, which would assist greatly in the investigation of the smuggling operation but offered nothing with which to approach the Home Secretary.

Allen thought again for a few moments, then said, 'All I'm prepared to tell you at this time is,' he hesitated as he looked closely into the three apprehensive faces surrounding him before beginning. 'The diamonds are being used both to build and finance a sophisticated control system, capable of controlling what they call "Donor Units".'

'And the hi-tech electronics capability they are designing are to be implemented in various locations. I'm telling you all now, this is big, they have already had trials and you lot wouldn't have a clue it was them that caused the tragedy. They are currently working in an underground base, which was built during the last war in complete secrecy and sealed up before Germany fell.

'It's been kept mothballed since then in readiness in the belief of the inevitable rise of the Fourth Reich. Anyway, that's all I'm saying for now, that's enough to whet your appetite, you take that to the Home Secretary and I'll tell you the rest when my immunity and the other demands are met. Okay?'

There was an outburst of questions thrown at Allen from both DCI Pearce and the Rear Admiral, Frank Tomlinson was so taken back by the revelations, he was stunned into silence. Once the initial outburst died down, Bartholomew-Smythe with a cynical tone retorted.

'Poppycock! It's all in your fertile imagination, some kind of story you've been dreaming up in a pathetic attempt to gain a pardon from the Home Secretary. This has been a complete waste of time as I thought!'

DCI Pearce, who by this time had simply had enough of the Rear Admiral's outbursts, demanded an end to his interference in the investigation. Advising him.

'If you feel you're wasting your time, please Rear Admiral, be my guest, you're free to leave whenever you wish.'

'How dare you speak to me in that tone, young lady? I'll see to it your superiors are informed of your outburst and that you're dealt with appropriately!'

Angela Pearce riposted. 'Good! Do it now and give us all a bloody rest!'

'Really! You're becoming intolerable, young lady.'

'Well! Sod off and make your report, Rear Admiral. And while you're at it, you'd better inform that chap you've got somewhere out in the bloody Atlantic what's going on! God knows what's going to happen to him when he gets to Kinshasa, going on what Allen here has told us already.'

Bartholomew-Smythe collected his belongings in temper and pulled the door open to leave, before doing so he couldn't resist to remark.

'You're wasting your time with him I can assure you, mere fiction. You'll be hearing from your superiors. I promise you. Good day to you!' He turned and quickly left the room, giving Angela Pearce little opportunity to retaliate. She sat and shook her head, then said.

'Stupid bloody fool!'

Allen looked at her and with a smirk, he remarked. 'I take it you don't like him much either?'

'That's unimportant Jason, we've both got our jobs to do and that's why I must insist you give us something to collaborate your story. You see, he's right, as we see it, this could all be a fairy-tale unless you show us some proof, something we can show the Home Secretary. Can you do that?'

'Look, the thing is, most of what I know is only from papers I read at Stein's flat They were all in German but that was no problem, I studied German at college before I quit. So, you see it's all in my head. I know the contact numbers, I don't know the exact location of the underground control base but I do know who Stein's prime contact is in Germany but most important I know what they plan to do with the system they're developing and the first live test targets chosen if the next range of proving tests actually prove successful, they intend to implement their donor units without delay.'

With some hesitancy, he added. 'The thing is, putting it bluntly, they have or will have very shortly, the power to render any defence system useless simply by utilising that country's own or another country's armament's against whomever and I'm not joking, I'm deadly serious. So, it's up to you.'

Frank Tomlinson had quickly grasped the contents of Allen's disclosure and ventured to remark. 'So, they haven't completed this system yet, is that what you're saying?'

'Yes and no. According to what I've seen, they still require further supplies of diamonds before they can make it fully functional. It's not anything like an actual missile system per-say, it's more a method of controlling third party missiles and the like at their will. That was in an update report dated sometime in February this year.'

'By now, they could have enough. I can tell you they planned to test it out sometime last month at random on some military aircraft but I've heard nothing to say they have and there's been nothing in the news or the papers, so I don't know how far they've got at present.'

'Jesus Christ! Is this for real Jason, you're not bullshitting us, are you?' asked DCI Pearce, somewhat dumbfounded.

Jason Allen tittered slightly before replying. 'Oh no! It's for real I can assure you. That's why I want away from here.'

'Then why are you laughing Jason, surely you see the danger in all of this, don't you?'

'There would have been little danger in it for me or for any of the loyal followers of the "Reichsbürger" movement, we were, sorry are to be advised of safe locations prior to commencement.'

'Once what starts, Jason? Where do they intend to attack? What do they intend to attack?'

'I've said all I'm going to say for the time being. Get me my immunity and I'll talk. You won't regret it, I promise.'

'Very well, Jason. I'll speak to the Home Secretary, that's all I can do but be warned you could be surrounded by all kinds of officials once this gets out. I hope for your sake, you're telling the truth.'

'Don't worry about me Detective Chief Inspector, I know where I stand.'

'Okay Jason, we'll leave it at that for the moment, I'll do what I can.' The two officers got up to leave when Jason called out.

'Did I hear you mention someone's out in the Atlantic and heading for Kinshasa?'

'Yes, Jason there's a small team headed out there to investigate the diamond smuggling operation, why?'

'Then tell them to mind the sewage!'

'The sewage? What do you mean?'

'Look, all I'm saying for now is to mind the sewage, the sewage system and its controllers at the mine. That's it, that's all I'm saying, if these guys find something out there, then you'll know I'm not "bullshitting", as you so eloquently put it before. Won't you?'

'Okay Jason, I'll make sure they get the message, we'll be in touch.'

DCI Pearce and DS Tomlinson left the hospital around 11.30 hrs and hurried along to the station where Angela Pearce updated the team and her superiors with the latest developments. She then contacted the Home Office which advised her the Home Secretary would be informed as soon as possible and to await further instructions.

She took the decision to inform the Admiralty of Allen's last statement for them to advise Larousse and his team who were due to reach Matadi the following day.

Speaking to Admiral Stevens direct for the first time, she soon realised he took the matter far more seriously than his subordinate Bartholomew-Smythe. After agreeing to contact Larousse and advise him of the latest developments, he explained contact had previously been made and that Larousse had been requested to withdraw from the operation but had refused for personal reasons.

Angela Pearce showed some concern as she pleaded with the Admiral to do his utmost to restrain Larousse from continuing before the "whole affair blew up in their face", as she put it.

The Admiral agreed to try and dissuade Larousse though thought it quite impossible given his courage and determination, which he knew to be paramount in any given situation.

Soon after speaking with DCI Pearce, the Admiral made immediate contact with the second Frigate on stand-by in the Atlantic, north-west of Ascension Island awaiting instructions to rendezvous with the KATRIANA for her second re-fuelling, prior to docking in Matadi.

After giving the rendezvous co-ordinates, he advised the captain fully of the recent developments and that he was to update Larousse on Operation Windcutter and the Foreign Office's communiqué. Also, to officially request Larousse's withdrawal and return, leaving the matter to the authorities to investigate as it was no longer considered safe for him to intervene at this crucial stage.

He added that in any event the two Royal Navy personnel. Lieutenant Chambers and Sub-Lieutenant Malhotra were to abandon the mission and transfer to his command for the time being. The captain accepted the orders and told the Admiral he would do his utmost to persuade Larousse to return, asking what his orders were if he refused.

The Admiral replied, 'If all else fails Captain, ask Larousse to contact this department direct through secure channels on board your Frigate but avoid doing so, if possible, he's no longer classified by our department and this operation is on "a need to know" basis.'

Admiral Stevens called his team together to discuss the latest findings. Whilst they were deliberating the probabilities of whether this so called "donor system" was responsible for the recent accidents with NATO aircraft and the French aircraft carrier, Bartholomew-Smythe having travelled back from Bristol by helicopter arrived around 12.30 hrs. Entering the room in his usual pontifical manner, he announced his arrival.

'Good afternoon, Admiral Stevens, Sir. I've just returned from.'

'Smythe! The duty office, now!' Admiral Stevens bellowed aloud, causing other members of the team to raise their heads and gaze in silence at Smythe as he stood in the doorway.

'Sir!' Questioned Smythe, looking bewildered.

'I said! The duty office. Now!' Admiral Stevens gave Smythe the sort of look which could curdle milk.

Smythe straightened his tie and raised his chin, an action he used regularly when about to encounter a superior in verbal upbraid.

The two men turned simultaneously and headed for the partitioned office, which afforded little privacy when being reprimanded. Once inside, the Admiral laid both hands on the desk whilst Smythe stood to attention and began.

'I intend to be perfectly clear about this, Rear Admiral. I've about had as much from you as I intend to tolerate. You walked out of the meeting with Jason Allen, is that so?' Inquired the Admiral as he paced the floor.

'Yes, quite so Sir, you see.'

'Be quiet! Smythe. Simply answer yes or no, is that understood?'

'Of course, Sir, what's this all about?'

'I said, be quiet and sit down.'

Bartholomew-Smythe was incensed by the Admiral's treatment, he began to breathe heavily through his nostrils as his lips tightened in temper.

'Now then Smythe, I believe you don't take our Mr Allen's story very seriously, is that so?' Without giving him time to answer, he continued. 'But then you wouldn't, would you and why? Because you didn't bother to wait long enough to listen to it fully. Did you?'

'Sir, I believe the whole thing to be a figment of his imagination and decided I would be wasting valuable time listening to his fairy tales.'

'Valuable time! Doing what? Smythe.'

'Investigating the smuggling operation, of course. Sir.'

Admiral Stevens continued pacing up and down then headed directly towards Smythe, bending over to look him in the eye he said, 'Had you bothered to sit through the meeting with Allen you would have found out how and where to concentrate efforts to discover the smuggling operation at the mine as a starting point. This information we now have thanks to DCI Pearce of the Bristol Police who persevered long enough with Allen to extract it amongst other things.'

The Admiral then detailed Allen's disclosures in full and concluded. 'You however decided the whole story to be a "waste of time", so you say.'

'Yes Sir, but.'

'No buts! Rear Admiral. You have disgraced this department for the last time with your pompous and arrogant attitude. This is an intelligence unit for god's sake! We listen! We listen to everything, no matter how concocted it may sound. If this Allen's telling the truth, even partially, then God help us all if we don't find this base and disarm whatever their developing before they start again. God help us.'

'What base, Sir?' Smythe uttered in a bewildered tone.

'Had you remained at your post during the interview, you would not need to ask that, would you!' Retorted Admiral Stevens.

'I can but apologise, Admiral Stevens, Sir. I must say however that although Allen's details of the smuggling operation may possibly be authentic, giving his involvement, I fail to see how on earth these people have managed to carry out major construction works unbeknown to anyone other than themselves. Surely Admiral, you can't be seriously considering the possibility?'

'Of course, we're seriously considering the possibility. My god, man! Haven't you been listening to me. I must say Smythe, I have serious doubts about your capability within this section and perhaps you should consider a post elsewhere.'

The Admiral looked at Smythe whose remorse appeared to be genuine. The rest of the operations team sat around the room in silence unsure if the Admiral had completed his scathing attack upon their colleague.

After a short silence, Admiral Stevens tapped Smythe on his shoulder, saying.

'Very well Jeremy but you must learn to control your attitude, everything we hear is of some importance no matter how trivial. I had intended relieving you of this operation, however, if you're willing to continue you must conduct yourself accordingly. Is that understood?'

'Yes of course Sir, I'm very sorry Sir.'

'Very well, let's see if we can get on with finding these bloody Nazi's then, shall we?' The Admiral replied with a little humour, which eased the tension felt by all in the room.

Admiral Stevens continued to brief the team with what little he knew, pausing for comments and suggestions by various team members. He summed up his report by advising the team they were no longer concerned with the smuggling of diamonds into Europe, that was for others to investigate and has already been implemented but their work would now consist primarily of locating this Operations Base and putting a stop to whatever plans the "Reichsbürger" movement had to instigate the Fourth Reich.

By now, the MOD had sanctioned the release of information on the various attacks which had already taken place to members of the senior staff, this included Admiral Stevens who naturally saw a connection between the proposed threats detailed by Allen and the recent attacks on NATO and Russian forces. He sanctioned the release of the information to the Rear-Admiral, advising him to contact Larousse and detail the same.

Staff at the Admiralty had already began the task of informing the mining companies concerned of Allen's disclosure that the sewage system was in some way utilised to convey the smuggled diamonds from the mine to an as yet unknown location for forwarding to whichever European port was designated.

They suggested the companies carried out immediate and thorough inspections of the sewage plants and questioned all concerned with its installation and operation.

***

Whilst all the activity between Bristol, London, Germany and the various diamond mining companies was at its height around 15.00 hrs the KATRIANA was pulling alongside HMS Argyle now lying off the coast of Liberia.

The captain welcomed Larousse aboard the Frigate, whilst taking him to his cabin, he began to impart the recent developments detailed by Admirals Stevens. 'Firstly, Monsieur Larousse, I am requested by Admiral Stevens to strongly request you to withdraw from any further action you may be intending forthwith.'

Larousse sat in a composed silence, awaiting completion of the captain's announcement.

'The reason being, information recently received has deemed your part in this operation invalid so to speak, Admiral Stevens has already informed the mining companies concerned of the smuggling method and they in turn are investigating the matter, consequentially your involvement now would only make matters worse. In any case, I have been officially advised to inform you that your shipping operations are no longer suspected as being involved.'

'That! Captain was straightened out, before I agreed to take on this operation, otherwise I would never have become involved.'

'Yes, quite,' the captain replied whilst he continued. 'I also have orders to take on board the two naval personnel travelling aboard your yacht.'

'Of course. There's no point in them staying now.'

'I must say Monsieur Larousse, you're taking this far more calmly than I had anticipated.'

'Perhaps Captain. The fact of the matter is, I have been involved far too long with the Naval Intelligence service not to realise what's been going on whilst I have been pounding the open sea for the best part of a week. I had already expected advice of this manner after my previous re-fuelling. You see Captain when I was first told of this escapade, I was furious.' Larousse took a seat and continued.

'To think my shipping line had been utilised as a smuggling operation was bad enough, then to be told the fact that the smuggled diamonds were for use in some Nazi plot or other brought my blood to the boil. However, having had the last few days to reflect on the situation I see there's no need for me to reach

Kinshasa and deal with a mere band of smugglers, whom I presume are hardly likely to know the what's, whys and wherefores behind it all!'

Larousse paused as he studied the look on the captain's face, a look of bemusement.

'I presume, therefore Monsieur Larousse, from your comments, you won't be continuing on to Matadi?' The captain hesitantly asked.

'What for, Captain? It's all in hand, is it not?'

'So, it appears, Monsieur Larousse.' The captain was unsure of Larousse's intention at this point, though he felt the need to inquire what it might be but deemed it would be rather abrupt to ask outright.

'Both of us have some time on our hands, perhaps you would care to join me for a small drink in my cabin.'

'I would be honoured and delighted, captain. Just one small request though.'

'Yes Monsieur Larousse, if I can be of any assistance.'

'My daughter, my captain André and Mr Cameron are aboard the KATRIANA, they are all rather anxious about developments, perhaps they could join us if it's not too much trouble?'

The captain answered with a tone of uncertainty about the purpose behind the request. 'Of course, no trouble at all. I'll have the Chief Petty Officer make the request immediately.'

Once all had settled in the captains' cabin, after half an hour or so of questions and answers, the questions put in the main by Robert and Katriana, the captain informed them he knew no more than he had already told them. With the initial feelings of anger felt by Robert now subdued, over the news, that the operation was to be abandoned, he commented lightly.

'Well, I suppose that's the end to that, I can only hope to see those in custody sentenced for a very long time but I must say, I wish I'd got my hands on one of them, just one.'

'Robert, you shouldn't speak like that, you're not like them,' Katriana said as she reached for his hand.

'I hate to say this sweetheart but I felt like one. I was looking forward to meeting one of them, face to face, you know? God almighty! What's got into me? I can't abide violence, I'm sorry. Look Captain, I'll have to go, I apologise I'm just upset. Please excuse me,' Robert said.

'Of course, Mr Cameron. I, that is, we, understand.'

Robert rose from his seat and headed for the cabin door, closely followed by Katriana who made her apologies as she also left.

The captain shook his head as he closed the cabin door behind them. 'Poor chap, he's taking it bad.'

'Yes, Captain he his. Never mind, down to business then!' said Larousse, changing the subject and causing the captain to wince.

'I beg your pardon, I'm afraid I don't understand your connotation, Monsieur Larousse?'

'Ah, Captain. It's quite simple really. I wish to speak with Admiral Stevens urgently.'

'Quite out of the question Monsieur Larousse, I have orders to inform you of the developments to date and nothing further!'

'Captain. Unless I speak to Admiral Stevens through your secure channel I will have no alternative other than to make contact via open channels. Now, considering this operation is still classified, I'm sure you wouldn't want radio ham's far and wide tuning into what I have to say? It's your decision, Captain.' The captain realising, he was in a dilemma, advised Larousse he would contact the Admiralty and request permission from them. Larousse agreed to wait.

Around 16.00 hrs, Admiral Stevens had granted Larousse's request and was awaiting what he considered, could only be a call for him to continue.

'Admiral Stevens, Sir! François Larousse.'

'Commodore Larousse, this is highly irregular, you are no longer classified.'

'Ah, Admiral, the Navy hasn't changed one bit, at least not for the better, it seems,' Larousse said contemptuously as the captain looked on in disbelief.

'I trust there's something you want, Commodore or are you simply here to belittle His Majesty's Royal Navy?'

'Yes and no respectively, Admiral Sir. The yes being, I wish to join forces with whatever operation you've launched against this operations' base.'

'Out of the question Larousse, you're a civilian, remember!'

'Ah! Admiral that fact appeared to be of little consequence whilst I have been sailing out here on your behalf.'

'That was different, your shipping line was involved and we merely gave you the opportunity to clear your good name!'

'Now Admiral Sir, you know that's not the truth, my shipping line was cleared before I agreed to take this job on.'

'Very well, that's correct. However, that does not give you any rights to follow up on the developments, I'm sorry, I cannot sanction your request.'

'Admiral, I must admit I expected something of this sort once those two dockers were arrested, I assumed quite correctly it seems, one or both of them would talk, then with the revelations of a Neo-Nazi plot, it was obvious at that point you would be making immediate inquiries, all of which I might add whilst I have been making for Matadi.'

Admiral Stevens interrupted. 'If your memory serves you correctly Monsieur Larousse, we advised you to withdraw at the time of your re-fuelling with HMS Somerset.'

Larousse's tone became indignant as he retorted. 'Yes! Admiral but we were unaware of the extent of the Nazi plot at that time, our main concern then was to expose the smuggling operation, nothing more!'

A short silence followed whilst both parties assessed their position. Admiral Stevens was first to speak. 'Tell me Larousse, what do you have in mind, have you formulated any sort of plan?'

'Yes of course Admiral, I have had time to think whilst we've been sailing out here. I propose a small group, myself and the men here with me now, including your two chaps,' go into the suspected area and flush these Nazi's out. You cannot seriously consider sending in a large force that would make no sense, surely you see the potential of my plan, a small covert group, far more effective in a situation such as this. Admiral, I am asking you as a loyal servant of His Majesty's Royal Navy to be granted the opportunity to see this through that is all I ask.'

'François, listen to me. Within Germany, we have NATO base's, regiments of men, equipment, armaments, etc. What could you hope to accomplish which they couldn't?'

'With all due respect Admiral, the NATO base's, etc. haven't exactly been successful in preventing the "Reichsbürger" movement establishing such a base in the first place. I'm telling you Admiral; you go in there with force and you'll live to regret it.

'Once they know what's going on and there's those who'll tell them, believe me! It'll be over. The consequences being, the "Reichsbürger" movement will seal up the base until it's safe to re-open and no one! And I mean no one, will find it, until it's too late.'

A few anxious moments passed without any conversation, then the Admiral replied. 'Very well, I shall put your proposal forward, it may be tomorrow before a decision is reached though, obviously, I can't say for sure whether it shall be accepted or not, in any case we have no idea as yet where this mystery base is, that is assuming there is one!'

'Very well Admiral Sir, I shall remain alongside HMS Argyle until I hear from you, for security reasons obviously.'

'Yes, that'll be in order.'

The remainder of the day and for some of the staff at the Admiralty, most of the evening was spent looking at wartime records and old and new aerial photographs of known German underground installations built for the Second World War, in a vein effort to locate a possible site, which had obviously been expertly concealed before the fall of the Third Reich.

Admiral Stevens' department became inundated with archive material from a wealth of sources once the alleged information had been passed between several differing factions of the security forces. The operations room had become a hornet's nest of frenzied activity even though there was no proof yet, that the allegations had any substance. The school of thought being, "Best to find out for sure".

***

During this activity at approximately 16.40 hrs news came through from the German Federal Polizei authority that Mark Blanford had been found dead in the Bavarian Alps. The Polizei advised they were treating the incident as a murder inquiry as the evidence pointed to the vehicles braking system having been tampered with. They also advised they had issued wanted notices to all stations to arrest Jürgen Steinbacher alias James Stein.

Receipt of this information immediately decided Admiral Stevens to concentrate their efforts in and around Bavaria for the time being. His staff studied detailed maps, geological charts, photographs from the air and from satellites in an attempt to pinpoint a suitable location for such an installation.

The task was mammoth in proportion even though it had been lessened by some degree by Mark Blanford being found dead near Walchensee in Bavaria, even so, there was no certainty that Bavaria was the place to look. But there had to be a starting point, so why not there.

By Thursday morning October 6th the small staff of volunteers who had worked through the night could only offer a couple of possibilities based upon areas of isolation with geological suitability for such vast construction works to have been carried out undetected through the war years. Admiral Stevens was quick to point out.

'It's not what happened during the war years that bother me, it's the fact, that is, if what were told is true and my god I hope it's not, that these people have managed to re-commission and further develop this underground base over the past three! Four! Five years! Heaven knows how long and under our bloody noses! How have they managed it? That's what I'd like to know.'

The searching continued.

***

Angela Pearce was told of Mark Blanford's death and the circumstances surrounding it when she arrived at the station on Thursday morning, together with a notification to meet with the Home Secretary, Suella Braverman at two o'clock at the Home Office, she and Frank Tomlinson immediately left for London to allow for any traffic problems enroute.

She hoped that the next interview with Allen would be more forthcoming once she informed him that Mark Blanford had indeed fled to Germany to escape justice and had subsequently been found murdered and that Steinbacher was the prime suspect, coupled with the strong possibility the Home Secretary was about to issue the pardon he had requested.

Upon arrival at the Home Office, Pearce and Tomlinson presented their identification and were taken to a room to await the Home Secretary who was apparently running late from a meeting with the Prime Minister. Upon her arrival, the Home Secretary duly introduced herself and began.

'Are we to believe this Allen character's story, what's your opinion?'

'I sense there's some truth behind it, Ma'am. But I can't be sure to what extent.'

'Well, I've just been briefing the PM with the details, she feels it's rather absurd to say the least but there again, she sees no point in ignoring the possibility, especially with the significance of the recent anomalies shall we say. However, the PM has decided to play it low key for the time being, she is prepared to authorise what's deemed necessary in the event Allen's tale is not the fabrication it appears to some.'

'Ma'am, am I to assume Allen's request is to be met in full?'

The Home Secretary continued to detail the government's position and advised Angela Pearce of her limitations under the Official Secrets Act.

'This matter must go no further for the time being. The PM has a very busy schedule in Berlin and Brussels over the next few days, so let's hope we can sort this out between now and before she returns from Europe next week.'

The DCI felt pleased with the Home Secretary's decision and comments. Even the provisos she stipulated were those of common sense, surely Allen would agree to the conditions, from which they could get down to serious discussion. Pearce and Tomlinson left the Home Office and returned post-haste to Bristol.

***

The news of Mark Blanford's murder was also transmitted to HMS Argyle and the Captain requested Larousse come aboard.

'Admiral Stevens for you, Commodore.'

'Ah! Good morning, Admiral. Good news, I trust?'

'In a manner of speaking, you could say. The thing is Commodore, one of the chaps who escaped from the docks to Germany has been found allegedly murdered, in some remote region of Bavaria.'

Larousse was quick to grasp the significance.

'Then that's where our search should begin, Admiral that is of course assuming my request has been granted?' There was apprehension in Larousse's voice as he questioned the outcome.

'Commodore Larousse, I have been instructed to advise you that the minister has granted you and your party an initial period of forty-eight hours, to commence once you arrive in Bavaria. If after this time you have discovered nothing, you must withdraw and allow the security forces to engage in a major operation, there is little time left to chance.'

'Admiral Sir! Forty-eight hours! That is indeed limiting considering we don't know where to start yet,' blasted Larousse.

'I'm sorry, I am simply advising you,' replied the captain.

Larousse thought it best to agree in principle. 'I am extremely grateful.'

'Commodore Larousse, I had nothing to do with it. It was Admiral Salisbury and your father who spoke up for you, directly to the Prime Minister, no less.'

'My father! Do you mean my father's been told about this, my god! The man's ill! The shock could have killed him. The thought of Nazi's again!'

'François, François!' The sound of a faint voice could be heard under Larousse's rambling.

'Father? Father! Is that you?'

'Yes my boy, it's me. I'm talking from home through a link of some kind. Lawrence told me, that is, Admiral Salisbury to you, he came to see me and told me all about it, we've been to see the Prime Minister. She's given us forty-eight hours from when you arrive to sort this mess out, are you up to it, my boy? Eh, can you handle it?'

'I can but try, father.'

'Try! Try! Have you forgotten all I taught you, François? Do it! Never mind try! Do it!'

'I will father, trust me,' Larousse said confidently, feeling the adrenaline pump as it had always done so under his father's direction as far back as he could remember. His father had groomed him well for the role he was to play in later life. It was not from fear of his father the adrenaline flowed but from a deep feeling of respect.

'Admiral Salisbury here, old boy. Admiral Stevens is arranging transport for you and your team, he'll give you the details in a moment, for now all I want to say is, good luck, may God go with you.'

'Thank you, Admiral,' he replied then his father reiterated the same message. 'Thank you, father, now don't you worry, you should go and have some rest.'

'Rest, François! I intend staying abreast of developments with Lawrence until this matter is resolved, so if there's anything we can do you must ask, do you hear?'

Larousse and his father argued lightly for some time regarding the situation, Larousse was concerned over his father's failing health. Admiral Stevens then intervened and advised Larousse of the arrangements made for their immediate transportation to Bavaria.

Larousse returned to the KATRIANA and called the crew, his daughter and Robert to a meeting in the main cabin. Once all had assembled, he calmly began. 'Katriana. Gentlemen, there's been a change of plan. We are no longer required to proceed to Matadi and thence forward to Kinshasa.'

There were immediate sounds of disappointment from the assembly.

'I'm afraid developments in Europe have outweighed the necessity to continue to Africa, the smuggling operation is being investigated by the mining officials and the security forces within their operation as we speak. However, all is not over for our part. We have been requested to continue with investigations in Europe as to the whereabouts of a secret underground base commanded by some faction or other of the "Reichsbürger" movement. The base is said to be the recipient of the smuggled diamonds, their purpose to initiate a German Fourth Reich.'

There was a sudden outburst of questions from everyone demanding to know more. Larousse informed them there was little to go on at present, only the word of a prisoner held in Bristol.

Robert on hearing this, ensured his voice was heard above all others. 'This prisoner! Is this prisoner responsible for the death of my brother?'

There was complete silence in the cabin. Larousse turned to Robert and answered.

'I believe he's held in question with that incident Robert, although I can't say for sure. In any case Robert, both you and my daughter must at this stage refrain from any further involvement, it's getting far too dangerous for both of you. On this, I must insist!'

'Insist all you like! But just you listen to me Monsieur Larousse, my brother was killed by these people and I intend to see this through. On my own, if necessary.'

'Mr Cameron. This is not a game, we're not playing an eye for an eye, a tooth for a tooth. This is almost bloody war! I can't have amateurs running around jeopardising the mission, I have been granted a mere forty-eight hours to locate and report the location of this underground base and I don't need you along to hinder my progress. Do I make myself clear?'

'Hinder! What do you mean hinder? I can help you, you stubborn bloody fool!'

Larousse was angered by Robert's outburst.

'Enough! I warn you Cameron, I've tolerated you for my daughter's sake but you're going too far. Tread carefully, I warn you.'

'Your threats Monsieur Larousse, I've told you before, they don't bother me. If you take a moment to think this thing through, you'll see that I can help you.'

'How can you help me, Cameron? All my men are ex-servicemen, they all understand discipline, orders, the dangers facing them in such a mission, they have had training all their life, they are able to sense danger, they are able to handle weapons, explosives, what can you do? Tell me!'

Robert looked around the faces in the cabin, all silent, awaiting his reply with apprehension.

'My god, man! Have you forgotten what I do! I'm a mining engineer, for god's sake. This underground base you're talking about, there's got to be an entrance! A concealed entrance. An entrance which must be used regularly without trace, well! Where would you start looking, eh? Tell me that!'

Larousse was astounded, he hadn't given the matter much thought until now, suddenly he could see an advantage in taking Cameron along.

'Very well Cameron, you've made your point, there's one thing though.'

'Yes?' Replied Robert.

'What about your phobia, Robert?' asked Larousse. 'Surely you don't expect us to turn about and sail to Germany,' he added sarcastically.

'So, what's the plan then?'

'We are being air lifted out by the Fleet Air Arm,' informed Larousse. 'Well, Monsieur Larousse, it seems I'll just have to take my chances.'

'Well! What a surprise, eh. You were never afraid of flying, were you?'

'Not entirely true. I'll avoid it if I can but when needs must, there's no choice.'

'Ah, very well Robert but don't say I didn't warn you. Tell me, where would you start looking?'

'Do you really think I'm that stupid?' Replied Robert.

'No, not really. Worth a try though,' answered Larousse jovially.

This change in tone allowed the others to indulge in spontaneous light laughter, all of whom except for Katriana began to relax and questions began flowing regarding the new destination. The general ambiance which had developed over the table between the group was suddenly shattered as Katriana shouted out.

'And what about me? Am I to stay out here in the middle of the godforsaken Atlantic Ocean with only the fish for company!'

Her father reached over to her and gave her a hug. He said.

'Of course not, I'm sorry my precious, you're going back to Marseille, back to mama where it's safe. Robert was to accompany you but that's all changed now. It's all arranged, there's nothing for you to worry about.'

Katriana stood up and with defiance in her voice, she rebuked her father's suggestion, saying.

'Papa! You never learn, do you? Nothing for me to worry about you say. No! What about you! What about Robert? I can't just sit in Marseille waiting for news, expecting the worst. You've put me through it this far, there's no way you're sending me home now, I'm telling you!'

Robert took hold of her hand.

'Katriana, sweetheart, your father's right, it's too dangerous for you, please do as he says.'

'For once you're talking sense, Robert. Listen to him my dear, there's no need for you to worry, we'll all be alright, trust me.' Larousse tried to console her, to no avail.

'Papa! Either I go along with you or God help you and you, Robert,' she added vehemently.

Larousse asked the others to leave the cabin for a moment. He then attempted to dissuade his daughter alone. Ten minutes or so had passed when he called them back.

'André, advise the Frigate's Captain there will be another two passengers for Bavaria and to cancel transport arrangements to Marseille.'

'Yes Sir, at once,' he said as though expecting it.

Robert attempted to reason with Katriana for a few moments, until Larousse interrupted.

'You're wasting your time Robert, take it from me, you'll soon learn.'

Once André had returned, Larousse advised the group of the transport arrangements to Bavaria and the fact they would be underway within the hour.

Chapter Seven

Within the previous hour, Angela Pearce had returned from London to Bristol hospital with a signed amnesty for Jason Allen from the Home Secretary, subject to a few provisos, together with a promise of a new identity and the other demands made if he could convince them there were grounds for such.

Jason Allen, who appeared to be overcoming his ordeal remarkably well, listened to DCI Pearce detail the terms and conditions laid down offering him the demands he had requested. Before he could answer in agreement or otherwise, DCI Pearce advised him that due to the discovery of Mark Blanford's body, a team had already been organised and were heading for Bavaria as they spoke and unless he had further "useful" information, there would be no deal.

'Its useful information you want, is it? Well, I hope you're ready for this, lady!' He said, raising his eyebrows, he continued. 'And I hope you're in time, because?' Allen paused awkwardly for a few seconds as he re-adjusted his position.

'Because what?' asked DCI Pearce anxiously.

'First, have you got a fag? I'm bloody desperate,' he asked sanguinely.

'Frank, give him a cigarette, for god's sake! Now Jason, because what?'

'Because remember I told you about a test sometime this month.' He did not wait for a reply, quickly continuing.

'Well, I know only of the British "Donor Unit" and its British targets and I also know it's been fitted with what they call a "Receptive triggering device". Some sort of computer wizardry, which is activated by a Wi-Fi satellite signal triggered from this underground base of theirs.'

'I presume several other donor units exist, for I've seen mention of their planning but no actual details. All of this depends on the success of the initial tests. Which as a matter of interest will at first appear to be nothing more than a series of terrible accidents.'

'The reason for this is to give them time to evaluate the system and program or re-program further donor units. Then! And believe me, then you're in for a bloody big shock and no mistake!'

Angela Pearce looked at Frank Tomlinson with apprehension.

'Well Jason, come on, let's have it,' she demanded with trepidation in her voice. Jason Allen continued.

'The first British target will be a couple of F35 aircraft I believe, if this and a number of small subsequent tests prove satisfactory, the next main British target will be fired upon from HMS Audacious,' Allen announced casually as he billowed smoke signals into the air.

'HMS Audacious? What's that, a ship, a naval base, what?'

'A bloody submarine. God! Don't you people read the papers, it's only one of the latest to be built, I can't remember, anyway that's the donor unit's target. Only the British unit mind, the Allied nations are all targeted for similar treatment. I think their phrase when they announce themselves will be "We will avenge" or something along those lines.'

DCI Pearce interjected.

'So, Jason, are you implying missiles from HMS Audacious will be trained against targets on British soil without the knowledge of naval personnel, either on-board or otherwise?'

'Who's a clever girl then?' He remarked sarcastically, continuing. 'The captain will wholeheartedly believe and be confirmed through correct procedure this to be no more than an exercise and follow it through. However, the missiles will be armed and controlled by those in the "Reichsbürger" base.'

'Christ Jason! This is for real; you're not bullshitting us, are you?' Inquired Frank Tomlinson, somewhat agitated.

'You could always wait a while and read it in the news if you like. That is, if there's anything left of Fleet Street,' Allen answered calmly.

'My god! What's going to happen? Do they intend to attack more than one target or what, do you know?' Interjected the DCI again.

'From what I've seen and read at Stein's place, the submarine holds a compliment of Tomahawk missiles. It would appear all can be controlled at will, their destinations simply a matter of co-ordinates being fed into a re-coding unit.'

'You say it will look like an accident Jason, why? What do you mean?'

'After the launch of as many missiles as they wish, the submarine will be detailed to launch one against its own co-ordinates. It will simply appear to have blown itself up due to a major malfunction, that's what makes it appear accidental, like I told you, remember? But there's another possibility and that's whether they carry on with the accident theory or decide to go all out and take the credit from the beginning. And I'm serious about this, I know opinions have been voiced in that direction quite strongly.'

'Jason, this might sound simple but surely if the Navy made contact with HMS Audacious and advised the captain of the situation, he would be forewarned to avert such a disaster?' Suggested Pearce.

'You can try it but I think you'll find the submarine is already under the control of those at the underground base. Any attempted contact will be intercepted and will be controlled by them. If it is simply normal instructions, they are relayed to the sub, if there is any mention of a change in routine, such as dis-arming the missile control system, it will be re-coded to read different. The reply from the sub will of course be re-coded to comply with the original order, so therefore no one will be any the wiser, will they?'

'Christ, Frank! This is getting out of hand. Get on to the station, advise them what's just been disclosed. We're going to need the Navy in here again. Go on, quickly.'

Frank stepped outside and radioed the Chief Superintendent at the station and relayed the request, the reply was of disbelief as expected, soon to change as the possibility of reality was realised. He returned to the room where the DCI was pacing the floor and chewing on the end of her pen as was the norm when she felt the need to concentrate.

'Jason, you realise what you're saying, don't you? You want us to believe these people can simply blow up almost anything they wish, simply by placing some sort of device in it, is that true?'

'Seems so. From what I've read anyway, yes.'

'And I take it, this is all done from this underground base, is that true?'

'Correct, with regard to them actually carrying out the destruction but the electronics are brought in from elsewhere; before you ask, I don't know.'

'Well Jason, do you know where this underground base is exactly?'

'No, not exactly but I can say you're looking in the right area, I know that because I saw several photographs of railway installations and such and on some of the carriages you could just make out places on the destination boards. Places such as, Innsbruck, München, Stuttgart, Salzburg, Zurich, all around the Alps, you know.'

'Yes Jason, that's all very well but can you be sure it's the Alps, I mean, you told us yourself, Stein's contact number was in Cologne, that's not in Bavaria.'

'As sure as seeing the mountains, there were snow-capped mountains in most of the pictures, anyway it makes sense if you think about it, an underground base, mountains, yes? No?'

'Yes! Yes, I see what you're driving at. Tell me, what else was in these pictures, Jason? Can you remember?'

'Two things struck me as odd, I must admit.'

'Yes, what were they?' she said quickly, egging him on.

'There were several pictures of an old railway carriage or wagon of some kind-no, more like an old carriage really, all different views but all at the same location.'

'The location Jason, do you know where it was?'

'Sorry, not for sure, I couldn't see any mountains in those but it was a railway yard and this carriage was on its own. I don't know for sure if there's any significance but why would Stein conceal photographs of an old railway carriage, it must mean something, don't you think?'

The DCI naturally sounded anxious as she detailed DS Tomlinson to make another call to the station.

'Quite possibly, Frank, have Interpol check on all railway yards in that general area to begin with. What was the other thing, Jason?'

Jason Allen was beginning to show signs of fatigue as he tried to shift his battered body into a more comfortable position, he continued. 'There were pictures of one mountain in particular, I've no idea which one but at least six or seven views including a couple of aerial shots, I'm sure one of your lot could soon find out which one.'

'And you're sure it was in the Alps?'

'An educated guess rather than sure, sorry best I can do on that but there's a lot more to tell.'

'Hold on a minute, Jason.' She halted his progress abruptly. 'What did you mean? One of our lot could soon find out which mountain it was?'

'Well, I'm sure if they saw the pictures, it wouldn't take long for someone in the know, like the German Polizei, the army or something to figure it out, there must be something on them that would be recognised. Like the fact among all the snow-covered mountains around it, it's not fully snow covered. I don't know why but it stood out to me, that's all.'

The DCI stopped her pacing around the room and quickly walked straight towards Allen. 'Tell me Jason, have you got those pictures?'

'No.'

'Well, what the hell are you playing at for Christ's sake, this isn't a game!'

The DCI was perturbed by Allen's cool reaction, throwing her pen to the floor in temper, she protested.

'If this is the best you can do Jason, then you can forget about any sort of deal, I'll tell you that for nothing!'

Angela Pearce was livid, she could feel herself losing control, she turned and walked towards the window, placing her hands on the windowsill, she took a few moments to compose herself. There was an eerie silence in the room for a while. Allen took the opportunity to smoke another cigarette from the pack the DS had left on his bedside cabinet in peace, billowing circles of smoke into the air and enjoying each and every inhalation to the full.

DS Tomlinson walked over to join his DCI and remarked on the possibility they could well be wasting their time with Allen, Angela Pearce reluctantly agreed. She turned and with her voice raised, she gave Allen the plain facts.

'Jason. Unless you can do far better than this, at the moment it all seems like a conjectured fairy tale. You are not offering any evidence just simple anecdotes. I'll have no alternative other than to inform the Home Secretary that this whole episode has been a total waste of time, well, can you see our position? You must give me credible proof of some kind!'

Allen lay back in his bed and laughed aloud even though it hurt him inside as he did so, he couldn't help it, knowing what he knew. The DCI had taken about as much as she was likely to take from Allen, she grabbed her handbag from the side of Allen's bed and instructed DS Tomlinson to follow her out. Allen, whilst attempting to halt his laughter, shouted best he could.

'Hang on, hang on a minute, I said I didn't have the pictures but I've got the next best thing. Photocopies!'

The DCI pushed Frank aside as she swung around to confront Allen. 'Photocopies! Are you saying you have copies of those photographs?'

'Yes!'

'What, all of them?'

'Yes, the only thing is, the quality is not so good, I hadn't time to go to a decent place to have them done but I think you'll find them okay.'

'Christ Jason! You almost made a right balls of that. Where are these copies?'

'I posted them off to my brother in Nottingham, he's at university there. I told him to keep hold of them for safe keeping, I'll need to speak to him before he'll hand them over. He knew I was involved with some group or other, he obviously disapproved but he's still my brother, you know, so don't be going in there heavy handed, do you get my drift?'

'Okay Jason, we'll get hold of him and you can speak to him on the phone, we'll get Nottingham Police to collect the copies, is that okay?'

'Yes, okay with me. But I do need to speak with him first as I said.'

Angela Pearce, seeing as she'd quickly decided to "get the ball rolling" so to speak, instructed Frank Tomlinson to return to the station and forward the information on to Nottingham Police to collect the copies and email them through to Bristol HQ immediately following Jason Allen's phone call. Then, to inform the various intelligence departments and Interpol, adding.

'The sooner we get started, the better.'

'Yes ma'am.' Frank left the hospital and returned to the station, one of the officers on guard in the corridor taking his place as the interview continued. During which time, the Nottingham Police had located Allen's brother and he took a call from Jason as requested. Following this, he took the officers to a safety deposit box in a city centre bank. From which all the documents were scanned and forwarded to Bristol HQ and the Admiralty for analysis.

As DCI Pearce continued to extract Jason Allen's statement, Larousse and his team were being taken by one of the Frigate's Wildcat helicopters to the French military and NATO facility at Port-Bouët, in a suburb of Abidjan, in the Cote d'Ivoire, the nearest mainland base from their location in order to board a French naval transport plane to fly the company to a NATO base close to Stuttgart Böblingen, in the southern side of Germany.

The base known as "Panzer Kaserne" is one of the almost 60 co-bases located in Germany and this one is run by the United States of America under German regulations. It is operated by the US army.

Didier was instructed to remain on the KATRIANA with a number of Larousse's staff and was told to make for Ascension Island on the Mid Atlantic Ridge and await their orders.

The information Frank Tomlinson relayed to the Admiralty was immediately conveyed to Larousse and his group to keep them abreast of recent developments. Larousse began immediately to brief his team of the situation, advising them that now they still had no knowledge of the precise location of the

Nazi base and the only leads they had pointed to it being located somewhere in the Alps, the suggestion being that it could be somewhere close to where Mark Blanford's body was discovered. There, he suggested was where their search should begin.

The Admiralty now in full communication with NATO had organised to supply the team with detailed maps of the area covering a twenty-mile radius of "Kochel" where Blanford's body was found. The maps were placed in the transport plane for them to study as they headed for Germany.

The final message relayed to Larousse advised him that, NATO bases in Germany and neighbouring countries had been put on "Yellow Alert". Failing to locate the "Reichsbürger" base within the forty-eight hours allotted to them, would render his operation cancelled and implementation of NATO armed forces enmasse. Larousse had no choice other than to reluctantly agree.

Transferring their equipment from the helicopter to the transport plane took a mere ten or so minutes and within the next ten, they were airborne and on their way to Bavaria. Larousse continued his briefing aboard, giving each of the team an objective and purpose. He began.

'Katriana. Gentlemen. First and foremost, I oversee this operation and you will do as I say. That goes especially to you Katriana, either you agree to this condition now and abide by it, no matter what the circumstances. If not, I warn you, I'll send you packing. It's for your own safety my dear, what's it to be?'

Katriana held Robert's left hand tightly in both of hers and looked deep into his eyes, Robert nodded gently, urging her to comply.

'Yes papa, I'll do whatever you say. I promise.'

Larousse reached out for her hand; she offered him her left while continuing to clench Robert with her right. Her father took her hand, saying. 'My precious, I promise you, you do as I say and we'll all come through this okay. You promise?'

'Yes papa, I promise.'

'Very well, my dear. And that goes for all of you. You included Robert, I have learned quickly how stubborn you can be, I must have your assurance also, we cannot succeed as individuals, we must work together as a team, of that I am certain.'

'Yes, I understand Monsieur Larousse, you have my full support,' Robert replied, maintaining the formal address.

'Ah, very well then, the rest of you I needn't ask. André, Marcel, Carl, Gerrard, you have all been with me for some time, let's make sure we continue the relationship. Lieutenant Chambers, Sub-Lieutenant Malhotra, I have no doubt in your abilities as officers and I know, you know your respective skills, let's hope we needn't have cause to implement them, eh!'

'Larousse took a moment or so to cast a glance at the eight faces all of whom were looking in his direction, expressions,' he thought, 'can say much more than words at times like this.' He looked at his daughter, whom to his surprise seemed remarkably calm and unaffected by it all.

He thought inwardly, she's so much in love with this Cameron she's hardly had time to think this thing through. Robert's face was a mirror image of his daughter's, bright eyed and undisturbed. André, was studious, patiently awaiting further developments in order to formulate a draft plan of some kind, the sort of thing he excelled at.

Marcel, he looked apprehensive, he had had the easy life of chauffeuring around since leaving the army. Carl worried him a little, he looked full of adrenaline, his eyes somewhat frightening, he gave the impression he was looking ready for a kill, he thought it best to keep a close watch on him.

Gerrard's face showed no sign of alarm, emotion or worry, the sort of expression perfectly suited to the job he carried out, in fact his composure left Larousse realising he himself was a trifle edgy. Chambers and Malhotra looked every bit naval officers, full of confidence and oozing with adrenaline, though not of the type Carl was pumping around his arteries.

'Katriana. Gentlemen, we must put our heads together, we have as I've said very little to go on at present, the security forces are sifting through the information passed on by the chap in hospital who's forwarded what information we have up to now.'

'Any further details will be relayed to us as becomes available, for the moment let's study these maps and see if we can suggest any suitable locations for an underground base. Remember it's an underground base which has remained completely secretive to the outside world for over sixty years! Any suggestions will be most welcome.'

The group began considering the options presented as they sat around studying the maps and offering locations in remote mountainous areas, marking them off as they decided their suitability warranted.

Shortly after studying the maps, the radio operator came through to the team and handed Larousse the information detailing Allen's description of the photographs he had seen. Larousse immediately advised half the group to concentrate their efforts around any railway lines traversing the region, the other half to continue with generalisation.

***

Bartholomew-Smythe had been dispatched from the Admiralty with all speed on receipt of the news from Bristol and had been taken by helicopter direct to the hospital.

He entered the room where Allen was continuing his statement, to a torrent of verbal abuse dished out by Allen, the content of which remarked upon the probability of him being illegitimate. Allen then demanded he leave the room, refusing to continue whilst he remained.

DCI Pearce asked him to step outside for a quiet word.

'Well Rear Admiral, I didn't expect to see you again, I must say.'

'Detective Chief Inspector, I am surprised to still be with His Majesty's Royal Navy after the call you made to Admiral Stevens. I have been sent to continue the interview with you by Admiral Stevens himself but first, I wish to apologise for my previous behaviour and will you do me the honour of accepting my most profound apologies?' Angela Pearce reached for Smythe's hand and shook it gently.

'Rear Admiral, apologies accepted by me, now you've only got Allen to convince so please don't go in there with your usual pompous attitude or we'll get nowhere, understand?' The Rear Admiral nodded in agreement.

'Before we go in, I'll update you on Allen's statement so far, it makes interesting listening, I'll tell you.'

She condensed Allen's statement highlighting the main points. Smythe immediately requested if there was any further information regarding HMS Audacious? DCI Pearce replied simply, 'Sorry, nothing.'

'Then I suppose it's time to sweet talk our friend in there.'

'Rather you than me, Rear Admiral.'

Smythe tugged her arm as she raised it to open the door. The DCI turned to face him; she could see trouble in his eyes as she pondered the reason.

'DCI Pearce, I have been authorised to brief you fully regarding the situation our end. Firstly, we do not want Allen to know about this for the time being but I'm afraid the sequence of events he has been detailing has seemingly already begun and there have been several casualties to date.' Smythe quickly briefed the DCI and informed her it must go no further for the time being. Amid shock and disbelief, she agreed to comply.

Bartholomew-Smythe then re-entered Allen's room and made his apologies to Allen for his previous treatment towards him, his apologies however were coupled with the fact that unless he continued the statement in his presence, for Naval Intelligence to act upon any information given, the Home Secretary would be informed of his unwillingness to co-operate fully, the consequences of which could be detrimental to him.

Allen, after protesting somewhat, reluctantly agreed, Angela Pearce was recalled into the room and the statement continued.

Part way through Allen's revelations regarding the papers he had seen at Stein's, he had to admit, some of which although he had been able to translate meant nothing to him, due to the fact they were of a technical nature beyond his comprehension, however he could be certain, beyond any doubt the "donor system" was a reality and that the first "live target" test to be carried out would be on the F35s and the next British target would without doubt be through HMS Audacious.

The actual date was not detailed on the papers he had read, only notification that once a final supply of diamonds had been received and the systems proven, all senior officers involved with the "Reichsbürger" project would be informed and required to attend, by order!

Smythe remained singularly persistent regarding the submarine.

'Mr Allen, tell me please. If their intention is to destroy, firstly, how do they locate its whereabouts?'

'No need, there's some sort of electronic wizardry fitted to it by one of their collaborators at the shipyard where it was built, all they have to do is send the signals and after the missiles are launched, it'll blow itself up, just like that!'

'So, you're saying it could be blown up under water, afloat, in dock, anywhere in fact, is that true?'

'So, it would seem, all I know is this receiver picks up the signal, arms the missiles and triggers them to fire at a target, that's why their called "donor units". They have, sorry, will have the capability to select missiles from any source fitted with this electronic gadgetry, anywhere and program them to do whatever they wish once this coding device is commissioned.'

'Some multi-national armaments manufacturer has been infiltrated by their scientists who have designed equipment on their behalf with the facility to receive the satellite signal without their knowledge. What I'm saying is this test is what it is, a test. I know of several targets in this country alone!'

'Several!' DCI Pearce exclaimed with consternation.

'Yes, that's why I'm talking to you now, it's not safe to stay here any longer than is necessary and I could be here a long time unless I talk, yes? Well, now you understand, eh.'

'Right Jason, where are they? You've got to tell us if you know!' Angela Pearce challenged.

Allen took his time giving the locations, much to the annoyance of all in the room. 'London's one. They really have it in for London!' He said, laughing a little. 'Thorp Nuclear Re-Processing Plant's another, that's after its commissioned and holding stock, of course. Eh? Flyingdales Early Warning Station, GCHQ near Cheltenham for obvious reasons. I don't know the order of attack but they will all be targets, I'm sure of that.'

'How long have they been setting this damn thing up for Christ's sake?' Demanded the DCI.

'Years, soon after the war ended, a few hard liners decided to rebuild the Fourth Reich or so I've been told, I can't be sure though, although I know it's only in recent times, the past ten years, I think. That this "donor system" has been developed. They've had a team of dedicated scientists working on the project for a long, long time.'

'Jason, are they the only targets?'

'Christ, no! Haven't you been listening to me! They've got targets all over the place, all over the world but I don't know the location of them all, only that they're placed to cause maximum disruption and damage. Like I said, you'll be bloody sorry when they start, they'll have the bloody world at their mercy. If you don't do as they say, they'll simply blow something up again and again until you do!'

'My god! I don't believe this is happening,' said DCI Pearce.

'Are you quite sure you're not exaggerating, old chap?' asked Bartholomew-Smythe.

'Listen! I've told you once, you pompous bastard! If you don't believe me, piss off now and read about it in the papers!'

'Rear Admiral! Please!' Angela Pearce dragged Smythe over by his arm to the window and speaking softly, she said. 'Listen to me you stupid bloody sod! We must take this seriously, he's our only lead, we've tried to talk to Matthey but he won't say a word. We may only have a day or two left, just try not to upset him, please! For all our sakes. If he's bullshitting us, we'll soon know, just give it time, okay.'

Smythe was a little ruffled by the DCI's manner, he being unaccustomed to a lady using such adjectives in his presence.

'Yes, quite. I think I'll leave you to do the talking, he obviously dislikes me somewhat. Can't think why?'

Angela Pearce shook her head in disbelief whilst restraining a guffaw quickly forming within as she returned to Allen's bed.

'Right Jason, I want less of the dramatics and more hard facts. We may not have the time to waste, understand!'

Allen realising she was obviously correct in her assumption agreed to simply detail all he knew without embellishment. He continued for some time giving all the information he had on Stein, the donor system and his involvement with the "Reichsbürger" movement. Once he announced that he had told them all he knew, he asked if it would be enough to grant him his deal. The DCI answered. 'Provided your statement is corroborative, I see no problem but then it's not up to me, is it?'

'I've done my bit, they better do theirs, you tell them!' Allen challenged angrily.

'Look Jason, I'll do what I can, you've been a great help and eh, listen I'm sorry for what happened to you, for what it's worth.'

'Yeah, okay. You're not so bad, for a copper that is! And don't forget I want out of here and fast. Somewhere in the country not a city, understand, okay!' he exclaimed.

'Okay Jason, I'll see you later, I'll have to go and get things moving, you get some rest, you look like you need it.'

'Thanks. Listen, let me know how you get on, will you?'

'I'll be in touch, okay.'

Jason nodded his head in approval as the DCI and Bartholomew-Smythe left the room. Heading down the corridor, Smythe couldn't contain himself.

'Really Chief Inspector, you can't seriously consider all he said to be true, can you? I must say I don't doubt some of it considering what has already occurred but I can't see one machine or whatever wreaking so much havoc, can you?'

'Does it matter Rear Admiral, I for one don't want to read it in the newspapers! Do you?'

'No! Of course not, though I still feel there's a degree of imagination there. I mean to say, defence installations, nuclear installations, mobile targets and missiles from differing powers strategically placed around the globe at the wanton call of a handful of Neo-Nazi's in some bunker in Bavaria, I'm sorry, I can't take this too seriously, I'm afraid.'

'Before you say anything, I shall make my report to the Admiralty detailing all Allen said along with my views on the matter and they can take it as far as they wish.'

'That's fair enough Rear Admiral, I'll be interested to hear their views also!' Replied the DCI.

Both parties made their way back to the operations room at Bristol Police Headquarters where they viewed the photocopies Allen had furnished them with. Once the first copies were sent through from Nottingham to various interested security departments, others were forwarded to the Admiralty, MI5, Interpol and the German Polizei.

The originals were being transported direct to Admiralty Headquarters with the aim of clarifying the images as best as possible given modern technology and time, precious time, as it had now become.

The final few hours of the day served to be extremely beneficial to the investigation, news came through from Germany advising the Admiralty the location of the railway yard was without doubt the engineers' yard at Murnau, in Bavaria. A small team of four detectives had been dispatched to the installation around 9 p.m. to question the staff and locate the vehicle in the photographs.

The officer in charge, Inspector Klaus Pfeiffer after showing the Yard controller the copy photograph was informed that the vehicle in question was solely requested by the "Engineering and Permanent Way Department" for use on the Oberammergau line tunnel examination duties, hence it's somewhat strange design and that special arrangements were made for its use when required by the Superintendent in charge of the yard, Herr Schnorr, who unfortunately was off duty somewhere on holiday until Friday evening.

No one could enlighten the officer's further as to its purpose, only that it was only used on the line to Oberammergau on examination duties mainly in an old tunnel repurposed for the area's water supply, the railway remaining the owners of the tunnel maintained it on the utility company's behalf.

Pfeiffer immediately asked to see a route map of the line in question. A few moments later, one of the railway staff brought in a large cardboard tube.

'Here is the map you requested, Herr Inspector,' the controller said as he pulled out the rolled sheet of paper and spread it out on the table. 'What is it you're looking for exactly?' he asked.

'I'm not sure, all I know at present is that carriage is suspected of being involved with an illegal operation of some kind or other. So, any information you can give me regarding its use would be welcomed,' he answered, averting the truth somewhat.

'Well Herr Inspector as I told you before, in the past fifteen years I've worked at this yard, that carriage has only ever been used on this route, it probably ventures out only five or six times a year. It's probably away for no more than a few days at a time.'

'I must admit, I've always thought there was something strange about that vehicle, Herr Schnorr wouldn't comment on its use, he was the only one in this office, in fact this section, who sanctioned the engineering train to include that vehicle when operating along that line.'

Whilst studying the route map, Inspector Pfeiffer casually asked. 'Are there any disused lines along this route?'

'No longer Inspector, they've all been dismantled. The Oberammergau line is a terminus now but the tunnel once went onward to Oberau to meet with the Murnau to Garmisch-Partenkirchen line. I do wish you would tell me exactly what you're looking for, Herr Inspector,' the controller asked.

'I'm trying to find somewhere else this carriage could be based without causing concern. Tell me, what does it carry when it's used?'

'I've seen it loaded with all types of materials mostly engineering, construction or electrical equipment, to be perfectly honest, most of the equipment is packed in cases or crates, so I couldn't say for sure exactly what's in there but I can say it always comes back more or less empty!'

'What about staff? Does the train consist of any workmen?'

'Yes, of course. Several people ride with the train when it's requested, that's something else I often wondered about.'

The Inspector was intrigued. 'Wondered about what?'

'The people, the so-called Permanent Way and Utilities crews.'

'Yes! What about them?'

'Their ages! Most of them looked a little too old to be doing manual work of that nature. Schnorr said they were specialists in tunnel and pipework engineering when I commented on their ages, how did he put it now. Oh! Yes. "Knowledge, something we are not born with, my friend". He thinks he's a philosopher, does Herr Schnorr.' He laughed.

'I see. So, what you're saying is, these workmen, that is if they were workmen were mostly middle-aged or there abouts?'

'Not quite, Inspector. Some of them have white hair!'

'Did they? Interesting! The workmen, did they also return with the carriage?'

'I can't say for sure, changing shifts and so on, you might not even notice its arrival for a few days, especially being out of sight from the control box as it is.

Sorry, it's the way the job is.'

'Never mind, you've been a great help. I may need to talk to you again. Okay?'

'Yes, of course Inspector.'

After questioning the other control room staff, the Inspector decided to take a closer look at the unusual carriage. He donned a reflective warning jacket and began walking along the trackside leading to the short siding where the carriage was stabled when not in use along with other departmental vehicles.

About mid-way from the railway control offices, the threatening sky gave way to a downpour, Pfeiffer dashed along, hoping to reach the carriage before he got completely drenched. Closing in on the carriage, he examined the copy of the photograph in order to clarify the identity, there was no mistaking the fact that this was indeed the carriage in the photograph.

It was also apparent the controller was indeed correct regarding it's out of sight position, for as he turned to look back, he could no longer see the Control building due to the curvature of the line.

The carriage itself was a full twenty plus meters in length with half the windows obscured in an off-white colour within the glass and the other half by metal plates riveted over seemingly previous apertures. At the front gangway end as he was looking at it, there was one window also obscured although this time temporarily by an interior blind, which had been drawn fully down.

The carriage lay towards the rear of the siding in front of several permanent way wagons used for ballast and track laying, plus track tamping machines and the like. At the rear, a concrete ramp had been built to assist loading requirements.

Pfeiffer hurried up the steps to the ramp platform and attempted to look inside the carriage, without success. He waited for a while until the rain eased off then walked its full length studying the vehicle closely.

"What could be so sinister about an old carriage like this?" He thought to himself.

The rear gangway end of the carriage had been cut back about three meters to provide a platform area upon which was mounted a mechanical arm for lifting purposes, there was also a door allowing access to the interior which was firmly secured.

Crossing over the platform and descending the steps on the opposite side, he walked along the full length again, this time checking the underside. He didn't quite know why he was doing so as he hadn't a clue what he should be looking for in the first place.

Disillusioned with what he'd seen so far, nothing more than an old railway carriage now past its initial role in life and seconded to menial duties with the permanent way team was all there was to report. He crouched down and scrambled under the carriage between it and the other vehicles on the line.

As he came up on the other side, he was alerted by a voice shouting from beyond the overgrown hedgerow adjacent to the dirt-track beside the lineside.

'What are you doing?' The voice shouted out, an old voice it was, quivering from the bushes.

'Hello! Who's there?' asked Pfeiffer.

'Who are you? What are you doing here?' Came the reply, the source still concealed.

'I am Inspector Pfeiffer of the Murnau Polizei. Look, here is my card.' He held it out at arm's length and swung his arm around to either side.

'Where are you?' Pfeiffer asked in a kindly tone.

A dishevelled old man certainly in his eighties emerged from the bushes and cautiously approached the Inspector.

'Let me see!' He demanded as he took hold of the Inspector's identification card. Reading it slowly as he held it close to his eyes, he snapped.

'Well! What are you doing here? This is my carriage, why are you here? What do you want from me?' He demanded.

'Hold on there, there's no need to get upset, I'm only looking around it.'

'What for? Have you come to take it away again? I'm too old to have nowhere to live. Every time you take it away, I must rough it out there for days. I'm sick of it, I tell you. This is my carriage! I live here, do you hear!'

Pfeiffer quickly realised the old man was obviously suffering from senility or similar, going by his reactions and his apparel. He quickly reassured him he was not there to remove his carriage only to look at it.

The old man was not so sure, saying.

'The last time you took it you had it a full week, I had to sleep out there in those bushes and it's not fair, I tell you!'

'Listen to me. Let's go and get a nice hot meal and we'll have a chat, just you and I, what do you say?' Pfeiffer thought the offer may lead to some information, though he couldn't say he would relish the thought of the old man's company.

'You're not here to take my carriage?'

'No, I promise you. But I would like to talk to you about it, if you will that is?'

The old man eventually agreed to join Pfeiffer and talk about his carriage.

Pfeiffer made excuses to his colleagues who continued to search the railway yard and surrounding area then took the old man to an outdoor Café-bar and provided him with most probably the best meal he'd had in a long time.

The old man wolfed down the various courses presented to him under the glare of onlookers and passers-by. Once he had finished his feast, Pfeiffer began asking him about the carriage.

'Tell me, what is your name?'

'That's not important, I don't want to be persecuted by your people and social workers and the like,' he refuted.

'Alright, I understand your feelings, there's no need for you to give your name if you don't wish to. All I want from you is any information you have on that carriage. Can you tell me anything, I mean for instance why do you call it your carriage?'

That was the worst thing Pfeiffer could have said.

The old man knocked crockery and cutlery off the table as he replied angrily.

'It's my carriage until they come and take it away from me! They don't know I live there because I always sneak out when I know they're coming and take everything with me so that they still don't know, see? But I'm left out in all weathers whilst they have it, it's just not right, you tell them, tell them to leave it be and leave me alone!'

'Yes, I understand your situation but I need to know how you get in and out without anyone knowing, all the doors are well secured and bolted, surely you have a set of keys or something? I would very much like to take a look inside.'

The old man laughed aloud, showing his bare gums to all in the immediate vicinity.

'Keys! Keys, you say. I haven't had any keys for as long as I can remember. No! No, I don't need keys you see, it's my carriage and I have my own way in, see. I operated this carriage many years ago, that is, until they finished me up on the pretence that the train was to be used solely by some specialists or other on the new water supply system in the Oberammergau tunnel. I had nowhere to go then, see. So anyway, this used to be my life and I wouldn't let them take it all away, not my carriage anyway!'

'Yes, I understand. But how do you get in?' Pfeiffer asked impatiently. He had to see the interior, he had to know what was inside.

'Hold your horses I'm coming to that. It's my trap door. They think it's fixed down but it's not, see? I get in from underneath and no one knows I'm in there. No one can see in. I bet you tried to, didn't you?' He laughed.

'Yes, you're right, I did and I couldn't see anything, you're rather resourceful old man, how long did you say you've been living there?'

'I didn't! You won't tell them, will you?'

'No! Most certainly not. You're being a great help. Is there any more you can tell me about your carriage?'

'Oh yes, there's plenty to tell. I was the operator of this carriage from when I started here in 1969 until 2001 when the railway yard controller Herr, fucking, Gunther Stoltz, evil bastard that he is, sorry, was, pensioned me off three years early saying I was no longer required as the duties for the carriage were to cease.'

'But the duties did not cease like they said, they still used it, they lied to me, that evil shit lied to me after all the time I gave to the railway, it was my whole life. His swine of a nephew, Felix Schnorr is now in charge here at Murnau yard, it runs in the family, evil that is.'

'I could tell you tales about what happened to me and old carriage "45629" from now to eternity, we had many a narrow escape from avalanches, landslips. Oh yes, I've got plenty stories!'

Pfeiffer notice the old man's ramblings were not giving him much in the way of information, so he held him around the shoulders, smiled and thanked the old man kindly for offering to detail his experiences regarding his career with the carriage.

He advised him the information he required would be more up to date, more to do with the carriage after he left the railway service proper so to speak. Then as an afterthought, Pfeiffer suddenly realised the old man had said something, which he hadn't quite understood.

'I'm sorry my friend, there was something you said earlier which has got me puzzled?'

'And what would that be?' asked the old man knowledgeably. 'You said, you were the operator of this carriage?'

'Yes, that's correct. For over thirty years.' Answered the old man proudly, Pfeiffer was puzzled.

'I'm sorry. I don't understand these things too well but surely your carriage has no engine! Or has it?'

The old man laughed again.

'No! No engine, my friend. Doesn't need one, it's a "slip carriage"! See!'

'I'm sorry. I still don't understand?' Reiterated Pfeiffer.

'A slip carriage! I'll explain. My carriage would be attached to the rear of a train heading further away. When we approached the location, it was due to stop at, there would be a marked post where the operator 'me' would "slip" the coupling, disconnect it from the rest of the train, you understand now?' Pfeiffer nodded in amazement.

The old man continued.

'Well, the train would continue onward without stopping at the station, the operator 'me' would brake gently creating a gap between the carriage and the train itself, see? Once the train had passed over the switch leading to a platform or yard siding the control tower would select that line to coast into un-assisted and the operator 'me' would operate the brake control to bring the carriage gently to a halt at the platform or end of a siding. Do I make sense now?'

Pfeiffer was still bewildered, he had never heard of such an operation before but somehow now, it all made perfect sense. The old man added.

'You see, although "45629" was my carriage and I was trained on its operation but I only ever used it as such on trials, I don't remember seeing anyone else actually using it as a slip-coach then the whole program of testing was dropped because a landslide blocked the line it was going to be used on and it was said to be too expensive to re-open.'

'I then staffed the carriage with others in the permanent way team, you know the track workers, eh! I really don't understand why it's still in use after all these years it's so old but I'm glad it is, it's my home, see.'

Pfeiffer understood some of the jargon then asked the old man to come back to the carriage in order for him to have a look inside. The old man told him he would have to be careful because they were about to move it.

Pfeiffer asked him how he knew. The old man told him that the yard staff always placed a destination card in a clip on the side of the carriage, indicating its intended movement and on what date. Pfeiffer asked what date was on the card.

The old man replied, 'The ninth. This Sunday.'

'This Sunday? Do you know the movement also?'

'Yes, this Sunday, the movement, same as always. Oberammergau Tunnel. See, soon after the war the line got cut back between Oberammergau and Mittenwald and the tunnel is now used for the water supply from the mountains, the right-hand side just has big pipes coming out. The track is still there on the left and is only in use to inspect the pipes and pumps or so they say.'

Pfeiffer asked. 'What do you mean "so they say"?'

'There must be problems with those pipes or something, they are taking my carriage away every month or two recently, I'm getting sick of living in the bushes, see.' Pfeiffer stopped him.

'I've got to have a look inside, it's very important. Will you help me?' he asked the old man.

'Well, I suppose so. You'll have to be very careful though, because they could come at any time to load all kinds of things on to it, that's why I was out in the bushes, see!'

Pfeiffer understood the old man's cunning. He placed his arm around his shoulders again, saying. 'Come on my old friend, let's get back to your carriage. I'll be careful, I promise.'

Upon their return, the old man took Pfeiffer down his secluded pathway behind the bushes to ensure no one would notice them. He checked the area for a few minutes before giving the Inspector the "all clear". Both of them bolted over to the carriage and scrambled under the underframe, Pfeiffer was amazed at the old man's agility given his age and appearance.

Once under, the old man released four secluded catches on the underfloor section and lifted the trap door up and into the carriage, he rose himself up and removed a vertical panel, which formed the front support of an internal bench seat, the old man wriggled himself upward into the carriage itself, Pfeiffer following closely behind. It was very dark inside and Pfeiffer wished he hadn't stopped smoking as he no longer carried a lighter.

'Where are you?' He said softly.

'Over here,' came the reply as a gas lamp was lit.

'I only ever light one of these, if I use too much of the gas in those bottles, they might get suspicious, see!'

'Yes, good thinking, you're not at all stupid, are you! You mean they might see the light,' asked Pfeiffer.

'No, the windows are all blanked out but I just use a little just in case. I'm happy here, that's all. I like to be alone, see.'

'Yes, I understand, I'll say nothing, I promise. You don't mind if I look around, do you?'

'No, help yourself. Not much to see though, just machinery and tools.'

Pfeiffer began conducting a thorough search, starting at one end of the carriage and working his way down to the other and back along the opposite side. Part way along, the old man's inquisitiveness got the better of him.

'What is it you're looking for anyway?'

'I only wish I knew. Something that doesn't quite fit in to the proclaimed use for this carriage would be a good start, I suppose.'

The old man chortled at Pfeiffer's statement. Pfeiffer looked around. 'What's so funny?' he asked, chuckling with the old man.

'It's what you said, see? I've never seen anything put aboard my carriage that could be used for tunnel work, only fancy mod-con machines and masses of wiring and boxes of gadgets. All a tunnel needs are bricks and mortar, see, some heavy-duty wiring for the power supply and communication and maybe a few brackets or something, see. Anyway, it doesn't need all the stuff they've been taking there for the last twenty or so years, I'll tell you for sure!'

Pfeiffer considered the old man's comments and satisfied himself there was a need to inform his superiors of his findings and to organise surveillance of the carriage as soon as possible. He thanked the old man for his help and wished him good luck. Both of them left the carriage as they found it and slipped un-noticed into the bushes.

Pfeiffer handed the old man one hundred euros and told him he would undoubtedly return. He omitted the fact there may be others with him. The old man gave him his blessing and bid him farewell.

On returning to the Polizei station, Pfeiffer immediately organised a surveillance team and posted them around the railway yard, he then informed Interpol as requested, who relayed the findings through the security services to the Admiralty.

Shortly before landing, Larousse's team had received the details of Inspector Pfeiffer's report and had decided "Oberammergau Tunnel" was indeed, a good place to start.

Chapter Eight

Returning to the morning of Wednesday October 5th in Murnau Bavaria, Steinbacher was again very uncomfortable as he patiently awaited the General's departure from the hotel. He had made a generous financial arrangement with the night porter to provide him with a bed for the night and advise him of any movement of the guests in rooms 312/314.

There had been none noted Tuesday evening through to Wednesday morning so far. The porter had advised the day staff would be unapproachable as they were under the watchful eye of the hotel director, who opposed such matters. He had therefore to maintain his own surveillance in daylight hours hence his return to the cramped seclusion of the car's boot.

With no movement up till now, he assumed the General and his aide were arranging base transportation together with others. He would have to be at the ready to intercept them before they reached the transport.

On Tuesday evening, he had also arranged to be supplied with a high-powered rifle from one of his old comrades who he knew cared little for politics, only for money. The rifle had been delivered in an attaché case for assembly. His plan was to follow the General and Oefner to the railway yard where they would be in open space, then gun them down.

He knew time was now closing for the imminent departure and for expedience, he opted to hire a car from a rental agency close by. Handing his identification over to the receptionist at the car hire company was probably the worst lapse of caution Steinbacher had ever made; for by this time, his details including all known aliases had been circulated throughout Germany to report on sight.

The receptionist handled the situation remarkably. On noting the name Gerhard Farbmacher on his papers, she detained him as long as possible whilst he completed totally unnecessary hire documentation. A few moments later, a detachment of officers from the Murnau Polizei entered the office and Steinbacher was arrested.

Steinbacher, whilst protesting his innocence to the officers, was bundled into the back of a Polizei BMW was informed he had been arrested and would be charged with the alleged murder of Mark Blanford. The car then sped off in the direction of Murnau Polizei Headquarters with Steinbacher in handcuffs in the back seat.

It is a well-known fact that the German Polizei have never been zealous with regard to investigating matters involving links with Nazi's, past or present. They would much rather have nothing to do with it, if the truth be told. It was no surprise therefore, to find that Steinbacher was taken to a cell and left there until Inspector Pfeiffer returned from his investigation the following day and was available to interview him, no one else wished to get involved with the case if they could avoid it.

It does no one any good in the promotion stakes to be seen helping convict any Nazis regardless of the situation. However, Klaus Pfeiffer was a new breed of German, he didn't particularly like Nazis but by the same tone, he didn't hate them either. He felt it was something which had happened before he was born, something which a lot of his countrymen at the time believed to be the correct course of action for their country and their future.

It was not to be and Pfeiffer had realised long ago, there was little he could do to change things. He realised when he was given the case that any hopes of promotion would be dealt a severe blow despite the result.

Once Pfeiffer had submitted his report appertaining to his investigation at the railway yard, the details were forwarded to the Admiralty together with the news of Steinbacher's arrest. Pfeiffer then attempted to extract whatever information he could from Steinbacher.

He was finding things very difficult, Steinbacher was well trained in how to handle police interrogation, trained by those who knew better. Trained by ex-SS officers no less. He gave nothing away.

***

Late on Thursday October 6th Larousse and his team touched down at the NATO air base at Panzer Kaserne near Böblingen, where they were met by the Base Commander, who somewhat unwillingly, provided them with an operations room and further details to study the area surrounding the "Oberammergau Tunnel", including new aerial photographs taken that very afternoon immediately after Pfeiffer's report had been relayed to the Base Commander.

Larousse was also officially advised his "forty-eight hours" would commence at 06.00 hrs the following morning. Friday October 7th. Failure to locate the alleged "Reichsbürger" base and or failure to eliminate its alleged weaponry, within the specified time would result in the deployment of NATO troops into the area forthwith and enmasse.

Lengthy discussions followed, some of which were heated, the Base Commander unsure of the reasoning behind a non-combat group being privileged to initiating the inquiry. Larousse explained the Admiralty's reasoning whilst emphasising his own position best he could.

The Base Commander partially satisfied with the account agreed to maintain a distance whilst the team attempted to infiltrate the "Reichsbürger" strong-hold though, under the proviso of; "any sign of trouble and we're going in!" Larousse agreed.

A hearty meal followed the discussions, after which, Larousse advised his team they should get some rest. All in agreement, they were shown to suitable accommodation for the night. Larousse however quietly requested he be taken to Murnau Police Station to talk with Steinbacher.

On arrival at the police station, Larousse and the Base Commander were informed that Steinbacher had been interviewed by Inspector Pfeiffer earlier but declined to comment on anything other than his innocence regarding the death of Blanford.

The Superintendent at the station however granted both of them permission to interview Steinbacher and wished them more luck than his Inspector had had.

The Base Commander, Leo Perzinski, an American of Polish decent, aged about forty-five, stood six foot, five inches tall, with a finely honed physique to complement his frame, a daunting individual at the best of times, even more so when dressed in his uniform as he was when he entered the interview room followed by Larousse.

'Good evening, Herr Steinbacher. I am NATO Base Commander Perzinski of the United States Air Force and my colleague here is a Monsieur François Larousse. A name, you no doubt know well?'

Steinbacher, though uneasy at the thought of being questioned further simply answered, 'I have nothing more to say other than I did not kill Mark Blanford.'

'It's not Blanford we're interested in, that's for the local Polizei to deal with. No, our inquiry is more of a military matter, I take it you understand, boy!' The Commander's southern drawl was vividly evident.

There was a short silence.

'When I ask you a question boy, I expect an answer, do you understand me, boy?' said Perzinski, raising his voice.

Steinbacher leaned back in his chair and mumbled a few profanities under his breath.

'What was that, boy? I didn't quite hear, if you've something to say, then spit it out, boy. I haven't all day!'

'I've got nothing to say to you,' he answered at length whilst remaining calm. Larousse interjected before the Commander could continue.

'Herr Steinbacher, we know a lot more about you than you might think.' Steinbacher raised his eyebrows slightly.

'Oh, you do, do you? That's nice for you,' he replied, unperturbed. 'Firstly, we have proof you and your colleagues Allen, Matthey and the unfortunate Mr Blanford, whilst employed by the Avonmouth Port authority, systematically handled a diamond smuggling operation emanating from SIBEKA'S in Zaire, utilising my freighter African Envoy IV, for transport to various European Port's.

'The purpose behind the smuggling is also known to us. And the fact that you are a high-ranking member of the "Reichsbürger" movement, we know also. The fact that you are being sought in England for the murder of a transport police constable, etc. In fact, there is very little we don't know about you including your aliases of Stein and Farbmacher.'

Steinbacher threw his body forward against the table and looking Larousse in the eye, he said, 'If you know so much about me, why do you want to speak to me so badly? Answer me that!'

'It's very simple, we want you to tell us exactly where the "Reichsbürger" secret base is located!'

Steinbacher looked astounded at the remark, he could not understand how they could have found out about the existence of the base seeing as he had never mentioned it outside of the secret meetings arranged for high-ranking party officials.

He certainly hadn't mentioned it to any of the other three in Bristol or to anyone else who was not sanctioned to receive such classified information. He was taken aback but not visibly.

'What base! I don't know what you're talking about!' He protested loudly. 'Ah, Herr Steinbacher, come, let's not play games, you know as well as I do, that your Nazi friends have built a base in the Tirol region, supposedly capable of controlling missiles, etc. of different world powers and are intent on inaugurating the Fourth Reich. Am I correct in my assumption?'

'I've never heard anything about any underground base in the mountains, I don't know where you're getting your information from but I should look to other sources if I were you. It's obviously someone's fertile imagination,' he refuted.

Larousse looked pleased with himself, leaning forward, he eyed Steinbacher over the table from about two inches apart, saying, 'Ah, now then. I never said anything about it being underground, did I?'

'Yes, you did! You said an underground base!'

'Oh no, you said it was underground, not me.'

Steinbacher, realising he had made the simplest of mistakes, the second in twelve hours, remarked, 'Well, I obviously assumed it would be underground, that is if it exists at all!'

'Oh! It exists alright and rest assured, we will find it and destroy it before it's too late. With or without your help.'

'Right, boy!' The Commander bellowed in. 'We want you to tell us all you know about this here base. Where it is. What it's capable of. How it's guarded. Where the entrance is. Everything! You hear me, boy!'

Steinbacher looked at Larousse whose expression showed little interest in the Commander's outburst and remarked cynically, 'Is he for real?'

'Don't you push me, boy! Or I'll have you breaking up stones until you die from exhaustion. I'm warning you!'

Larousse took the Commander by the arm gently and led him over to the door. Speaking softly, he told him they stood little chance of getting anywhere whilst he adopted an aggressive tone. The Commander replied that he would get the information out of Steinbacher if he had to beat it out of him, adding the comment.

'I hate these God damn Nazi bastards!'

Larousse requested he be allowed five minutes alone with Steinbacher, after that he would leave the rest up to him as he needed to get some rest before tomorrow. The Commander agreed and left the room. Steinbacher looked puzzled as Larousse returned to the table alone and sat down.

'What's going on now?' he asked, adding. 'Gone for that pick-axe, has he?'

'Ah, you may well jest while you still can Herr Steinbacher, however the fact remains that unless you help us to locate and destroy this base your friends have built, then you're in for a very long spell of imprisonment. You're facing two charges of murder and another of attempted murder. The truck driver, remember?'

Steinbacher shrugged his shoulders. Both men sat facing each other in silence for several seconds, Larousse continued.

'In short, you're going to go to jail for the rest of your life. Now understand this! If you're convicted by a civil court, you'll go to a civil prison; however, if they decide to convict you in a military court then you could end up doing what the Commander has already got planned for you.'

'So, what are you saying? Are you offering me a deal or what?'

'No promises I'm afraid, I'm in no position to offer you any deal, all I can say, is that I'm willing to help you if you'll help me. Look!' Larousse raised his voice to gain his audience's fading attention.

'We know your friends have already tested this system of theirs with some effect. We know the next possible test subject is to be launched from one of the UK's Royal Navy's submarines. We know their base is located in the area around Oberammergau. We know they have been using an old railway carriage to supply equipment to this base and we know this carriage is on the move again on Sunday, this Sunday. We could wait until then and simply follow it in!'

Steinbacher threw himself back into the chair whilst raising his hands in the air and placing them behind his head. Shaking his head slightly from side to side, he commented lightly.

'I don't know what you want me for, you know more than I bloody do already!'

'So, what are you saying, can you help us or not?' asked Larousse, outright. 'With what! I've never been to the base, all I ever seen were photographs and a few plans. Honestly, you know more than I do!'

'Well, I'm sorry, you'll just have to suffer the consequences of your actions, I can't help you any further. Goodbye.'

'Hold on!' shouted Steinbacher.

'I never killed Blanford, you've got to believe me. I brought him over here to help him but this General Stoltz of theirs, the bastard, he had him shot in the knee by his second in command for stealing some of the diamonds. We tried to escape but they tampered with the brakes on the car and it went over the edge. I was lucky, I could jump out but poor old Mark, he couldn't make it!'

Larousse looked at Steinbacher, without feeling any remorse, he said, 'You still murdered the Police Constable on Bristol Docks. That's where you made your first mistake.' Larousse rose and walked over to the door, turning back, he said, 'If you think of anything which might help us, I would be grateful.'

In the few moments it took for Larousse to walk to the door and ask for it to be opened, Steinbacher considered his situation. He had already realised his support for the Nazi movement had been obfuscated by the actions of Oefner, under the General's direct orders. He was convinced this was not the way forward for the "Reichsbürger" movement.

If he spoke out now, his actions could eliminate most of the present hierarchy, most of whom were in very high-ranking positions. His dilemma was further fuelled by the desire to "get even" with the General for the attempt on his own life and seek retribution for Blanford's death at his behest.

He made a snap decision.

'One moment!' He shouted. Larousse swung around. 'Yes?'

'Listen. Can we have a talk? There's something I need to say.' Larousse returned to the table and sat down.

'Before you start, you must understand, there is nothing I can promise you. I have no authority in this matter. My task is simply to find this base and destroy the alleged missile system within. But I promise you I'll put a word in for you, that's the best I can do, okay?'

'All I can tell you is where to find General Friedrich Stoltz and his aide, Oefner. Axel Oefner. You'll have to take it from there.'

Larousse was not impressed. He replied, 'Why should we be interested in locating this so called General, we have a far greater task ahead of us and precious little time as it is.'

Steinbacher sat back in his seat and raised his hands behind his head.

'He's got full knowledge of how the system operates, he was in charge and it's his legacy, so to speak. And anyway, I want him! I want him bad enough to tell you where to find him.'

Larousse felt his heart miss a beat. Allen's tale of an underground base had not been collaborated until now, that is.

'Ah, so you do know of the base it seems,' Larousse said, trying to maintain his composure.

'You must understand, Monsieur Larousse. I have been a member of the "Reichsbürger" movement since I was a teenager. I believe in the cause as a whole; nothing will change my views towards it. The only reason I'm prepared to tell you where to find the General is for him and Oefner to be dealt with for Mark Blanford's murder. I assure you; I had nothing whatsoever to do with it.'

Larousse had listened to Steinbacher's case against General Stoltz, feeling little remorse for his predicament. Considering the matter for a few moments, he replied.

'Herr Steinbacher. I'm afraid this General and his aide are of little significance to me or my operation. I doubt very much if either of them will talk before your friends initiate the test launch they have planned. With this in mind, I feel if you wish to settle a score with them, you should discuss the matter with the Commander who's waiting in the corridor or the Polizei themselves.'

Steinbacher paused to consider his options before replying.

'The only thing I can offer you is some photographs of the general area around the base, that's all.'

Larousse smiled.

'Ah! The photographs. I'm afraid we already have those.'

'Impossible!' Blasted Steinbacher.

'I brought them over here with me. Surely you don't think me that stupid?' Larousse chuckled slightly before enlightening him to his plight. 'Photographs of the mountains surrounding Oberammergau. Photographs of the tunnel mouth. Photographs of an old somewhat strange looking railway carriage. Photographs of schematic drawings, etc. Do you wish me to carry on?'

'How! How did you get hold of them?' He shouted.

'Betrayal is a terrible enemy, Herr Steinbacher. You ran out on the two men you left behind in Bristol and left them to face the consequences of your previous actions.'

'But? But Matthey and Allen knew nothing of the Base. They thought the diamonds were for Party funding, nothing more.'

'I'm afraid you underestimated one of them. Your apartment was broken into, more than once in fact and the documentation you held there was photocopied by one of them on a regular basis. He's given us the full story to date.'

'Matthey! I knew he couldn't be trusted the stinking fat shit,' Steinbacher said as he thumped the table.

Larousse laughed a little before enlightening him.

'I'm afraid it was Jason Allen who gave us the information. Matthey hasn't said a word since his arrest.'

Steinbacher was noticeably stunned. Shaking his head, he said.

'I just don't believe it. If anyone would have talked, I would have put money on it being Matthey. Mind you, I do see his reasoning, it's the same reason I'm sat here talking to you. If General Stoltz had prevented Oefner shooting Mark Blanford in the knee, this situation would never have arisen,' remarked Steinbacher, somewhat disconcerted.

Larousse interrupted him before he could continue, advising him that he must return to the NATO base as he had an early start in the morning. He compelled him to comply with the Base Commander and give any information he had to him, who would in turn pass on the relevant details as required.

Larousse returned to the NATO Base in the very early hours and got what rest he could in the few hours before setting off for Oberammergau.

***

Early the following morning Friday October 7th around five thirty, Herr Schnorr the Railway Yard Controller returned to his home after his short break away. Oefner had slipped out of the hotel and was keeping watch for his arrival, still nursing his facial wounds from the chill of the early hours.

Allowing him a few moments to ensure he had not been followed given the fact that Steinbacher was still at large as far as he knew. He cautiously approached the front door to the handsome bungalow. Giving a coded knock reminiscent of railway signalling calls, Schnorr eased the door open gently, the security chain still attached.

'Herr Oefner?' Schnorr was a little unsure of Oefner due to the bruising and laceration which had by now been stitched together. 'Herr Oefner! What are you doing here?' he asked on full recognition.

Oefner pushed the door to the limit of the chain. 'Let me in, you fool,' he commanded.

'Of course, Herr Oefner, one moment,' he replied nervously.

'Herr Schnorr. I have been sent by General Stoltz on a matter of extreme urgency. We have instructed the movement of the "Base Transport" vehicle in your absence for Sunday. However, it seems we will have to alter the movement plan in favour of tonight at midnight.'

'The operation has had to be moved forward due to the actions of a traitor in our midst, we have no option other than to take immediate action to complete implementation of the missile system and carry out the first test before he betrays us. Do you understand?' Oefner shouted as he removed and smacked his previously concealed black coloured riding quirt against his right leg.

Herr Schnorr looked frightened and immediately agreed to Oefner's demands. 'I shall contact Control immediately, Herr Oefner.'

'You must ensure absolute secrecy regarding the deployment of the Base Transport vehicle, many important Kammeraden are travelling with it on this occasion. Understand!'

'Ya wohl! Herr Oefner,' Schnorr replied as he saluted.

Oefner raised his quirt and tapped his forehead in response, he wished he hadn't, for as he hit the wound, the pain increased. Schnorr asked if he was alright and if there was anything he could get for him. Oefner simply demanded he carry out his order.

Schnorr lifted the receiver and telephoned the railway control office at Murnau yard. He advised them of the alteration and that the Permanent Way and Tunnel Inspection Unit would be required for midnight. Tonight. An emergency repair had to be undertaken.

The Control staff naturally sanctioned his request.

Schnorr was uneasy over the situation, he had always been given fair warning of impending movements and was therefore able to deploy crews sympathetic to the cause though not necessarily full-blooded "Reichsbürger" members.

He enlightened Oefner to his fears that he may be unable to contact the normal crews who turned a blind eye to their operations for the sake of the Fatherland and the Reich.

Oefner riposted.

'Herr Schnorr! You are to carry out your orders! Now may I suggest you get started? If the normal crews can't be found I suggest you use another, we will deal with them if necessary!'

'Ya wohl! Herr Oefner.'

'We will contact you in Control later. Guten tag.'

'Guten tag, Herr Oefner.'

Schnorr was perplexed at the prospect of the forthcoming arrangements to be made, wishing to himself he had never been talked into assisting them in the first place. Casting the thoughts of doubt from his mind, he began calling the various departments in order to arrange the crews required.

***

By this time, Larousse and his team wishing to make the most of their "forty-eight" hours had driven to the area around Oberammergau and were surveying the northern end of the Oberammergau Tunnel just after 06.00 hrs Friday morning.

The normal railway service itself terminated at Oberammergau station and the tunnel itself was around a kilometre south. The line between station and tunnel was only lightly maintained and therefore overgrown in most places as it was only accessed by staff supposedly maintaining pipework for the area's water supply.

The surroundings were mountainous, affording beautiful views of the Tirol Zugspitze range had they had the time for sightseeing. Having given the surrounding area a sound reconnaissance, they moved on towards to the northern end carrying out similar checks for something out of the ordinary, there was nothing that they could identify as being out of place.

Larousse advised the members of the small group to surrender their mobile phones for safe keeping to André who would be remaining with one of the vehicles until they all returned, he then suggested that Katriana and Robert, the only two members of the team still in civilian clothes, head into Oberammergau itself and ask some of the locals; cautiously, if they had seen anything strange recently. They agreed and took one of the cars and a radio to report back.

Larousse opted for a slow drive south along the northern mountain pass avoiding the tunnel itself. Traversing the mountainous pass served little purpose, nothing unusual was seen from the roadside. They stopped several times on the short journey to study the aerial photographs old and new, hoping to identify a recent structure or perhaps a major change in the rock face. Nothing out of the ordinary.

With the short journey southward complete, Larousse and the team studied the maps. There was no road within easy distance to the south of the Oberammergau Tunnel so therefore it was assumed if the base was at this location and approached by rail as they knew from the best of their knowledge it to be, then their search must remain along this road including the entrance to the rail tunnel itself, knowing there was no other railway junction within the vicinity and no disused lines either.

Turning their unmarked four-wheel drive Range Rover around, they traversed the route again, this time South to North with all eyes trained on the mountainous slopes and craggy rock formations. Once again disappointment was the result, there was little they could see which had changed from any of the old or new, photographs, taller trees a few road improvements, a new building and such.

Larousse commented.

'If only we knew how their system works, what does it need, perhaps the operation is carried out here but the signal sent from elsewhere. It's like looking for a needle in a haystack!'

Marcel was driving Larousse and his team, he suggested they take the road to Ettal and perhaps have a word with some of the locals there. Larousse agreed.

On the approach to Ettal, there was a seemingly unused dirt track leading off to the left, the sign at the junction although a little tatty proclaimed "Fischen und Baden Verboten".

'Marcel! Stop! Back-up, take that road on the left!' Larousse swung round in the seat.

'Gentlemen, according to the map the river Ammer flows along here, let's have a look, shall we!'

A few hundred meters on, there indeed was the river Ammer, flowing gently along.

'Have we anything to take a sample with?' asked Larousse.

'Sir, I have some plastic containers among my equipment and some sealing tape,' answered Chambers.

'Excellent, Chambers. Get a few out. There's a tributary further upstream, do you think you can make it?'

'Sir, I'll try my best, Sir,' Chambers replied as he viewed the mountain rising ever upward.

'Good! I want you to take a sample of the water from both sections of the river beyond the tributary, then one from here. Malhotra. I want you to go downstream and do the same. Understand?'

'Yes Sir! May I ask why, Sir?'

'Ah! The answer to that is simple. Why is there a sign stating, "No Fishing or Bathing" and displaying skull and crossbones in an area renowned for pure water. In addition, I'm not so sure there would be fish this far upstream, eh?'

'Yes, Sir, I see.'

'Now listen, both of you, I want you to report back each and every fifteen minutes, just in case you're spotted, or you get into trouble on the rocks, okay.'

'Yes, Sir,' both men answered together.

'Andre, you get as close as you can in the Range Rover to pick them both up. This is our insurance, men. If we fail to locate the base within the allotted time, analysis of those samples might help to pinpoint the source so make sure you mark the location. I'll meet up with you all once you're through. Okay.'

'Sir. Yes, Sir.'

Both men headed off in opposite directions, leaving Larousse to decide his next move.

'Carl, you and Marcel stay guard over the equipment here while Gerrard and I go into Oberammergau and have a word with the locals. Gerrard. Let's make ourselves look like tourists.'

'Sir?' Gerrard asked, slightly bemused.

'Come, come, Gerrard, I've seen your knees before.'

Larousse opened a hold-all containing an assortment of "loud" clothing he had requested from a bewildered Perzinski. Selecting shorts and T-shirts for both of them, he handed Gerrard his, saying.

'We've come for the fishing.'

Gerrard looked amused as he stripped out of the camouflaged combat suit, which at this stage bore no markings of origin.

The two men walked the short distance into Oberammergau, the time 07.30hrs.

***

Meanwhile, the railway yard Controller in Murnau had dispatched a clerk to exchange the movement labels on the permanent way train, advising of a change of movement to the ground staff.

From the bushes, the old man had seen the clerk remove and replace the labels. Waiting long enough for him to clear from view, he boldly walked over and removed one from a ballast wagon. He held it close to his eyes to read the information. Noting the date had been altered from midnight Sunday to midnight tonight, he thought he had better inform the nice young policeman who had been so kind to him.

Without realising the urgency of the situation, he decided to walk into the town and talk with Inspector Pfeiffer himself, thinking also that he might just get another decent meal for his troubles. He returned to the bushes and collected his old bag, which contained all his worldly goods and set off for the town centre.

His task was hampered by the frantic movements of people and vehicles through the early morning rush hour traffic, his passage causing many a frayed temper amongst the motorists as he stepped out in front regardless of their presence. He retorted with a few choice phrases and gestures to the embittered motorists.

Still a good hour's walk from the Polizei station, he almost came to blows with a driver who had swerved to avoid him and rammed another car in the process. The driver was clearly distraught with the event, shouting and yelling at the old man and knowing he had no hope of claiming against him for damages. The matter had been reported by someone to the Polizei who quickly attended the scene.

Whilst the driver was explaining how the accident happened, the old man was thanking the officer for sending a car for him to see Inspector Pfeiffer. The officer laughed as he listened to his remark, then repeated it to his colleague who joined in, leaving the motorist bemused at the situation.

Once the formalities and necessary documentation was over, the old man was taken to the station for an interview. He was sitting in the interview room, feeling quite perky after his ordeal until the interviewing officer walked in. Pulling a pen from the inside pocket of his jacket, he threw it down on top of the pad already lying on the desk.

'Well! What have you got to say for yourself, Herr? Herr! Well, what's your name, Herr what?'

Avoiding answering the officers' direct question, he replied, 'I'm here to see Inspector Pfeiffer, that's why I've come. To see Inspector Pfeiffer, see.'

'What on earth are you babbling about? You've been brought here because you caused an accident between two motor vehicles! Understand!'

The old man looked out the window for a moment then replied, 'I've come to see Inspector Pfeiffer, he'll want to see me, see. Sent me a car, he did. That was kind of him, I must remember to thank him.'

'You can see your Inspector Pfeiffer after I'm finished with you, okay!'

The old man began to rock back and forth on the seat, as if looking into oblivion, kept repeating, 'I'm here to see Inspector Pfeiffer, see. Here to see Inspector Pfeiffer I am, see. Here to see Inspector Pfeiffer, he sent me a car, see. I'm here to see Inspector Pfeiffer.'

'Okay you win for now, I'll get hold of Inspector Pfeiffer but after he's through with you, you've got me to deal with. Damaging property is an offence, do you understand?'

'Here to see Inspector Pfeiffer, see,' the old man continued to reply. The officer left the room and called the Inspector's office. 'Inspector Pfeiffer.'

'Yes, speaking.'

'This is Sergeant Friedrichs from the traffic division.'

'Yes, how may I help you?'

'We have a nutcase down here who insists on talking to you.'

'What's his name, I know plenty of them,' answered Pfeiffer. Friedrichs laughed.

'He won't tell me his name, some old man who's got the hots for you, Inspector.' Before he could laugh at his quip, Pfeiffer replied.

'I'll be right there!' And slammed the phone down.

Friedrichs was startled by the reaction, wondering why the old man could be so important to Pfeiffer. A few moments later, Pfeiffer entered the traffic department and asked for Friedrichs.

'Over here, Inspector,' he shouted.

'This old man's nuts, I'm telling you. Don't take what he says too seriously, Inspector.'

'Quickly! Sergeant, what's the story?'

'Well, he was picked up by two officers after he'd caused an accident between two motorists, then apparently he thanked them for you sending a car to pick him up. Since then, that's all he's said, that he's here to see you. Does it make sense to you?'

'Okay I'll take it from here, thanks Sergeant.'

'Do you want me to sit in, I could do with a laugh.'

'No, that won't be necessary.'

Friedrichs shrugged his shoulders and left him to it. Pfeiffer entered the room; the old man was still rocking back and forth repeating the same sentence.

'Here I am old friend, Inspector Pfeiffer, remember?' The old man stopped rocking and replied.

'Of course, I remember, it's you I've come to see, see!'

'For a minute there, you had me worried,' Pfeiffer said with relief.

'Oh that! That was just for him, come in here shouting at me, I'll take that from no one, no one you hear!'

Pfeiffer laughed then walked over to shake the old man's hand. 'Tell me my friend, what can I do for you?'

'You can buy me breakfast, if you want to, that is.'

Pfeiffer couldn't risk refusing him even if he'd wanted to. The old man had helped him from the beginning and he thought he may have more to tell.

'Yes of course, no problem. What's your fancy?'

'Something hot and filling, eh.'

'I know just the place, come on.'

Both of them walked out of the station together to the amazement of the others as Pfeiffer held the old man around the shoulders. Not realising the urgency, the old man ensured he had eaten his breakfast, had seconds, drunk his coffee and had some more before he whispered to Pfeiffer.

'I've got something for you, see.'

'Oh! And what's that?'

'This! See.' The old man pulled out the crumpled label from his jacket pocket and handed it to Pfeiffer as if still guarding it with his life.

Pfeiffer eyed the label and shook his head.

'You've gone to the trouble of bringing this here to me, you shouldn't have bothered, I could have got one myself yesterday.'

'No, you couldn't! Not one like that, see.'

Pfeiffer's eyes paid a little more attention to the label this time, then he realised.

'They've changed the date!' he exclaimed. 'Yes. Thought you'd be interested, see! Eh!'

'My friend, I can't thank you enough. Listen, this is really important. I'll have to get back to the station, you don't mind if I leave you, do you?'

'I've got to go back also, I'll come with you, see. I've got to see that other officer over what happened this morning, see,' the old man said sadly.

'Forget it. I'll straighten it all out for you, you've been a great help. Listen old friend, keep away from the carriage today, you could be in great danger. Please for my sake, will you?'

The old man thought a little though said nothing.

'Look, here's a hundred and odd euros, all I've got on me. Will you take it and get some alternative accommodation for now? Please my friend, it's for your own safety.'

'No! I don't want your money, all I want is for you to help me keep my carriage, you understand. You help me, see,' the old man said disconsolately.

Pfeiffer took hold of his hands and clasped them tightly.

'I'll do what I can but you must understand, it's not up to me. I have no authority over railway property. I'll put a good word in if all goes well tonight, okay?'

The old man shrugged his shoulders and replied, 'I suppose so. You be careful tonight, Herr Inspector, see.'

'I will. I've got to go, sorry. I'll be in touch.'

With that, Pfeiffer quickly scurried away in the direction of the Polizei HQ.

***

Robert and Katriana were still busy, asking around the shops and Café bars which were just opening for business in Oberammergau if anything strange had happened lately in the area. Their inquiries met with a mixture of intrigue, scepticism and humour from the locals. In short, they had learned nothing of any value.

Robert suggested they try looking around the railway lines for anything odd, seeing as the locals thought nothing of any importance had ever happened in Oberammergau since they built the tunnel water supply and upgraded the main road, everything nowadays passed by un-hindered.

Walking down to the railway at the northern tunnel portal, both gazed along the single-track line into the distance southward, then into the gloom of the tunnel itself. There was, as the locals had pointed out, nothing unusual. Robert turned to Katriana and put his arm around her shoulder.

'Looks like we drew a blank on this, sweetheart. I can't see anything out of place, can you?'

Katriana rested her head on Robert's arm and rocked it gently from side to side. Putting her arms around his waist, she pulled him close to her.

'Papa will be furious if he's wrong about this place. We better go back and tell him there's nothing here, maybe he'll think of somewhere else while we still have some time.' Robert agreed and both returned to the car and radioed in for instructions.

By the time Robert and Katriana returned to the rendezvous spot by the river, Larousse and Gerrard were just heading back from their own little chat with the locals in the town. On seeing them crossing the bridge in the distance, Katriana pointed to them and laughing, she said.

'Robert, look! There's papa and Gerrard, what on earth are they doing dressed like that?'

'God knows,' Robert replied, joining in the humour of the situation.

Robert pulled the car up beside the Range Rover and Katriana immediately jumped out and ran back a little way until she could see them walking along. Shouting out and pointing towards them, she cried out.

'Papa! Papa! What are you doing, you look so silly, both of you.'

Larousse raised his arm and waved back at her. Katriana was doubled up in a fit of giggles, Robert ran to support her.

'Darling, I know it's funny but I mean, come on!'

'Robert! Just look at the state of them both. T-shirts and shorts finished off nicely with a pair of hob nail boots and you're telling me to come on!'

Robert hadn't noticed the boots until now, he couldn't help himself; they did look an awful sight.

'Ah! So, you think it's funny, do you?' Larousse asked whimsically as he stomped up to the car.

Katriana reached for her father and kissed him.

'You should see yourselves, surely you didn't talk to people dressed like that, papa? I'd die if you did.'

'You had better try and postpone your appointment with your maker, my precious. Gerrard and I have obtained a little information, which could be helpful. You, I take it, being dressed a little feminine, given the terrain and situation that is, have squeezed masses of information out of the residents of Oberammergau, no doubt? Eh!' Larousse replied wryly, causing the flurry of laughter to subside.

'Sorry, papa. No one's seen anything. Have they, Robert?'

'Katriana's right Sir, they're all saying that nothing ever happens there since the tunnel was converted to a water supply route. Some said the mountain no longer gets a full snow covering in places but that's about it.'

'Okay then, let's see what we've got at the moment,' said Larousse. 'Firstly. A "no fishing or bathing" sign in an area of normally pure water.

Secondly. In our chats with the people of the town, we were informed that the river is polluted to some extent, hence the ban. Apparently, the ban was imposed shortly before the war ended.'

'The reason given then was "Ingress of a sulphurous substance permeating from within the mountain itself". That was the official jargon, needless to say, this has remained the reason since.'

'So perhaps this is not the place after all?' Posed Robert.

'Don't be so hasty, Robert. We have photographic evidence of this location. We have the information from that chap in Bristol, that the base is underground. We have the fact, that somehow an old railway carriage is utilised, yet we don't know how but I suggest we concentrate our efforts in this direction for the moment.'

Robert shook his head in frustration.

'Katriana and I have been down to the entrance of the railway tunnel near the town, there's nothing unusual there. Everything looks well so normal.'

'No, perhaps not. Neither is there anything unusual on the road to the town of Ettal other than the no fishing sign. Nevertheless, there's a connection involving the railway somehow. It's got to be under there, somewhere. All that remains, is for us to find it!' Larousse replied as he and the others all turned to survey the vast bulk of the mountainous terrain behind them and realising their task ahead would not be an easy one.

Robert had a quick realisation.

'Hold on, do you think the lack of snow could be due to heat from inside the mountain, I mean if there is a base under there somewhere surely there is some form of heating, eh?'

'That's a fair possibility Robert, did the people say where on the mountain.'

'No not really, they just sort of pointed in that direction.' Robert raised his arm, showing Larousse.

'That's a coincidence, that's the direction of the river. Seems like a good place to start eh.'

***

Inspector Pfeiffer hurried back to the Polizei HQ and immediately relayed the new information through to the NATO Commander whose Base was still on Yellow Alert pending developments. He in turn forwarded the information to the Admiralty.

Shortly after 10.00 hrs, Larousse was contacted by radio from the NATO Base advising him and his team of the movement alteration of the suspect carriage. Larousse thanked the Base Commander and requested they collect the water samples taken from the river and have them analysed as soon as possible to pinpoint the type and source of any pollution.

Perzinski agreed and ordered a helicopter to proceed immediately to a suitable landing spot on the outskirts of town, the co-ordinates of which were given to Larousse for rendezvous.

Larousse gathered his team together and told them of the change of movement. Correctly or incorrectly, he surmised the Nazis had brought forward their plans because of Steinbacher's arrest. The reason was, in fact, immaterial, all that mattered was that Larousse's "forty-eight" hours had diminished to, in reality, to only fourteen or so, that is if the plug hadn't been pulled on him altogether. He knew they had to locate the entrance before the train set off from Murnau.

He knew Perzinski was ready and waiting to trail any entrance to wherever it led, he had to be there first. After a little thought, Larousse decided to go for the long shot of searching the railway tunnel itself. He told Robert and Katriana to drive to the agreed co-ordinates and rendezvous with the helicopter. Then to return and stay with the car and man the radio in case of any developments.

He ordered all communication to be by secure radio from the NATO vehicles direct to him and he would forward any change of plan onward. All phones to be left in the Range Rovers for the time being.

He split the other members of the team into two groups. André, Carl, Marcel and Malhotra in one and Gerrard, Chambers and himself in the other. Both teams boarded a Range Rover each and headed for the northern portal where the groups alighted and adorned themselves in fluorescent safety jackets as worn by railway maintenance personnel.

Larousse asked for a volunteer from both teams to act as lookouts. Marcel and Gerrard took the initiative. Passing out handsets from the equipment, he advised Marcel to walk along the railway about five hundred yards and await his signal.

He then instructed André to wait with the car, Carl and Malhotra to proceed through the tunnel cautiously along the wall adjacent to the refuge recesses.

Leaving the other three men behind, they began entering the tunnel itself. Larousse called to commence the operation ensuring first, the lookouts gave the "all clear". The signal though was weak given the mountainous terrain. The team, using heat seeking instruments combined with activity sensors and high-powered lights began the painstaking inspection of the tunnel walls and floor for any abnormalities.

Within ten minutes whilst the tunnel search was underway, the helicopter arrived and collected the water samples leaving Robert and Katriana at a loss to occupy themselves, they returned to the original location and sat quietly together on a fallen tree adjacent to the dirt track.

Holding each other close, their arms entwined, Robert commented.

'You realise this is the first time we've been completely alone since we met.' Katriana's eyes lit up as she raised her head off his shoulder.

'Yes, darling! You're right, I hadn't thought of it with all that's going on. Papa must trust you now, of that I'm certain. He's never left me alone with anyone hardly. You've done it, darling. Papa likes you and I love you so very much,' she said sensually.

'He'll be gone for ages,' she added not as an afterthought, more of an invitation.

They gazed into each other's eyes as they slipped down slowly on to the grass below. She reached to caress Robert's face as he lowered himself alongside, they kissed each other long and hard and for several minutes as they rolled about on the ground beneath them before either of them began caressing each other.

Robert, who had self-imposed a discipline in his life whereby; if ever he met a woman, the right woman, he would know who. She would have to feel the same love for him as he did for her before he would consider making love. He was not your typical "wham-bam-thank-you ma'am" male. Robert was a gentleman.

At the age of thirty-two, he had only had two women in his life, the first lasted only twelve months and she was a mistake. He was young and immature; she was slightly older in age but wiser where men were concerned. He soon found out the truth and vowed he would never allow himself to be used again.

Two years had passed before he met Diane, he never bothered in between, he'd had opportunities, several but Robert knew what he wanted and he hadn't yet found her until Diane came along.

Diane, his ex-wife, was the girl he'd been waiting for and at the time, she was right, his instincts back then told him. The two of them were right, right for each other. In the months leading up to their marriage, he built on the foundations laid and was certain beyond any doubt that he'd found true love. He was happy, she was ecstatic, they were the "perfect couple", everyone said so.

But eight years on, the magic had vanished, there was the usual catalogue of arguments and conflict between them both, usually over money and the lack of it. He knew in his heart he'd done all he could to save the marriage, he still had feelings for her but the love, the magic, it had vanished.

The past three years had been difficult, life at the factory had taken its toll, a woman or the lack of one was the least of his worries. But throughout, his principles had remained, the offers had been forthcoming but the commitment was absent.

Now however, everything was different, suddenly, through the strangest of circumstances he'd found the right person again, right for him and he knew in his heart he was right for her. Love had come back into his life and he was gloriously happy, she seemed ecstatic. The time was right but caution was still his restraint.

Robert and Katriana's osculation's only subsiding for want of air, they began exploring each other's body and Robert running his hand up and down along her shapely legs, each stroke inching higher and higher up her thighs, though not between as yet.

Robert was maintaining his self-imposed discipline even now, even though his body was aroused beyond belief he was still holding back, he feared Katriana may be offended if he made his move so soon, he was prepared to wait a little longer, as long as it took, next week, next month, three, six months whatever!

Katriana though, wanted Robert and she wanted him now, she was not generous with her favours as a rule but she instinctively knew when it was right and now was the time, she'd waited long enough.

They kissed and caressed each other for several minutes more before Katriana took hold of Robert's hand and guided it slowly but directly to her left breast. She'd had enough of this "taking it easy" attitude, she wanted him and she was determined to get him while the going was good, while her father was well out of the way.

She could feel Robert's heart pounding harder against her as he skilfully and gently released the uppermost buttons on her blouse and slid his hand in and over her brassiere. Running his hand around her supported half-clad breast, Robert kissed her hard, their passion forcing their mouths to open and their tongues entwined.

Robert worked his hand around her back and with the precision of a surgeon, he unclipped the brassiere, eased the straps and pulled it down away from her breasts. She released her grip on him and eased him away slightly as she removed the garment and spread her blouse out to either side. Saying softly.

'I hope you approve, my darling.'

Robert gazed down at her perfectly formed breasts, which had remained firm although laid on her back. Her nipples a deeper brown in colour to her already well-tanned body were protruding with excitement, he placed his hands upon her breasts and fondled them both as he answered.

'Beautiful, absolutely beautiful. You're beautiful, darling. I love you so much, sweetheart,' he said genuinely. For he wanted her as much as she him, he hadn't considered the consequences of their actions, neither had she. They were in love with each other and they were about to prove it.

She reached for his trouser belt and unclipped it, then the clasp of his trousers followed by the zip fastener, teasing him a little she ran her hand slowly up and down the prominent bulge, which showed on the outside of his trousers.

'Who's all excited then?' She whispered, then wet and pouted her lips.

Robert was doing all he could to control himself, the movements of her hand generating the most intense feelings within him every time she moved it sensually up and down.

'Is my darling excited?' She teased again. 'Oh God. Yes!' He replied breathlessly.

'I shouldn't tease you, should I?' She smirked and pulled her hand away and up under his shirt.

'God! I love you so much, Katriana. I love you and I want you,' he said as he lowered himself down and began to suckle and caress her breasts. She began to writhe in ecstasy, he had found her sensitive spot, she moaned with delight as he teased her nipple between his teeth.

Although the two of them were locked in a vice like grip, she struggled to reach down and undo her tight-fitting jeans, once open, she pulled them down a little, leaving Robert the option to proceed further. Robert took the initiative and slowly worked the garment from under her, she kicked out to cast the jeans a few feet away as they reached her feet.

Katriana spun Robert onto his back, her long brown hair falling to the side of her face, her breasts falling forward but still firm to the touch. Robert reached down to find she was wearing very skimpy black panties.

'Black panties, eh!' He said approvingly.

Katriana smiled. 'I wanted to look my best for you, darling. I've been wearing this type for days!' She added in frustration. Both laughed, then kissed.

'Do you like them?' She asked softly.

'Oh sweetheart, especially on you. You look terrific. God, I love you.'

Katriana investigated Robert's eyes as he pulled her panties down ever so gently, running his hands around her bottom as she moved slightly to assist. She stopped what she was doing to Robert and sat upright throwing her hair back, she looked deep into Robert's eyes.

'You do love me, Robert. Truly love me, don't you?' She asked before continuing. She knew, mere clarification was all that was needed.

'Like I've loved no other, sweetheart. I fell in love with you when I saw you sunbathing that very first day. I thought at the time you'd have nothing to do with me. I've never been so pleased to be so wrong about anything in my life. Until now that is. Because I love you more than anything. More than you could possibly imagine. And that's the truth. I swear.'

Katriana reached into her bag.

'Robert, I want you to have these my darling, just in case.'

'In case of what?' he asked, as if he needed to.

'No arguments darling, just take them please, for me, please,' she said softly. Who could resist her feminine charms, certainly not Robert. He opened the small box to reveal a pair of exquisite platinum gold cufflinks with an abstract etched design and a small diamond in one corner. Robert looked down at them.

'I can't take these Katriana; they look horrendously expensive to me.'

'Robert, they are for you. Please just for me.'

Robert looked uncomfortable with the gift but took them to please her. 'Promise me you'll wear them Robert, please.'

'Yes, of course I will, I'll wear them every day.' He unfastened his shirt sleeves and fitted the cufflinks.

Katriana lowered herself down, pulled Robert close to her and kissed him gently, whispering in his ear. 'Make love to me Robert. I want you to make love to me, faire l'amour'a. I love you, my darling.'

French or no French, Robert needed no persuasion, he knew he truly loved her from the beginning, now he knew she truly loved him also. Words of love had been said but action was stronger than words.

Both of them made passionate love for almost an hour beside the deserted dirt track, oblivious to the fact their climatic screams and moans could have been heard for quite a distance; luckily for them, they weren't.

***

General Stoltz and Oefner were busy contacting various Party hierarchy who had previously been advised of the impending live target test of the donor missile system and had made their way to pre-arranged locations, their task, to advise them the matter had been brought forward forty-eight hours as a cautionary measure.

The necessary arrangements had as usual been impeccable. All the required members had been notified and by now all had arrived in the Murnau area to await transportation to the base.

The arrangements regarding the transportation of staff to and from the base was a complex, tried and tested series of movements coordinated throughout Europe and for an important event such as this, even beyond. Many had already arrived in the Murnau area in readiness for the glorious event they all fully anticipated.

To get there, the method involved the co-operation of many distant outposts of the "Reichsbürger" movement. The arrangements covered each individual for absence from their given positions within Industry and Commerce and secretive changeovers and accommodation enroute to safe houses within the Murnau suburbs. From there, the collection and processing for transport to the Base was a simple affair.

Whilst the General was looking through his code book for the contact number of a fellow Kammeraden, the telephone rang in the hotel room. Both the General and Oefner looked at it suspiciously as they had informed no one of their location. Oefner lifted the receiver.

'Guten Morgen!' He answered bluntly. A voice speaking softly in German answered.

'The Polizei are on their way to arrest you, Kammeraden.' Oefner wasted no time replacing the receiver whilst exclaiming. 'Die Polizei!'

Stoltz and Oefner frantically collected the paperwork and small notebooks they had been consulting to decipher the constantly changing codes implemented by the "Reichsbürger" for security's sake and stuffed them into the briefcase. Then swiftly, both men exited the hotel room and chose to scurry down the stairs rather than be captive in the elevator.

They located the driver as they passed casually through the foyer and signalled him to leave the building immediately. The three men walked smartly and confidently away from the hotel entrance in different directions to avert any attention and were several hundred yards away before several Polizei cars and vans arrived and surrounded the hotel.

The General cursed Steinbacher for betraying them. He was right to do so, for Steinbacher had indeed made a statement to the Polizei and given the location. Although that was the only information he had given, the General was obviously unaware of the fact and therefore assumed the worse.

Pfeiffer was in command of the police team; he entered the hotel and identified himself to the receptionist on duty. He requested she give him the room number of Herr Stoltz or Herr Oefner. The receptionist swiftly glanced down the registration list and advised the Inspector no one had registered under either of those two names.

Pfeiffer quickly realised they were obviously using false identities and requested the room numbers of anyone who had registered in the previous few days. He was given a list of seventeen names occupying fourteen different rooms.

The hotel exits having been sealed off, he and three officers headed for the first room. Satisfied the occupants were not who they were looking for they continued to the next. It was at the seventh inspection, rooms 312/314, where they found the doors wide open and a few items of clothing scattered within. The occupants had obviously been expeditious.

Pfeiffer realised immediately that Stoltz and Oefner had been "tipped off" from someone inside the Polizei HQ. He was not surprised; he knew of the network of Kammeraden and how strong the bond was between them.

Posting a couple of officers to search the rooms and take any statements, he ordered the others to return to HQ. He himself decided to take a short stroll alone to focus his mind. It was whilst strolling alongside the river Ach, he decided to return to the railway yard and have another word with the Control staff. He was convinced the carriage he had been through with the old man was indeed one method the "Reichsbürger" used for transport to the secret base.

Pfeiffer then made his way alone to the Murnau Railway Yard where he requested permission to talk with the controller.

'Herr Inspector. Please come in. My name is Herr Mayr. My colleague has informed me of your previous visit. I must say, it is seldom we receive a visit from the Polizei, let alone two in the same number of days.'

'Please forgive the intrusion, Herr Mayr. The investigation I am conducting seems to revolve around the old carriage stabled just out of sight around that bend,' Pfeiffer said as he pointed in the general direction.

'Herr Schnorr's "toy", we call it. It seldom moves out of the yard without the direct orders from Herr Schnorr,' Mayr answered comically.

'So, I'm led to believe,' replied Pfeiffer.

Mayr led the Inspector over to a desk where upon laid a large thick ledger. 'Look for yourself Inspector, this ledger goes back as far as 1991. The others are in store up to then if you wish to see them also. In all that time Schnorr's "toy" has been authorised by him alone for the same duty time and time again. I have asked Herr Schnorr in the past what's so special about the carriage.' Pfeiffer interrupted.

'And?'

'Nothing. Inspector. He maintains the coach is for the specific use of the Civil Engineers and Permanent Way staff for maintenance of both the old tunnel and water supply installation at what is now the end of the line at Oberammergau.'

'Yes, I have been told so already. I have also been told it only travels on the line through the Oberammergau Tunnel. Is this correct?'

'Correct, Inspector. I for one fail to see the need for the inspection of the Tunnel on such a regular basis, no other tunnel structure within a hundred kilometres' radius receives the attention lavished on the Oberammergau Tunnel,' Mayr answered cynically.

Pfeiffer was systematically flicking through the ledger mentally noting how many times Schnorr had authorised the use of the carriage.

'It would appear Herr Mayr, Herr Schnorr has already sent the coach out four times this year alone. Five! Counting tonight,' Pfeiffer remarked.

Mayr was bemused.

'You know about tonight's movement already, Inspector. How? We only heard of the change early this morning.'

'We have our sources, Herr Mayr,' said Pfeiffer candidly, thinking of the old man. Just then the internal telephone rang.

'For you, Herr Mayr,' called one of the assistants.

'Reports of men in the Oberammergau Tunnel, Herr Mayr. Have you authorised this activity?'

'No. I know nothing of it. One moment please.'

'Excuse me a moment Inspector, I must check on any Permanent Way movements booked to work in the Oberammergau Tunnel area today. A coincidence, Herr Inspector?' Mayr quizzed.

Pfeiffer was quick to react.

'No need, Herr Mayr. They are my men. I shall take full responsibility for the situation. Please do not reveal it's a Polizei matter just yet,' he answered.

'Very well, on your head be it. Had this been still an active line I would have thrown the book at you and no mistake.' Mayr returned to the telephone.

'Emergency work in progress. I'm sorry, we only found out ourselves earlier this morning, no need to worry. Please update the network accordingly and advise. Thank you.'

'What's going on, Inspector?' Mayr asked, outright. 'I wish I knew, Herr Mayr,' said Pfeiffer.

'You obviously know more than I do, Inspector. I am responsible for the safe running of the network within my district and I don't take kindly to others, Polizei or otherwise, hindering the safe and punctual passage of my trains. Do I make myself clear!' Mayr protested strongly, his previous air of informality turning to an aggressive outburst.

Pfeiffer stood in silence for a few seconds, he knew he could tell him little of the circumstances and hoped the matter would simply fade away. Unluckily for him, Mayr had other ideas.

'Well! Herr Inspector, I am waiting for an explanation. You obviously fail to see the potential dangers in wandering around live railway facilities, if there is any planned works on any line, our drivers are warned to keep a look out at the location for staff safety, you must be aware, Herr Inspector the overhead power supply carries 25,000 volts! Your men are in great danger if they stray too close. I think it best we close the line down and shut off the power for the time being.'

'I am sorry Herr Mayr, this is a Polizei matter. There's nothing more I can say for the time being, I must ask you to bear with me on the matter for the moment. Also, you must not change any operational plans already in force. This is a Polizei order, I'm afraid.'

'Herr Inspector. The Oberammergau Tunnel is literally a dead end now. In fact, the southern end was sealed up some seventy or more years ago, just after the war if my facts are correct or perhaps you know nothing of this either.'

Pfeiffer obviously had no knowledge of this so asked Mayr to get full details from the relevant department. Mayr protested in a demanding tone.

'What the fuck is going on, Herr Inspector?'

Pfeiffer composed himself and quelled Mayr's temper by asserting his authority.

'Herr Mayr. This is an international matter which requires the utmost co-operation of all concerned. I take it you understand your position. You would be foolish to continue in this vein. There is no more I can tell you for the present. Do I make myself clear, Herr Mayr!' Pfeiffer retaliated abruptly.

Mayr stood in silence as he eyed Pfeiffer. He took advantage of the moment to consider the Inspector's statement.

'Very well Inspector, I understand your position. Tell me, can I be of any assistance?' He genuinely offered.

'Yes, I'm sure you can, Herr Mayr. I have men located around the area of Schnorr's carriage, simply keeping watch you understand.'

'Yes,' Mayr answered cynically.

'The thing is, we don't wish to move in and foil any plans those people have for using the carriage. We don't know why they use it, as yet but we are sure it's significant to their operations.'

Mayr interrupted. 'How can I help, Inspector?'

'Both of us know Herr Schnorr is on duty tonight whilst the coach is on the move, correct.'

'Yes, he arrives for duty at around 21.30 usually to commence the 22.00 shift,' Mayr answered.

'Now then. The coach is due to depart apparently with the ballast train at midnight. Could you arrange for another train carrying personnel to follow a safe distance behind undetected, of course?'

Mayr thought for a few moments.

'Without Herr Schnorr's knowledge, I presume?' he asked candidly. Pfeiffer nodded.

'I would say, impossible. He would see the movement immediately on the track circuit diagram. There's no way round it I'm afraid, once a train is on the move its prescribed route is illuminated on the panel,' said Mayr.

'Then it will have to be done without Schnorr present. Would you be willing to fill his position tonight and make the necessary arrangements I've already mentioned?' asked Pfeiffer.

Mayr took a seat at the operations desk.

'What's Herr Schnorr done, Inspector? Is it drugs?' Mayr quizzed.

'I am sorry. I'm unable to comment further at present,' answered Pfeiffer bluntly.

'Inspector. Do you realise what's involved in making an addition to the working timetable under normal circumstances, never mind what you're asking me to do?'

Pfeiffer walked over and stood alongside him.

'I haven't a clue. All I need to know is can it be done and have we time to do it?'

Mayr began pencilling in the necessary arrangements as he reiterated them to Pfeiffer.

'First of all, we need coaching stock.'

'Something that can also carry any equipment we may need,' added Pfeiffer.

'Okay, freight stock should do. One van or perhaps two, have you any idea how many personnel are involved?' Mayr inquired quite naturally.

Pfeiffer coughed slightly and said in a low voice.

'You had better put together a full train, if that's possible?' He answered sheepishly.

'A full train! Are you out of your mind? What the devil are you moving, a bloody army?'

'Not quite, Herr Mayr.' He hesitated. 'Perhaps part of the local NATO detachment at Panzer Kaserne.'

'What! You are crazy or something. What in hell's name is going on?'

'I've already told you; this issue is extremely sensitive; I can give you no more information for the time being but we need the train and we need its existence to be known only to the very few. Do you understand?'

'Have you received NATO orders for this operation, Inspector?'

'Not as yet but I'll soon arrange them, you have my word.'

'I thought not. The NATO base has rail vehicles of its own. They need not request the authority's stock.'

Pfeiffer pulled him to one side.

'This is highly confidential. Keep your voice down, Herr Mayr.' He paused for a moment.

'Listen, I'll tell you what I can when the time comes, for now though, all I need is for you to organise a train that will follow that carriage when it leaves at midnight. Will you do that or must I jeopardise the operation by announcing to all and sundry? Look, I'm asking you to trust me on this, its vitally important.'

Herr Mayr looked at Pfeiffer, he could see the torment in his eyes. The man was desperate.

'I will receive official confirmation from NATO. Yes?'

'Of course. I will see to it, trust me on this.'

'Could we utilise NATO stock that would prevent any awkward questions from the networks' stock controller?' Mayr inquired.

'Yes of course. I can organise that immediately if required,' answered Pfeiffer as he thought it best to keep matters in hand.

'Where do you intend following the train from? From here or elsewhere?'

'Could we move it from the NATO base to somewhere close to here, somewhere it would not be spotted?'

'Yes, no problem. There is a junction running in from the south, we could position the train there prior to midnight.'

'Well then, what else do we need, Herr Mayr?'

'Well secondly, we need to request in advance a locomotive from the depot and a train crew to man it and the train.'

'Would Schnorr have any way of knowing about this prior to his shift starting tonight?' Pfeiffer inquired.

'Not necessarily. That's not his direct responsibility.'

'Good,' replied Pfeiffer. Mayr asked.

'What about Herr Schnorr?'

'You can leave Herr Schnorr to me, I need him out of the way this evening. What else do we need from your operational side, Herr Mayr?'

'This is where it gets a little tricky. We must advise Central Control who automatically forward the information by computer to all sub-controls throughout the prescribed route. All movements of any kind are treated in this way, that's why I received that call before. You see Inspector, no one cleared your men to be at the Oberammergau Tunnel.'

'Yes, I see the problem.'

Both Pfeiffer and Mayr continued to discuss the dilemma for some time before a draft proposal was agreed. Pfeiffer advised Herr Mayr he had to leave and make further arrangements and that he would contact him later. Mayr assured him he would make the arrangements if possible. But must receive written orders before any movement could take place. Pfeiffer assured him they would arrive.

***

Unfortunately for Larousse and Perzinski, Pfeiffer had failed to fully contemplate the controller's remark concerning the automatic computer notification system. He failed to realise the ramifications of its use throughout the network and most importantly, the fact that the section of railway under scrutiny was within the same network.

Therefore, when the main area control at München received the notification regarding unauthorised personnel in the Oberammergau Tunnel, simultaneously all other offices and departments received the same!

The consequence; within the hour, strategically located Party members had been informed to initiate "stage two alert" procedures and investigate the possible threat within the Oberammergau Tunnel. The area was already on stage one alert since General Stoltz had advised of Steinbacher's betrayal.

The exterior guard had mobilised themselves to pre-determined locations surrounding the entrances and taken up vantage points on the route from Murnau to Oberammergau. Several "Reichsbürger" members mingled with the townspeople asking simple questions or seemingly enjoying a coffee or two from Café-bars suitably located to view the movements of others.

Their orders. "Hold suspect persons and interrogate". All the exterior guards had forged police papers to assist them in their duties to the "Reichsbürger". They also had the facilities of an old building in Oberammergau in which they coordinated the defence of the base from outside interference. If anyone was found to be asking awkward questions, they were to be brought in for questioning and held.

***

Leo Perzinski was giving the officers under his command an appraisal of the on-going situation in the event Larousse and his team failed to make any progress before the suspect carriage moved off at midnight. As he was concluding, he was advised an Inspector Pfeiffer wished to talk with him on the phone.

'Perzinski speaking,' he said on picking up the phone.

'Commander, I have arranged with the Murnau railway controller, Herr Mayr, the movement of a NATO train to follow the suspect carriage tonight at midnight. He is forwarding you the prescribed route and agreed stand-by location, we need to move fast. I think they are informed of our involvement.'

Perzinski replied, 'No problem, I'll organise men and equipment immediately.'

'Any other news?' Pfeiffer inquired anxiously. 'Afraid not. Still early days though,' said Perzinski. Pfeiffer began. 'You got the message about the—?'

Perzinski interrupted. 'About tonight! Yes, we got the message okay. We are reworking something right now, just in case, you understand,' he said hopefully. 'Look Commander, this whole thing could turn nasty. There's a Nazi General and his aide wandering about in Murnau at this very moment. We don't know what their up to. All the information we have is that he was on the telephone most of the time he was in the hotel,' Pfeiffer stated, sounding uneasy.

'Inspector. I fail to see the problem here. You and this Larousse guy are convinced this odd ball railway car has something to do with getting these Nazi guys to their secret lair up in them there mountains. Well, it's simple. We guard the car and prevent its movement, that'll stop them from using it and we can send in an assault team to flush the bastard's out,' Perzinski retaliated robustly.

'No! No! That's no good. We're no closer to finding this base now after what! Forty, fifty, sixty years in the making who knows. No, I think we should consider the only option open to us.'

'And I suppose you know what that is, Inspector,' Blurted Perzinski with some annoyance.

'I have a suggestion, yes.'

'Go on, let's hear it.'

Pfeiffer began detailing his plan. Perzinski sat and listened throughout and agreed the plan had potential. Both men talked for some time analysing the logistics of the operation in terms of manpower and equipment. The only thing Perzinski was concerned about was the impact their actions would have if it were all a waste of time and there was no base to be found. Pfeiffer answered.

'If my information is correct and I believe it to be so. That carriage will be bursting at the seams with "Reichsbürger" trash at midnight tonight and all we need do is follow them right to the door. Our actions will be vindicated once the world knows we managed to prevent the rise of the so called Fourth Reich!'

'Okay, Klaus. I'm with you so long as my superiors back me. I take it yours already have.'

Klaus Pfeiffer sat silently; his head bowed for a few seconds although this could not be seen.

'Klaus!' Perzinski repeated, looking for an answer. Pfeiffer laughed a little. 'I'm going it alone, Leo. I'm sorry to say but I can't afford to trust this to any of my colleagues at H.Q. Earlier this morning, someone tipped off this General and his aide we were coming, we missed them by minutes I'm sure of it. At least that's all he or she knows, I haven't forwarded any other details of this investigation to anyone.'

'My God, man! You've got to be tearing yourself apart. You mean you're working on this alone?'

'Almost Leo. I might as well be, no one in the force likes to get involved in anything to do with the "Reichsbürger" I just got lumbered with it, call it bad luck. I do have a few men keeping a watch at the marshalling yard, that's all. They know very little of what's happening, best for their sakes.'

'Christ Klaus, you're in deep shit, boy!'

'You said it,' Pfeiffer said dejectedly. 'Oh, I almost forgot the controller, Herr Mayr must have written orders from you before he'll go along with the plan, is that a problem?'

'Hell no! I'll get a courier to take them along right away.'

Pfeiffer could feel the relief flow throughout his body. 'Thank God,' he thought. Otherwise, his whole plan would have been scuttled had Perzinski refused but then he thought he agreed far too easily considering. He prayed Perzinski wasn't simply treating this as an excuse to mobilise his troops and "kick some ass" as the Yanks had a way of putting it!

***

Almost mid-day and the search of the tunnel was halfway to completion. The verdict from both search teams to date. "Negative". Larousse and the two groups gathered around a personnel refuge almost at the centre of the tunnel.

'This is hopeless. We've completed the search almost as far as the line goes and we've found nothing. Those bloody overhead pipes are playing havoc with this equipment, you couldn't get any readings at all once we were a few meters in. Could you?' asked Larousse.

'No Sir. The interference and confines of the tunnel must be affecting the sensors, they're just going haywire like you say,' answered Malhotra.

'Modern bloody technology! A total bloody waste of time they've proved to be, eh!' Remarked Larousse angrily.

Malhotra and the others nodded and mumbled in agreement.

'We'll have to continue as planned, even though it looks as though we've drawn a blank on the idea of them having an entrance in here,' advised Larousse.

Outside, Robert and Katriana having recovered from their exertions were quickly becoming bored with simply sitting around and waiting for any radio contact. Against the explicit orders from her father, Katriana suggested they return to Oberammergau, have a bite to eat and try asking the locals a few more questions. Robert agreed, adding.

'It's better than sitting around doing nothing.'

They left a note jammed in the fallen tree as previously directed by her father should they need to, then took the car and headed for the town. When they arrived, they found it somewhat busier than before. The Café bars along the main street were well patronised with a mix of tourists and locals alike.

The shops in general seemed to be doing good trade considering the town had been by-passed. They walked through the main street casually as if tourists themselves, they had a few short conversations with several shopkeepers and passers-by, asking them what the town was like since the by-pass, had it changed much, was there ever any strange things happening around the railway or the tunnel. Their questions met with equally strange responses from most if not all concerned.

'They think we're a bit mad, I think sweetheart,' said Robert.

'I know it's so embarrassing, Robert. I feel a right fool, don't you?' She thought for a moment. 'Robert! I have a great idea!'

'What's that, darling?'

'Why don't we pretend to be journalists, I don't know from some magazine or other, like say; Cosmopolitan or Vogue or something like that. They might not look at us as if we're stupid then, what do you think?'

'Good idea! But those two are just fashion aren't they, I think. What about saying we're freelance, there's no need to name any actual magazine then, just in case.'

Katriana thought it the perfect solution, she decided it was time for lunch and a nice cup of coffee whilst they formulated a quick plan of action before taking to the street again. They made their way to a vacant table at one of the cafés.

Ordering a coffee and a Bavarian specialty dish each, they made short work of the meal to make several notes on how to tackle their first subject. Twenty minutes or so passed before they decided to quiz the waiter when he returned. Just to test his reaction.

Having asked him a few simple questions regarding any strange goings-on, in or around the tunnel, the waiter shrugged his shoulders and dismissed himself.

Robert sensed the look in his eye as he walked away.

'He like all the others thinks we're a couple of cranks. Did you see the look he gave us? So much for the cover, eh?'

'Well darling, what would you think if a total stranger asked you the same questions?' She smirked.

Before Robert could answer, a voice asked quietly behind them.

'You are asking about the Oberammergau Railway Tunnel. The railway tunnel. Ja?'

Both turned to face a man aged about fifty who had stooped down to speak to them. He was dressed perhaps a little shabby for his stature and physique which both failed to notice. He wore an old washed-out cardigan which sagged at the front from over-use of the pockets, trousers that hadn't seen a pressing in many months, the collar of his shirt was soiled and slightly torn from friction round the neck, the shoes well-worn though undamaged and unpolished, serviceable.

The man himself seemed disinterested in his appearance but his physique belied the outward appearance. His hands were firm and strong looking, his facial structure that of a fit man, the two did not add up but neither Robert nor Katriana noticed in the split second it took them to acknowledge the stranger.

Quick as a flash, Robert answered.

'Yes, that's right. We're with a publishing firm who specialise in water filtration matters and we've been told there's problems in the old railway tunnel with the water supply being contaminated. Do you know of any?'

The man's face beamed a wide grin.

'Wunderbar!' he exclaimed excitedly. Reverting to reasonable English, he prompted.

'You have been reading my work, my reports and my letters. Ja?'

'Which reports, Herr? I'm sorry, Herr?' asked Robert, requesting his name. The man's smile vanished, he asked sternly. 'You are from the magazine.

The magazine I wrote to about the tunnel.' Katriana swiftly replied.

'We're from a firm who publishes many magazines. We were sent to cover a story on the Oberammergau Tunnel, perhaps your reports are the reason it was meant to be kept under cover for a while. I'm sure you understand.'

The man's expression was one of distrust. He stood upright and moved to walk away, saying. 'You people, journalists, you are all the same!'

'Wait!' shouted Robert.

The man turned back to look.

'What can you tell us about the tunnel? You can tell us; we'll see it gets to whichever magazine you contacted. If it's any good, we'll find you a market for it?'

The man pulled up a chair and beckoned them to close in.

'I know plenty. How much will you pay?' Robert and Katriana looked at each other, more for inspiration than a figure.

'We need to see what you have before we can give you any idea of fees, Herr?'

'I have told your people time and time again. No one takes any notice.'

He bent down to whisper. 'I can't tell you anymore here, it's too crowded.' He looked around before continuing. 'I have collected masses of notes over the years, masses of evidence for you to look at, if you're genuine, that is?' He paused and glanced around yet again.

'All kinds of comings and goings. I have a few pictures even. I tell you now, you won't believe what you see but it is true, I will show you. I will prove it to you.'

Robert and Katriana both nodded and whispered in agreement to joining him. 'It is all at my house, you wish to see it, yes?' Nods of final approval were given as they stood up from the table and walked away with him. 'It will make a great story for you. You'll both be famous, you'll see,' he said with a jolly smile. Katriana asked for a moment's privacy, the man stood to one side. After a few minutes, both Robert and Katriana decided to take him up on his offer, advising him they would have to contact their superior, who as it happened was already in town, as they put it. The man agreed and asked if they had a car. 'Yes, just around the corner,' answered Robert.

'It's only a few streets away but I'm not so good on my feet these days. You don't mind, do you?'

'Not at all, Herr?'

'Just call me Max for now,' he answered, then shuffled off with them towards the corner.

'You can call him when you get there, you can give the directions then, that's the best plan, eh,' suggested Max. They both thought it best and agreed.

The three boarded the car and Max directed them along a few back-streets and stopped at a rather dilapidated double wooden door set into the stonework of a once impressive building, now sadly in a state of decay.

'One moment and I shall open the gate. Please drive straight in, I'll close it behind you. I must have my privacy, you understand.'

They looked at each other with eyebrows raised as the doors were being forced open with a fair bit of effort from Max as they wondered if indeed, they had made a wise decision. The stranger seemed genuine enough, though something bothered Robert about his appearance or was it his mannerism, he wasn't sure.

'I don't know about this, Katriana. I think we should contact your father before we go inside, there's something strange about him but I can't put my finger on it.'

'He's just, well odd I suppose. Let's see what he's got first Robert, I would hate to get papa thinking we were on to something to find it was all a waste of time, he's got so little time left now.'

'Yes, okay. Five, ten minutes at the most. If he doesn't come up with anything, we'll make our excuses and leave, okay.' She agreed.

With the wooden doors opened, Robert drove the car through and entered a fair-sized cobbled courtyard, glancing quickly around them they could see that the four walls surrounding them all had numerous large double wooden door entrances, perhaps garages.

The whole place resembled some sort of military establishment most of which looked to be in the same state of decay throughout. Above them was a balcony to the left and right and simply windows to the front and rear. There was an old clock tower above the entrance, which had also sadly succumbed to the effects of negligence and nature.

'I'm sorry about the facilities. We were once a powerful family in this area but times change. I simply refuse to part with the old family home. My home. What's left of it? Come, follow me, I live at the rear of the house now, it's a lot quieter.'

'House?' Robert whispered to Katriana, twisting his lips in disapproval. They both raised their eyes again to each other, thinking to themselves that Max was no more than an eccentric.

Robert nudged Katriana and said, 'Let's forget it, he's a nutter.'

'No Robert we can't do that, we'll stay a few minutes as we agreed. He's probably lonely. Anyway, he just might know something.'

'I doubt it,' replied Robert as they followed Max to the door.

'I never find the right key when I want it,' said Max as he fumbled with a large bunch. Eventually, he inserted one key into the upper lock and turned it, then another into the lower lock, turned it and pushed the door open. Still fumbling, this time for the light switch, he apologised for his delay saying his eyesight was failing him also. Robert couldn't help making an audible sigh. Katriana tugged at him.

'Robert!' She whispered hard from embarrassment.

Switching on the light, which was of low wattage and therefore of little use, Max closed the door behind him and fumbled for the key to the next door.

'Only one more, sorry about this,' he said. Then turned the last lock and pushed the door open. 'Please, go through while I switch on the lights.'

Robert and Katriana stepped cautiously into the room giving that the illumination was negligible. Suddenly, the door slammed behind them with an almighty crash as if steel slamming against steel, then almost immediately the sound of an automatic lock was heard clunk into place as the lights were switched on to reveal a hive of human activity together with a reception committee!

'Oh shit!' said Robert softly whilst Katriana grabbed his arm. 'What's all this then?' Robert asked casually. 'Max! What's going on? Where are you?' He shouted as he moved to step forward. Immediately, two men from the reception committee lunged towards him and restrained him.

'Now just a minute. I don't know who you people are but we're not here to cause you any bother.'

A few agonising moments passed in silence as both Robert and Katriana surveyed the bustling scene in front of them. There were men hurriedly packing papers, books, computers, equipment of all kinds and stacking them in crates and boxes for removal. A few computer terminals were still active as men and women sat entering and processing data as required without even heeding their presence.

Robert looked round the room with his eyes only. He daren't move his head. There were no windows, only two doors, the one they came through and another leading off to the right. The walls and ceiling were covered in sound-proofing material, obviously to prevent the outside world knowing of the existence of any activity within rather than ensuring the neighbours were not disturbed.

There were boards and charts being taken off the walls, communication equipment being wrenched out rather than removed, nothing was being overlooked, when they vacated the premises, they wanted no one to know anyone was ever there.

Katriana tugged at Robert's arm and nodded towards the rear of the long narrow room. Robert focussed on the subject matter; it was quite incredible; several men were busying themselves clearing all traces of debris left behind.

Everything! Behind them others were scattering materials randomly over the floor from wheeled containers as they dragged them along ahead of them.

The floor, which in turn was being carpeted in a thick layer of dust being blown from a machine of sorts. The distance was too great. Robert had difficulty focussing on the items being deposited but he felt sure they were old, pretty old.

He could see old newspapers, the paper itself yellowed from age and exposure to the light. Magazines, note-paper, partial cigarette packs, wrappers of various kinds, cigarette ends and as the men came closer, what looked like old used matchsticks and so on, general detritus which is left when a building is closed.

'Nothing was in great numbers, just enough,' Robert thought, 'to convince outsiders that no one had used this building in a very long time.' This was their intention. Robert concluded. Whoever "they" were? It didn't take much thought, they had to be the Nazis!

'Where are we, Robert? What is going on here?' Whispered Katriana with fear in her voice.

Robert shook his head.

'God knows, sweetheart. But I think we're in deep shit if you'll pardon the expression,' he answered, then stepped forward.

'Look. There's got to be some mistake here. We haven't done anything wrong,' he protested.

'Then why are you here?' Came a voice he recognised.

'Max! Is that you?' Robert turned to the sound of Max's voice, the man guarding him dealt him a severe blow to the stomach, Robert saw it coming, tensed his stomach muscles but feigned the expression of pain as he thought of Katriana, he couldn't take them all alone. He dropped to the floor as if in agony but not so.

'Robert! You bastard, Max! You shit,' screamed Katriana. The other guard held her back.

'What's going on?' said Robert, struggling to raise himself or so he hoped it seemed.

Max entered the room, dressed in the uniform of a Nazi Colonel. He laughed aloud. 'Ha-ha-ha! You are as good an actor as I, Herr?'

'You know why we're here; you told us you had information on the railway tunnel, remember?' Robert turned again, this time the guard allowed him. 'Holy shit!' He said under his breath. 'What's this? Amateur night, what the hell's going on here?'

'Your name, Herr?' Demanded Max.

'My name is Cameron, Robert Cameron and this is my wife and assistant, Kate.' Robert reacted quickly, he instinctively knew he daren't mention Katriana's name was Larousse, God help her if he did, God help her if they found out!

'We are here to investigate claims of there being a serious water pollution problem within the tunnel which according to sources, requires excessive maintenance work.'

'I do not believe you, Herr Cameron,' shouted Max.

'I couldn't care less what you believe. Why are you dressed in some kind of Nazi uniform, anyway, is this some kind of pantomime?' Robert quizzed, attempting to bluff their way through.

'Do you take me for a fool? Herr Cameron?' Bellowed Max.

'I don't know what to take you for, Max. Remember, you were the one to invite us here, we never asked to come.'

'Enough! We know there are others searching the tunnel at this very moment, you do not fool me, Herr Cameron. Take them away! We'll deal with them later once we have their comrades,' instructed Max.

'You've got this all wrong, Max. Look, I can prove it.'

Max simply waved his arm and Robert and Katriana were led away protesting to a secure and of course, soundproof room. Their fate hanging in the balance.

Chapter Nine

Fortunately for Robert and Katriana, Herr Oberst, Max Wittenberg had no time for interrogation now. The stage two alert ensured that he and whatever men could be spared from reverting the old building to a scene of dereliction were about to challenge the intruders in the railway tunnel, they were the priority for the moment.

Max having yet again changed into his civilian attire, not those of the eccentric but those of his regular choice. He instructed his subordinates to maintain a constant vigil on the two prisoners. He emphasised the constant need to listen in on their conversation and report anything of significance directly to him.

He ordered a small section of the room to remain looking like an office environment and the rear screened off for the time being. He then advised he would be joining the others outside to "hold" those in the tunnel and bring them in for questioning.

He ordered a car from one of the concealed bays in the courtyard and instructed a guard to move the prisoner's car into its vacant space. He and three others then proceeded cautiously out through the doors and headed for the northern end of the Oberammergau Tunnel where he rounded up his men keeping watch over the entrance.

Marcel and Gerrard were still on the lookout at opposing sides of the tunnel for anything suspicious and had agreed to move from their positions nearer to the tunnel mouth due to the fact their radio communication equipment had proved to be useless the further the team headed into the depths of the tunnel.

The only method both had left of contact, was the use of handheld air horns supplied as a back-up, which they were to sound to warn those inside of any activity and should communication fail, two long blast every fifteen minutes would serve to advise all was satisfactory.

Marcel noticed the unmarked car draw up close to the lineside fencing and three well-built men in their mid-twenties alight, they were followed by a middle-aged man who began gesturing instructions to the others as they climbed the fence and headed towards him. All the men were neatly dressed in differing suits and gave the outward impression of being Polizei or similar and all appeared to be carrying weapons other than the older man.

Marcel decided to face the situation and bluff his way through as they had pre-planned beforehand.

'Guten Tag!' Exclaimed the older man as he approached, holding an identification wallet, then asked him in German the reason for his being there. Marcel advised him his knowledge of German was very limited. The man repeated the inquiry in commendable English and announced himself as, Chief Inspector Neugart of the Polizei. Anti-Terrorist division. Marcel answered.

'Emergency inspection of the water supply pipes, Chief Inspector. Serious complaints of water quality have arisen. There's a team of engineers inside carrying out a visual. I'm the lookout. To advise if a train is approaching or anyone such as yourself should arrive, you understand,' Marcel answered, in truth, rather unconvincingly.

'Why were we not informed of this?' asked DI Neugart.

'No idea. We were sent here earlier this morning direct from München.'

'From München! Nonsense! I am in direct contact with München Control and I would have been given advance notice of your arrival,' Neugart challenged angrily.

'Look. I'm only doing my job. There's an emergency remember, we're here to inspect the supply, that's all I know. What's the problem? What's this got to do with Anti-terrorist Polizei?' Marcel answered calmly.

'Emergency repairs authorised by München! Do you take me for a fool, you don't even speak the language! How many of you are there?' asked Neugart, avoiding answering Marcel's query.

Neugart continued to demand answers from him in an onerous tone. Marcel became alarmed, his gut feeling told him something was far from right with the stranger's method of questioning and the fact the other three men had cautiously, systematically, encircled him whilst the questioning proceeded.

This, he concluded was not the actions of any authority, anti-terrorist or otherwise. Something was very wrong, their assertion inexorable to his explanation. He had to think quickly, he had to think of Larousse. He daren't undermine Larousse's position by giving their small number, especially as the man had obviously no knowledge of such, so Marcel decided to embellish the facts a little.

He answered, 'Oh, there's me and my opposite number at the other end, then there's another two forward lookouts at one and two kilometres either way. Then there's the other two, one in each sub-control, north and south, just in case we must halt the supply completely, you understand. There's the support team standing by with the emergency repair train at Murnau, that's about fifteen kilometres north of here.'

'I know where Murnau is! Get on with it!' Neugart interrupted in temper. 'Sorry. Well, that leaves our own team in the tunnel.'

'And you are how many?' he asked impatiently.

'Oh! There's fifteen of them in there, they'll be having a break about now I expect,' he said, glancing at his wristwatch.

'Fifteen! Are you sure?' Blasted Neugart, sounding exacerbated. 'Oh, quite sure. The supervisor and two teams of seven.'

'Any women in your little group?' He inquired candidly.

'Women! Wish there was. No. No women,' Marcel answered whilst pondering the reason why he had posed the question in the first place.

'You have no women, no one named Kate for instance?'

'Kate? I don't even know a woman called Kate.' Marcel's heart missed a beat; he could only imagine Kate to mean Katriana! Where did he get the name from? It was too much of a coincidence, the situation frightening. As he pondered, Neugart announced.

'You will have to go with my men to headquarters, we must verify your story. For security reasons, I'm sure you understand,' he said authoritatively.

'I'm sorry but I can't leave my post. I'm the lookout. For reasons of safety, I'm sure you understand!' Replied Marcel ardently. He needed time, time to get a message to Larousse, time to ensure Katriana was safe. But there was no time.

Neugart removed his identification from the inside pocket of his jacket and presented him with a cursory glance. Marcel could but read the name and rank before it was folded up and replaced in his top pocket.

'You are under arrest. Take him to HQ.'

Before he could say anything, Neugart signalled to one of his men to take charge of the equipment Marcel was holding.

'Do not worry. If what you say is true, you have nothing to fear. Hans here, will take your place until we verify your story. Now please come with us,' asked Neugart civilly.

Marcel's indecisiveness was apparent to all but himself, he knew he couldn't take on the Polizei, nor did he know if indeed they were genuine. He was sure they were impostors one minute and not the next, what if, the German authorities had advised the "Reichsbürger" of the concealed base situation he pondered.

He decided to go along with them but had one card up his sleeve, a way of warning Larousse, a way they surely could not question. He decided it was the only chance he had and he had to try.

'One moment, Chief Inspector,' he said. 'Yes, what is it?' asked Neugart.

'Your man, does he know the signals?' He queried. 'I'm sure he'll manage,' he replied abruptly.

'No! You must make the correct signals otherwise there might be confusion,' Marcel announced with conviction.

Neugart, who simply wished to get him away decided it would be easier and more convincing if he let him advise them.

'Okay, inform Hans of the signals. You take note of these,' he said to Hans. 'One long blast of at least five seconds, followed by two short blasts of two seconds if it's an emergency. Our teams have installed sensors to take readings and if those prove to be dangerous, we must advise those in the tunnel.' Marcel was indeed playing for time and he knew it.

He continued. 'Three short blasts of two seconds if it's an inquiry such as from an official like yourself that I can't deal with, such as this situation which I have to say is becoming a little disturbing and finally one long blast of three seconds followed by two of two seconds if it's simply a lack of communication via normal methods. Have you got that? Shall I write it down for you?' Truth was Marcel doubted even he could remember the nonsense he'd just rambled.

'Hans?' Hans nodded in agreement.

'There will be no need, Hans has it in hand. Please follow me.' Marcel was guided away by the arm to the waiting car.

Of course, the horn codes were a figment of his own imagination, he only hoped Larousse would notice there had been a significant change to the arranged double blast and act upon it if necessary.

Marcel was driven to the same location where Robert and Katriana were being held. Neugart continued to question Marcel regarding the contaminated water inspection until they were upon the double doors, where he began enlightening him to the fact the outside of the station bore no resemblance to a Polizei station for obvious anti-terrorist reasons. Marcel began to feel uneasy about the whole situation as the doors were opened and the car drove through into the courtyard.

Once inside the building, he became confused as the sight of a dozen or so personnel working at their desks and computer terminals, others plying back and forth with papers and such. He was allowed a few moments to digest the scene after which he concluded that he was indeed under scrutiny of the anti-terrorist division. Perhaps he'd been over cautious giving the circumstances.

Neugart ushered him to a desk where an officer began taking his personal details in the correct and proper manner adopted by regular Polizei personnel, whereupon Neugart informed him he would be taken to an interview room where he would be questioned further, and his story double checked.

Marcel, even though almost convinced all was above board, decided he should avoid telling them the truth about the tunnel, simply because the Polizei themselves could not be trusted given the possible "Reichsbürger" connection. He was duly led away to a room and locked in.

Max had taken the car again and headed back to the tunnel, gathering his men from there, he closed in on the portal.

'Where's the lookout?' he exclaimed.

'Sir, he's gone inside, he went in shortly after you left, saying he heard voices,' answered one of his men.

'Damn it! I ordered you all stay at your posts! There's nothing for it, we'll have to go in and flush them out. No rough stuff, we're supposed to be Polizei, remember!'

Max and the others began the slow task of walking the tunnel.

Larousse and Chambers, realising something had either gone wrong as no horn signal had been sounded for at least twenty plus minutes, perhaps some new information had come to light which warranted immediate attention, both turned about face and headed for the exit. He confided to Chambers he had not given Marcel any specific instructions regarding contact in case of difficulty, an oversight he admitted he could come to regret and therefore could only assume there was a degree of urgency relating to the silence of the warning horn.

The tunnel search now deemed abandoned; they made their way swiftly northward with apprehension as time passed. Carl and Sub-Lieutenant Malhotra had also heard no 15-minute horn and had decided to proceed with haste to the portal, they of course were somewhat closer than Larousse and Chambers.

Heading swiftly, Carl and Malhotra soon reached a position from which, with caution, they could observe any movement at the tunnel mouth. Malhotra suggested they act cautiously until they could at least see Marcel or Gerrard and that all looked safe.

Thirty or so minutes later, the figure of a tall man, much taller and stockier than Marcel stepped into the portal and silhouetted himself against the arch as he sounded a differing tune on the air horn. Both Carl and Malhotra knew for certain something had gone wrong.

There was no sign of Marcel but who was the man blowing the warnings on the horn. They agreed between them that he bore no resemblance to any of their party.

Luckily the Oberammergau Tunnel was constructed relatively straight with only the slightest of curves within. Malhotra suggested they retreat to the first curve and pray Larousse and Chambers had heard the blasts and had taken similar action.

Their assumption was correct, as they came out of the bend, they could see the powerful beams of light from the two high intensity lights coming towards them, though still some considerable distance away. Chambers noticed the lights of Malhotra and Carl in the distance and signalled to Larousse to stop for a moment.

'It must be Carl and Malhotra,' said Larousse, somewhat breathless. 'Yes. I'm sure it is Sir,' answered Chambers.

'Come on, let's go. Something's not right, I can feel it,' muttered Larousse anxiously.

'May I make a suggestion, Sir?' Inquired Chambers. 'Yes, of course.'

'Switch off our lights for a moment then signal Malhotra in Morse code, both of us can read it without any trouble, they may know something we don't!'

'Excellent suggestion! Ask them, have they seen Marcel, and do they know what's going on!' Instructed Larousse.

Chambers carried out his instruction. The reply came back. "Marcel gone. Stranger in his place".

Larousse was worried by the reply, he told Chambers to advise them to await their reaching them before continuing. This he did and they replied affirmative.

Several minutes later, Larousse and Chambers had caught up with Carl and Malhotra. They were discussing the situation and the best way to handle it, realising that all they knew for sure was that Marcel had been removed and his position covered by someone unknown to them. Larousse began to study the facts available.

He had eliminated the German Polizei and the railway authorities due to Pfeiffer. He also eliminated Perzinski and his troops, all of whom had no reason to remove Marcel. The only feasible alternative could be an outside authority becoming involved. The unofficial alternative could only be the Nazis.

The four men crouched down aside a refuge to discuss the best method of escape if in fact the Nazi's were indeed behind the disappearance of Marcel. After a short while, they heard footsteps. Larousse looked at the others with dismay. Shaking his head, he commented.

'It must be the railway authorities after all. It was a long shot anyway.'

'I don't know about that, Sir. It's Gerrard, look!' said Carl, a little surprised. Gerrard was heading towards them, beckoning them to join him.

'Come-on! Come-on!' He said in a low but demanding tone.

Larousse and the others took no time collecting their equipment and reached Gerrard. He advised the group Marcel was no longer at his position and it looked very much like Polizei had taken him away. Once in relative safety, Larousse asked Gerrard if he knew what was going on. Gerrard described the fact he'd noticed several unsavoury characters lurking around the area close to the tunnel mouth watching every move.

When he saw Marcel being led away, he decided there had to be a problem and it would be safer to go inside than stay behind. He also felt sure that once he'd disappeared inside, it was not long after he began to be followed.

Larousse decided to split the team up and make their way south through the tunnel. He judged that there must be an old exit in the distance and if it was blocked, they had equipment to unblock it. His final orders to all were to exercise extreme caution and rendezvous at the river with his daughter and Robert.

From where, they would attempt to locate the whereabouts of Marcel. He noted they only had eight hours left before the suspect train left Murnau at midnight.

Max Wittenberg (Alias DI Neugart) sensing their pursuit of the unauthorised men in the tunnel was doomed to failure after half an hour, decided to retreat to the base and question the three prisoners. He left one volunteer to walk the full length alone and report back.

Returning to the secluded building, he was advised of a notification from General Stoltz, decoded to read.

Tighten security immediately. Transport of strategic personnel at 23.59 hrs ETA 01.00hrs Ensure personnel are armed and in position. Standby to activate defences. Ensure reception arrangements are in order. No mistakes, Herr Oberst.

His second in command, Hans, advised all was indeed in order and that all personnel had been deployed barring the reception guards, as was normal practice. Max instructed him to ensure they were alert in their duties as the future of the "Reichsbürger" movement depended upon the success of the operation tonight.

He conveyed his concern regarding the situation in the tunnel, whilst speculating upon the growing possibility of outside intervention. The fact that an unknown group were in the tunnel and the two he caught earlier asking questions seemed more than coincidental, of that he was sure, especially so close to the operation deadline itself.

'Have you heard anything from those two?' Max asked, referencing the voice recordings.

'Only the woman, she sounds worried. She keeps talking about her father and what he'll have to say when he finds out.'

'Women! Her father is the least of her worries and the man?'

'He's very cool. Keeps telling her it will be okay.'

'The other man, has he said anything?'

'Not a word. He just sits there,' replied his second.

'Right, we'll play this Polizei nonsense for another few of hours or so with the other man. Separate those two and question the woman first, she appears to be the most nervous.'

'Herr Oberst. Let me deal with them now and save us some time,' pleaded Hans.

'No! We cannot be sure they're not who they claim to be, we only have some seven hours left before the deadline, we cannot allow any further outside interference. We shall keep all three of them here until the test is completed, after which we shall have to deal with them,' instructed Max. His aide reluctantly agreed and went below to carry out his orders.

***

Klaus Pfeiffer and Herr Mayr had completed their arrangements with Perzinski for the procurement of a locomotive with crew to haul the NATO train to follow behind the suspect carriage when it departed at midnight. The train had reached the dedicated siding near the Oberammergau branch junction and was on stand-by awaiting orders.

Pfeiffer contacted his few trustworthy men staking out the railway yard for an update on the situation there. "Negative movement" came the reply. Pfeiffer could only assume they were awaiting the cover of darkness and instructed them to maintain a constant vigil. He subsequently contacted Perzinski, enquiring if Larousse had made any report to date. The reply was "Negative" again.

Perzinski expressed his concern at the length of time Larousse had been out of contact and that he feared for his and his team's safety. Pfeiffer agreed there was indeed cause for concern with under seven hours before the departure of the train from Murnau. Though he insisted there was to be no military intervention until they found the underground base, as had been the agreement.

Perzinski agreed in principle to comply, then informed Pfeiffer he had taken the step of dispatching a detachment of men and equipment to close in on the area under the auspices of a NATO exercise, under direct orders from his superiors. The Admiralty had thought it best considering the time factor regarding the movement of the suspect carriage and had requested their mobilisation forthwith.

Pfeiffer could do nothing regarding NATO orders. He merely accepted the given situation and advised he was returning to Murnau Control and would maintain contact.

Simultaneously, Larousse and the two teams had by now reached the old southern portal. It had been bricked up as expected without any means of egress they could only use their explosives to blast a way out. The two naval personnel carried out the task within a few minutes and the group exited the tunnel confines into an overgrown area of dense bracken, trees, etc.

Utilising cutting equipment they carried in their packs; they reached a mountain road around half a kilometre from the exit. They cautiously approached the road and still wearing the reflective jackets, they easily flagged down a passing vehicle, which was a large Mercedes box-van.

The driver naturally expected some accident or other had occurred on the mountainous road and was shocked then to find five men emerge from the bushes. Larousse asked politely if he would take them to Oberammergau; the shocked driver agreed saying it was indeed fortunate the van was empty to fit them all in. Larousse and Chambers sat in the cab, the others in rear.

Larousse on checking the map throughout the journey halted the driver close to where André with the Range Rover was parked some distance from the northern tunnel entrance. He bid the driver good evening and passed him a 100 euro note asking him not to breathe a word of this to anyone for twenty-four hours. The driver who had been pretty shook up on seeing all manner of military grade equipment loaded, breathed a sigh of relief and agreed.

Satisfied they were not being watched the team made their way to the riverside rendezvous. Larousse's heart dropped when there was no sight of Katriana, Robert or the car. Taking a risk of making radio contact with Perzinski, he inquired if his daughter or Robert had made any communication.

The reply was of course "negative". Larousse was outwardly perplexed. 'First Marcel. Now my daughter and that fool Cameron! We must find them.

If those Nazi bastards have harmed her, I'll tear them apart limb for limb! I promise you!' He screamed.

'We'll find them, Sir. Don't worry,' said Chambers with the others backing his statement.

'They're on to us. That's for sure now. Just over six hours to go, if we don't find this bloody base before then, God help us all!' Submitted Larousse.

He took the calculated decision that the Nazi's would be on the lookout for them, especially close to the tunnel. He opted to mount a short surveillance on the northern end seeing as it was closest to the town where he surmised, they must have a base of some kind with Marcel having been taken from there.

Moving to a vantage point in the hills affording a view of the tunnel entrance without causing suspicion, they had a panoramic view of the town of Oberammergau. Looking down upon it, you would be hard pressed to believe there could be anything as sinister as an underground Nazi base nestling beneath such an idyllic location.

The town of Oberammergau lay just north of the Zugspitze Mountain, at 2963 meters, this was also the tallest mountain in Germany and in the Tiroler Zugspitze Arena group of mountains. As you descended the pass from Ettal into the valley, you reached the town of Oberammergau, a small quaint village with a population of about five thousand.

The village is very close to the German Austrian border and best known for its woodcarvings and the finely frescoed buildings were indeed a beautiful sight. A passion play is performed here every ten years which brings in many tourists. There are several Ski Schools located in the area with a proliferation of cable cars, ski-lifts and chairlifts were commonly known as the "circus" and provided skiers access to many slopes surrounding the area.

In the summer months, the town was also a popular holiday resort being favoured by hill walkers and climbers wishing to tackle the Tirol Arena. All this history and the beauty of the location meant very little to Larousse and the team with the situation becoming more critical by the minute.

After thirty minutes or so, Larousse became impatient for something to develop, something which would assist him in finding his daughter. He decided to head into the town with Carl to attempt to locate the missing car, hoping it would lead them to the Nazi's lair.

Carl had suggested the move, feeling somewhat responsible, as his prime duty was the safety of Katriana. Larousse assured him he was not to blame and that if anyone was at fault, it was himself or that bloody fool Cameron. With that, the two of them drove down into Oberammergau and began the painstaking search of every street for the missing car. He had instructed Chambers and the others to maintain vigilance on the tunnel and radio any movement direct.

***

Pfeiffer contacted Perzinski to confirm that Herr Mayr had organised the train movement and that he should ensure the NATO railway vehicles were equipped and stabled in readiness for the deadline. Perzinski advised this had already been done and he was awaiting orders.

Mayr was still reluctant to fully comply before knowing all the facts, he demanded to know what was going on and he demanded he had a right to know.

Pfeiffer took him to one side.

'Your grandfather. Was he in the army or—?'

'The Luftwaffe,' Mayr interrupted, adding. 'He was an air traffic controller just as I am a railway controller. Now enough of this. I demand to know what is going on!'

'One more question, Herr Mayr,' pleaded Pfeiffer. Mayr nodded.

'Your views on the war. Would you say we as a people were right in our actions?'

'I would be proud to fight for my country. All true Germans would say the same. But no, I cannot condone the actions of our people under Hitler, not all of them you understand, only those indoctrinated to his principles. Many mistakes were made, and I feel ashamed over the way things got out of control. What happened to the Jews and such, it was barbaric.'

'Very well, Herr Mayr. I'll tell you the truth but it must go no further. Do I have your word?' Pfeiffer presented Mayr his hand. Mayr reached out and shook it.

'You have my word as my honour, Herr Inspector.'

Pfeiffer spent the next few minutes condensing the details of the situation to Mayr. After which Mayr had to sit down for a while. The blood had drained from his face, leaving him almost grey in colour. Pfeiffer wondered if the shock had been too much for him to take and asked him if he needed medical assistance. Mayr refused and attempted to compose himself under the strain.

Once he regained his equanimity, he confessed that all along, even as far back as when Herr Schnorr implemented his "toy", he thought something illegal had been going on but nothing like what Pfeiffer had just described. Mayr then assured Pfeiffer he would assist in any way possible. He only had to ask.

The only thing left for Herr Mayr to do was to ensure Herr Schnorr would not be missed at the office tonight, so he fabricated an urgent leave request which was granted by the senior controller at München provided he had someone to cover his post. Mayr obviously volunteered or so it seemed.

***

Max Wittenberg and others had begun interrogating the three prisoners; Robert, Katriana and Marcel individually for some time now without any joy. Neither of them would stray from the basic story they first told. Max felt the urge to believe the couples story though it was impossible to verify without causing concern, he of course could not just let them go, they would have to wait until the morning, after the test, nothing could jeopardise this.

The other man's story however could not be true. Had they been engineers as he stated, they would not have absconded from the tunnel using explosives when he and his men approached. He decided to allow Hans Fassbinder, his second in command to question him alone.

Marcel was handcuffed and removed from the faked interview room and taken to an interrogation room below ground. Until now, he had almost come to believe he was in the custody of an anti-terrorist Secret Polizei Unit. That is, until he was frog marched along the damp, dimly lit underground corridor to a room where he was thrown in and the door slammed closed.

He stumbled to his knees in the dirt below him, he could see nothing and the room was in total darkness. Rising to his feet, he walked slowly, cautiously, consciously aware that circumstances had taken a turn for the worse. He slowly stepped along the floor, feeling his way towards a wall.

Once he reached a corner, he paced out the size of the room, about four meters by six meters, as he stood contemplating his situation. Suddenly, piercing jets of water struck his body, coming at him seemingly from all directions. He moved around the room attempting to dodge the high-pressure jets, after a short while he realised it was useless.

He sat down where he'd stood and covered his head to prevent the force hitting his eyes and ears. The force was tremendous, he had no choice but to suffer the pounding.

Fassbinder closed the water valves off after five or so minutes, then opened the door and switched on the light. Two bare bulbs dangled from a simply assembled cord with basic bayonet fittings, they hung around three to four meters above his head.

'Are you ready to talk now?' he asked. 'Who are you and what were you and those others doing in the tunnel?' He demanded.

Marcel raised his head. 'Go to hell!' He replied.

Fassbinder smiled as he reached for a switch outside in the corridor. Turning the round dial slightly clockwise, it energised a circuit, which sent a current of electricity through the flooded floor. Marcel was dancing with pain, jumping up and down, in and out of the water, he looked for something to grab hold of above him and to his dismay, there was nothing he could reach.

After what seemed like an eternity, Fassbinder turned off the current. Marcel desperately needed to sit down but was too afraid to do so in case the current was turned on again.

'Why are you doing this? I've told you all I know,' he pleaded.

'You know perfectly well why. If you won't talk perhaps, I can persuade your young lady friend or her accomplice to. Eh?'

'Young lady? I don't know any women from around here.'

'Oh, you must know this one. She's very pretty at the moment, anyway. Can you picture her now? Her name is Kate, she has long brown hair, a fine figure and as I said, she's very pretty. For now.'

'I'm telling you, I don't know anyone from around here.'

'Who said she's from around here? I would say she's French, perhaps. Maybe I'm wrong, maybe she's English, eh? Then there's her husband, they tell us they're from some magazine or other, he is English without doubt.'

Marcel's heart sank, he could only mean Larousse's daughter and Robert Cameron. They must have been captured too. He concluded. The switch went on again and Marcel resumed his dance.

'Oh, what a shame, you were dancing so well before, perhaps you need a partner. I shall introduce you to our young lady guest, you can dance together. Eh!' Laughed Fassbinder.

Marcel slumped to the floor as the switch was returned to off. 'You barbarian!' he exclaimed loudly.

'Such aggression. I hope you have better manners when you're introduced to your dancing partner,' Fassbinder replied as he shut the door, switched off the light and gave a swift bolt of current once again.

When he returned five minutes later, Marcel was opposite the door kneeling in the dirty water stooped over in the middle of the room, looking decidedly worse for wear. Fassbinder opened the door and pulled Katriana to his side. Marcel looked up at them, giving Fassbinder a contemptuous glare.

Katriana, once realising in the dull glow from the hallway, only took a sharp intake of breath and lifted her hands to her face in shock, at the same time showing she was handcuffed also. She shouted out.

'What are you doing to that man?' Katriana had wisely maintained her "no knowledge" position.

Marcel was indeed a sight, he and his clothes covered in the filthy water he was kneeling in, the room flooded up to just above his knees, his hands buried in front of him seemingly supporting him from falling over. Katriana was devastated at the sight of Marcel in such obvious pain; she broke down, crying. 'Enough of that!' shouted Fassbinder as he pulled her further forward.

Laughing and jesting, he shouted at Marcel.

'Here is your dancing partner? Kate, why don't you join him, I feel sure you know each other already.' Fassbinder laughed.

Katriana turned in horror as Fassbinder energised the circuit once again. Marcel rose to his feet quickly and began jumping in agony. Fassbinder switched off the power and Marcel dropped to his knees, seemingly exhausted whilst Katriana sobbed even more for him.

'Very touching. Now for the last time! Will you tell me what I want to know?' He shouted as he held Katriana tightly by the arm, almost forcing her into the room.

'Okay, okay. I'll tell you,' Marcel said breathlessly as he looked up at him in the gloom.

Fassbinder was pleased with himself; he reached for the light-switch and turned it on. Immediately, the fuse blew and together the lights in the room and the corridor were put out of action.

It was what Marcel had been waiting for. While he had gone to fetch Katriana, he had thrown plentiful handfuls of water at the light fittings in the room and as soon as the lights were switched on, they short circuited and blew the fuse. Instantaneously as the fuse blew, Marcel tossed handfuls of mud in the general direction of the door then lunged forward at his captor.

After a short struggle in the dark, Marcel knocked him a blow to the head with the edge of his handcuffs, which rendered him semi-unconscious. He bundled him into the room and removed the handcuff key from his pocket and cuffed Hans' arms behind his back, he then slammed the door closed.

He couldn't resist the temptation of switching on the current, which he hoped would be on a different circuit and letting him feel the pain he obviously relished in whilst administering it to others. Unfortunately for Fassbinder, Marcel had no idea the current flow was graduated on the switch and administered the full force. In a few moments, Fassbinder lay dead in the muddy water although no one knew this.

Marcel's only thought was to get Larousse's daughter to safety. In the darkness of the corridor, he could see nothing. He called her name softly.

'I'm over here, Marcel. Please help me! We must get Robert out; they're holding him in a room upstairs.'

'We can't risk going back there on our own Mademoiselle, there's too many of them, we must escape somehow and find your father before sleeping beauty in there awakens,' he said. That's assuming he's not been captured too. He thought but dared not mention.

'Come on!' said Marcel as he took hold of her hand and guided her along the wall.

They fumbled around in the dark, feeling their way along the corridor to the end where another door led into a similarly filthy room with a stale dusty smell in the air.

'What's that smell?' asked Katriana.

'Coal! We're in a coal cellar! That means there must be a hatch or something leading to the outside. Feel for the stack,' he urged as he let go his grip.

'Stack of what?' Whispered Katriana. 'The stack of coal, Mademoiselle.'

'Why?' She asked in wonder.

Marcel realised Larousse's daughter had in all probability never seen the inside of a coal cellar in her life and no doubt she would have no knowledge of delivery methods either.

'Please, Mademoiselle. If there's enough coal in here, we may be able to climb the pile and reach the delivery hatch. It's our only chance,' he whispered.

'Oh, I see? I think. I'll go this way.'

Without the aid of light, they cautiously crept through the darkened cellar, occasionally stumbling over pieces of coal previously scattered around. Inside the cellar, there was several pillars supporting the building above, as they negotiated their way around, Katriana tripped and let out a low scream.

'Schhhh,' urged Marcel, hoping to quieten her.

Katriana getting up on her feet she felt for the item she had tripped over, she tugged at Marcel's hand.

'Look Marcel, it's a shovel.'

'Okay, keep hold of it,' whispered Marcel.

'Look! There's a chink of light over there, up at the top of the wall!' she said elatedly.

Marcel couldn't believe their luck. It was indeed one of the coal hatches and with good fortune, their passport to freedom.

Time was of the essence now. With Fassbinder next door who may be missed or raise the alarm at any moment, they hurriedly climbed the coal heap to reach just short of the opening. Quickly, they piled the coal up from either side using the shovel until Marcel could reach the doors.

Gently pushing them apart, his hopes grew for their impending escape only to be dashed by the sight of an old rusty chain retaining them from the outside.

'What's wrong?' asked Katriana as Marcel sat down, holding his head in his hands.

'It's chained up. We can't get through,' he said with despondency. 'Let me try,' said Katriana.

'It's no good, Mademoiselle. We'll have to find another way.'

'Well at least let me try, Marcel. We've nothing to lose. Come on, hold me up,' she said.

Marcel felt slightly embarrassed as he put his arms around her waist and lifted her up.

'Higher Marcel! I can see someone. He's walking a little dog. It must be the street outside!' She cried with joy.

'Bitte! Bitte!' She shouted "please" in German as Marcel pushed her up under her bottom, by now he was red to the face, even though he could see nothing in the darkness, he could feel an area of her buttocks.

'Please mademoiselle, hurry. I can't keep you up much longer the coal is moving under me,' he advised as he struggled to keep balance on the shifting coals.

Katriana shouted again, a little louder this time. 'Bitte! Bitte!'

The man she could see walking his dog was looking everywhere for the source of the call, the dog was barking and pulling its owner in the general direction. Katriana, fearful he would fail to spot her, reached down, removed her shoe and banged on the underside of the steel cover.

Marcel by now was acutely embarrassed as he struggled to maintain her position, touching between her legs and almost full buttock in the process. Katriana was not the slightest interested in her decorum, all she wished for was to escape. She banged the shoe frantically against the steel sheet, the stranger came running over to investigate.

'What has happened? Are you injured?' he asked in German.

'Nein mein, Herr. Holen Sie schnell Hilfe! Holen Sie die Polizei!' (Fetch help quickly. Get the police!) She pleaded.

The man bid her to wait a moment as he juggled with the chain which was only wrapped around the handles. A few seconds later, he'd unravelled it and pulled open the small steel double doors.

'Schnell! Schnell!' He shouted as he grabbed hold of her hands and dragged her up and out.

'Please help my friend, he can't reach,' she asked.

The man lowered the metre or so of chain down to Marcel, trapping the other end with one of the doors. Marcel took a leap to reach it as the coal level had dropped somewhat with all the activity. Clinging on tightly, he lifted himself up until he could reach the ledge.

The man grasped at Marcel's hands and opened the door fully, allowing the chain to drop. Marcel caught it as it descended and asked Katriana to reach down for it. As she leaned in, she grabbed it and passed it up and out as the man raised Marcel out fully. Katriana instinctively took hold of the chain as the man looked at the two of them cautiously.

'Danke! Vielen Dank!' Reiterated Katriana several times as she hugged and kissed the stranger on the cheeks. The stranger asked them what had happened as he looked them up and down again, noting their condition. Marcel, avoiding causing any alarm informed him they got locked in and this seemed the only way out.

The stranger commented on how lucky they were he was passing by at the time, as this was a rather quiet spot in the town where very few townspeople ventured.

Marcel thanked him for his kindness then asked him the quickest way to the town centre, which he obliged by pointing in the general direction. Although eager to vacate the vicinity, Marcel took the time to close the doors over and wrap the chain around the handles to lock them.

The man looked puzzled by his actions. Marcel enlightened him. 'We wouldn't like a small child to fall in, would we?'

The man smiled and told them they should perhaps see a doctor as they both looked a little worse for wear.

Both thanked him again and bid him Auf Wiedersehen, then hurriedly ran off in the general direction of the town centre. Several streets away, they reached the main route through the town. Katriana held Marcel back, telling him how both of them had been lured into the trap by someone posing as a local.

They decided to make for a telephone off the main street from where they could call Perzinski at the NATO Base and alert him to the Nazi keep and the fact Robert was still held captive within. 'Katriana also hoped for news of her father, had he and the others been captured also?' she wondered.

Running towards a telephone, they attracted the glances of several people who were outwardly shocked and bewildered by their filthy condition. Ignoring the looks and remarks, Marcel suggested Katriana make the call whilst he stood guard, just in case.

She lifted the receiver and dialled the operator, once connected she requested a call be put through to NATO HQ at Böblingen for the attention of the Base Commander and the charge reversed. The operator advised she would try but deemed their acceptance unlikely.

'Just tell them it's François Larousse's daughter, it's very urgent,' she remonstrated in German.

A few moments later, the call was patched through to Perzinski aboard the NATO train.

'Miss Larousse, are you alright?' Perzinski asked in an anxious tone. 'I'm alright, my father?'

'He's fine, he's out there looking for you at this moment. I'll contact him right away. Give me your location.'

'Listen! The Nazis are here alright, I've seen them. Marcel and I have only this minute escaped, Marcel's with me but they've got Robert. He's being held in an old building at the edge of town, you've got to help us, please,' she beseeched Perzinski.

'Okay ma'am, no problem there. First though, give me your location and I'll relay it to your father, quickly ma'am, we don't have much time left,' replied Perzinski.

Katriana looked around her, it was difficult in the fading light of the early evening to read any street names, so she detailed the spot by relaying the description of a couple of shops and a small hotel.

'Tell him to hurry, please!'

'Yes ma'am, just you stay out of sight till you're sure it's your father, got that, ma'am?' Instructed Perzinski.

Katriana agreed and replaced the receiver. She ran the few short steps to Marcel. who was keeping a vigilant watch on the street corner.

'Perzinski's calling papa, he'll be here soon. Oh, please papa, hurry, please hurry!' She murmured as she hopped up and down in a nervous fashion.

Marcel took hold of her shoulders, guiding her to a recessed doorway in a shopfront.

'We'll wait here for your father, Mademoiselle. It'll be alright, don't worry we'll make it,' he said, comforting her. She put her arms around Marcel's neck, rested her head on his shoulders and began to sob.

'What about Robert? What will they do to him? It's all my fault, if I'd done what papa told me to, none of this would ever have happened. Oh god! What a mess.'

'Now then Mademoiselle, you shouldn't blame yourself. It'll be alright, you wait and see.' Marcel wished he could believe what he had just said himself.

Within ten minutes, they heard the roar of a powerful engine round the bend at the end of the street. Marcel took a cautionary glance out from the seclusion of the recessed doorway.

'It's your father, mademoiselle! It's Monsieur Larousse!' He shouted with delight.

The powerful Range Rover hadn't completely stopped before Larousse threw open the door and jumped out to embrace his daughter as she ran to the safety of his arms. He looked her up and down as she ran towards him. What had she been through?

'My precious! My precious little girl! How could I have been so foolish? Come, we must get you away from here at once!' He said, guiding her over to the Range Rover.

'Papa! They've got Robert. You must help him, papa!' She squealed, resisting his guidance.

'Cameron! He's been nothing but trouble since we found him on the yacht. My darling, there's no time to go looking for him, there's only a few hours to the deadline. Look at you my precious, we must get you away from here.'

'No, papa! I am not leaving here without Robert. I mean it!' She pulled herself from her father's grip.

'Forget him, my dear. You're young and very beautiful, you'll soon find someone else, someone.'

'Stop it! Stop it!' She shouted aloud. Then tearing herself from his embrace once again, she dashed over to the vehicle, reached in below her father's seat and withdrew a small automatic pistol she spotted being hidden there by Lieutenant Chambers earlier in the day.

'I'm not leaving without Robert!' she said decidedly as she began heading to the old building.

'Don't be so foolish, Katriana! Now put down that gun immediately,' Larousse demanded.

'No, papa! It's my fault we got caught. I persuaded Robert to come back into the town and ask some more questions. Just look at Marcel, they electrocuted him, I saw them do it, it was horrible and I imagine my poor Robert's being dealt the same punishment.'

'My precious, leave this to us. He's not worth risking the whole operation for. Let's stick to what we came here for. To find and destroy a Nazi base somewhere in those hills.'

'You go and find your precious base, papa! I'm going to help Robert. Why can't you understand, papa? I love him, I love him so very much. Why won't you help us? Please papa, I'm begging you,' she cried as she dropped to her knees from exhaustion and despair.

Larousse ran to her aid. Holding her tight, he said, 'I'm so sorry, my precious. It's all my fault.'

There was no reply from his daughter, he lifted her head up to find she was unconscious. The stress was too much for her to bear. Had she simply fainted or was it more serious?

'We must find a doctor! Quickly! The telephone book from the kiosk!'

Marcel ran over and ripped the book from its mounting with a surge of adrenalin forcing its way through his body at the sight of Katriana laid out on her father's knee. Had they come so far for nothing? Her appearance had saved his life only minutes previously simply from her being captured herself.

'You've got to help Mr Cameron, Sir! If they hadn't been caught, I could be dead now. It was electric shock treatment they tortured me with before the bastard brought your daughter down threatening to give her the same unless I talked. Please Sir, I beg you also, please help him.'

Larousse fumbled through the book as he thought the situation through. 'Put my daughter in the car, there's a surgery close to the station, we'll take her there.'

'And Cameron, Sir?' Reiterated Marcel. 'André, what do you think?' asked Larousse.

'It's getting dark now François, there's not much else we can do until the train arrives shortly before 01.00 hrs.'

Larousse continued to give the matter some thought as they proceeded to the doctor's residence at speed. Pulling up outside, he knocked frantically on the large carved oak front door, a few moments later a heavy-set lady answered asking their business before opening the door.

'There's been an accident, my daughter is hurt. Please can you help?' Larousse speaking in German, pleaded whilst holding Katriana in his arms, flanked by Marcel and André.

The woman looked through the security eyelet placed in the wooden door before opening it, she saw their plight and opened the door swiftly. The conversation continuing in native German.

'Yes, of course! Please bring her through,' she said with genuine concern. 'Put her in there on the couch, I'll fetch Herr Doctor,' she said, scurrying away. Moments later, the doctor entered the room. 'What has happened?' he asked seeing her condition. 'An accident Herr Doctor, she's collapsed.'

'What kind of accident?'

'We're not sure, doctor. I was asking her that when she just collapsed,' answered Larousse.

'And she is?'

'My daughter. Katriana. Katriana Larousse.'

'What has happened? She's covered in coal dust. What are these marks on her wrists! Has this woman been handcuffed? Are you on the run from the authorities?' The doctor quizzed openly.

There was a brief pause from Larousse and the others as they looked at one another.

'We are the authorities, Herr Doctor. We're here to prevent a major international incident taking place in this vicinity tonight.' Larousse calculably advised the doctor to see his reactions.

'Here! In Oberammergau! You must be mistaken Herr Larousse, nothing much happens in Oberammergau barring the odd skier or mountaineer coming to grief on the slopes,' he replied casually.

'Please leave the room all of you, while I examine her.'

They stepped outside into the hall. The housekeeper showed them to the doctor's study. Larousse checked no one was listening then advised Marcel and André he'd decided to attempt a rescue mission. Both were elated at the news, confirming they thought he was doing the right thing.

Larousse held back his real reason for his decision. The fact that he was afraid Robert may talk before the train conveying the Nazi hierarchy had commenced its journey. This being the one and only lead they had left to locate the secret base.

The doctor entered the room a few minutes later. Speaking in English, he began.

'Your daughter is going to be fine, Monsieur Larousse. I take it I am speaking to "the" Monsieur Larousse, head of the worldwide shipping and industrial conglomerate?'

'You are, Herr Doctor. You say my daughter is going to be alright, what happened?'

'She'd fainted. Too much stress, too much worry. It's not good for you, you know.'

'That'll be the accident, eh?' Ventured Larousse.

'No. No accident. She's been subjected to an ordeal much worse than a mere accident, I'm afraid,' replied the doctor.

Larousse could only think of one thing. She'd been raped.

'If they've touched her, I'll kill every one of them, the nasty swine,' he roared, just managing to avert saying the word Nazi.

'Please, Monsieur Larousse. Don't try to deceive me. Your daughter was delirious when she came around. She was rambling a little, she mentioned a man called Robert and how she had to save him from the Nazi's. This makes sense to you, I take it?'

Larousse failed to answer.

'Monsieur Larousse. There's something I must tell you. Something which I hope will help you to understand my position.'

'Go ahead please.'

'My family are all Austrian's, going back many, many generations. In 1938 after Austria's annexation just as Hitler was about to occupy most of Europe, my father arranged passage on one of what would have been your grandfather's ships at the time, passage for the whole family, secretively through the British department your grandfather joined before France fell.'

'My grandfather and father always held your grandfather in the highest esteem for what he did to help our fellow Austrian's and others and how he risked his own life and seen the ruin of his European companies as Hitler advanced. Yet still, he helped the oppressed people of our country and others. We owe him a great debt and I would be privileged to assist you, his grandson, to seek out and rid my people of this accursed Nazi trash once and for all!'

Larousse was astonished. The doctor walked over to him and presented him his hand.

'My name is Kurt von Rauch. I'm so pleased to make your acquaintance.' Larousse stood up and exchanged a firm handshake with the doctor. 'Please if I can be of any assistance whatsoever, I am at your disposal,'

offered von Rauch. 'My daughter?'

'Please do not worry, Heidi is looking after her, she has retired from nursing and looks after the house for me now. Your daughter needs to rest, the poor girl's exhausted.'

Larousse decided to confide the situation to von Rauch in the hope a little local knowledge would help their plight.

Larousse asked Marcel to describe the building they had been taken to and if he could find his way back. Marcel nodded and began to tell von Rauch about the derelict looking building on the outskirts of the town and its operations room within.

Explaining also how they were posing as either a middle-aged eccentric or Anti-terrorist Polizei to lure anyone in who asked questions in the town or anyone in the vicinity of the rail tunnel, which was how they'd captured him. He admitted he was duped by the officialdom of the arresting officer as he explained the circumstances.

After Marcel detailed the whereabouts of the building he had been held in, von Rauch appeared totally devastated. He walked slowly almost trancelike over to a drink's cabinet. Opening it, he said, 'I think you gentlemen had better sit yourselves down and join me in a drink.'

'I'm sorry, Herr von Rauch. We have no time to socialise,' Larousse replied cynically.

'Please, this could prove important,' he said as he began pouring out four brandies. The doctor continued. 'That building you describe was commandeered by the Nazi's when they arrived all those years ago.' He paused momentarily, obviously overcome with emotion as he passed the three men their drinks and sat himself down in a high-backed armchair.

'It was used as a holding camp for Jews rounded up locally from the surrounding area. Once they had become exhausted and their numbers large enough to justify their transportation, they were herded like cattle in trucks down to the old railway yard and packed into cattle wagons or anything the train could pull.'

'From there they were transported to Dachau, Sachsenhausen, Ravensbruck, Buchenwald and other such horror stories synonymous with the Nazi brutality of the war. The building you have described to me was found after the war to contain torture equipment so barbaric in its nature it made the local people so repulsed, they vowed it would never be used again and have subsequently petitioned on several occasions for its demolition and for the land to be left bare for one hundred years as a mark of respect. As far as the townspeople know, it's just some odd eccentric who owns it.'

Larousse and the others looked on in sympathy as the doctor's eyes began to puff, and a tear flowed out down his left cheek.

'Why can't they leave us alone! The horror of what happened over seventy years ago is coming back to haunt us. Why us? What do the Nazis want with us after all this time? You must stop them! We cannot allow them to regenerate the horrors which took place in that building years ago!'

The doctor was obviously more than upset at the thought. Larousse assured him they were doing all they could and that others were standing by but firstly, they desperately needed to find an underground base they had been informed of by one of their own.

'Underground base? What! Here in Oberammergau? Impossible. I have been here all my life. I have seen no sign of any such activity, you must have your facts wrong, Monsieur Larousse. My god! I hope you have,' he said as he wiped the tears from his cheeks.

'No. We have proof positive the base is here or at least in this vicinity. We have been led to believe it was built during the war and sealed up until the time was right. Listen, I'm trusting you implicitly now, Herr Doctor. What I am about to tell you will come as a great shock so be prepared.'

Von Rauch nodded with apprehension. Larousse began.

'At midnight tonight, an engineer's train will depart from Murnau carrying what we believe to be the "creme-de-la-creme" of the "Reichsbürger" hierarchy. They are being secretly, they think, transported to this underground base to oversee a test launch of a secret missile system the Nazi's have developed, the target British locations!'

'We have been told if this test is successful, strategic worldwide targets are already destined for the same treatment. In short, the Nazi's aim to hold the world to ransom unless we can locate this base and prevent this test.'

'Good God!' The doctor said. 'What on earth are you doing about it? How many of you are there?'

'We're only a small team. We have until about 01.00 hrs to locate and blow this base out of existence if we have to.'

'My god! That's only three hours from now!' He said, panicking. 'What can I do to help?'

'Stay here, doctor and look after my daughter. Don't go outside just in case. We'll go back to that old Nazi building; we have one of our team still imprisoned there. We must get him out first,' said Larousse.

'Of course!' The doctor had a sudden recollection. Jumping to his feet, he rose his hands high in the air before swinging them back to place his fingertips on his forehead.

'My god! I'm such a fool! Why didn't I think of this before?' He shouted.

'What?' Exclaimed Larousse in curiosity.

'The Jewish prisoners!'

'What about them?'

'They were exhausted when they were loaded into the trains.'

'I don't mean to be callous doctor but most Jewish prisoners were badly treated, tortured and such, they're bound to have been exhausted.'

'No! No! The stories I have heard over the years saying these Jews, the ones from the holding station, they never left that building. Never! Yet they were totally demoralised by the time they were taken away to the trains.'

'How do you know that you yourself said my grandfather helped your family to escape.'

'Yes, yes, he did. But we came back after the war. My father was also a doctor. People talk to doctors for things other than medical problems.'

'What are you getting at, Herr Doctor?'

'The Jewish prisoners. Could they have been used as slave labour to dig this secret base, do you think?'

'Anything's possible but how does that help us.'

'They never came out of that building until they were taken to the trains! Understand. Never! My father and I often discussed the plight of the Jews. Many, many times, he told me of the townspeople's heartache and how they felt so useless when truckloads of them would pass through the streets on their way to the death camps.'

'The people of Oberammergau had told him of their condition and how weak they looked. From what? How could so many men women and children become almost skeletons so quickly? They never left that building!'

Larousse glanced around at his two comrades, then the reality hit him. 'You mean they dug a tunnel from the prison building to the underground base, is that what you're implying?'

'Well. It makes perfect sense, don't you think?' said von Rauch.

'Yes! Yes, I do. If I am thinking straight, that means there must or at least could still be an entrance from that building down to this base. Come on men, we must start there.'

Larousse and the others jumped to their feet.

'Please?' said von Rauch pitifully. Larousse looked at him.

'It's far too dangerous, Herr Doctor. I cannot allow it,' he answered. 'Monsieur Larousse, I owe you, my family owe you. Please let me help.'

Larousse could sense the turmoil the doctor must be going through. 'It could be very dangerous.'

'I must help my countrymen. I cannot sit back and see the Nazi's overrun us again. Please,' he pleaded.

After a quick word with André and Marcel, who thankfully had by this time cleaned himself up thanks to Heidi who had furnished him with some of the doctors' clothes, Larousse agreed to allow the doctor to come but warned him to do as he was told. Von Rauch agreed then said he would return after he had spoken with Heidi and looked in on his daughter.

'She is going to be alright, isn't she?' Larousse asked again, notably concerned.

'Yes of course, I'll give her a sedative, she needs the rest, your daughter's a brave woman, she's been through a lot.'

Larousse looked at von Rauch.

'Katriana is a head strong and determined young lady, sadly foolish at times I must admit. However, after what she's gone through today, I agree she must also be brave.'

Larousse then went out to instruct Chambers who was still in the Range Rover with the engine running. He contacted Perzinski to update him on his situation. Perzinski acknowledged and advised Larousse he had a message patched through for him from the Admiralty. Larousse asked him for the details.

'Admiral Stevens said the information you sought regarding a German National who died in Hamburg eighteen months ago was a guy named Dieter Schäffer, a young student of electronics.' Larousse interjected. 'Dieter Schäffer! Shit that was his name! Are you sure, Leo?'

'That's the information I have here, why what's the problem, Larousse?'

'Dieter Schäffer, if it's the same chap, he was only my daughter Katriana's boyfriend at the time of his death. Jesus Christ, this is getting out of hand,' Perzinski added an observation.

'The report stated "accidental death" apparently.'

'That's what they've all said so far, Leo. The thing is the African Envoy was docked in Hamburg at the same time, so I need to know if Dieter was caught up in this Nazi shit, you know, trying to get inside information from my daughter or was he simply an innocent caught up in all this fucking mess.'

'Can't help you there, buddy.'

'No, no of course not. I'll see what I can find out but I'll have to be very tactful, she's no fool, my daughter.'

'Best of luck.'

'Oh, before I go, how long before we get the results of the samples Leo, any idea?'

'One to two hours for a basic screening, a more in-depth study may take several.'

'Okay, keep me informed, it may help. Out.'

'Roger, out.'

Whilst Larousse was inwardly contemplating the recent revelation, he instructed Chambers to collect the other team members and bring them to the doctor's house to discuss a rescue plan for Robert.

Chambers quickly collected Carl, Gerrard and Sub-Lieutenant Malhotra from their position in the hills and brought them down to von Rauch's. He told them of Marcel and Katriana's escape and that they were going in for Cameron. They were ready.

Von Rauch offered Larousse the use of his house to formulate a plan. Larousse thanked him and called the group in.

'When did you eat last?' asked von Rauch.

Larousse shook his hand as if to dismiss the suggestion.

'You are guests in my house. I insist you have something to eat before embarking on such an undertaking. A doctor's advice, you understand. Come you have some time whilst formulating your plan of action. Please, I insist.'

Larousse glanced around him at the five faces staring in anticipation of something more substantial than the army packs they had been given at the NATO Base.

'Very well doctor, something quick, not too fancy, okay.'

'Of course. I'll have Heidi see to it immediately.'

***

Meanwhile, Max Wittenberg decided Fassbinder had had long enough to interrogate the prisoner.

'Sergeant!' He yelled. 'Tell Fassbinder to get up here at once, we have to implement evacuation procedures,' he ordered.

'At once, Herr Oberst,' he replied.

A few moments later, the sergeant came rushing back into the room.

'Herr Oberst! Herr Oberst! Herr Fassbinder, he's dead! The lights are all off in the cellars. There's no power.'

'What! How? The prisoners, what about the prisoners?'

'Two have gone Herr Oberst, the man we arrested at the tunnel along with the woman!'

He was interrupted.

'What do you mean gone? Find them, you fool!' He raged.

Several of the guards mounted a search for the missing prisoners although their efforts were hampered using torches as new fuses continued to blow with the short circuit.

'Search the building from top to bottom. We must find them,' Wittenberg screamed.

'Schnell! Schnell! Close the base, evacuate to the tunnel, schnell!' He bellowed; Max knew he may only have minutes now to secure the building. He had to leave it looking as though it was disused. Those were his orders.

Max Wittenberg was frantic; he could only contemplate his superiors' reactions at the news that two prisoners had escaped.

'Any sign of them yet?' He screamed down to the cellars as he paced the floor.

'Nein Herr Oberst, nothing,' came the obvious reply. 'Get up here, all of you! Now!' He ordered.

When the dozen or so men returned to the operations room, he instructed them the game was over. The prisoners had to be found before they could talk to the Polizei or anyone else. He asked for four volunteers to go into town and search for them. The sergeant was the first to step forward.

'No Peer. I need you here.' Peer returned to the rank. Four others came forward one by one.

'My God,' he said at length. 'Is this the best you can do? God help us if we pull this off tonight,' he muttered.

'The rest of you, get into your uniforms. You are true soldiers of the Fourth Reich now! No more pretence. The time has come to stand up and be counted. We must defend the base until the test tonight is carried out successfully. The "Reichsbürgersbewegung" depends upon us. Do your duty well, my comrades!' The men left swiftly as instructed. Whittenburg called Peer back.

'After you change into your uniform Peer, get me the remaining prisoner,' he said in quiet annoyance.

Robert was unable to hear the commotion from his soundproofed room. He was laying down wondering why they were taking so long with Katriana, why they hadn't taken him for an interview first. He was in a dilemma. But not for long.

The door to the room swung open violently, crashing against the wall. Robert jumped upright simultaneously to see the figure of the sergeant, Peer in full Nazi uniform and brandishing an automatic machine gun across his chest.

'Oh shit!' Robert said softly as he quickly realised the gravity of the situation. He decided their only chance was to continue the bluff for as long as possible.

'My wife?' he asked, 'What have you done with her? Is this some kind of weird joke?'

'Schnell! Schnell!' shouted the sergeant, avoiding commenting. Pushing Robert from behind with the gun barrel, he guided him up the stairs to Wittenberg.

'Herr Cameron. Please be seated,' said Wittenberg civilly. Robert took a seat across the desk from him.

'What is all this?' asked Robert, acting bemused. 'Some kind of charade.'

'Charade. Hardly. You Herr Cameron are soon to witness the birth of the Fourth Reich. You should consider yourself very privileged, very privileged indeed,' replied Wittenberg.

'Why me? What have I done to deserve such a so-called honour?' He replied sarcastically. 'Where is my wife?'

'Do not be so flippant, Herr Cameron. Just consider yourself alone as the lucky one.'

Robert's heart sank as a feeling of deep despair infused itself through his body. 'My wife! What have you done with my wife?' He demanded.

'Oh, the woman, yes of course, you were both reporters for some magazine or other as I recall. Your wife though, I think not.'

'You know damn well we're journalists! What's happened to her? I want to see my wife now.' Robert protested as he rose from his seat only to be thrust back down at the point of the sergeant's gun.

'I'm sorry Herr Cameron that will unfortunately be impossible. Your wife and or "assistant" is no longer with us, she tried to escape I'm afraid along with another prisoner whom we think you knew. Another husband perhaps, I am sorry for both of them, of course.'

'You bastard! What have you done to her?' He shouted as he lunged across the table at Max. The sergeant prevented his reaching him with a severe blow to the head with the butt of the gun. Robert fell in a heap to the floor. Max jumped up to survey his prisoner's condition.

'You bloody fool, Peer. I wanted him conscious; I must find out why he and the others are here and what they know. Take him back and wake him, then make ready the passage to the base, ensure the entrance is well camouflaged. I'm not sure we can maintain our position here for much longer.'

Although Robert was indeed badly hurt, he was not as Max expected totally unconscious, he had overheard the mention of a passage and decided to play along with his condition a little longer if possible.

Peer called two guards over, instructing them to take him below and put him in the room containing Fassbinder's body.

Robert had no idea who this Fassbinder was and wondered if someone else had stumbled onto the Nazi plot and had suffered at the hands of this madman called Max. He could not think straight though, his mind racked with pain, not the physical kind but much worse, what had Max done to his beloved Katriana. Was she still alive or would he find her lying alongside this stranger Fassbinder.

Chapter Ten

Klaus Pfeiffer had given the order to arrest and detain Herr Schnorr at his home address or upon his arrival at the Murnau Railway Control. He was not to be allowed access to the Control office at any time, regardless. Three officers were dispatched to Schnorr's residence and had awaited his arrival as there was no answer when they knocked.

Schnorr had panicked, the sight of Oefner on his doorstep in the early hours of the morning had his nerves on edge. By lunchtime, he could no longer just sit and wait. He surmised there was a problem, a major problem if Herr Oefner had taken the risk of meeting with him personally. He had to get away from the house, he needed to calm down. A drink was what he needed.

Schnorr had taken himself into the old town, where there were bars aplenty. He moved from bar to bar, drinking heavy in one and hardly any in another, the hours had dragged on until it was time for him to "book-on", as he attempted to book-on at the railway control offices at 21.45 hrs that evening, he was intercepted by two of Pfeiffer's team and placed under arrest.

Pfeiffer was advised of his arrest by radio, he instructed them to take Schnorr to the Polizei station, charge and detain him for standard blood tests, etc. At 22.00 hrs, he received a call and asked to explain exactly what was going on with Herr Schnorr to his superiors.

Pfeiffer concluded from this there indeed had to be a "mole" at HQ as this simply appeared like a normal arrest, so why the call? He knew then he now trusted no one at HQ therefore avoided answering in detail the request, simply fabricating the story that he was passed information by a member of the public stating a senior railway controller was seen noticeably drunk whilst making his way to work and was allegedly involved in some drugs dealing, which was also under investigation.

He knew he could not return to interview Schnorr just yet for fear he may have no alternative other than to disclose the full facts and possibly alert the

"Reichsbürger" mole within the station. After convincing his Superintendent to allow him a few more hours to ensure, there was some substance to the information he had received, he returned to meet with Perzinski.

Soon after speaking with HQ, a call came over the radio direct from the officers watching the railway yard informing him of activity surrounding the carriage under surveillance.

'What's happening?' asked Pfeiffer.

'A small locomotive and van carrying a group of men has arrived and they are walking along the line checking the area,' came the reply.

'What are they doing exactly?'

'Checking all the wagons, Sir. Inside, underneath, all over in fact.'

'Don't let them see you! Let them board the train and allow the train to leave. Understand.'

'Yes, Sir.'

'Keep me informed of any developments between now and the departure of the train, then keep up the surveillance until you're sure it's clear. They will no doubt have contact of one form or another, I don't want them spooked by anyone, okay!'

'Yes, Sir, of course.'

Pfeiffer replaced his radio handset and turned to Perzinski.

'Things are moving, Leo. That was one of my men, the locomotive has arrived and there's a group checking around the area of that old carriage and the engineer's train.'

'Good, at least we know for sure something's happening. God damn it! I hate this sitting round,' commented Perzinski.

'Yes, I know what you mean but I don't think we'll be sitting around for long Leo. We better make a move and get things underway.'

Perzinski agreed and made a few calls to the section commanders involved in the operation and advised them to be ready within five minutes. Situation. Go!

***

Back at Doctor von Rauch's following a warm and satisfying beef dish of Heidi's own concoction, Larousse and his team felt ready to tackle anything.

'May I use your study again, Herr Doctor?' asked Larousse.

'But of course,' replied von Rauch, gesturing towards it. Larousse took out his communication pack and contacted the NATO train.

'Commander please, Larousse speaking.'

'Larousse! How's things? Your daughter, she's okay, is she?' Inquired Perzinski thoughtfully.

'We are at a doctor von Rauch's in Oberammergau; Katriana is going to be fine, thank you. Anything happening your end?'

'It's official! We have taken up position. We have full NATO backing on this since your daughter confirmed the situation. Our original plan is unaltered for the time being. Troops are already positioned on the outskirts of Oberammergau.'

'Good, anything else I should know?' asked Larousse.

'Men reported at the engineers train in Murnau yard, checking it out, you know?'

'Fine. Listen, there's a change of plan my end. That bloody fool, Cameron, is still being held captive in the building where my daughter and Marcel were held. The doctor here has given us reason to believe there may be an entrance to the base from within that building!'

'I have to that is we are all agreed, we must try and rescue Cameron from there before they make him talk or worse! In any case, there's no more we can do outside, it's too dark and the bloody railway tunnel was a wild goose-chase. You and Pfeiffer follow the train as planned, any developments let me know immediately, and break radio silence if necessary. Got that?'

'Yeah, sounds like you lost out with your tunnel idea, seems they only use that carriage for transportation to the general area, what do you think?' asked Perzinski.

'Let's not be too hasty. You stick to your plan and follow that train! It will lead us to something, that, I'm sure!' Larousse added.

'Just be aware, the radios will not work once you are so far inside the tunnel, okay.'

'Okay, the time is now 22.50 hrs check.'

'Check.' Larousse confirmed, glancing at his watch.

'We should be there around 01.00 hrs. Have a couple of your boys keep a look out on the tunnel entrance, we've arranged a stoppage of all other traffic between midnight and 08.00 hrs along the line from Murnau. Listen Larousse, you be careful, you're one hell of a guy!'

'Thanks, I will.' Larousse smirked and shook his head. Replacing the receiver slowly, Larousse looked around at his small group sitting around the doctor's dining room table. He only had three words to say.

'Its official, men!'

After a short silence, Larousse detailed the two most vulnerable members, Marcel who had been through enough but refused to quit and Gerrard who was the eldest, to keep watch on the tunnel mouth from a distance and report what they see, when they see it, no-matter how insignificant.

The doctor was detailed to carry out surveillance on the suspect building and man the radio, relaying anything of significance from the vicinity where Robert was being held.

Himself, André and Chambers would enter the building through the coal drop, whilst Carl and Malhotra would create a distraction at the main doors and hopefully rescue Cameron in the process; second, render whatever was in the building inoperative and third, try to locate the tunnel, if indeed there was one. Any further action would depend on the outcome of this first phase.

***

Klaus Pfeiffer and Leo Perzinski were boarding the specially arranged train now standing at the siding in Murnau. Higher authorities including the Admiralty in London had been kept advised of the latest developments and had authorised use of heavy armour if required. The NATO Base was now officially on "Full Alert".

All manner of supplies, ammunition, etc. had been loaded onto the train whilst both Perzinski and Pfeiffer joined by other officers sat and discussed possible scenarios in the comfort of a saloon coach attached directly behind the locomotive.

At 23.45 hrs, Pfeiffer's men at the railway yard reported several vehicles arriving at the loading dock and at least forty or so men boarding the coach quickly and quietly through the door at the rear. Also being loaded was a crate, which was lifted onto the open platform of the carriage and fastened down.

The contents of the crate were yet unknown. Perzinski gave the order for the NATO train to be moved into position and with a sudden jolt, they were on their way.

In the Murnau railway yard, all had returned to normal, the vehicles conveying the "Reichsbürger" hierarchy had disappeared as quickly as they had arrived. A few moments later, the small electric locomotive rolled into the siding and was attached to the front of the short ballast train, then the train was propelled to attach the suspect carriage at the rear.

Following a brake test, the driver called Control for clearance and awaited the signal. At 23.59 hrs exactly, the signal was switched to "off" and the driver eased his charge over the network of tracks leading out of the railway yard and onward towards to Oberammergau tunnel.

***

Inside the Nazi's coach the atmosphere was somewhat sombre, many of the occupants were understandably concerned with the security of the operation, given the fact one of their own (Steinbacher) had informed the Polizei of General Stoltz whereabouts only the previous day.

General Stoltz shrugged off the possibility of anyone knowing anything further, stating that Steinbacher had never been told of the precise location of the secret base and had never been involved at high level discussions regarding it.

One man stood up to make a statement. He was ex-SS Oberst, Conrad Braun's grandson. Commander of a Panzer division during the war and now his grandson bearing the same name was promoted to Reichsführer (Field Marshall) by the Neo-Nazi's, for his unquestionable loyalty to the "Reichsbürgersbewegung" and his level of almost infinite financial support to the project since its inauguration. In typical Hitler fashion, he began.

'Fellow members of our Reich! We are only a few hours away from achieving our destiny! Our God given right! We have waited a long time to see this day dawn on the fatherland. We have at last world domination at our fingertips and there is nothing, nothing! That can stop us attaining our goal. Once this final control cubicle we are transporting is installed into the mainframe and systems re-booted, the British submarine HMS Audacious will be under our control and the target chosen destroyed; then we announce to the world the "Fourth Reich" is here and here to stay.'

A rousting cheer and applause interrupted Braun's address, he continued. 'Then we will go on to prove the strength and flexibility of our "donor missile system" to the rest of the world and show them all that their country could easily be our next target. Before long, they will at last bow to our superiority and I for one have waited a very long time to see this day dawn. I so wish my father and grandfather could be here. So! Let us hear no more defeatist talk this night. Let us bask in the glory that will be ours this night! To the Reich!'

Amid frenzied accolade and cheering within the coach, a voice repeatedly called for order. The voice was that of a much younger man in his mid-thirties. As the coach quietened. all eyes looked towards him.

'One moment, Herr Reichsführer. I am not afraid to say that I and many of my generation within the Party have serious misgivings regarding tonight's operation. Yes, we want the same goals as previous generations did seventy years ago but we have everything to lose if it all goes wrong.'

'Most of you here are ex-SS in heritage, which means you have all looked after each other since our country's defeat in 1945. I and others in a similar position have no one to turn to if anything goes wrong this night. We will be locked away for the rest of our lives or worse.'

'I still say we should postpone this test for a few months, at least until we are sure the location of the base is safeguarded giving the developments of the last day or so.'

The dull chatter within the coach subsided as Braun stood up and walked slowly towards the offending young officer, who rose slowly from his seat to confront the Reichsführer. Looking him straight in the eye with a wicked glint, Reichsführer Braun said softly.

'You should consider yourself very fortunate. If this was wartime, I would have you shot for insubordination, Herr Lieutenant.'

The Reichsführer's threat only served to inspire the young Party officer to retaliate.

'Had we carried out less killing of our own during the last war, who knows, we may have actually stood a chance of winning the bloody war then!'

Braun raised his hand to strike the young man but was stopped by another. 'Stop this nonsense!' shouted General Stoltz, angered by both men's outburst.

'This is neither the time, nor the place for such foolishness. We must work together for the future of the Reich and put the past behind us, forever! Now both of you sit down and stop this bickering. We are embarking on a momentous journey, the inevitability of which will see the fatherland triumphant! Nothing can stop us now; within an hour we will be in the underground base and by 03.00 hrs we will rule the world! Sieg heil!'

As the young Lieutenant sat down, a chorus of Sieg heil was shouted several times whilst the others raised their arm in typical Nazi style, he realised as he did so himself, he had no hope of postponing the planned uprising. He was for that in principle, though couldn't help feeling something was not quite right. The Reichsführer had calmed himself somewhat and moved away from the irritating young man.

***

Back in the old building, Robert Cameron had faired rather better than poor Marcel under his short captivity with the Nazis. He had been fortunate Fassbinder had been killed before he dispensed some of his brand of questioning upon him. Unfortunately, however, he was not in a position to know this.

When Max Wittenberg decided to make his withdrawal from the old building in Oberammergau and retreat into the base itself, he decided to have his prisoner accompany him, "for insurance" as he put it.

Sometime before Larousse had decided to mount an assault on the building, Max Wittenberg had already made his move. Robert had remained handcuffed as he was led out of his detention room and down to the basement, still protesting his own and his wife Kate's innocence as to what was happening. At the entrance to the room where Marcel was tortured, he was halted.

Inside the room working with the aid of portable lamps were two guards cleaning the floor of excess mud and water. The water was being drained at the far corner and the mud pushed into a grid in another, the task completed the guards swilled the floor with a hosepipe brushing the excess to the drain.

Once satisfied the room was clear, Max opened an electrical control box in the corridor, the power supply to which was already blown by Marcel's actions were immaterial.

Max pushed the box hard from below, the effort needed clearly showed in his face as the veins in his neck became more pronounced, eventually the box, metal in construction and measuring perhaps 60cm x 40cm x 10cm was seen to slide upward, the cables leading into the top easily manipulating themselves by provision of flexible hosing, the box had not raised more than fifty millimetres when Max ceased his efforts, he then pulled and jolted the box at the left side, which allowed it to swing open revealing a master switch behind, he inserted a key turned it and pulled the lever down into position.

An electrical thump was heard as the lever made contact; Robert's eyes swung immediately to the source within the room. As he looked on, he saw a panel in the floor begin to raise slowly, his mouth agape, he began to realise exactly what was happening, he surmised his troubles were just beginning.

His fears increased when he demanded to know what happened to his "wife, his assistant". Robert, even yet maintaining his cover as a journalist. Max Wittenberg's reply left him shaken and distraught.

'The young lady and another troublemaker we found snooping near the railway tunnel have been dealt with. I'm afraid Mr Cameron, you are quite alone.'

Robert demanded to know what he'd done with "Kate". Wittenberg smiled and spoke.

'She's the last of your worries. In a few hours' time, the whole world will be at our mercy. You included.'

'What exactly do you mean by that?' Demanded Robert.

Max Wittenberg ignored the question and turned to go, then thought for a moment.

'You said you and your assistant were from some magazine or other, is that correct?'

Robert was quick to correct him, stating.

'Not one magazine, we are freelance journalists covering a series of reports about problems in the water supply from the tunnel. I've told you that already. Why?'

Wittenberg turned back towards him. Walking slowly over, he brushed Robert's shirt down and straightened his collar.

'If you are who you say you are,' he said slowly, precisely. 'How would you feel about covering the biggest story of the Twenty First Century? It will make you famous, I guarantee it.'

Robert thought for a moment.

'I'll need Kate to help me, to take shorthand notes, dictation, you know?'

'Not possible!' smacked Wittenberg.

'I do not have the time nor the patience to negotiate. Give me your answer now!'

Robert thought his only chance would be to go along with the suggestion, though he quickly realised he had no journalistic experience and wondered how soon his captor would realise the truth.

'Okay, I agree. But what about my equipment. My cameras, tape recorder, notebook even. I've got nothing here, have I got time to collect them. You could have a guard accompany me; I promise I won't try to escape. I mean if this story is as big as you say, I'd be foolish to consider escape.'

Stopping him in his tracks, Wittenberg called for silence.

'We will provide you with all the relevant equipment when the time is ready, until then, you must do as I say. Understand?'

Robert looked down at the now fully open entrance to the underground tunnel and swallowed hard. It was an impressive sight, a truly massive slab of concrete measuring some 1.5-meter-wide by 3.5-meter-long and a full 40-centimetre-thick was now raised clear enough to allow passage down the steps it revealed.

Robert knew he had no choice, if he tried to run they would surely kill him instantly but he thought of Katriana, he couldn't stop thinking of her, if they'd harmed her, he would demand vengeance but vengeance had to be planned, he thought; there was no point in heroics at this moment, he would continue to play the role of the freelance journalist a little longer.

Robert reluctantly agreed as he watched Max return the key to its original position then remove the master switch and relocate the control box to its rightful place on the wall. From behind, a guard loosely threw a few handfuls of dust over the box and floor to further conceal the fact anyone had tampered with it.

He considered for a moment and concluded, that if Larousse or the others were to locate this building it would be quite improbable, they would find this operating switch. He suddenly became cognizant of the fact he had to somehow draw the attention of the others to this room at least.

As he was guided into the room, he protested a little to delay them a few moments as he teased with difficulty at one of his gold cufflinks. Approaching the entrance, he dropped it onto his shoe to deaden the tinkling sound it may have made striking the floor, twisting his foot slightly, the cufflink slid off silently to the damp floor.

Robert flicked it slightly with the side of his foot towards a small still slightly muddy mound and prayed with all his heart it would not be noticed, at least not by the Nazis.

Most of the equipment and office paraphernalia from the old building had already been removed and was being taken down into the tunnel and stacked along the walls. Wittenberg decided there was no need to carry it any further as it would impede their progress, so the final detachment of guards closed the entrance and accompanied Robert through the long tunnel in a small electric golf buggy type vehicle to the main base. Wittenberg had proceeded quickly ahead and was at the entrance to welcome his guest.

'Herr Cameron. Welcome to the military headquarters of the German Fourth Reich!'

Robert stepped forward through the massively engineered steel entrance door and was totally overwhelmed by the sight before him. Here, under the Tirol Mountains was the base Larousse and the Admiralty hoped never existed. The base they presumed was a figment of Jason Allen's fertile imagination.

As he stood there in awe of the engineering marvel, he could be forgiven for thinking their mission was doomed to failure. He could not envisage Larousse and the others breaching this fortress before the Nazis carried out their threat. He kept hearing Max Wittenberg's words.

In a few hours' time, the whole world will be at our mercy. 'Surely Herr Cameron, you have some comment to make?'

Robert looked over at Wittenberg.

'It's incredible, absolutely incredible!'

Max pulled him aside and instructed the guard to close the door and seal it. 'We could be here for some time, Herr Cameron. That is of course, only if the outside world decides not to take us seriously to begin with. Don't worry though, we're quite self-sufficient, I assure you.'

'I'll bet you are,' said Robert. Max called Peer over.

'Peer, I want you to take care of our guest. He will require video and SLR cameras, etc. a notepad and a recorder. He's going to capture for posterity the birth of the Fourth Reich as it happens.'

'What are your intentions?' asked Robert bluntly.

'Interviews later, Herr Cameron. I have work to do. I suggest you do the same.'

Max pulled Peer aside and instructed him to remove the handcuffs and keep a close watch on his movements.

'What if he asks questions?' Inquired Peer.

'Tell him, if we don't like what he writes we'll destroy it later, together with him, if need be. Let him do his job, we are making history this night and he can record the event.' Peer acknowledged.

Robert realised he was in one hell of a predicament. He knew that somehow, he had to find a way of stopping this war machine getting into action. As he walked around the complex accompanied but unhindered by Peer, he noted through his engineering abilities, several small details that may prove advantageous given the correct circumstances.

He quickly grasped the fact all major systems were hydraulically operated from the rails of neatly attached pipework surrounding him and leading to the entrance door, hoists and a traverser platform. Suspended some thirty feet above the floor was what could only be the main control room and at the furthest point, he could see the massive hydraulic platform, which he immediately recognised as their main means of entry from the railway, so the theory of the carriage being utilised as transport was indeed correct, he surmised.

Robert was inwardly pleased with what he saw, for he, being a mining engineer had a vast knowledge of hydraulics which his captors were, of course, ignorant of! Robert's mind was now working overtime to formulate some sort of plan. He knew he was now in the key situation to prevent the "Reichsbürger" implementing their threat. The only problem was, how on earth he could stop it.

As Robert was guided around the facility, continuous updates on the current situation were being broadcast over the loudspeaker system within the base. Although in German, Robert could understand most of the information, it was not long before he understood the arrival of the train was imminent and that an unidentified train was following closely behind. The announcements called for urgency in reception of the carriage when it arrived.

***

At Doctor von Rauch's, Larousse and the team headed out to the Range Rover and drove around the rear of the doctor's residence where trees and foliage gave them some security. They removed several of the boxes of equipment still stored away.

All bar the doctor adorned army issue camouflage dress and daubed their faces with camouflage cream. Weapons Officer Malhotra supplied each member of the group with an automatic pistol including silencer, an automatic machine gun and a bag of grenades, other cases contained belts and boxes of ammunition, enough to sustain them a couple of hours, by which time reinforcements should have arrived in the event of massive resistance. They also possessed a couple of handheld rocket launchers and enough explosives to wage a small war if need be.

The doctor looked on in amazement as the five men transformed themselves from mere civilians to a small combat unit, each one loading and checking their weapons and equipment. They exhibited more than a degree of professionalism as they carried out the duty.

'Looks like you've done this before, gentlemen,' said von Rauch.

'We are all professionals in our own field, Herr Doctor,' replied Larousse as he loaded a magazine into the machine gun, clicked it and primed it for use.

'Right, men! This is it. Marcel, Gerrard. Here are your night vision binoculars, both of you go with the doctor and find a suitable spot each to keep an eye on both tunnel entrance and the suspect building. The only trains due past midnight will be the one we're waiting on followed by Perzinski, so keep vigilant.'

'Lookout for anything unusual but be very careful, they know we're here now, so they'll be looking out for us also. Maintain radio silence until you're sure there's something happening, we don't know what to expect but that train is our only lead, so keep a good eye on it, okay?' Larousse then turned to von Rauch.

'Doctor von Rauch, will you take them to the tunnel entrances and meet us back at the old building, we'll take a drive round the area to see if there's any sign of it being guarded, okay?'

'But of course. I know the perfect place for both. Come gentlemen, my car is over here.'

The doctor led Marcel and Gerrard to his car and they drove off towards the northern end of the tunnel, it being the furthest away. Larousse and the others boarded the Range Rover and headed for the Nazi's lair. Within minutes, Carl and Malhotra were pretending to be drunk and banging the entrance doors, Larousse, and his team, comprising; André, Carl and Chambers had gained entry to the building by the same method his daughter and Marcel had managed to escape.

Concerned with the noise of the coal as it cascaded downward underfoot, he instructed his men to proceed slowly. Once all were inside and off the coal heap, they slowly opened the door to the corridor, all was in darkness. Taking his torch, he shone it along the passage and breathed a sigh of relief when there was no sign of a guard.

Proceeding along the corridor, they came to a staircase leading upward. Larousse tapped Chambers on the shoulder.

'Come on, let's see what we've got?'

The two cautiously climbed the stairway until they reached a set of double doors, trying to open them very slowly, they soon realised they were locked.

'We'll have to blow them,' said Larousse with dismay. He'd hoped to surprise his foe without announcing to the town he'd arrived.

'Okay Sir. I'll set it up,' answered Chambers quietly.

Once accomplished, Larousse instructed Chambers to join Carl and continue along and see if there was another stairway, if so to signal by flashing his torch twice and set up the same charge. There was no other, his daughter was indeed correct.

Only one doorway. The charges set; they retired back to the safety of the corridor. Double checking their weapons before the blast, Larousse then gave the signal to blow.

In a matter of seconds, the group made an assault on the room behind the now missing doors; nothing, no one. The large room was empty bar for a few pieces of old furniture. The floor, the furniture, the debris, all of it, everything covered in dust, the room gave the impression of having been unoccupied for many years.

'Where are they? The bastards!' shouted Larousse in temper. Taking a moment to think, he quickly ordered a search of the building.

'Katriana said this was the room they were led into from the courtyard, it must be, there's no other way from the cellars but she said it was used as some sort of computer control centre. There's no way this room's been used in years, I mean just look at it, it's filthy. We must have got it wrong, we'll have to do a thorough search.'

Katriana had forgotten to mention the transformation procedures she'd witnessed with Robert. Larousse was therefore unaware. They split into two groups and worked their way through the old building from either end until they met each other at the far side of the squared complex.

'Nothing, Sir,' said Carl.

'No. Same here. Okay, let's look for what might be an entrance to this underground base, knock the walls, floors, check inside the cupboards and closets, check every room again, this time thoroughly. We'll keep going in the same direction, that way we'll cover each other's path.'

They spent best part of forty-five minutes searching the entire building. Max Wittenberg had made a superb effort in decoying the unwanted guests, his collection of forties memorabilia in the form of old cigarette packs, posters, bottles, papers and such had played a significant part in delaying any intruder, for who could doubt the facts before them.

Larousse had to risk it, he called the doctor and asked him to return home and speak with his daughter to clarify this was the correct building.

Von Rauch replied this was the building his daughter had described, there was no other similar building in the town. He was in the right place, the only place. But he agreed to return in any case to verify her description. He made his way from the vantage point towards his home, eager to confirm the location.

Larousse called them all together.

'The bloody train will be arriving soon, we'll have to go down to the tunnels, there's nothing here. This whole thing's becoming a farce, this can't be the building. Come on, let's go,' said Larousse, somewhat disillusioned.

'Quiet! What's that? Sh!' said Larousse on hearing a faint sound outside. 'Someone shouting, Sir. A woman, I think.'

'Christ almighty! It's my bloody daughter. What the hell's she doing back here? Quickly, let's get out there before one of those Nazis turn up.'

Larousse and the team ran towards the sound of Katriana's voice.

'Papa! Papa, quickly, where are you?' Came her voice as she ran up and down the street, hoping to attract her father's attention.

'Stand back, my dear! The door's locked,' he shouted.

'Okay, papa,' Katriana replied as she moved away. With that, he shot the locks off the door with the automatic rifle and forced it open. Running out into the street, he grabbed Katriana by the arm and dragged her into the doorway.

'Papa! You're hurting my arm,' she complained bitterly, as Carl and Malhotra joined them on hearing the raised voices.

'Never mind that! What the fuck do you think you're doing, Katriana! Are you trying to get yourself killed?' She gave him a look of shock; her father was not renowned for using profanities.

'It's too dangerous for you out here. Anyway, I told you to stay at Doctor von Rauch's. And in any case, he's supposed to have sedated you, how have you managed to come round so quick?' Her father raged with his voice kept low but demanding whilst maintaining his grip on Katriana's arm.

'I don't know. Too tense, I suppose. Never mind, Heidi brought me. Listen, papa.'

'No! You listen, Katriana. Is this the right building?'

'Of course, papa! Do you take me for a fool?'

'No, no my dear but there's nothing in there, you said there was some sort of control centre, the place has been empty for probably for the last fifty years. No-one has been using that building, you must be confused.'

'Confused!' Katriana was livid. 'Look along there, that's the steel hatch Marcel and I climbed out of, that leads up to the room behind here, I'm not the one who's confused here!'

'But its filthy inside, no one could have been working in there like you say.'

'Look, papa. If you would just listen! I forgot to tell you, they did that, they had a machine spread dust and they were throwing old papers and things down, I'm telling you this is where we were, I should know. Now you listen to me, papa. I've remembered something from when they took me down to see Marcel.'

'Yes, what!' Interrupted her father anxiously.

'When they took me down, the one called Max, the one who captured Robert and I, he said to the other one, the nasty one, remember?'

'Yes, yes of course. What did he say?' Larousse interjected, his patience beginning to break.

'Please, papa. He, Max that is, he said, "You better clean up this mess, Fassbinder?" Yes, Fassbinder, I'm sure that was his name, the nasty one that is. "You better clean up this mess when you've finished. We can't be seen by our superiors looking wet and filthy when we retreat to the base".'

Larousse looked a little at a loss for a few moments until his daughter enlightened him further.

'Don't you see, papa? The room Marcel was in was filthy, deep in water and mud up to his ankles. Max must have meant him to clean it out before they could go through it to the base! The entrance must be in there.'

'My god. You've got a point, my precious. There's only one room in the cellars that's wet. Come on, let's go.'

They started towards the stairway when Larousse stopped and turned to see Katriana following.

'I'm sorry, my dear. I can't allow you to come with us, it's too dangerous, anyway, you've done your bit, I'm very proud of you.'

'Papa, I don't want patronising. I'm going with you; Robert needs me, I know he does. I've got to go, you must understand. Why can't you understand. I love him, papa.'

Larousse hugged his daughter for a moment, then said.

'You must understand, my precious. I'm afraid of losing you because I love you. You and your mama are the most important things in my life, I won't see you endangered, anyway, what would your mama say? We're dealing with fanatics here, there's no telling what they'll do if they get hold of you again especially if they know who you are, you were lucky last time.'

'What do you mean, papa?' Larousse knew he had no time to be gentle. 'Look Katriana, this is going to come as a terrible shock to you, please sit down.'

'Is it Robert? Oh, please papa, tell me he's okay. Please,' she cried.

'I don't know how Robert is, none of us do. This has to do with Dieter I'm sorry, I need to ask you this.'

'Ask me what papa, what can Dieter have to do with this, you know he's dead, papa. Poor Dieter.' Katriana sobbed on her father's shoulder.

'Did Dieter ever ask you anything about my work, anything at all?'

'What, what do you mean, papa? What has Dieter got to do with any of this?'

'Katriana, did he or did he not? That is all I'm asking.'

Amid the tears, she managed to tell her father he only asked in general what her father did for a living and just general conversation any boyfriend would ask about possible in-laws. Larousse was stunned.

'You mean you were thinking of getting married and you never mentioned it to me or your mama?'

'You, Papa, were never here, I did talk with mama, she did like Dieter and at least she came with me to his funeral.'

'I was in Australia, Katriana.'

'Oh, you remember where you were, that's a surprise, papa. What the fuck is going on, papa? Tell me, tell me now,' she protested.

'Less of the profanities, young lady.'

'Enough, Papa! Tell me.'

'Look Katriana, I don't know if Dieter was involved with this Nazi trash or was just an innocent victim of an accident but at the time the African Envoy was in Hamburg, that's all I know at the moment.'

'Dieter would never have been involved with these monsters, I know him, I mean knew him. He was a lovely man not a bloody Nazi.'

'Look my precious, it's all too sinister. Can't you see there is a connection between Dieter, you and this mess we are in. It's just too dangerous, I won't allow you to come with us and that's final.'

Katriana gave her father an ultimatum she'd wished she'd never have to. 'Papa. If I don't go with you now, you'll never see me again. I mean it!'

A tear formed in Larousse's eye as he kissed his daughter on the cheek and spoke.

'Then so be it, my precious. I would rather know you are alive and well, than know I led you possibly to your death. Goodbye, my child. I must go now. Please, let us not part in anger.' Larousse held his arms out and Katriana rushed into them, sobbing.

'I'm so sorry, papa. I love you so very much but I loved Dieter and now it's Robert I love. I never thought my falling in love would have come to this. I am truly sorry, papa. Goodbye, be careful, all of you. Please bring Robert back to me papa, please.'

Larousse said simply, 'I'll try, we'll all try. That I promise you, my dear. Go back to Doctor von Rauch's. For your own safety. Please,' pleaded Larousse.

She pulled herself out of her father's grip and ran off towards the street exit in floods of tears. Larousse stood motionless with his shoulders rounded and his neck bowed down, he looked a broken man. The sight of his daughter running away broken-hearted caused him severe pain. He assumed she was running to safety but Katriana had other plans.

She had to know first-hand if Robert was still alive, she also needed to know if Dieter was who she thought he was, she just had to be involved. She decided there was only one thing left to do. André meanwhile walked over to comfort his old friend.

'François my friend, don't worry, she's upset that's all. When it's all over, she'll come round, you wait and see if I'm not right.'

Larousse shrugged his shoulders and shaking his head, he said.

'That's assuming we get out of this in the meantime, I take it.'

'Come-on François, think positive. We'll all make it, you'll see.'

'I don't know André. I've had it with all of this. We're in this above our heads. How have I been so foolish to get so involved in something that should have been left to the bloody army or those boffins in Whitehall? My God, when I think of the trouble this has caused, was it worth it, is it worth it?'

'It is François, if we manage to prevent another reign of Nazi tyranny. It must be. Come François, we must try, for your daughter's sake. You don't want her living in a world of Nazi domination, do you?'

'No of course not, André. You're right as usual, let's go. Come on men, we've work to do.'

Just then the doctor radioed that his house was empty. 'Both Heidi and your daughter have gone!' he exclaimed.

Larousse put him wise to the situation and asked him to wait for their return. With that, they hurried down to the cellars and headed for the only room which was wet inside. Upon reaching it, each man was detailed to a certain task. André; to checking every square inch of the walls. Carl; to the ceiling, just in case. Malhotra; to bailing out. Chambers; to sweeping the water away along the corridor. André to keeping a look-out. Larousse whilst double checking all around the room was waiting patiently for news of the train's arrival as it was now imminent.

Suddenly, André realised that Katriana had said Marcel was ankle deep in muddy water when she had seen him earlier but now the level of water had dropped significantly and was no longer as muddy as she had described.

Advising Larousse of the fact, it became obvious the room had probably been drained somehow and then more water added to camouflage the entrance to the tunnel. With vigour, the team emptied the floor of water and mud and began the painstaking search for the entrance.

Their task was hampered by the fact there was no electricity supply to the building. Max and his men had sabotaged the supply at the main distribution board before leaving. So, with their powerful lamps they had been using in the railway tunnel and a couple of hand torches, they inspected the walls, ceiling and still rather wet and dirty floor for any sign of an entrance.

Carl satisfied himself there was no possible way out through the ceiling of the room and joined with the others bailing out, as he did so he caught sight of something which glistened through the murky water for a split second. With the aid of his torch and kneeling in the shallow water, he felt from side to side the murky space ahead of him.

A few moments later, he felt something as his hand passed over it, lifting the object up he shone his torch onto it, it was a gold cufflink. He studied it momentarily, then he realised.

'Monsieur Larousse. Sir, a cufflink. I'm sure it's one Mademoiselle bought in Lisbon, in fact Sir, I'm positive,' Carl said as he handed it to Larousse.

'Bought them in Lisbon! How can this be here?'

Carl knew he had no choice but to enlighten his employer.

'Sir, your daughter bought them for you together with a brooch for Madame. She asked my opinion, that's why I remember them.'

'That does not explain how it got here, Carl.'

'I understand Sir, perhaps she gave them to Cameron instead, it's only a suggestion, Sir.'

'Oh, I see. I have certainly not been her favourite person this last week or so, that poor girl of mine is so confused and I'm to blame.'

'Sir.'

Larousse composed himself but felt guilty none the less.

'No matter, this means either Cameron was down here suffering the same torture as poor Marcel or he deliberately dropped it in here as a clue to his whereabouts. Let's hope it's the latter, eh.' Smiled Larousse as he placed it in his breast pocket.

'Good old Cameron, perhaps he's not such a fool after all, eh!'

Several minutes later, Larousse received a coded message through from Gerrard telling him the train was approaching the tunnel and all appeared normal. He passed on the information to the others and assisted in the search himself.

'Sir I've found something, it looks like a seam in the concrete, very tight though and the water doesn't flow through, it may just be a joint from where the concrete was laid,' said André.

'Joint or no joint, it's a start. Come on let's scrape it out, see if it opens or not,' replied Larousse.

They traced the seam along and found it to be almost four meter's long by one meter wide with only a few millimetres gap around it as they dug out the deposits of mud with their knives.

'Chambers, bring the sensor in and try it round this seam, let's see if it tells us something,' commanded Larousse.

Chambers did as he was bid and returned with the sensor. Probing the area to the outside of the seam, he verified the density of the material below was obviously solid, passing over to the centre of the area the reading changed confirming there was indeed a void below.

Tracking the sensor along the length of the area, he found the reading changed the closer he passed to the outer wall confirming the space below was closing in. Moving away towards the inner wall and corridor, the sensor showed the space below becoming larger and more distant. He advised Larousse there was without doubt a void below. Elated, Larousse called out.

'This has got to be the entrance, there's a bloody tunnel under here leading to their secret base in one of those mountains outside, it must be, we'll have to go for it and hope we're right. Lieutenant Chambers, do your stuff and blow this bloody floor section to oblivion, quickly we haven't much time and the train will be in the tunnel any minute now.'

'Yes, Sir. All of you, stand well back along the corridor, this will be one hell of an explosion,' said Chambers.

Everyone took Chambers' advice and retreated a safe distance away to the left and right of the corridor as he prepared his explosives and set the charges. He was about to blow the charge when Gerrard called to inform them the train had entered the tunnel travelling at an estimated speed of 30kph or so.

Larousse acknowledged him and told him to watch out for Pfeiffer and Perzinski's train following a safe distance behind. He advised him of their current situation and the fact radio contact may fade as they head deeper underground.

With that, Larousse gave the order to blow the charge. Chambers detonated his handiwork by remote control. Before the dust settled, the team ran into the room, weapons at the ready. Before them, they saw what had eluded them throughout the mission. The secret entrance to the Nazi lair.

Unfortunately, the explosives had only partially exposed the entrance due to the fact the floor section they had blown had been a heavily reinforced steel and concrete panel, hydraulically operated by two rams much too powerful for the task itself but good insurance against an attempted entry such as this.

However, pleased they were with themselves, they now faced a delay whilst they cleared enough of the fractured concrete and mangled steel rodding to gain access. Larousse chose not to use further explosives for fear it may focus the attention of the local Polizei on them.

The first double explosion as they blasted their way into the upper floor was one too many, the second much larger one was pushing their luck. Although the shock waves would have been felt some distance away, they were confident the authorities would be baffled by the source seeing as it was contained below ground, at least for a short while.

A few minutes later, Marcel's voice sounding as though in a state of panic was shouting for Larousse on the radio.

'Sir! Sir I'm sorry, I've got to give you this straight, I can't code it.'

'Give me what? What's happening, Marcel?'

'Sir, I have gone through the tunnel almost to the other end and the train, it's gone past me, it never stopped, Sir. I timed it from Gerrard's message, it couldn't have stopped in the tunnel! But Sir, the thing is, there's no carriage at the rear! It's gone,' he said in disbelief.

'What! Are you sure, Marcel?' Replied Larousse, astounded at the statement. 'Yes, Sir, positive. There's no carriage on the train that just passed me, only the locomotive, some stone carrying wagons and a van. I assure you.'

'Okay, Marcel. Gerrard, did you get that?'

'Yes, Sir. I don't believe it, it passed me a few minutes ago and the carriage was definitely at the rear,' confirmed Gerrard.

'Okay Gerrard, listen; I want you to go down to the railway and stop the NATO train, tell Pfeiffer and Perzinski what's happened, be careful Gerrard, they may have men down there. The NATO train will be travelling slowly now so you should have no difficulty in stopping them, okay?'

'Yes, Sir, straight away.'

'Tell them we've found an entrance and we'll be going down the tunnel shortly. Tell them to forget radio silence, if they don't know we're coming now, they never will.'

'Yes, Sir. I'm on my way,' Gerrard said as he scrambled his way down from the cover of the trees towards the railway line.

Larousse's team having cleared a space large enough to pass through they cautiously took the first steps down into the tunnel over the debris. The tunnel had been expertly constructed to last a considerable number of years. The entrance slab was over 40cm thick and the hydraulic rams 150mm in diameter.

The tunnel walls had been smoothed off with cement render and waterproof lights set in at regular intervals. There was room for three men to walk abreast through the tunnel comfortably with numerous set-back refuge points. André looked on in sadness as he commented.

'Those poor prisoners, they must have been put through hell down here, François.'

'Here as elsewhere, André. They were nothing to the Nazis. Once they had outlived their usefulness here, they would have been forwarded in those cattle trucks to a concentration camp and gassed or shot. After digging this though, it may have come as a relief to some, can you imagine it André, being stuck down here until you drop, unbelievable cruelty.'

'They must have been sick to do what they did to these people and the other six million like them. One thing for sure André, we'll do all we can tonight to prevent it happening again, agreed?'

'Agreed, François,' answered André with determination.

With that, the team descended further down the tunnel and headed into the unknown at the other end.

Chapter Eleven

With only moments to spare before the NATO train would pass him, Gerrard scurried down the slope leading to the tunnel mouth, as he charged through the bushes and bracken in his path, the sharp thorns of some bushes ripped into the flesh on his hands and face.

There was no time to consider his own safety, the train was almost upon him. He couldn't afford the time to ensure a clear passage down the road, he had to take the chance; he presumed, if the Nazis were watching, they would be watching the road rather than the hillside itself with any luck.

Out of breath, Gerrard finally lost his footing completely and tripped over a protruding rock concealed by the vegetation. He tumbled over and began the descent of the steep slope ever faster downward; he lost grip of his torch to grasp at anything to arrest his fall, his efforts were ineffectual as clumps of grass and bracken either slipped through his fingers or were torn up in the process.

His body being constantly battered and bruised, he rolled uncontrollably until he landed hard on his back alongside the track. Winded and exhausted, he raised his head partially, attempting to focus clearly through his now watering eyes, he could almost make out the outline of the train approaching through the darkness.

There it was a dark shadowy box like object almost upon him. He struggled to his feet and waved frantically from the trackside, still the train crept steadily forward.

Would they see him, he questioned himself. It was doubtful, the normally compulsory light affixed to the locomotive had been ordered off for fear the Nazis may observe their presence. To compound matters, the location itself was too dark for even the evening light to penetrate as the hillside shadowed the light from the moon.

Gerrard prepared himself as the train came closer, waving his arms at first, he soon conceded his doubt was accurate. With the train only ten or so meters away, he began running alongside the track ahead of the train, as the locomotive coasted gently by, he leaped for the handrail leading to the door of the driver's cab. He'd caught it but it was made of chrome plated steel and was slippery, he gripped it as tight as possible with his right hand as his feet were dragged from under him.

The ballast and sleeper ends protruding outward from the rail itself were catching his shoes and drawing him further down as he attempted to reach with his left hand the other handrail. With a determined effort, he swung around and caught hold of the handrail, dragging himself off the ground and placing his feet on the first step of the locomotive's bogie. Ensuring he at last had a firm grip with his left hand, he knocked and battered at the cab door to alert those inside to his presence.

Both Pfeiffer and Perzinski had travelled in the locomotive's cab when the train had moved off from the stabling point to follow the suspect carriage. They couldn't believe their ears when the knocking was heard. Pfeiffer opened the cab door inward at the same time Perzinski drew his pistol to cover the possible breach by one of the Nazis, both were grateful to see it was Gerrard who luckily had just managed to climb up and in just before the train entered the Oberammergau Tunnel.

'Stop the train driver!' shouted Gerrard. 'What's happened?' Perzinski called out.

'The carriage has disappeared,' shouted Gerrard in a perplexed frenzy. 'What do you mean? Disappeared?' Quizzed Perzinski anxiously.

'It was at the rear of the train when it entered the tunnel here but it had gone when the train passed Marcel who was stationed near the other end!' He explained breathlessly.

'They must have stopped in the tunnel and disconnected it,' suggested Perzinski instantly.

'No, Sir. I very much doubt it. Marcel and I arranged to time the passage through. There was no time for them to stop, disconnect and then regain the speed to pass Marcel when it did,' Gerrard advised.

'Marcel came back through the tunnel and confirmed the carriage had just disappeared.'

'Well, where is the bloody train now?' Demanded Perzinski.

'It looks as though it carried on to the end and is just waiting there, because there is no way out at that end, it's all bricked up. Apart from the hole François made earlier, that is.'

'Then what do you suggest did happen to the carriage?' asked Perzinski with a tone of cynicism in his manner.

'I've no idea, Sir. But it's got to be in there somewhere,' Gerrard concluded. Pfeiffer thumped the rear bulkhead of the driver's cab in anger.

'Of course!' He declared.

'Of course, what?' Urged Perzinski.

'The carriage detaches itself! The old man told me about it yesterday. How stupid of me, I totally forgot about it.'

'What are you talking about, Pfeiffer?'

Pfeiffer explained the principles of the Slip-coach to Perzinski who was as surprised as he had been when the old man described the system the day before. He could not understand why he hadn't realised the significance earlier.

Perzinski advised his command of the situation by radio then told the driver to proceed slowly into the tunnel. The troops opened the sliding doors on all wagons along the train and stood ready and armed.

Whilst the train headed into the very dimly lit tunnel, Larousse and his team continued along the tunnel they had discovered from the old building. From what they could see, their tunnel seemed endless. Undaunted, they continued forward and downward as fast as they could on the slight slope towards the Nazi base.

Larousse contacted Perzinski direct by radio, advising him to send a detachment of men to the old building to remove the numerous filing cabinets and boxes they found on entry stacked against the walls of the tunnel, he added. 'Leo, there could well be some very important information within those cabinets and boxes.'

Perzinski agreed and contacted the commander of the back-up group sent by road to carry out the order. Whilst in contact, Perzinski was informed of the water samples taken at the river and sent for testing.

'Your samples have returned a result, Larousse,' he advised. 'What does it say?'

The test show presence of contaminated water, corrosive liquid, oils and vapours as well as flammable gases.

'Do they have any idea what gives rise to these findings?' asked Larousse.

Possibly due to use in cooling of electrical installations or contamination from hydraulics. 'Is what it states.'

'Good enough for me, looks like they have some sort of power plant down there.'

Larousse was ready to make his next move, then added. 'Leo. Were all three results the same, do you know?'

'Hell, no. The upper west flow tested normal, the upper east flow was heavily contaminated, and the joint lower flow was moderately contaminated.'

'That suggests the pollution starts about a mile, maybe a mile and a half in, under the mountain just east of the track bed in the tunnel if my calculations are correct.'

'It seems so Larousse, is your tunnel headed in that direction?'

'Affirmative, Leo.'

'Then this is it, we have to move forward together now, you carry on, on your side whilst my men find where this carriage has been hidden, okay.'

'Affirmative. Best of luck. Out.'

'You too. Out.'

***

Inside the Nazi base they were plainly aware, by this time, of the intruders approaching from both directions. Their superbly concealed security monitors had noted the movements from the first entry Larousse and his team made at the old building and their unofficial connection to the railway's signal and telegraph system alerted them to the passage of the train following close behind.

Max Wittenberg had cleverly and deliberately kept any show of force to a minimum whilst the base was under his guard. This he believed would avoid attention being drawn by outsiders. Now however, it seemed he may have no alternative.

He decided once the Reichsführer with General Friedrich Stoltz and the other Party hierarchy were safely inside the base and all entrances rendered impenetrable, he would begin initiating small disorientating counter attacks on the forces closing in on them.

This action he confidently predicted would give them the few hours required to install the final re-coding unit still loaded aboard the secluded carriage.

The tension inside the underground base was immeasurable, the imminent arrival of the final electronic re-coding cubicle had been long awaited by all concerned. The integration of this unit would present the ultimate weapons technology of the 21st century.

Once all connections were made, a systems verification procedure and "booting up" of the computer systems would be carried out to prove the circuitry and functions, upon satisfactory completion, the "donor missile system" would at long last become fully operational, from then on, the successful outcome of the first test target would be inevitable. And from that the Fourth Reich would be born.

***

Max Wittenberg took time to reflect whilst awaiting the General and the others arrival. He recalled the day some twenty years previous when General Friedrich Stoltz took him aside at one of the secret meetings and detailed the story of a secret base known in wartime only to a handful of senior officers in the then, German High Command.

Including Stoltz's grandfather, Heinrich. He detailed its conception, building and purpose and then bestowed upon him the honour of protecting the secret location of what was now deemed to be the birthplace of the impatiently awaited Fourth Reich.

Friedrich Stoltz's tale of the secret base had been passed from grandfather to father and thence to himself. The family, following cessation of hostilities in 1945, were loyal to the "Reichsbürger" movement as the new nationalist deemed to call it.

Stoltz continued detailing how during the Second World War, the Nazis and prominently his grandfather himself, an honoured civil engineer in peacetime had conceived and built the most extraordinary and unique specimen of civil engineering excellence for its time.

One and a half miles from the northern portal of the Oberammergau Tunnel lay the station, the old building was close by and from there, they conceived to tunnel almost halfway through the Zugspitze range some three miles distant. They systematically utilised Jewish prisoners of war to excavate a pedestrian only tunnel, this led from the old building under the outskirts of the town and then under the mountains to an area adjacent to the railway tunnel where Nazi geologists had studied data and believed a cavern was to be found.

The prisoners, men, women and children old enough to carry a mere few rocks were sent down the tunnel day and night, their meagre rations soon wore off under the intense pressure the Nazis put on them to dig still further with each day.

Within a matter of a couple of months, sometimes only weeks, even the strongest of the prisoners were reduced to a mere shadow. Undeterred, they pushed and worked every one of them until they dropped from exhaustion or worse.

The idea behind all this frenzied activity was the brainchild of a certain ex-Nazi Youth Party member now drafted into the SS as Lieutnant; Heinrich Stoltz. At the time war broke out, he was a mere twenty-six years of age and gifted beyond his youth with an exceptional civil engineering forte.

It was he who had proposed the plan in 1942 in front of the German High Command to construct a top-secret mountain base in the Tirol region. From this base, he proposed would be launched the ultimate force in modern warfare being developed by the Nazis at the time, the V3 rocket.

He presented his plans with a view of the not-too-distant future and how in the meantime, he envisaged the Reich's scientists developing still further the infant rocket technology and specialised weaponry.

The High Command dismissed the plan initially, deciding to mothball it for future consideration, much to the disappointment of the young Stoltz. Though in 1943 in response to the Fuhrer's demands for better weaponry now being developed, they reconsidered and approved its implementation, channelling, as they did, a greater flow of Jewish prisoners through the transfer camp at Oberammergau and then on to Dachau in Bavaria, from which many of whom would never see the light of day.

Soon after, Lieutnant Stoltz was transferred from duties at the Abwehr Offices in Berlin to Camp Commandant at Oberammergau Transit Camp as it was known.

The previous few months leading up to Stoltz's appointment at Oberammergau had seen the Jewish prisoners secretly prepare the camp for its changing role, from what had been up till then merely a transit camp, to a place where the local population were told the Jews now broke up rocks to assist in the Reich's war effort.

Indeed, so secretive was the project that although a tunnel was being dug from beneath the camp buildings, trucks would bring in quantities of large boulders from outside to be broken up, thus camouflaging the removal of material from the tunnel.

Needless to say, the prisoners were under sentence of death by firing squad if they dared speak of such work once they moved out of the camp for transfer. The guards had similar treatment threatened should they have loose tongues.

Stoltz's plan provided for a pedestrian tunnel leading directly from the camp administration building, which could be sealed up if necessary, once the main entrance had been established. This administration building was a mere quarter of a mile from the location of the "old building" which belonged to one of the hierarchies, the tunnel therefore passed directly beneath the "old building" allowing a connection to it should it be necessary.

Before the war ended though, Stoltz had managed to excavate the pedestrian tunnel through to its desired place under the Zugspitze Mountain, which opened into a vast cavern as the Reich's geologists had predicted from their surveys.

Once the cavern was cleared and a floor level provided, the task of building the main entrance began. Stoltz decided from the outset that the entrance should remain secretive to only a select few. No one should be able to witness the comings and goings of the supplies and materials needed to transform a bare cavernous area, into what could possibly become the most important military installation the German Reich would ever see.

His obsession with secrecy led to one of the most innovative ideas of the war. The idea sprang to him whilst he waited at Mittenwald for a train from München to Innsbruck a year or so before war was declared, though he believed it then to be inevitable. He saw something at the station, which completely took him by surprise.

At the time, he was tempted to raise the alarm at the sight before him, for in the distance the Innsbruck direct express which normally passed through Mittenwald without stopping was fast approaching and at the rear, a carriage had become detached and was coasting along behind, to his mind at that moment, obviously out of control.

However, he noticed the others including railway staff on the platform who couldn't fail to notice it were taking little heed of its plight. He approached a railway worker and asked had he noticed the detached carriage, saying he was quite concerned.

The railwayman replied that it was a relatively new idea, which he believed had come from England and was on trial in the area for twelve months. He explained that passengers could now catch the prime time express out of

München and providing they board the rear coach, it and only it, would stop at Mittenwald!

The young Heinrich Stoltz was captivated by the engineering of such a principle and had to delve deeper to find out more. Having inquired as to which platform it would arrive at, he deferred his journey until later and rushed over in time to see the strange vehicle come slowly and precisely to a halt at the end of the prescribed platform.

Once the passengers and driver had alighted, Heinrich Stoltz approached the driver and asked him quite politely if he would explain the principles behind the detachment of the carriage whilst in motion, explaining at the time he was interested in engineering matters.

The driver was only too pleased to describe in detail the method of uncoupling the coach and allowed him to view the inside of the driving cab and its controls, which were simply an uncoupling and braking device and little else. Satisfied he understood the method and design, Stoltz thanked the driver and bid him good day. From the events of that day, Heinrich Stoltz was to formulate his plan and establish the most secret of all Nazi underground establishments.

From the conception of detaching a vehicle from a moving train, Heinrich Stoltz had designed an elaborate system powered again by hydraulics, to receive vehicles direct from the railway tracks into the vast cavern below the mountain without anyone seeing a thing!

With the Nazis in control of the railways, there was no problem installing the necessary equipment to control the operational side. All signal and telegraph equipment were channelled through to the base control centre who were able to relay false details to the next section controller who would take the appropriate action where necessary assuming the previous control in either direction had issued those instructions.

By way of a bonus, all information regarding movement of trains through the Oberammergau Tunnel came through as a matter of course. This was naturally a precautionary measure as even Stoltz recognised that not all Germans' not even all military personnel were in support of the Third Reich, this therefore was a simple solution to utmost secrecy.

The next major obstacle was the building of the machinery and track work capable of handling the stowage of rolling stock needed to supply the base. This was Stoltz's "Piece-de-Resistance". For here built within the cavern from prefabricated sections, he provided a hydraulically powered traverser platform, twenty-five meters long and capable of handling a couple of loaded wagons or a full-length carriage.

With the precision with which both the platform and the reception housing were installed, it was quite impossible to detect their location from inside the tunnel.

Operation was simplicity itself. When a vehicle was due to arrive on the traverser platform, all signals turned to danger in both directions to prevent anyone accidently viewing the opening of the entrance. Marker lights rose secretly upward to assist the security approved Nazi driving the train in locating the platform.

Once the vehicle was positioned on the platform, the full twenty-five metre section would be released from the reception housing, the rail joints connecting each section of track were made to retract at each end then a hardened steel rectangular box would rise through the ballast, thus allowing the platform to be lowered enmasse into the base.

To prevent any delay due to an unforeseen fault, the loaded platform would be replaced with an identical empty platform whilst the loaded platform was lowered into the base. The six massive hydraulic rams would silently but quickly lower the section of track complete with ballast down to cavern floor level where it aligned with another track in the form of an internal Base Traverser, which served a series of short stabling sidings.

Once the vehicle had been moved from the platform to the traverser via a powered capstan, the empty platform would be returned and the main platform would then be raised up and positioned in readiness for the next delivery, the rectangular steel box would descend and the platform would vibrate enough to ensure the ballast secluded the entrance and no one would be any the wiser as to the fact it even existed.

The whole operation took no longer than four minutes. All movements were carried out in very faint light for security, plus the deployment of Nazi guards posing as Railway Permanent Way Staff at the tunnel entrances themselves on pre-planned railway maintenance movements was in times of war essential.

With the completion of this main entrance, all ancillary equipment thought necessary at the time was installed to operate all manner of machinery. Water was the power source for all hydraulic systems, this being drawn from the ample water courses on the Zugspitze Mountains. Any overflow was channelled back to the water course further downstream.

A control room was built and equipped with the specialised instrumentation and machinery controls needed to operate all systems within the Base, including the launching platform which rose high within the cavern to a point where a small section of the mountain's craggy exterior rock face would have been opened out to provide a passage for launching.

Luckily for the Allies, the new V3 rockets destined for use at Oberammergau failed to arrive before the end of the war. Shortly before which, Heinrich Stoltz still obsessed with secrecy, ensured that no one engaged on the building of Oberammergau RaketenabschuB Stutzpunkt (Oberammergau Rocket Launching Base) lived to tell the tale.

The final batch of prisoners were shot within the confines of the base, their clothes removed and their bodies carted away on one of the then frequent train movements carrying supplies. Even professional people and tradesmen engaged in the building process, under duress one may add, suffered the same fate.

They were then dressed in the Jewish prisoners' clothes to prevent anyone suspecting they were anything other than Jewish prisoners of war sentenced to death for trying to escape or otherwise. Stoltz eliminated all, bar his SS colleagues and proceeded to close the base up in the hope another day would dawn.

There was one more item Heinrich Stoltz ensured was constructed. In the six months following that first meeting, Stoltz with the aid of his two colleagues alone had gained entry to the base through an entrance concealed by the drainage channels within the railway tunnel, which ran the full length to disperse the rainfall and melting snow from above as it endlessly peculated its way through the rock.

Simple gravity drainage for the tunnel length would have been inadequate, therefore the railway engineers of the day had provided four remote water collection sumps with pumping equipment set below track level within the tunnel equidistant from each other, with two main pumping stations, one at either end outside the tunnel to disperse the water to the nearby rivers, streams and reservoirs.

The concealed entrance lay within the second remote collection sump from the northern tunnel portal. The four rectangular sump tanks measuring one metre wide, by ten metres long, by three metres deep, horizontally positioned and sunk below the track bed provided the catchment for the endless ingress of water. Once above a certain level, the remote pumps automatically cut-in and forced the excess water outward to the main pumping stations and thence to the river courses.

The second tank however had been temporarily by-passed then re-engineered by Heinrich Stoltz to include a retractable cylinder capable of holding one person which was raised up through the tunnel floor into one of the refuges provided in the tunnel wall for maintenance gang safety purposes.

The operation was of course hydraulic, with all moving parts sealed to prevent water seepage from the tank into either the cylinder itself or the passage below the tank leading to the base. Once completed, the temporary measures were removed, and the tank functioned as normal.

At the time of building the passage and the elaborate entrance system, only three people knew of its existence as all prisoners employed in the excavation and engineering were shot before they ever saw the light of day. This was Heinrich Stoltz's escape route. He had no need to worry about the other two who knew of its existence, he had shot them himself to protect this secret escape route.

From then on, until a day in July 1987, in which Heinrich Stoltz son Gunther, then 38 years of age and naturally indoctrinated into the "Reichsbürger" movement attended with his father Heinrich, then 74 years of age, one of several secret gatherings of aged ex-WW2 Nazis who remain obsessed with the concept of a Fourth Reich, within which was held secret talks discussing a new and daring plan.

The plan was put forward by a revered member of the group, a man holding the self-imposed title of Reichsführer, no less, detailing a pioneering system of "Missile command" under development at his direction at a secret location. In his plan, he advised there were three prime matters which needed to be addressed quickly and requested the "Reichsbürger" group consider the plan carefully and offer suitable recommendations.

The first:
A vast supply of diamonds would be required to fund and equip the project over the next ten or more years. This would involve finding a suitable source and the provision of a reliable method of transportation.

The second:

A top-secret location would have to be sought in which to build the systems' infrastructure over the next ten to fifteen years whilst the system was under development.

The third:

Two volunteers from the group would be needed to coordinate and manage each of the previous project requirements.

Heinrich Stoltz sat in silence at the meeting, listening to the various suggestions raised by his Kammeraden. Pleased with the fact that after 42 years, his secret had been kept from even the hierarchy of these once powerful figures in the SS.

Heinrich Stoltz ventured to say very little regarding his secret until at the third meeting held in January 1988, he saw proof positive of their indeed being such a system in the making. From this knowledge that there was now indeed a hope and real possibility of raising the Fourth Reich, he bestowed upon those present the details of the Oberammergau Raketenabschuß Stutzpunkt. Though not its precise location.

Amid frenzied shouting of disbelief and denial, luckily contained within the confines of a luxuriously appointed Board Room, where on this occasion the Party members were being accommodated by a sympathiser, such is the way these things had to be done, came the call to order from the chair. Once a semblance of order was obtained, the gauntlet was thrown down to Heinrich Stoltz from the chair to justify his claim.

Stoltz calmly described the history of the Oberammergau Base to the "Reichsbürger" hierarchy and offered some of them the opportunity of inspecting it first-hand. All present denied any knowledge of its existence and several concluded Stoltz to be no more than a romancer or even a madman.

Uncompromisingly, Stoltz suggested that two members of the group, the Chairman and the Scientist in charge of the Missile Command System plan should accompany him to inspect the facility the following evening. The other members at the meeting protested at being brushed aside by Stoltz and demanded they be included in any proposed visit.

Stoltz reiterated the fact that the secrecy of the base had been protected for 42 years and until the group approved its implementation for use in the proposed plan, he would ensure its location would remain so, insisting those who viewed it must proceed to it blindfolded.

There was an outcry. But Stoltz remained adamant. Eventually agreement was reached.

In the six months leading up to his disclosure, Heinrich Stoltz had made several visits to Oberammergau with his son Gunther, to reconnoitre the area and make presentable the interior of the base. He knew the task would be impossible alone, so therefore, he decided from the outset to impart his long-kept secret to two of his most loyal and trusted friends; Otto Oefner and Hartman Wittenberg, both of whom he trusted implicitly.

He realised also, of course, he was no longer a young man and perhaps the day would soon come when he would no longer be with us but until now, he felt no need to divulge the location of the fruits of his labour all those years ago. But now! With the distinct possibility of the birth of the Fourth Reich within his lifetime, the temptation was too great to ignore.

Soon after that first meeting of the Party hierarchy when the proposed, 'Donor Missile Control System plan was announced, he summoned both Oefner and Wittenberg to his beloved Bavarian home in Walchensee, where he proceeded to disclose the facts surrounding the "old building" and proposed operation of his vision of years ago in the underground base.'

The two men sat in silence as if entranced by some master hypnotist as he relayed the details to them. His descriptive flair had them almost able to visualise the scene inside the cavern with all the comings and goings of a war machine in action. Their adrenalin was pumping through their bodies faster and faster as Stoltz finally described how, if the rockets had been delivered six months before the surrender of Germany, he was convinced the German Nation would not have succumbed under the Allies.

The history lesson over, Stoltz then offered them their chance to make history. To play a significant part in bringing about the Fourth Reich sooner, rather than later. He advised them of the new system under development and the fact that once he was convinced of its power, he would propose the use of the Oberammergau Base.

Both men offered their allegiance and swore the old SS oath. Heinrich Stoltz concluded by warning them both if they spoke of this to anyone before he had sanctioned such, he would kill them instantly. They understood and agreed with full conviction.

The following day saw Hartman Wittenberg, head of security and charged with the task of selecting possible operatives to man the base from the vast files of sympathisers to the cause. Caution here was of the utmost concern, a mole within the base could ruin the whole operation.

Otto Oefner was seconded to Stoltz as his Aide. He would organise the operations outside the base and recruit key railway personnel to assist with the transportation arrangements.

In the six months following that first meeting in 1987, Stoltz with the aid of his two colleagues alone had gained entry to the base through the old building. Once inside, Hartman Wittenberg and Otto Oefner could only stand and look on in amazement at the sight confronting them.

A vast cavernous area, which had been transformed from bare rock into a self-contained military installation far ahead of its time. From the wide beam cast by their lamps, they could see part of the main floor area. Although the whole cavernous area was dusty and covered with debris and pools of water where the corrugated steel roof cladding had given way to the endless percolation of rain and snowfalls over the intervening forty-two years, the sight was magnificent.

The whole area was neatly laid out with supplies ranging from various oil drums, sacks, barrels, foodstuffs, weapons, ammunition boxes and the internal transport trolleys and electrically powered tractors to draw them. Masses of electrical control equipment capable of supplying power to the base direct from the plentiful natural water supply ensured no detection by others, this base was fully self-sufficient.

The traverser could be seen with two old railway wagons still in place. On the accommodation lines, two other old wagons could be seen, their contents half removed and neatly stacked on trolleys for transport to the storage area. Behind them, two oil tank wagons lay coupled together their filler pipes still attached to feed the large storage tanks.

The control room situated above the main floor was protruding outward from the rock face with no obvious support from beneath or above and no visible entrance from anywhere, its whole construction covered with a smooth armoured plating offering little means of attachment to anyone wishing to scale its face.

Stoltz gave his two trusted friends a few moments to come to terms with the sight before them, then suggested they get started. They prepared and tested the generators and power circuits. Once the lighting was reinstated, the expanse of the cavern could be appreciated in full.

The two men could hardly believe their eyes. In the distance stood the massive hydraulic platforms ahead of the traverser, the six-massive chromium plated hydraulic rams each shimmering in the light as if still new. Next, they inspected the hydraulics and found them in need of repair due to the seals bonding to the metal with lack of use. Engineers would be required from the files, suggested Stoltz.

Before the January 1988 meeting when Heinrich Stoltz decided to enlighten his Party Kammeraden to his long-kept secret, the base was made presentable, though not functional. This would require many months, perhaps years of dedicated work to repair and double check all systems for fool proof use.

Hartman Wittenberg and Otto Oefner felt justifiably proud of their respective positions as they gazed upon the base as it was meant to be. The one thing they could not penetrate yet was the control room. Stoltz was holding back on the method of entry until the base was approved for implementation. As indeed, he was resisting the temptation to deploy the engineers and others until such times as he was given the Party's approval.

The day following the January 1988 meeting, the two invited guests arrived at Stoltz's Walchensee home, accompanied by four other members of the hierarchy. Stoltz, being no man's fool, easily tricked the two to part company with the other four and travel with him whilst they followed.

He insisted they travel in his two vehicles using his own drivers. A mechanically minded member of Stoltz's staff had long ago installed a device to cut the fuel supply by use of a simple separate fuel tank attached to the underside of their car providing just a small supply of fuel with an electric fuel pump, so that this, the car following Stoltz, would appear to have suffered a fuel supply fault after some distance as the fuel gauge still exhibited well over half full, thus averting any suspicion from Stoltz.

It would then take "some time" for the driver to diagnose and repair the trouble, naturally! Only the two invited guests arrived at the secret location, blindfolded to boot!

Their approval was inevitable, within a month an account was set up for the funding of the refurbishment of the Oberammergau Base and it's upgrading to modern standards. Over the years, many of the then even new systems were replaced yet again by more technologically advanced state of the art electronic systems.

Automatic advance warning, security monitoring, defence and deterrent weaponry were mounted to operate remotely in the tunnels. The hydraulics were overhauled and tested regularly. All the old control systems and platform for the rocket launching equipment were removed and the control room refitted and made ready to accept and interface with the high technology of the latest 21st century developments of the new missile control system as and when it arrived, piece by piece.

Sadly, for Gunther Stoltz his father Heinrich, the brainchild of the Base died in 1992 aged 79. He went out of this world a very happy man as he was assured by his son Gunther, the project would be in safe hands. In Gunther Stoltz's case, himself then 43 years old, he also had a son; Friedrich who in 1987 was only sixteen years old but showing great promise in following in his father's footsteps.

The scientists developing the new missile system had by the year 1999 requested a greater and more stable electrical supply than the present water-based system to power the implementation of their proposed banks of computer servers. This task was given to Friedrich Stoltz, the founder's grandson at the age of 28, who had been educated in the family tradition of civil engineering.

At times, it seemed as if there was no stopping the imminent war machine as it grew and developed, Stoltz, Wittenberg and Oefner were enthralled with the developments, knowing as they toiled, the world slept on oblivious to the impending threat of the Fourth Reich.

As the years marched on, each had their own offspring continue where they left off as they had indoctrinated each into the Nazi dream of world domination.

***

Thinking of Fassbinder brought Max Wittenberg back to the present time and the task at hand. Wittenberg ran a tight ship. His hand-picked team of men from cleaners to engineers to guards all believed in the cause and were prepared to die for it.

Oefner on the other hand was more of an oppressive figure, especially when he had to choose an individual important to a specific function. Once he selected a prospective candidate from the sympathisers' files, he browbeat them into assisting him and the Party.

Such was the case of Herr Schnorr. He was no Nazi in reality, just a confused little man who signed a paper years ago as a youth and unfortunately the position he now held as controller at Murnau was a prime target for the likes of Oefner.

Steinbacher's three assistants, David Matthey, Jason Allen and Mark Blanford also passed through the Oefner regime as they were seconded from Neo-Nazi rallies and so forth, not the ideal recruitment policy given the importance of the operation but little or nothing was done to improve it. Stoltz made the mistake of entrusting Oefner implicitly with his own methods.

Oefner was also responsible for having Hans Fassbinder attached to Wittenberg's section, a decision Wittenberg learned to live with, though not to enjoy. He frequently voiced his opinion regarding Fassbinder's treatment of the men under him, men who had volunteered to assist the Reich only to be mistreated by a man obsessed with power and heading further and further out of control as the time approached for the first test.

It was fast approaching the moment when the Nazi hierarchy's carriage would be brought to rest on the hydraulic platform from which it would be lowered down into the base then the whole place sealed up and made impenetrable.

Max Wittenberg considered the position. He happily concluded that within a few hours, government and world powers would be at the mercy of the Fourth Reich.

Chapter Twelve

The moment arrived approaching 01.00 hrs when the order to prepare the platform to accept the carriage was given. With complete and well-practiced efficiency, the underground crews began the task.

Max Wittenberg had adorned his dress uniform of Oberst (Colonel), the uniform was a slight improvement over the old SS style, still in black with a slightly different and more stylish cut for the early 21st century. Rank was once again depicted on the collar of the tunic in company with the SS flashes. Jackboots, of course, were a pre-requisite to ensure the new style bestowed upon the bearer and the onlooker a powerful image indeed.

As he marched across the floor to the reception platform of the traverser, Max Wittenberg instructed one of the guards to bring the camera equipment to the platform. He then announced over the speakers for the guards to bring the prisoner to the traverser immediately. Within two minutes, both requests had been fulfilled. Max lifted the video camera and held it in his hands as he announced.

'Herr Cameron. In a few moments, you will witness the arrival of the highest members of our "Reichsbürger" movement right here on this platform.'

Robert looked up at the engineering feat in awe. Six powerful hydraulic rams bedded into what seemingly appeared to be simple rock, there was a rectangular outline; however, Robert remained puzzled regarding the possibility or the probability of any kind of operation which could be made through solid rock.

Wittenberg continued. 'They have all come together this night from across the globe to witness our resurgence. The birth of the Fourth Reich. The Rebirth of the Oberammergau Raketenabschub Stutzpunkt. Now known as the Oberammergau Donor Missile Base, to you.'

Robert had a reasonable understanding of German and had easily identified the term.

'Rocket's!' Replied Robert, feigning concern. 'Surely you don't intend launching rockets from here, how?' Robert was interrupted.

'Of course, Herr Cameron, you would not know this. The Oberammergau Raketenabschub Stutzpunkt was created during the war by our own Herr General Stoltz's grandfather, you will have the pleasure of meeting him very soon. Had our glorious Third Reich received the new proposed V3 rockets then nearing completion, we would have won the war without doubt.'

Robert interrupted this time. 'So, you're telling me you have some 70-year-old rockets you intend to launch from here, impossible, I have seen no launching area or anything capable of such a thing. I think you are bluffing, Herr Oberst.' Robert gave Wittenberg his appointed title to flatter him rather than provoke him, he hoped it would serve for him to elaborate somewhat.

Wittenberg obliged to a point, continuing, 'Are you a journalist or just a fool, Herr Cameron? Do you honestly think we Germans have sat on an old 70-year-old rocket design and are intent on using them now, after all this time, really is that the best you can do?'

'Well, that is what you said, more or less.'

'Oh no Herr Cameron, we the "Reichsbürger" movement have developed the old Oberammergau Raketenabschub Stutzpunkt base for 21st century warfare, we have re-titled it the "Donor Missile Base"; the "Reichsbürger Resurgence" will rise here this day, the Fourth Reich will dominate the world.'

Wittenberg was in an awe inspired moment, his emotions playing out for all to see, it was indeed a theatrical performance to encourage all those around him. Cries of "Sieg Heil! Sieg Heil! Sieg Heil!" reverberated around the cavernous area. He continued.

'We no longer need to manufacture our own weapons of war; our brightest minds have over many decades toiled with the advanced technology available and now at last, we have wanton control of many nations' armaments at our fingertips.'

Robert was stunned into silence as he grasped the gravity of Wittenberg's statement, for a moment he lost his composure, saying.

'You call it 21st century warfare, the rest of the world will simply call it terrorism. You're nothing but a bunch of madmen.' Wittenberg slammed the desk with his swagger stick.

'Do not try to infuriate me Herr Cameron, I could have easily had you shot in the cellar, remember.' Robert's heart sank, he couldn't help himself.

'Is that what happened to Kate, my wife, is she dead? I demand to know, you barbarian.'

'Your wife is of no concern to me and you should consider your own position, you are only here because I want you to report to the world the power we hold, you will see first-hand our donor missile system in action, we will strike our first target at 03.00 hrs, Herr Cameron. We will avenge!' He shouted aloud.

More chants of Sieg Heil followed.

Robert thought he had better play along a while longer whilst he thought hard what on earth, he could possibly do to stop the madness. He started by asking.

'If what you say is true and you can fire these "donor missiles" at will, what makes you think all of Germany will be in favour of your actions this day. I for one do not think the German people will wish to tolerate another era of fascism, they, the ordinary Germans like most nations don't want another war, you only have to look at the current situation with Russia invading Ukraine to see the world as a whole are against Russia for starting that unprovoked war, why on earth do you want to wage war, its bloody madness.'

'Herr Cameron, there will be no war. You have no idea what our system is capable of, how else do you think we the "Reichsbürger" intend to convince our German brothers and sisters we can have world domination? We understand that the world I'm afraid will not react kindly to our demands. They remember the mistakes of our glorious Reich seventy years and more ago only too vividly. Therefore, we have a program to follow whereby the world leaders will ultimately succumb to our overall power and you Herr Cameron are being privileged to witness a new day dawn.'

He handed the camera over to Robert and continued.

'I offer you the privilege of recording for future generations how the Fourth Reich began right here, right now, this very day. You must write your story telling the world how futile their attempts at destroying this base would be. I will show you in person how powerful our weaponry and defences really are and I want you to make this clear to the outside world before there is any need for further bloodshed.'

'Why does there need to be any bloodshed if what you say is true?'

'Unfortunately, as I have said Herr Cameron, merely announcing to the world the fact the Fourth Reich is at long last a reality will not be enough to ensure their cooperation. They may consider counter attacks or some other absurd retaliatory show of force, which we already know is being mounted against us.' Robert continued his pretence.

'What retaliatory show of force, I don't understand.'

'I would like to believe you, Herr Cameron but the fact remains that you and your wife were caught snooping and asking awkward questions while at the same time, there is an approaching NATO detachment making their way to the tunnel as we speak. There is also a smaller force who think they have penetrated the tunnel you recently passed through.'

Robert knew this could only mean Larousse found his cufflink and was close by. Max continued.

'Therefore, we must provide a demonstration to convince those in authority we have the awesome power at our fingertips to render their defences ineffective. Surely you understand the necessity for such a demonstration?'

'What kind of demonstration?' asked Robert.

'Oh, quite a simple one really. It is our intention to destroy London.' Max smiled at the thought, he then added.

'Oh yes, I forgot to mention the fact, although this is indeed the Oberammergau Donor Missile Base, the missiles which will destroy the target will be fired by one of King Charles 3rd's very own precious Royal Navy's submarines. HMS Audacious to be exact.'

'From its own complement of missiles, several will be launched under direct orders from your Admiralty or so HMS Audacious' Captain will believe. Ingenious, don't you think?' Max smiled again with a smug look of certain satisfaction.

Robert considered the statement.

'So, it's true,' mumbled Robert in a low voice, though not low enough as Max had overheard him.

'True! Of course, it's true. What did you mean "it's true"?' Max bellowed. 'Are you saying you know something of our plans, Herr Cameron?' The thought agitated Max.

'No! No, I said is it true.'

'I know what I heard, Herr Cameron. You distinctly said, "So, it's true", did you not?'

'I don't know what I said! God almighty, this is a bit of a shock you know, I'm just not thinking straight. I assure you I know nothing of your plans, how could I, eh?' Robert responded quickly, hoping to convince him, knowing that if he failed, he may no longer be a luxury he could afford.

Robert promptly changed the subject and reversed the line of questioning by Max into a plea for clemency from himself as the significance of the target struck him.

'London! My God. Surely you realise, there will be millions of innocent people in London. My God, you're insane! You're provoking another world war! For Christ's sake, have you no shame, think of the innocent people, please! I beg you to call this off,' pleaded Robert.

'Call it off! You fool, we have brought forward the event because of recent developments threatening us from beyond these impenetrable walls. We intend allowing you no mercy before bringing you all to your knees. The Fourth Reich has waited long and patiently for this moment, do not be so foolhardy Herr Cameron as to think a mere plea from you would sway our destiny. I think not. And I add, any interference from you and I will have you shot on the spot. Do I make myself clear?'

In the few moments, it took Max Wittenberg to utter those last words, Robert had become nauseated from the sudden awareness of what was shortly to take place. He thought of the thousands, more likely millions of innocent people who would be massacred at the hands of this handful of lunatic fanatics.

He could hold himself no longer, the revulsion of the pictures forming in his mind of the devastation, which would result from their actions caused him to vomit. He had no control over his actions. Wittenberg stepped aside in the nick of time, avoiding the ghastly mess as it splashed on the concrete floor.

Robert was still retching beyond his control. Wittenberg ordered the guard to take him away and have the disgusting mess cleaned up before the hierarchy arrived.

The guard dragged Robert by the collar towards the amenity block and ordered him to make himself presentable and quickly, as the approach of the hierarchy was imminent. Both returned to the platform just as the announcer informed the train was now approaching the platform.

Robert was handed a TV grade shoulder mounted camcorder plus a 35mm camera together with a bag containing various lenses and such. One of the guards clipped a small voice activated recorder to his shirt. Wittenberg took a moment to brief him.

'The camcorder will activate by pressing the trigger on the hand hold. You will begin recording immediately and include a positive commentary as you do so, therefore you are to record the event as it happens. I will be watching and listening. The voice recording will of course be edited and analysed as will the sound and vision track from the recording. So, for your own sake, do not be foolish. Keep your report positive, unbiased and factual, remember you are witnessing history in the making. Take heed of what I say, Herr Cameron. I warn you.'

Max turned to the guard. 'Keep an eye on him at all times,' he ordered as he made his way to the arrival platform.

Robert positioned himself, trying to look as though he was a journalistic professional. He replied, 'Herr Oberst, I am a journalist not a TV reporter, I am not comfortable with this type of technology, may I just use the SLR?'

'Nien! Herr Cameron,' bellowed Wittenberg.

'You will record this moment in time or you will be shot here and now!'

Robert nodded as he conceded to his demands. His composure was weakening as he could see no positive outcome to the series of events he was witnessing. From overhead, he heard movement from the armoured steel shutters of the control room, as they released each shutter retracted a mere two centimetres and slid slowly, precisely, behind the lower panel downward to provide the operatives with a visual of the Party hierarchy arriving.

Robert was positioned next to a monitor showing live pictures from the camera located to view the reception platform. With the camera on his shoulder aimed at the monitor, he pressed the trigger. A green light illuminated in the bottom right corner of the screen.

Robert could see the train passing at a fair speed through the tunnel, he couldn't understand at this point how anything could possibly be alighting from this train, it was travelling far too fast. As the train cleared the monitor screen, he looked on in amazement as small transparent globes rose from under the track and through the ballast to protrude and illuminate gently the general area.

A few moments later, following the passage of the train which had completely passed the platform by, Robert could see in the distance a shadowy shape of a lone carriage coasting towards the platform unaided. It was the carriage in the photographs, he was sure of it.

He stood transfixed as he saw the driver slow the carriage down and position it almost dead centre between the dull glow of the illumination. This achieved, the marker lights of the hydraulic platform were retracted into the ballast, simultaneously a clamping system rose through the ballast and gripped the front and rear sets of wheels. The lights within the base were dimmed to a mere glow. All armed guards were in position, ready to defend against attack.

Robert asked if he could get closer to see the operation from a better vantage point. The guard agreed and ushered him forward.

'This is fantastic. I've never seen anything like it. Can I film up into the tunnel, just to prove how it's done?' asked Robert.

'Yes but no tricks. Understand?' Replied the guard.

Wittenberg noticed Robert repositioning and shouted over to him.

'Herr Cameron, the arrival you are currently capturing for posterity will not, naturally, be disclosed to the outside world, this will serve to inspire future generation of the "Reichsbürger" movement that is all. Ensure you report fully the magnificence of the spectacle. Understand?'

Robert nodded in agreement and moved down onto the traverser and began filming again. He grasped to a point that the carriage would be lowered somehow into the base but looking at the mass of rock above, he thought it impossible. To his amazement, he heard a dull noise, this was the locking mechanism releasing.

Once the platform was free, to his amazement a massive section of seemingly solid rock began to lower, slowly at first until it was at a point where the rock section cleared the overhead rock face, from then the platform tilted slightly downward a little speedier, he calculated, to assist the release of the carriage by gravity alone. To his amazement a second platform was replacing the missing one in the tunnel.

Robert could only admire the feat of engineering he was witnessing. As the carriage cleared the rocky overhead obstructions Robert considered his options, he would have to choose his moment well and he quickly surmised he had two options.

'The first, to jump up and on to the platform in a bid to escape, which,' he thought, 'would be pretty foolhardy given the lack of cover afforded by the flat platform and the large void he would have to scale to reach the tunnel floor, this in addition to the amount of guards strategically placed to prevent such foolhardiness, all of whom were wielding automatic weapons of one sort or another.'

His second choice, less effective perhaps was to use the second cufflink, which he had previously placed in his pocket when the handcuffs had been removed for fear, they may notice one was already missing. He concluded this to be the safer of the two actions considering the situation, hoping against all hope, once again it would get noticed.

Here at least, as opposed to the old building, he knew Larousse had been through and carried out a thorough inspection, the appearance of a cufflink may give just cause to delve deeper. It was a million to one chance but Robert felt it may be more beneficial to be held by the Nazis than if he did escape. An opportunity may present itself, if not now, perhaps later.

Within a split second, he decided on the latter, he reached into his pocket and removed the second cufflink, the last cufflink. As the platform came to rest, it aligned with the internal traverser and the clamps released, luckily for Robert, the guard had taken his eyes off him to follow the arrival of the hierarchy.

He used the motion of placing the camera gadget bag on the platform holding the carriage and removed the 35mm camera to take a few still pictures, at the same time dropping the cufflink onto the platform floor. Quickly, he snapped-off a few still shots and retrieved the bag before the carriage rolled off onto the traverser and its momentum controlled by a retarder braking mechanism on the traverser.

Immediately, the carriage cleared the platform, it began rising beyond his shoulders. The guard saw nothing amiss with his actions thankfully. The last action was the return of the empty platform and the combined retraction of the clamps, the marker lights and for a few moments once the platform had quickly returned to tunnel ground level, it vibrated to allow the loose ballast to settle as it closed any voids and served to disguise its existence once again.

Locking in place of the platform confirmed by the dull electrical thud he had heard previously. The base returned to normal illumination.

His heart was pounding with fear now as he drew his arm back praying, he had not been seen by any of the other guards. In truth, Robert had been fortunate. All grades of personnel had their eyes focussed on the arrival of the hierarchy of the "Reichsbürger" Party, some of whom had never been seen in Europe before, some naturally were direct descendants of escaped WW2 Nazis.

This was the biggest event for the Nazi Party since the coming to power of Adolf Hitler. It was a time to reflect. A time to honour. A day to remember. No-one within the complex wished to forego such a moment in history. The "Reichsbürger" movement would at last be able to show its awesome power.

The order still in place for complete silence duly obeyed and the hydraulic platform locking into place and confirmed secured by the control room staff, the lighting was restored to full power. Robert breathed a long sigh of relief as he looked at the monitor. It showed the rail tunnel unchanged with no visible sign of his cufflink, he was duly pleased with his efforts.

Robert knew instinctively he had to reach the control room for any hope of alerting Larousse and Perzinski's NATO team to the location of the entrance, he just wondered how.

The few seconds between the lights being restored and the door of the carriage opening seemed like hours to Robert as he watched through the viewfinder of the camcorder as it filmed endlessly on. He attempted to detail the events in the manner a professional journalist would do and he knew it would have to sound convincing.

The intense atmosphere within the base as everyone awaited the first member of the hierarchy to step out from the carriage caused him to perspire, more so with apprehension than with fear itself. He suddenly thought to himself. 'Perhaps this Max Wittenberg wants the event recorded but will the others who have just arrived? They may find his presence unacceptable. What then?'

He looked on nervously as the Guard of Honour were ordered to attention on the reception apron, awaiting the disembarkation of the revered members of the "Reichsbürger". Whilst the German National Anthem was being played over the loudspeaker system.

The traverser rolled along to align with a short length of track surrounded by a raised concrete deck. The carriage was transferred from the traverser by a powered capstan to the short section of track and the handbrake applied. Robert had the video camera on "record", he captured on film the arrival of the forty plus Kammeraden as they filed out of the coach one by one in their black overalls.

He had no knowledge of who was who at this stage, only that they were all Nazis intent on destroying London and possibly the rest of the world as he knew it. He vowed to himself that no matter what happened he would do his utmost to prevent them.

If not for his sake, then for the sake of Katriana, if indeed she was still alive. She had to be alive, this was the reason he was doing what he was doing and it was to ensure her future, whether it be together with him or otherwise.

As he pondered his situation while watching Max greet each and every one of his guests of honour in person, he could see little hope of a successful conclusion. With the final guest taking his place on one of the internal transport vehicles, Max ordered the immediate removal of the crate and its transport to the control room for installation. Robert decided to keep a watchful eye on this crate in the hope it would lead to the control room entrance.

Whilst following the transport vehicles with one eye, he was making sure the guard thought him to be filming the general comings and goings as the base swung into defensive mode. The announcement came over the speakers that the train following had entered the tunnel mouth and was proceeding very cautiously through the tunnel.

Noise to be kept to a minimum. The lighting dimmed yet again for fear of the slightest escape through the recently disturbed ballast surrounding the platform. Max ordered the tunnel guns to fire if there was any sign they knew the location. If not, then to let them pass unhindered.

He commented briefly to one of the Party members, though Robert overheard him, saying, 'It will take them days, weeks even, to find anything. By that time, we will be giving the orders.' Robert shuddered at the thought as Max called out. 'Herr Cameron. Come here.'

Robert was escorted over by the guard.

'Herr Cameron, may I introduce you to Herr General, Friedrich Stoltz. The grandson of the designer and builder of the Oberammergau Base you stand in today.'

'General Stoltz,' Robert replied, gritting his teeth at the thought of having to be pleasant to such a man but for the moment, it seemed sensible to do so.

'Herr General. This is one of the people I caught prying and asking questions about the railway tunnel. He claims to be a journalist from some magazine or other. So, I have given him the task of recording the events of the next few days or as long as it takes for the world to see how futile any reprisals will be. We will be able to remember this day for many years to come, Herr General,' Max announced boldly.

'Excellent, Max! Just what we need to stir the blood of the youth in our country. Once Germany and the German people see we at long last hold a dominant position, they will be behind us all the way, just as they were in 1939. Now come, we have work to do.'

Max advised the control room from his portable handset clipped to his tunic; he required entry. As he did so, a section of the control room underside lifted upward partially and slid inward as on the front panels, again the engineering of which was impeccable.

This revealed a concealed collapsible stairway. Once the panel had slid clear under the floor, the stairway began lowering from one end to ground level complete with banister rails forming either side. Robert stood apprehensively as Max ushered his fellow Party members to the stairway.

He watched as the forty-plus hierarchy ascended the stairway into the control room. Then came the moment he'd been waiting for, praying for.

'Are you joining us, Herr Cameron?' asked Max in a sociable tone. 'As you wish,' answered Robert, seemingly unconcerned.

'I always considered journalists to be inquisitive people, you seem a little distant from your work, Herr Cameron.'

'I think I'm still in shock, to be quite honest. I just can't take it in, you know,' he replied, knowing his misgivings were beginning to show, he knew he had to make a greater effort otherwise his presence would no longer be tolerated. His distractions were however twofold.

First, he couldn't stop thinking about Katriana and if or not she was still alive and if so, where were they holding her. Second, he had to somehow prevent this base and the weaponry within being commissioned by whatever means and he knew whatever was in that crate may hold the key to the operation, otherwise why would it be so important at this stage.

Max interrupted his thoughts, agreeing with his excuse then inviting him on a guided tour.

'Come, let me show you around.'

Robert followed him up the stairway and into the control room. 'Raise the stairway,' ordered Max.

Robert cast his gaze across the control staff to catch sight of the operative controlling the function. He noticed from a bank of controls one lever out of alignment to the others and displaying a red lamp. Once the stairway had been heard "clicking" into its housing in the floor section, the lamp changed to green and the lever was returned to its neutral location.

He also noted the hierarchy were nowhere to be seen, strange considering over forty of them entered only moments before.

Satisfied he now knew the lever controlling the staircase, he continued to familiarise himself with his surroundings. All displays were of course in German, some of which he found difficult to translate, others were simply numbered numerically with the addition of an alphabetical code, which meant absolutely nothing to him.

Robert concentrated for a moment on what the combined code symbols could translate to; he knew "Bahnsteig" meant platform in German; so, would their controls be marked "Bahnsteig" or just alphabetical or numerical. He could see nothing in the codes that made any sense to him but still he persevered, toying with translations knowing his first objective would be to find the controls governing the opening of the railway platform and the tunnel entrance to the old building. Robert found the task more difficult than he'd imagined.

Max ushered him towards a steel panel at the rear, as he walked through the control room filming the various banks of computer and electronics equipment, most of the controls remained a mystery to him, simply levers, buttons, key operated switches and a multitude of computer-controlled functions and displays.

He had to think straight, he had to be positive, he had to be lateral and the stress was beginning to outwardly show by his repeated filming of certain sections. His stomach was churning again, his revulsion returning as he could think of no way to stop this madness. Those in the tunnel outside had by now passed by the platform, he noted this on the control room monitors.

It was down to him and him alone. Suddenly, the steel panel he was adjacent to clicked and began sliding open to reveal a lengthy corridor behind. Robert could hardly contemplate how all this excavation had been carried out unbeknown to anyone, it was indeed awe inspiring.

General Stoltz returned through the open doorway with several of the hierarchy now shorn of their black overalls and sporting their "Reichsbürger" Dress Uniforms detailing clearly their level of authority. Stoltz began taking an interest in Robert's movements and became uneasy at his presence, he strongly suggested to Max, he should be limited to the general area and not the control room.

Max stated he only wished him to witness the transmission for the launching of the donor missile and the destruction of the submarine. From then on, he would be held in a detention room where he would remain until it was necessary for him to tell the story to the world and then only if the facts were doubted.

Stoltz reiterated he was not content with the freedom of movement allowed to continue; he told Max he would have him accompany him to the sitting room once the final re-coding unit was brought up. Max agreed to Stoltz's wishes. Robert had just about overheard the conversation and realised this final unit could be something they desperately required.

All systems in the base had now returned to normal following the passage of the train. Below the control room, the transport vehicle carrying the crate containing the re-coding unit had arrived. Max ordered the hoist to be lowered. At the opposite end from the stairway, a floor panel opened as before and an overhead travelling hoist was positioned centrally above the opening. As the cable travelled downward, Robert inquired as to what was happening. Max was happy to oblige.

'One final section of our equipment must be installed before we are fully functional. This will take approximately one and a half hours. After which, all that needs to be done is to calibrate the readings before the final test can begin. Please do not try to be a hero, Herr Cameron. There's absolutely nothing you could do to prevent our demonstration taking place. If you do try something foolish, I re-iterate I'll have you shot on the spot, do you understand?'

Robert smiled with a contemptuous looking smirk, which needed no elaboration.

'You don't approve of our methods, Herr Cameron?'

'I have never approved of tyranny, Herr Oberst,' he snapped.

'Enough! You are here at my request, may I remind you. I can easily have you removed permanently, if you wish,' hissed Max.

Before he could answer, the ground crew advised the unit was ready to hoist. Max swung around and ordered them to continue. Moments later, the metal cased electronic cabinet having been un-packed from its wooden crate was raised up above the control room floor, the floor panel was returned to the original position and the unit lowered and unleashed from the crane then wheeled along on its built-in retractable castors to the open doorway leading to the corridor.

One tunnel monitor operative interrupted proceedings momentarily by advising the approach of the unauthorised train, which was reversing and almost upon them. It seemed to be coming slowly to a stop close to the platform.

Max rushed over to the monitor whilst ordering the unit be installed immediately.

'Is everything locked in position?' He shouted out.

'Ja wohl. Herr Oberst,' came the reply.

'Yellow alert!' He called.

The noise died down and the lights dimmed again. He watched the train come to a standstill and Max deliberated as to how they could have come to stop so close to the platform. Could it be just luck, he doubted the fact.

'Herr Oberst! NATO soldiers in the tunnel!' The operative announced. Max returned to the monitor.

'Soldiers. I presume you know nothing of this either, Herr Cameron?'

'NATO soldiers, how the hell would I know anything about NATO soldiers?

But one thing's for sure, they know about you, it seems,' Robert answered with some satisfaction over an interjection from the far end of the control room.

'That man! Is the NATO Base Commander at Panzer Kaserne, Böblingen. Some half-breed Polish American, I believe. Perzinski is his name.' General Stoltz enlightened the onlookers.

'I do not understand, Herr General. Where have they got this information from and why now?' Max asked, somewhat bemused.

'Herr Steinbacher, I can only assume. He was our supply agent in England until he and his men got careless. I tried to have him eliminated.'

Robert's blood boiled as he heard the General mention the word eliminate, for that was what he'd done to his brother, perhaps personally! Or perhaps not but certainly by his orders no doubt.

The General continued, 'But I'm afraid he managed to escape. He, my friend is the only weak link in the whole operation.' Stoltz solemnly declared.

'If only you knew.' Robert thought to himself.

'What are they looking at?' Quizzed the monitor operator. Robert's heart missed a beat. He swallowed hard. If they identified his cufflink, it would surely mean the end for him.

In the tunnel, Perzinski had ordered his men to alight in pairs from the train at fifty-meter intervals as it proceeded through. One soldier had caught sight of a reflection whilst waving his torch and found it to be a cufflink. The soldiers had of course been advised the tunnel had been thoroughly searched, therefore if anything seemed unusual, it was to be reported immediately.

Perzinski, Pfeiffer and a few others were examining the piece of jewellery, wondering if it was indeed a sign of some sort or merely a lost item. Luckily for Robert, they had their backs to the secluded camera monitoring the tunnel. Pfeiffer was first to comment.

'It must be a signal, it's too clean to have been here for any length of time. In any case, Monsieur Larousse and his men combed this tunnel earlier, if it had been here, then they would have found it,' stated Pfeiffer with some certainty.

'Okay, supposing this is some sort of signal, what the hell does it mean?' Quizzed Perzinski.

'I have no idea. But whatever it is, it must be here somewhere. An entrance or something.'

'Entrance! Where the hell's an entrance in this God-damn hole! Its sheer rock for Christ's sake, Klaus. Where would you start?' Screeched Perzinski, his voice echoing along the tunnel.

Pfeiffer looked around. 'Anyone have any idea? This must be the place; it simply must be,' he said forlornly.

There were no forthcoming suggestions. Only eyes wandering and scanning the rocky interior.

'That bloody carriage of theirs couldn't just disappear through the bloody walls now, could it? Let's be serious about this Klaus, there's no way, look at them, its God-damn solid rock with a fucking mountain above,' screeched Perzinski.

'Listen, Commander. This is all we have to go on. The carriage came in the tunnel but it is not at the end of the train down there and it has not come out, correct?'

'Yes but that don't mean it went through the God-damn bloody walls, Klaus! Now, does it?'

'No, so where else could it go?'

'If I knew that we wouldn't be standing here arguing about it, would we Inspector,' retorted Perzinski, by now a shade perplexed.

Robert stood watching the saga develop on the monitor screen, praying that they kept the cufflink out of view. Then he saw Gerrard limping towards them. His heart pounded harder, would Gerrard remember him wearing them, it was a long shot and he couldn't be sure if he would, he couldn't be sure he'd even seen them let alone remember.

Max laughed a little at the situation.

'Your friends out there, they seem to be having some difficulty, Herr Cameron. I don't suppose its everyday a whole railway carriage disappears before their very eyes.' He laughed.

Several members of the control staff joined Max in the humour regarding the plight of those in the tunnel.

'No matter, there is no chance of them locating the platform, our mission will not be interrupted, I assure you,' said General Stoltz when the laughter subsided. 'Take the control cabinet to the server room and begin installation immediately,' ordered Stoltz.

A small team of technicians wheeled the innocent looking grey steel enclosure measuring approximately 1.8 meters tall by 50 centimetres square along and through the open doorway and along the corridor to an opening part way down on the right.

Stoltz watching the progress whilst Robert commented.

'So, you're the man behind all this then,' he asked to avert their eyes from the monitor.

'That is correct, Herr Cameron. My grandfather designed and constructed this work of genius during the war believe it or not. The war we should have won! The High Command would not implement its use in time, had they had done so! I assure you; the outcome of the war would have been very different. Very different indeed. You! Young man, would be under the rule of the German Nation and you would have been grateful.'

Robert glared at Stoltz as he uttered those final words. He gritted his teeth at the thought. Had they won the war, he would not have been under the rule of the German Nation but under the rule of the Nazi Party, that was the difference, a vast difference.

Stoltz sensed the communication.

'You do not believe me? You wait and see, Herr Cameron. We are not the barbarians people make out. We are simply born into this world to be its leaders and after tonight's little demonstration, the world will quickly be begging us to do just so.'

'So, tell me General, what is actually going to happen?' asked Robert, averting his annoyance at the General's inference.

'Come with me, Herr Cameron. I'll explain the principles of the system while the technicians complete the commissioning.' he added, 'Do not try to be a hero, Herr Cameron.'

The General guided Robert together with Peer for company close behind through the armour-plated doorway and along the corridor, which led on the left to extensive comfortable living quarters cut deep into the bare rock itself. His intention merely to remove the intruder from the vulnerable control room rather than impart any prime knowledge of the "donor missile system".

Max smiled as the General led Robert along the corridor and away from the hub of operations. He watched them both closely until he knew they had passed through the bottom doors to the sitting room area where the other Party members had congregated to partake in a celebratory drink or two while watching events on a large split screen monitor.

Robert's eyes gave away his thoughts as he cast them rearward. The General sensed he wished to be where the "action" was and informed him they would return once the time had come to carry out the test. Changing the subject, he continued.

'As you can see Herr Cameron, we are completely self-sufficient down here. We have everything necessary to make a long stay both a comfortable and relaxing one. Would you care for a glass of Schnapps?' asked Stoltz sociably.

Robert declined the offer. One, would no doubt lead to another among the premature celebrations he could hear emanating from the room just ahead of him. In any case, this was no time for clouded judgement.

In the tunnel, Gerrard could shed no light on the mysterious cufflink. Perzinski therefore persuaded Pfeiffer to continue to the end of the tunnel and if nothing could be found, they would return to the same spot. They marked the area with a yellow aerosol and posted a couple of men on guard. The train moved off and returned southward and away from the Nazi base. The base returned to normal once again.

***

Larousse and his team meanwhile had almost reached the end of the tunnel from the old building. In the short distance ahead, they could see a large steel door in the rock, which had no visible means of operation. It appeared the door slid one way or the other to open but which was the dilemma.

Naturally, their passage had been carefully monitored and Max had been kept advised. Larousse held back from the steel door in the distance, knowing instinctively there would be some sort of armed response from within.

'Okay men, this is it. Behind that door is where we need to be. There's a good chance some of us won't make it so I just want to say, thank you to all of you for coming this far. To my team, André, Marcel, Carl. You did not sign up for this level of danger, you are free to return without malice, I hope to see you all soon on the other side. Chambers, Malhotra and I have no choice, we must continue.'

He struggled to say those words, for he truly meant them, he knew what he was facing and he knew neither one of them may survive this night.

The others thanked him but agreed to continue regardless, they all shook hands. Max witnessed the scene and commented, 'So touching, suicidal fools!'

'Chambers. I'm sorry it's you who must go in first. Do you think you can blow it?'

'Depends on how thick it is, Sir. How deeply the fixings are into the rock and what the door itself is made of. But we won't know till we try, eh! Sir,' he commented lightly.

'Hold on. See if you can find any cameras anywhere. They must surely have surveillance down here. If we can knock them out, we stand a better chance,' said Larousse.

The men crept forward slowly, their eyes fixed on the tunnel walls for hidden cameras. The task was almost impossible, two cameras were built into the steel door and disguised as rivet heads, another was positioned further up the tunnel to view the door itself, this was simply a Wi-Fi operated lens sunk through a small-bore hole in the rock and no larger than the end of a pencil, it was impossible to find among the various tones in the rock face.

This was one of the technological improvements the "Reichsbürger" had carried out when they authorised the refurbishment of the base together with improved defences as Larousse was about to find out.

Back in the Base Control Room, their movements were being studied carefully.

'One man is preparing explosives, Herr Oberst,' advised a technician.

Max Wittenberg casually looked down at the monitor screen. In a low voice, he spoke as if to justify his actions both to himself and the others.

'We have no option, Herr Kammeraden. We cannot allow this mere token opposition force to attempt a forced entry at this stage, we must initiate our defences and hold them back. In any case, in just under one hour the world will know the hidden might of the Oberammergau and the resurgence of the German Reich!'

Max walked away from the monitor and gave the order. 'Open fire in the building access tunnel.'

With that, several secluded automatic weapons came into operation. The bullets ricocheted off the tunnel walls as they fired indiscriminately within its confines. Larousse and the team ran back for cover, miraculously no one was killed though André took a flesh-wound in the shoulder. The guns continued to fire for several minutes then stopped as quickly as they had started.

Larousse took two hand-grenades from their plentiful supplies, primed them and tossed them as far as he could along the tunnel.

'Take that, you Nazi bastards!' He shouted.

A few seconds later amid the dust still rising from the gunfire, the explosions sent a shockwave through the rock and debris scattering along towards Larousse and his team. General Stoltz jumped up and dashed back to the control room.

'What was that?' He cried aloud.

'The men in the building access tunnel Herr General, they've reached the door. We opened fire, they have retaliated with grenades,' replied Max.

'Open fire again. They must not get through that door. What's happening in the railway tunnel?'

'The train has moved on, Herr General. They have posted two men on guard at several locations. It appears they have found nothing, a mere coincidence.'

'Good. Let them keep going back and forward, they could be there for days the bloody fools,' said General Stoltz, seemingly unconcerned.

Robert had seized the opportunity and followed the General into the control room. He'd overheard the gist of the conversation. He surmised the General was more concerned with the tunnel from the old building than the railway tunnel. He concluded that this must be their weak link.

Now he had to find a way of helping Larousse breach it. If he could only get Larousse through that door without getting shot in the process. That was the dilemma.

***

Katriana, after deciding what she had to do, had given Heidi the slip and ran all the way to the northern portal of the railway tunnel, she had discarded the shoes Heidi had given her for they were too large and were holding back her progress.

Two soldiers had been posted to guard the entrance, Katriana persuaded one of the men posted there to help her reach the Inspector and the NATO

Commander. She told him she had vital information from her father and that he couldn't get through. He assisted her along the tunnel till they met up with the two men posted guard where the cufflink had been found.

'Where are they?' She asked breathlessly.

'Gone to the other end of the tunnel, ma'am. We ain't found nothing yet, only a cufflink or something,' the soldier answered.

'Cufflink! What was it like? Did you see it?'

'No, ma'am. Commander's got it, I think.'

In the control room, the monitor operator noticed Katriana's arrival in the tunnel.

'Herr Oberst. Eine Frauline!' He announced with astonishment.

'Ah! Herr Cameron. I see your wife or shall we say assistant, is at the sharp end of your little assignment, eh,' said Max wryly. 'She looks a little worse for wear I would say,' he added sarcastically.

Robert's eyes lit up as he caught sight of Katriana on the monitor. His heart pounded hard sending a shiver through his body, she was alive that was all he needed to know, he looked at the monitor, she was in such a bedraggled condition and was performing for all to see, waiving her arms and shouting at the soldiers; she looked like some sort of raving lunatic to those in the control room.

'She has a temper your wife, eh! Herr Cameron.' Robert smiled and gestured in agreement.

'I think it is time for the truth, don't you? Please Herr Cameron unless you co-operate, I will be forced to open fire in the railway tunnel also and I guarantee your lady friend there will not escape this time.'

Robert riposted.

'You harm one hair on her head and I'll personally see you to damnation!' Robert said with vehemence in his voice.

'Strong words Herr Cameron, especially from a man whose time on earth is running shorter and shorter. Choose your next comment carefully Herr Cameron, I could have your friends there shot any second and all I have to do is push the button.'

Max turned to Peer the guard.

'Take him away, Peer. He's outlived his usefulness for the time being.'

Peer gestured to Robert with the butt of his rifle to follow him. Robert considered attempting some kind of suicidal retaliation to attract the soldiers but thought wiser of it, he still had some time left to formulate a better plan. He had no choice but to do as he was told for the time being.

He was led out of the control room and placed in another room off the corridor and the doors locked behind him. He sat for a few moments, contemplating his future or what there was left of it. He could only think of Katriana and how grateful he was to find she was still alive, at the same time he knew she was still in grave danger.

Max had meant what he'd said and he would open fire in the tunnel. He knew he had to do something. Think of something. He put his mind to what he had seen around the base. Was there anything he could do by way of a diversion?

***

While he thought, Larousse had decided to mount another attack on the steel door. Chambers had prepared his explosive charge. Larousse fired a few rounds towards the door to attract their attention. It brought about the desired effect. Within a few moments, the tunnel was a gloomy dust ridden cavern, this gave Chambers his chance, he rushed forward through the cover of the dust to the door.

Placing his charges, he signalled he was ready, the dust had settled some so he had to move quickly but not quick enough it seemed as the same method was employed again by Max. Chambers ran back when the firing stopped.

'All, okay?'

'Yes, Sir.'

'Blow it!' Commanded Larousse.

An almighty explosion ensued, throwing dust and debris up the tunnel towards them yet again. The control room retaliated with another blast from the guns although two of them had been dislodged with the blast and were now rendered useless. When the dust settled, it was obvious nothing much structurally speaking had been disturbed.

'My god! How thick is it!' said Chambers.

The group sat contemplating their next move. Whilst in the railway tunnel, the blast has been felt underfoot by Katriana and the guards.

'That'll be papa! He's reached them, I know it, I know it,' shouted Katriana as she jumped up and down with joy. It was then she realised how badly cut her feet were as she lifted and upturned each to inspect the wounds.

In the distance, the rear of the train could be seen reversing towards them.

'Here they come! Oh hurry, please hurry,' Katriana called as she waved frantically at them.

A few minutes later, Perzinski and Pfeiffer ran to join her, Gerrard limping behind.

'What the hell are you doing here, ma'am? Don't you know it's bloody dangerous out here,' Perzinski challenged.

'Never mind! The cufflink, you found a cufflink.'

'Yeah, that's right. Here it is. Probably fell off some bloody train or something years ago, why?'

'It is! It's Robert's, it's Robert's. He's alive, Robert's alive,' she shouted as she jumped for joy and hugged and kissed Perzinski, Pfeiffer, Gerrard and three soldiers.

'Wait a minute, ma'am. How do you know that belongs to Robert Cameron?'

'Because my dear Commander, I gave them to him. They were supposed to be a present for my papa but we had an argument and I gave them to Robert instead. I know they are his. I'm telling you. You must believe me,' she implored.

'Look Miss Larousse, we would dearly love to believe you but how do you explain them being here, I mean, look around you. This ain't Ali Baba's cave, you don't say "open sesame" and the bloody wall moves, come on ma'am, be serious,' Perzinski joked.

'You laugh all you want; I'm telling you Robert was here and they've got him. Now you answer that.'

'She's got a point, Perzinski. If he was here, there must be some way in.'

'Come on Pfeiffer, just look around you. For Christ's sake, do I have to spell it out?' Perzinski started to bash at the rock face both sides of the tunnel to prove the point.

'There's no way, absolutely no way through this fucking mountain! I'm sorry, ma'am.' He concluded.

'Commander, I understand what you're saying but I'm telling you! Robert was at this spot. Where exactly was the cufflink found?'

'Right there.' Perzinski pointed down to the sleeper where he'd marked the spot in yellow.

Katriana reached down and pushed aside some of the ballast. 'Right here, you mean?' She asked.

'No, no. On the sleeper, on the sleeper itself. Christ, there!' He reached down and pointed to the exact spot in an exacerbated manner.

'You bloody fool. Robert was trying to signal, can't you see that. He placed it on there for you to see it. He knew you were coming through, and he left you a signal and you ignored it, you stupid bloody fool.' Katriana broke down and turned to Pfeiffer for support.

'If anything's happened to Robert, I'll never forgive you, any of you,' she cried whilst still on her knees.

'Ma'am. Look at this sensibly. How can a railway carriage, I mean ma'am, have you seen the size of the thing? How can it simply disappear at this spot and your friend Robert find a way to mark it. Now I think you've been through enough, look at your feet for God's sake, they're torn to shreds. Listen, I'll have one of my men take you back to that doctor's in the village.'

Katriana turned on Perzinski.

'Don't you patronise me, Commander! I'm telling you Robert is somewhere close and so is this bloody Nazi base you're all searching for. If you won't look for it, I fucking well will! Sorry,' she added.

She stood up and started pressing against the walls, feeling in between the cracks, bashing stone ballast pieces against the rock surface, anything. She moved along a few meters and done the same, she ran back to where the cufflink was found, eventually she got down on her knees and began shifting the ballast chippings around the track.

'I think she's losing it,' Perzinski whispered to Pfeiffer.

'Leave her, she needs to do this, just give her a few moments,' said Pfeiffer, feeling a little saddened at her plight as he looked at her fraught state.

As the two men talked with disregard to Katriana's frenzied digging, she felt something smooth protruding upward some distance under the ballast. She began tossing the granite chippings in all directions, two, three at a time.

'Look! Look!' She cried out. 'What! What is it?' asked Pfeiffer.

'Some sort of light, I think. I don't know, take a look.'

Pfeiffer knelt beside her and helped her move some of the ballast.

'My God, Commander. She's right! There's a light fitting here. A light fitting buried under these stones! I don't understand it, why is this there. Shit, what the fuck. Sorry, Mademoiselle.'

'Well, I'll be dammed, ma'am. Looks like you're on to something after all! There is something going on here,' admitted Perzinski to everyone's relief.

He shouted out. 'Get back, all of you. If those bastards have any cameras down here, they'll know we're here now. They'll know we've found the entrance to their God-damn rat-infested shit hole! Back! Get back!'

Chapter Thirteen

Perzinski pulled his men back about fifty meters from the area where the underground lamp was located. He sent in a team of ten men to investigate along the track on either side of the lamp. Tossing the ballast chippings aside, they worked their way along a short stretch, quickly uncovering several lamps as they proceeded.

One soldier called out. 'Sir! Looks like some sort of metal seam under here.'

Perzinski and the others moved in slowly to examine the find, hoping against all hope the Nazis had no surveillance.

The Nazi technicians were working at full stretch, connecting the all-important final re-coding unit to the system allowing arbitrary selection of any donor target and carrying out the necessary circuit testing as they progressed. The tunnel monitor operators had been assisting them for a short while in making necessary connections to the circuitry, which caused an interruption to the signal from the tunnels. Max Wittenberg, meanwhile, was pacing the control room floor somewhat agitated by the arrival of NATO troops at the eleventh hour.

Thinking to himself he concluded the blame lay with the traitor Steinbacher; had he been silenced when the opportunity presented itself, the world would have known nothing until the test had been completed successfully, after which, the ultimatum would have been issued and pity help any power who refuted its claim.

He was partially correct in laying the blame with Steinbacher, though not in branding him a traitor to the cause. For had it not been for Jason Allen and his nocturnal forays into Steinbacher's flat, the Admiralty, NATO and the others would indeed have remained none the wiser to the events taking place within the Tirol Mountains.

Wittenberg's thoughts were disturbed by a monitor operator who upon receiving pictures from the tunnel announced.

'Herr Oberst. There are troops disturbing the ballast around the reception platform.'

Wittenberg was both astounded and slightly bewildered by the fact they could have known in a tunnel three and a half miles long, almost to the spot, exactly where to start looking. Whilst maintaining a degree of equanimity, Max called Robert's guard to the control room.

'Tell me, Peer. Did our troublesome guest come in close proximity with the hydraulic platform at any time whilst filming the arrival of our Party members?'

'Herr Oberst. He was filming the procedure as requested but yes, he was alongside it several times throughout the operation.'

'This is most important. Did he get close enough to the platform at any point where he would have been able to place anything on it, something that may attract attention?'

'Very unlikely, Herr Oberst. I was watching him the whole time as you ordered. He only placed the camera bag down to remove the still camera but he removed it again before the platform rose above him.'

'You idiot, Peer! I told you to watch his every move. The troops in the tunnel have located the platform all too easily, he must have placed something there when you thought he only placed the bag down, are you sure you saw nothing, was he carrying anything else?'

'Nein, Herr Oberst. He had nothing bar the camera equipment; I am positive.'

'Is it all accounted for; did you check the bag?'

'Nein, Herr Oberst. I know he never removed anything bar the camera; I was always watching him as ordered.'

'Get me the bag, you fool.'

'Herr Oberst!' Peer countered. 'Now!' Screamed Wittenberg.

Max was indeed perplexed. Had Cameron drawn their attention to the platform or could it have been what General Stoltz had warned him about many times in the past. The fact the ballast may take the regular form of the platform beneath as it's disturbed before the passage of trains reverts the situation as the vibration jostles the ballast chippings into an irregular pattern. The cause mattered not, Max realised he would have to take defensive action very soon, he decided to confer with the General first.

Peer brought the camera bag as directed. Max removed everything and checked the items back one by one; he confirmed the contents were indeed complete. Peer breathed a sigh of relief.

'Never mind, it's too late now. Ask General Stoltz to join me quietly. Then prepare the guard for an assault on the platform,' said Wittenberg disconsolately.

Peer made his way swiftly to the well-appointed sitting room. Where within, the Party hierarchy were being "entertained" with old newsreel and propaganda films from the thirties and forties in the run up to the big event. Stories of Nazi heroics and successes in the Second World War were being bandied around the room from the descendants of ex-Luftwaffe, Wehrmacht, Kriegsmarine and of course ex-SS and Gestapo officers present, those of whom had been clever enough or rich enough to slip the net close to the end of the war in Europe.

Not all had committed war crimes but many whose offspring were present had and they revelled in detailing the past conquests of their grandfather's or father's power to those who understood! The guard arrived and quietly gave General Stoltz the message.

'Danke. Tell Herr Oberst I shall be along momentarily.'

'I think the matter is rather urgent, Herr General,' insisted Peer politely. 'Oh. Sehr gut, kommen sie,' Stoltz replied as he laid his glass of Schnapps on a table and began following the guard to the door, his limp more pronounced when perturbed.

'Trouble? Herr Stoltz,' called Conrad Braun as he surveyed the whole assemblage from one corner of the room. His father's SS training coming into play after all these years just waiting, he knew instinctively a problem had developed by the manner in which the message had been passed.

'Nein Herr Braun, it is probably nothing. Oberst Wittenberg wishes to see me that is all,' replied Stoltz.

Braun knew better; being the son of an ex-SS Oberstgruppenfuhrer (Lieutenant-General) during the war; he maintained his natural scepticism and offered to accompany the General.

Stoltz of course, had no choice.

'But of course, Herr Braun, delighted,' said Stoltz, feigning amiability. Stoltz was very wary of Conrad Braun. He was a powerful figure in the Party.

He had done voluminous amounts to bring about the present-day regime, albeit behind closed doors. He had personally financed countless schemes to increase Party funds and popularity amongst the youth of Germany and beyond.

A formidable figure in the world of commerce, he portrayed an impeccable image to the outside world of a hard-dealing businessman, a cover he had perpetuated and retained under his grandfather and father's guidance since the family fled from the Allies in 1945.

Conrad was an only child born in 1962 when his father himself was 48 years of age. The family then returning to their beloved Germany in 1966 seemingly from the Copper Belt area of Africa, his father had purloined many of the Nazi treasures stolen during the war to portray an industrialist of some standing in the African Copper Belt. Conrad had an unchallengeable identity to the outside world and was a multi-millionaire to boot.

Presently, he was now jointly in command in the Reichsbürger Party hierarchy and relished in his self-appointed title of Reichsführer. He was quietly though impatiently awaiting the moment when he would be in overall control as was his idol, Adolf Hitler.

He inwardly concluded this would transpire soon after the successful destruction planned for 03.00 hrs. He had his own network within the main body of the Party who were becoming impatient as was he. One hour though, was not long to wait after all these years.

And he knew at the age of sixty, he had but one chance left to see the rise of the long awaited Fourth Reich. He truly believed the destruction he and his comrades had planned for so long would awaken and arouse the minds of the younger generation to follow their lead and see his beloved Germany to a long overdue victory. He contemplated in silence for a moment that this would be his finest hour, even in death, if death it was to be.

Marching together along the corridor with Stoltz, his joint in overall command, Braun composed himself from his thoughts and remarked without need to refer to his wristwatch.

'One hour to go, Herr General. I sincerely hope we find all is in order.'

'But of course, Herr Braun. The base is quite impenetrable, I assure you.'

Stoltz thought it best to mention the "small problem" now, to avoid a scene. 'We have sighted a detachment of NATO troops in the rail tunnel but it is unlikely they will cause us any disruption within the next hour.' Stoltz checked his wristwatch; the time 02.00 hrs precisely. He raised an eyebrow to Braun's sense of timing.

Entering the control room, Braun demanded, 'Herr Oberst! A report please.'

'Herr Braun!' Replied Oberst Wittenberg uneasily as General Stoltz gestured with his eyes from a few paces behind that he had no option regarding his accompanying him.

'Herr Reichsführer, Herr General. In the tunnel, the troops they have located the platform. I do not know how they could have located it so easily Sir, the ballast problem as it settles perhaps? I am not sure. All necessary precautions have been observed otherwise, I assure you,' Wittenberg proclaimed nervously.

'Stoltz!' Demanded Braun. 'Ya Wohl, Herr Braun?'

'How secure is the platform against explosives?'

Showing little outward sign of alarm, Heinrich Stoltz attempted to diffuse the situation.

'They would bring down the mountain above them before the platform gave way, I assure you it is made of—'

'Enough! Enough. We do not need a lesson in metallurgical hypothesis for the moment. What we need is to decimate that force at once! You do have defences positioned within the tunnel, yes?'

'Of course, Herr Reichsführer.'

'Then might I suggest you use them, you fool! My God, what is the problem here? In the old days, we would have wiped them out before they even came close! What about the other tunnel, are there troops there also?'

'Yes, Sir,' said Max sheepishly.

'Herr Oberst! You oversee security here. Might I suggest you secure your charge immediately! Open fire in both tunnels. Now!' Yelled Braun.

Max issued the order without further consideration.

The concealed guns rattled out a death-defying rally of shots within both tunnels, which had the troops and commanders alike running to take cover. A young private close to Katriana lunged forward at her and pulled her down to the ground, shouting out.

'Hit the deck, ma'am!'

She fell to the ground with a thud from the weight of the young soldier's body above her, winding her slightly in the process. For a full two minutes, the concealed gun emplacements rattled out, spreading their spray of ammunition in a controlled angular pattern to effect almost total coverage of the area most vulnerable.

Braun, meanwhile, made the decision to announce fifty minutes in advance of their planned time, their intention to provide a display of the Fourth Reich's power at precisely 03.00 hrs and advise the world powers of the resurgence of the German Reich.

He passed a package over to a member of the communications staff for immediate broadcast. Both General Stoltz and Oberst Wittenberg questioned the contents of the package, knowing the chosen transmissions were already pre-recorded.

Braun explained that the initial test involving the destruction of London in his view was foolhardy. Before he could continue, they both asked what he had changed and questioned why. He explained the facts to the onlookers in the control room who had all noticed the tension rising.

'I have ordered this replacement digitally engineered satellite communique to be broadcast to all major powers and be transmitted immediately. The transmissions are already prepared in all relevant languages for broadcast to the selected countries governments on classified wavelengths known to them to be used by defence departments to avoid initial panic.'

'The aim is to create as little disruption as necessary unless the leaders of the various governments oppose us. If so, the same broadcast will be transmitted throughout the world on commercial stations thus alerting the public immediately, the obvious result of which would be utter mayhem.'

'Herr Braun, you are not in a position to alter the planned attack on London,' Stoltz remonstrated angrily and omitting his "Reichsführer" title deliberately.

'Herr Stoltz. This final item of control equipment being installed is programmed to select the targets, yes?' Braun questioned, also omitting his "General" title.

'Of course, you know that we all know that but it has been pre-programmed to destroy London in a symbolic act of retribution, we all agreed on this first action as far back as I can remember,' Stoltz yelled. Braun looked him in the eye and replied in a calm voice.

'Perhaps it was back then but now it has been reprogrammed hence the eleventh-hour installation of the final cubicle. My associates are directly responsible and loyal to me and me only and it was those same associates who designed, developed and integrated all this equipment you see before you.'

'You Stoltz and your father and grandfather were responsible for building this base, nothing more. So, when I told them to change the agreed target, they did so without question, I suggest you all do the same. Do I make myself clear!' Before anyone could reply, the technician advised all was in readiness for the transmission. Braun gestured to him to commence. Stoltz, Wittenberg and the others began questioning what Braun had changed as the technician set things in motion. Braun simply said.

'I suggest you all keep quiet and listen.' Within a mere few seconds throughout the world, all government defence departments received the same targeted communiqué translated into their native language: This example was sent to the British government.

***

'Attention. Attention. To the British Prime Minister.

The Astute Class Submarine HMS Audacious of His Majesty's Royal Navy, currently at sea is now under direct control of the German Fourth Reich. At precisely 03.00 hrs, a missile will be fired at GCHQ in Cheltenham. Three hours later at 06.00 hrs precisely, an unspecified number of missiles from its full complement will be armed and fired at the City of London.

The targets will be completely destroyed regardless of defensive action. There is no possible defence to this action and there will be no compromise. We wish you to understand beyond doubt the futility of any reprisals. We advise you now that we have the capability to destroy all your defence installations systematically if retaliation is initiated in any form.

Our demands are simple and if met accordingly, will result in no further loss of life or disruption. We the officers of the German Fourth Reich regard this as an act of retribution. We are gifting you three hours following our demonstration to surrender yourselves to the rule of the German Fourth Reich.

If any attempt is made to retaliate, we will be forced to intercept and destroy military and non-military targets both in the United Kingdom and beyond. This broadcast applies to all nations. We will await your unconditional surrender forthwith.'

***

The broadcasts caused dramatic scenes amid the defence departments throughout the civilised world. Communications were blocked as officials attempted to verify the source and if indeed it was not simply an elaborate hoax. The Admiralty and NATO agreed to distance themselves from any previous knowledge of the matter to other powers, at least until 03.00 hrs when and if, GCHQ or any target named by Allen and or indeed HMS Audacious was destroyed, they would have no choice other than to confirm the worse.

They did not believe even at this stage GCHQ to be a possible target, regardless of the fact the Nazi base was no longer deemed a figment of Allen's imagination but he had told them it would be London. But GCHQ it was. It had been singled out together with the Pentagon in the Nazis' quest for retribution.

The Admiralty chiefs were immediately summoned to "Chequers" where the Prime Minister was being taken in haste away from London. The Ministry of Defence received the details over the secure line and were hurriedly preparing countermeasures.

They now knew for sure London was to be targeted and they only had three hours and forty-five minutes in which to evacuate the most senior personnel and members of the Royal Family, of which there were many in the city.

Prior arrangements had been made to some extent with the mobilisation of personnel and helicopters at the ready. Within minutes, the night sky was being crisscrossed with the passage of several hundred choppers making their way to strategic landing sites to pick-up their cargoes of privileged personnel and carrying them to safety. It was deemed unwise to announce any details to the media, believing panic would only ensue leading to the inevitable.

So, it was then. For the UK, GCHQ followed by London were left to their fate. Some stalwarts from both camps refused to leave and decided to brave out the storm, just as their predecessors had done in the blitz. The clock ticked by so slowly for those in the know.

03.00 hrs seen creeping steadily nearer with no word of reprieve. Passions were exchanged, skeletons un-earthed, quarrels settled, others began. Words of endearment were spoken where none had existed for so long. Prayers were spoken. It was a time of reconciliation for many awaiting their fate, some with their partners or friends, others with God, some with only themselves.

In the control room, Stoltz looked a dejected figure, Wittenberg looked incensed. Wittenberg was first to hurl abusive questions at Braun, demanding to know the reason for the change. Braun replied.

'Very simple, Herr Oberst. We gave this much thought over the years and I decided that destroying London whilst being symbolic presented us with greater difficulties. Our quest should not begin with destroying a city like London or anywhere else.'

'We the Fourth Reich wish to seize power around the world and in destroying London in a symbolic act of retribution would enrage the world in an instant. I have chosen to show our depth of control by destroying the British Intelligence, Security and Cyber Agency and the American Department of Defence at will.'

'The world will realise it would be futile to retaliate as they would be unable to utilise their own defence systems even if they tried.' The assembly within the control room stood silent, trying to comprehend the latest development, however Braun soon launched into abuse directed at Wittenberg.

He demanded Wittenberg's explanation of how the troops in the tunnel could have located the platform so easily. Max could only offer the obvious possibilities of the prisoner Cameron, having somehow managed to have placed some sort of object on it to attract attention or the movement of ballast, which he had previously warned him of.

Braun was furious with his subordinate. Shouting and screaming, he chastised him before all present.

'Eine idotisch Wittenberg!' He bellowed. 'The location of this base has been kept safe for over seventy years and now in our moment of resurgence and retribution, you allow one man! One man, to jeopardise the whole outcome of the Fourth Reich's rise to overall power. I hope you are satisfied with yourself, Wittenberg.' He concluded abruptly as he lashed his swagger stick against an operative's desk.

Max had had enough, he retorted. 'Herr Reichsführer. I protest! I only suggested that as a scenario, that is all. It is plainly obvious to me and others that NATO must have known of the location long before now! Just look at the monitors, there's a whole NATO detachment out there, thanks to our trusted friend and now a traitor; Jürgen Steinbacher.' He paused and looked directly at Stoltz, continuing.

'You, Herr General should have killed him when you had the chance, not let him escape as you did!'

'How dare you challenge my authority, Herr Oberst? Steinbacher is no friend of mine. I'll see you're court-martialled for this outburst!' Screeched Stoltz.

Braun interjected. 'Gentlemen, gentlemen. Enough of this bickering. We'll soon settle the matter. Bring the prisoner here to me, I'll soon find out the truth,' he said with a cynical grin.

'But Herr Braun, I must protest, it is too dangerous to bring him to the control room, he could—'

Braun interjected again. 'Herr Stoltz! Do as you are ordered. Have him brought here now!'

'Yes, Herr Reichsführer, at once.'

Stoltz issued the order under duress. Peer made his way to the room Robert was locked in.

***

In the tunnels, the guns had silenced for a few moments, allowing the forces to count the cost. Larousse and his team were lucky enough still to be out of range when it started but the story was far different for the NATO troops in the rail tunnel.

Fifteen troops' dead and over thirty injured from the indiscriminate gunfire. Leo Perzinski was wounded in the right arm by a bullet, Pfeiffer was lucky he had survived unscathed. Katriana was still lying on her side facing the tunnel wall, the soldier still on top, Pfeiffer called out to her.

'Frauline! Mademoiselle Larousse, are you alright?'

As she came partially out of shock, she screamed aloud feeling a warm trickling sensation running down between her breasts, she instinctively knew it had to be blood but whose? She was too shocked to feel any pain and too frightened to move, she began to shake uncontrollably.

She realised at last her father was right, it was indeed too dangerous, would she ever see him again? Was he alright? Was Robert alright? Would any of them make it? It was all too much, she screamed out, 'Bastards! Filthy Nazi bastards!'

Pfeiffer scurried over to her aid. 'Frauline, come we must get you away from here,' he said as he reached her.

He pulled on the young soldier's arm, the soldier rolled over and down to the gravel floor of the tunnel. Katriana couldn't fail to notice her jeans and blouse badly blood stained from the young soldier lying dead at her side, his eyes open and staring into oblivion.

She pulled the soldier's body close to her and rocked him back and forth whilst stroking his head. She closed his eyes as she stared into his face.

'He's so young,' she whimpered to Pfeiffer.

The tears were gushing from her eyes now. She let them. She had to cry. She owed her life to the brave young man.

'I'm so sorry, so very sorry,' she mumbled to him.

'He saved my life, Inspector. It should have been me lying here not this innocent young man. I, I don't even know his name. I should have listened to papa; he might still be alive if I'd listened. I'm so sorry,' she sobbed uncontrollably.

Pfeiffer tried to calm her down by putting events into perspective. He explained, had she not been there they would be none the wiser to the fact that this was indeed the location to begin searching for an entrance. She was the only one who could have recognised the cufflink belonged to Robert. It was fate and nothing more. He concluded.

Katriana was not entirely convinced the argument was valid considering the outcome. She rested the young man's shoulders onto the tunnel floor. Pfeiffer urged her to move away towards the northern exit, she couldn't move, not just yet. Katriana pleaded for a moment to compose herself, she sat up against the wall resting her head on Pfeiffer's shoulder.

Pfeiffer could do no more than give her time to come to terms with what had happened, then he would get her to safety out of the tunnel and back to von Rauch's. She had done her bit; it was up to the rest of them now.

***

At that moment, Robert was frog marched in to meet Conrad Braun. Peer edged him forward with the butt of his rifle digging into his kidneys until he was only a few feet away from Braun. Braun looked him over, walked around him and then stood face to face with only the protruding stomach of Braun preventing their noses touching each other.

'So, you are the cause of our little problem in the tunnel, are you?'

'Glad to be of service,' replied Robert with indifference.

'Do not be so facetious, Herr? Herr? What is your name?'

'The name is Cameron and its Mister, to you.'

'You are pushing your luck, Herr Cameron. Tell me, what did you use to attract the attention of your friends in the tunnel? Oh yes, we know about that.'

Robert stood and stared Conrad Braun in the eyes, giving him a cold glare yet refused to answer. Braun raised his eyebrows to Peer, who immediately drove the butt of his rifle into Robert's kidneys. He almost dropped to his knees but managed against all odds to remain almost upright.

'Will you answer my question now before I begin another form of interrogation on you? One which I have to say is particularly unpleasant.'

'Go to hell! I have nothing to say,' retorted Robert.

Braun almost laughed but a smirk was all he could muster. He struck Robert across the face, causing his nose to bleed profusely. Robert drew his head back to look at Braun, he made no attempt to stem the flow, he just stood firm and stared boldly at Braun.

'You will be pleading to talk to me later but first there are more pressing matters which I must attend to. Oh! Just in case you surmise your little effort may pay dividends, let me assure you it was all in vain. Look for yourself. Our platform areas are heavily fortified, there's at least twenty or thirty dead and many more injured. Even more would have been had it not been for the cover afforded by the train itself.' Robert looked at the monitor.

Braun continued, 'Your friends have absolutely no hope of breaching this base before we initiate our missile system, from then on, it's only a matter of time.' Braun pulled Robert closer to one of the monitors.

'Here, look there, see what you've done. I hope it does not play on your conscience in this your final hours, so to speak.' He laughed.

He forced Robert to look as he pulled on his chin and directed his view.

Robert swallowed hard as he followed the view from the hidden cameras showing the devastation as they panned the area. He could see the dead being cautiously dragged back towards the train, the injured being assisted and the futility on their faces of not knowing where to begin.

He realised they were trapped in a hopeless situation; how could they fight against secluded weapons. How could they breach the hydraulically powered platform?

His thoughts turned to Katriana and if or not she was safe, when suddenly, as the camera panned round yet further, he could see her in the distance, she was slumped against the wall with the German Inspector holding her to him, her hair was bloodied and covering her face.

Her body was motionless, as Robert looked agonisingly on, he could see her clothing around her breasts was drenched in blood. Robert's stomach twisted in agony. His whole body succumbed to the revulsion he felt at that moment. The revulsion this time far greater than that of before.

Robert quite naturally assumed the worse. His complexion changing almost immediately to a pale white as the nauseous sensation overcame him and he vomited and purposely directed its path right down the front of Braun's tunic.

Everyone in close proximity to Robert who could see for themselves what was about to happen had moved back a little to avoid the spillage with the exception of Braun whose eyes were fixated on the carnage in the tunnel. His moment of ecstasy was short lived.

'Get him out of here!' Screamed Braun, as the vile mess tricked down his front.

Peer moved towards Robert from behind, holding his rifle limply in his right hand. He too was disgusted at the malodorous sight. He reached out to grip Robert on the shoulder and guide him out. But in those few seconds, Robert realised a weakness, his rationality for his own safety became secondary now.

Katriana was dead.

He could avenge her death and stop this madness if only he had the courage. There was no choice. Instantaneously, he recalled his martial art training of many years ago, though he wondered if he could carry it out successfully given his state of mind.

He concentrated himself as he remembered the motionless figure of the woman he truly loved. In a state of controlled rage, he lunged his right elbow back with such a force into the base of Peer's rib cage, then he spun round bringing his tightly clenched fist upward crushing into his jaw, following a quick retraction the second blow with the base of the palm of the hand caught Peer fully under the nose, forcing the facial bone structure to fracture and travel upward into the brain. He was not dead but doubtless would be better off had he been.

As Peer fell back from the force of the attack, he unwittingly clenched the trigger of his rifle and released a volley of shots which rattled off the walls, ceiling and several banks of electronic equipment before falling to the floor. The final few shots terminating in the body of two technicians and a door guard as he made a dash for the corridor.

Robert pounced on the rifle as it fell from his grip, he let off a burst of fire over the technicians and the others before they had time to react. One, two seconds, that was all it had taken. Robert couldn't believe it had been so easy.

He composed himself instantly and took control.

'Right! Now then, you Achtung! You Nazi shit!' He ordered. 'I know how to use this and I'm not afraid to do so,' he said as he quickly locked the control room doors, sealing himself away from the hierarchy and others.

'I assume these doors are just as impregnable from the other side as this, eh?' Quipped Robert. 'Okay. All of you down that end. Now!' He ordered, pointing the rifle.

Braun, Stoltz, Wittenberg and the control room staff eased their way to the far end of the room with Robert watching their every move.

'Please, Herr Cameron. The guard needs medical attention, surely you can see that,' said Max.

'Dial 999.'

'What is 999?' asked Max, somewhat bemused.

Stoltz advised him, 'In England 999 is the emergency services.'

'So, you'd rather he dies then?' asked Max.

'Personally, I don't give a shit.' He looked around at his captives for a moment before continuing. 'It's not up to me. You lot call off this bloody madness and no doubt there's a medical team in the tunnel, they'll take care of him. Otherwise, shut the fuck up.' He gave them a few seconds to answer.

'Okay then, you don't obviously care about him.' Robert for compassion sake, knowing full well the injuries he had inflicted on the guard, he quickly released two shots from the automatic rifle, one to the head and one to the heart. He had no regrets.

'Right, you three, throw down your weapons and kick them over here, one at a time mind,' demanded Robert.

Robert had other things on his mind. The missile control system to be exact. He had no knowledge of electronic weaponry or the methods employed to launch the donor missiles. But he knew there were scientists travelling in the NATO train who would, it was them he had to get into the base and he was at last in the right position to do so.

His first task then was to lower the platform, then the old tunnel door where Larousse and his team were. He could understand some German but several of the controls were unmarked by name, merely by number. His dilemma of course was not to operate the control, which set the defences off.

He gingerly collected the guns as he moved forward, glancing at the bank of levers, switches, buttons and lights. Behind him, the sound of banging alerted him to the presence of the base guards attempting to gain entry, he flinched slightly from the sudden noise, looking behind for a split second, why?

He did not know; he knew the doors would hold. Max Wittenberg thought he would though. He had his eye fixed on Robert, just waiting for the opportunity. It had now presented itself.

He drew a small pistol from below his officer's cap but in the process of doing so, Robert caught sight of the movement. He blasted a few shots at him, knocking the pistol out of his hand and tearing into his flesh. He looked dispassionately at him and spoke.

'I told you I could use this. I should finish you scum off right where you stand. But then I'd be no better than the thugs you employed to kill my brother. Would I?'

As he announced that Stoltz said aloud, 'Cameron! My God, you're the policeman's brother, from England, the one who was killed on the dock.'

'Correct, so now you understand, eh?'

'That was a terrible mistake Herr Cameron, an unfortunate occurrence.'

'Oh! It was unfortunate alright, un-bloody-fortunate, for Bruce. But I'll see you all rot somewhere for it. You Nazi shit.'

As the conversation continued, Robert told one of the technicians to attend to Wittenberg's hand. He meanwhile continued to search for the platform controls. He asked outright if they would tell him, thinking the technicians may not be as pro-Nazi as the hierarchy. He was wrong, each man stood his ground and refused to co-operate.

'All of us here would rather die than betray the Reichsbürger!' shouted Braun.

'That can be arranged,' replied Robert.

'As you wish,' said Braun, challenging him. 'You are not like us, Herr Cameron. We are dedicated to Germany leading the world, we are prepared to die for it but are you prepared to pull the trigger? I think not,' Braun said as he stepped forward.

'Stop right where you are! Pull the trigger, eh. I'd put a single bullet right between your eyes for what you've done, you murdering bastard! So, don't! Give me any more of your philosophical bullshit. Okay!' Robert said as he pointed the rifle right between Braun's eyes.

Braun stepped back gingerly.

'Right! Get back all of you, right back.' He shouted as he tried again to make sense of the mass of controls. Looking at the clock, he noted it was now 02.30 hrs.

Braun noticed his glance; he commented as though unperturbed by events. 'Thirty minutes, Herr Cameron that is all! In thirty minutes, the world will see first-hand the awesome power of the Fourth Reich and you Herr Cameron, you will be swept away along with everyone else who opposes the Reich,' Braun announced ebulliently.

'I have no time for political chit-chat so just keep quiet and stay where you are,' retorted Robert.

Looking at the bank of controls, he tried to visualise a system of operation somewhat akin to a mining situation which of course was his forte. Unbeknown to those in whose company he was, of course. Had they thought seriously enough of him as anything other than the journalist he proposed to be, he may not have been granted the courtesy of seeing the complex as he had done so far.

Robert continued to study the various controls between glancing over at his captives at the far end of the room. He knew that instead of raising and lowering a cage in a mineshaft he had to lower the platform; therefore, a panel featuring perhaps a simple push button to raise and lower the marker lights he had noted protrude out of the ballast.

Then there was some kind of locking mechanism, he had heard this operate but a more robust switch, he thought would be required as he knew this should need a greater current, finally the platform itself, it called for something very heavy duty, it must take masses of power to operate the six hydraulic rams required to move the immense bulk of stone and steel.

Satisfied he had found nothing on the control desks he could consider robust enough, he began checking the electrical boxes affixed to the walls, as he moved around, he noted three personnel, one technician and two guards not moving away with the others as he closed in. Pointing the rifle at them, he said.

'Verschieben, bitte.' They stood firm, Robert shouted out.

'Move over, schnell!' As he waved the rifle, the three slowly, very slowly stepped to the side.

Robert ordered them to join the others, quickly. As they cleared the area, he saw a switchgear box labelled Bahnanschluss, he understood that basically the word "Bahn" in German meant railway and it was a possibility he would have to try it.

There was nothing else in the vicinity, he had hoped for two or more switches, this was a single heavy-duty pull-down lever mounted on a steel enclosure. Quickly he had to think, time was not on his side. He quickly reconsidered and concluded with some luck the whole system operated via a bank of relays rather than individual switches as he had first thought.

His heart missed a beat as he cautiously pulled down on the switchgear. He heard audible confirmation some circuit or other was functioning. Correctly, he assumed a sequence must be followed to energise each circuit both electrically and then hydraulically.

The first sequence would raise the marker lights up and through the ballast as he had seen earlier. He moved over to one of the monitors, watching the railway tunnel monitor, he could see the troops who had closed in somewhat from the cessation of fire run back for cover towards the rear of the train, which had by now reversed to within a few feet of the platform to afford the men a little more cover.

He knew they had heard something also. Automatically, the monitor switched to a four-way split multi-view image of each joint as it separated and retracted, simply a matter of visual confirmation, he could also see the lights rising. Robert was joyous yet controlled.

'Don't even think of it,' he shouted as he noticed movement from the group of Nazis.'

Once the joints cleared, the picture returned to normal scanning. Taking his eyes off the control panel to look out on to the main floor below, he could see the various grades of guards assembled below awaiting the imminent arrival of retaliatory forces.

Two things puzzled him though; first, there seemed to be a far greater presence of guards than he'd noticed before. And second, they hadn't attempted any breach of the control room.

The control room staff together with Stoltz, Braun and Wittenberg were becoming quite agitated by Robert's progress. Braun nudged one of the technicians to make a move to prevent his going any further but his attempt was caught again out of the corner of the eye by Robert, who blasted a few shots off in the general direction to dissuade him.

Turning back to the monitor, he could see movement of the platform itself. Robert was ecstatic!

In the tunnel, on noting the movement of the platform, Pfeiffer tugged at Katriana to get up, Perzinski commanded his men to be at the ready as the platform was seen to physically lower slowly. They couldn't believe their eyes, the expressions on their faces said all that could be said.

Utter disbelief! Robert looked around the room again quickly in the hope of seeing the control which operated the door to the old tunnel and Larousse.

Casting his eyes around the room quickly, he noticed a singular control mounted on the back wall. Turning to face his captives, his thoughts lingered for a moment as he wondered whether it was a case of not being able to see the wood for the trees, for there just behind him on the wall was a rather older looking panel with heavy twist type levers.

He toyed with the theory, that if the old tunnel was built first as he assumed was most likely, then the controls could well date back to the war years themselves. He decided to take the chance and give it a go.

The trouble now, was he knew from the design he had to twist both lever's outward simultaneously otherwise they would interlock as was the style of such old equipment, consequently this meant he had to release the hold on his rifle for a moment in the process.

He did so with lightning speed. In an instant, the levers were twisted illuminating both green lamps on the panel as the locking bars were drawn back and the door released.

Robert immediately retrained his rifle at his captors some of whom had attempted to move forward from their position. One guard had reached a rifle and was raising it.

'Halten sie es!' He shouted out as he fired the rifle. The guard was wounded in the arm and dropped the rifle.

'Don't try to be heroes now, I warned you I could use this. Soon this place will be swarming with NATO troops, look for yourselves,' he said, pointing to the monitors.

At that moment, he caught sight of Katriana running with Pfeiffer to join Perzinski at the other side of the line, he couldn't believe his eyes.

'Good God! She's alive!' He said in amazement as he gazed at the picture just a moment too long.

His momentary lapse of concentration cost him dearly, a technician was close to the control, which operated the trap door below the hoist. The same trap door Robert was now standing on, with his eyes fixed to the monitor and the sight of Katriana.

In an instant, the doors opened and Robert fell the thirty or so feet to the floor, landing on the trolley and thankfully the wood and polystyrene packaging which the re-coding unit had been delivered in.

As several guards rushed over from the platform area by orders of Max Wittenberg over the speaker system, Larousse and his team dashed through the open door from the old tunnel and mowed them down with rifle fire.

Larousse darted over to Robert who was lying on his back almost knocked unconscious from the impact. He slapped him around the face to bring him round, as he came round amid the gunfire surrounding him, the first thing he said was, 'Katriana, she's alright, she's alive.'

'Yes, Robert she's alive, she's going to be okay and she's at a doctors in the town. Now come on!' said Larousse.

'No! No. She's not! She's here, she's with Pfeiffer and the others. I saw her only a moment ago. God, I thought they'd killed her but she's alright. I've just seen her.'

'Here! My daughter's here!' Screeched Larousse.

'Yes, in the tunnel, I managed to open the platform just before I saw her, it took my mind of things I'm sorry Monsieur Larousse, I was so relieved to see Katriana alive, I honestly thought they'd killed her.'

'That's okay, Robert. You've done your bit, we couldn't have got in without your help, I'm proud of you, Robert and I don't mind saying so. But my god! That fucking daughter of mine, wait till I get my hands on her. Come on, let's get you to safety,' said Larousse as he helped Robert back to the others.

'Cover us!' shouted Larousse as he made a dash back towards his group.

In the control room, Braun had ordered the platform and the tunnel doors closed the instant Robert had departed the premises, however the operation was not a swift one and the platform had lowered over a metre and a half before it was halted.

When Perzinski saw its descent halt and then begin to raise again, he ordered the train to reverse quickly, as it did so, the last wagon was pushed off the edge of the rail onto the platform, its wheels digging into the gravel and sleepers before the rear of the wagon jammed hard under the far end, the next wagon followed suit causing the platform to lock partially open. Even the power of the hydraulic rams could not crush the mass of metal as it twisted under the immense forces.

Several troops attempted to slide through the gap left by the platform failing to close but were being picked off one by one by the base guards as they came through. Braun ordered the tunnel defences to be deployed. Perzinski ordered his rocket launchers to blow holes in the walls wherever they saw gunfire.

The whole melee lasted a few minutes as the tunnel guns were blown out of the walls. He then ordered the platform to be blown wide open and in no time at all, a gaping hole emerged allowing the troops to scramble in. Meanwhile,

Larousse and his team were waging a little war of their own at the other side of the cavern, unable to render assistance.

Sub-Lieutenant Malhotra had assembled a missile launcher and was aiming straight for the floor of the control room. The armour piercing shells were having little effect on the plating let alone the floor. The shutters had now been drawn upward over the windows, effectively sealing the control room off from attack.

Robert pulled Larousse to one side to tell him there was a large area behind the control room dug into the rock itself, if they could blast through the rock below with the missiles, they may find an easier way through. Larousse agreed it was worth a try and instructed Malhotra to aim for the area below the control room and maintain a barrage at the same location.

With each impact, huge amounts of solid rock from beneath the control room were gouged out and the debris scattered across the cavern floor but still it remained impenetrable.

'What is that floor made of, for Christ's sake?' Squawked Larousse.

'God only knows, Sir,' answered Malhotra. Those in earshot smirked at the humour of the reply before getting back to the business in hand.

Once the group had secured their position, Chambers, Carl and André were deployed to draw some of the fire off the NATO forces attempting to breach the platform area whilst Larousse and Robert covered Malhotra. The resistance however was fierce from the Nazi guard, each man hand-picked and sworn to fight to the death, they were brainwashed to believe it was a matter of honour.

Profligation of life was commonplace within the order. Dozens of grenades and multiple clips of ammunition were released in their general direction but still, they held their position and kept the NATO troops at bay in the rail tunnel.

Communications between Larousse and the NATO forces were once again restored. Larousse having discussed the situation with Robert regarding the Nazi threat advised they only had fifteen minutes left in which to destroy the control room, otherwise the threat would become reality and at the present, they could find no possible way of dealing with it.

Perzinski advised he had several cases of high velocity missiles, which might just do the trick if only they could get through, Larousse advised him to get his team clear and make sure his daughter was taken out of the tunnel immediately as he intended to train a few of their own missiles on the area below the platform in thirty seconds. Perzinski gave the orders and retreated to a safe distance.

Three massive explosions one after the other shook the cavern walls and dislodged several key structures as the missiles scattered boulders and pieces of mangled steel from both the platform and the wagons upon it. Perzinski ordered the troops in and in a matter of moments, the cavern floor was a scene of hand-to-hand combat between the NATO troops and the Nazi guards.

Larousse, content now that his daughter was safe at last, returned to the problem of the control room. Looking up at the fortress, he could see no sign of structural damage given the awesome firepower it had been subjected to.

'Robert, how did they get up there?' asked Larousse.

'A metal stairway swings down from below and is retracted into the floor, right there,' said Robert, pointing at the panels.

'Is that the only way in? Are you quite sure?'

'The only way I've seen. I was led up it after their top brass when they arrived.'

'But there is another area behind this, you say?'

'Yes, it's vast. There are sleeping quarters, refectory, showers and a bar even! It's quite a little home from home up there, I'll tell you. There is also a locked door marked Elektrischer Schaltraum. Next to it, one marked Serverraum.'

Larousse was quickest as he was used to using German more so than Robert. 'Those are electrical switch room and server room. We must get in there. There must be another way up there. All that equipment couldn't have been dragged through their control room, it's just impossible, impractical even. There must be another way in, there simply has to be.' Larousse thought a moment. 'Okay Robert, what do you think about this? The bastard who designed this place.'

'Herr General Heinrich Stoltz,' interposed Robert. 'Who?' said Larousse.

'One of the top brass. His grandson is up there now. He told me all about this place and how his grandfather built it during the war.'

'Did he now? I don't suppose he told you about another way in, did he?' Robert sensed Larousse's mood.

'Sorry, you were saying?'

'Yes, I was. Look, this Stoltz chap, he managed to disguise the entrances so well that they remained a secret for over seventy years, right?'

'Yes?' Answered Robert with some intrigue.

'Well, assuming he maintained the theme throughout, he would have disguised the entrance to the area behind the control room in the same way, agreed?'

'Go on.'

'How much have you seen up there?'

'I was taken out of the control room and down the main corridor past several rooms leading off from it and placed in a locked cell below. Christ!' Exclaimed Robert with sudden realisation.

'I think you may be right. When I was taken downstairs, there was a series of corridors and all of them leading off to my right, which from here would put them on the left just past this end of the control room.'

'Excellent, Robert. Now we might get somewhere,' said Larousse confidently.

Larousse instructed Malhotra to train the remaining missiles on the area below and to the left of the control room. With one already in the pipe, he blasted it at the target. As the dust settled, a sight to gladden the heart came out of the gloom.

The sight of yet another steel door, which had been camouflaged by a rock cladding blending perfectly with the craggy walls of the cavern. Although the door had suffered little damage itself from the impact, the sight of it brought new hope to the team. Larousse contacted Perzinski and told him to throw everything he had at that door.

In the control room, Stoltz broke into a cold sweat as the alarm sounded to notify that the entrance had been damaged.

'What is the significance of this alarm? Herr Stoltz,' demanded Conrad Braun.

'Herr Braun. Reichsführer. They have located the secure entrance to the control room and living quarters. It was sealed up upon completion. They must have come across it by accident but we are quite safe in here, I assure you,' replied Stoltz sheepishly.

'Safe! You call a NATO detachment currently poised to wipe out our brave Kammeraden, who together have brought about this day and indeed the Fourth Reich. And believed you, when you said this base was impenetrable. Safe! Eine idotisch Stoltz.' Braun thumped down on the panels in temper.

'We must help them, Herr Braun. Bring them in here, they will be safe in here,' rambled Stoltz in a state of hysteria.

'Of course, we must help them, you fool. Wittenberg! Instruct our Kammeraden to join us immediately,' ordered Braun.

'Ya Wohl, Herr Braun.'

There was little need to ask, as the door to the corridor was opened, the honoured Party guests were all clambering inside to safety, some with the presence of mind to bring along supplies from the refractory and of course, the bar.

'What has gone wrong, Herr Braun? Can we still carry out our mission?' Came the cry from the stalwarts in the bunch.

'Of course, gentlemen. We may be under attack but our capabilities are as yet unaffected. Here, see for yourselves, the re-coding unit is relaying the details of the targets to the submarines at this very moment. The captain will assume it's a mere exercise and comply with the instructions to the letter.'

'The one thing he is unaware of, is the re-coding unit whilst transmitting instructions is undermining the submarines own internal communications. The captain will undoubtedly double-check the armed condition of the missiles before launch and their target. To him, all will seem in order and the missiles will be fired.' Braun looked elated at the prospect. He added.

'Yes, gentlemen we have eight minutes to go. I am confident we shall succeed despite our current problems.'

'Herr General, Sir. Why not carry out the mission now before it is too late, perhaps then they will withdraw when they hear of the results, after which we could threaten to carry out another series of attacks,' shouted Axel Oefner as he pushed his way through among the hierarchy and the doors were locked behind them.

'I'm afraid that is impossible. As much as I would like it, I grant you,' came a well-educated voice from within the crowd. He continued.

'You see the problem is, all systems have to be programmed to a precise instant in time. The donor missile system has been pre-timed to respond to the signal we send out at exactly 03.00 hrs; the timer in the re-coding unit has programmed our equipment to be energised at just the precise moment.'

'It has taken into account the milliseconds it takes for the signal to reach the satellite and then for the signal to be transposed to the missile control system on the ground or in this case the submarines. It is a complicated matter I assure you, hence the last moment arrival of the final re-coding unit.'

'I had to wait until verification of the weekly re-coding had been completed by both the English and the Americans from our information forwarded by our agents in Whitehall and the Pentagon. From this code, the chosen missiles will be armed and fired at their prescribed target.'

'Nothing, absolutely nothing can stop its launch provided the timer is functional. At the same time, the signal being transmitted also jams all retaliatory ground defence systems within target range of destroying our missiles and there you have it, quite simple when you say it quickly, don't you think?'

'What about the fact the launch is forty-eight hours ahead of schedule?' Came another voice from the crowd.

'No problem. The re-coding unit has already been adjusted to suit. But these things take time.'

Braun put paid to any further questions by announcing.

'All very well providing we are not all blown to pieces before 03.00 hrs. Eh!' He said, somewhat dismayed as the troops below maintained their assault.

'How is our glorious Fourth Reich intended to continue if we are all killed here inside this godforsaken mountain, answer me that?' Oefner shouted out, somewhat paranoid.

Braun took the stage.

'Gentlemen, gentlemen. You all know as well as I do there are many more of us on the outside, we are but a handful of followers, an extremely important handful at present, I grant you but there are others waiting to take our place if indeed we do not make it through this night.'

'However, rest assured tonight's operation itself will succeed and retribution against the Allies will be final. The English and American's will be healing their wounds as London and Washington cease to exist at 06.00 hrs Those of us fortunate enough to live through the events of tonight will survive as leaders of the Reich itself.'

'Remember we have other facilities under construction at this very moment, capable of carrying out similar attacks in the very near future, the technology is available to us, so all is not lost. I for one am willing to die here this night. For our Fatherland! Sieg Heil!'

The speech finished to a rapturous round of applause as General Stoltz edged his way through the overcrowded room to Axel Oefner. Max Wittenberg had caught sight of the pair obviously planning something or other, he too made his way through the crowd towards the corridor door.

'Axel,' Stoltz whispered. 'I have no mind to die here like those idiots, we have to get out of here, are you with me?'

'Of course, Herr General. But how?'

'Remember the first time you came here with Wittenberg and myself?'

'Of course, Herr General! The tunnel leading to the water tank.'

'Yes, Axel. We must make a break for it now; we have no time to lose. Nobody but you, Max and I, have knowledge of it, we must make a run for it but only the two of us, the others must await their fate in here, agreed?'

'What about Max?'

'Too obvious, the three of us together, understand.'

'Agreed, Herr General.'

'This is what I want you to do, Axel.' Stoltz detailed his plan to Oefner. There was very little time left so speed was of the essence. Both men jostled their way through the crowd to the doors leading to the corridor, as the members of the hierarchy toasted themselves to a final glorious farewell, Oefner released a few rounds from his automatic pistol towards the lights whilst Stoltz operated the door control.

Both men slipped out as the others dropped for cover. Wittenberg seized the moment and jostled his way through with them. As Stoltz sealed the door operation from the corridor, Max Wittenberg confronted him.

'So, you intend to let us all die in there, you traitors!' He said vehemently as he pointed his pistol at them.

'We would rather fight to the death out here than be caught, is that not so, Axel,' contested Stoltz.

'Do not think me so stupid, Herr General. You are an insult to the Reich. I too know of your escape route, oh, don't worry it's still there, quite secure, I assure you. I knew you were planning something. So, for your sake, you had better take me along. I, like you, have no intentions of becoming a martyr to the Reich.'

'Of course, Max, come, there's no need for the gun, please join us if you wish but we must hurry, you see there's something I must do before this night's through,' said Stoltz alarmingly.

Chapter Fourteen

With most of the Nazi guard on the main floor eliminated by the overwhelming NATO assault, Perzinski and the remaining NATO troops forced their way through from the tunnel, attempting to reach Larousse. Their first impressions on seeing the interior of the base left them speechless.

Pfeiffer found the sight totally beyond belief. He knew the "Reichsbürger" movement had gathered momentum over the past ten or so years, their actions against foreign aliens residing within Germany had been a disgrace to the country and its people alike.

Apartment blocks in various cities, used to house certain alien minorities had been deliberately set ablaze in an effort to "persuade" those who survived to leave. The "Reichsbürger" conception being Germany for the German People.

Germany akin to other European countries throughout the eighties and nineties was suffering from a shortage of housing, jobs and general social infrastructure. The influx of aliens from beyond its borders plus the flow of ex-East Germans after the re-unification had caused an upsurge in population throughout the industrialised regions.

The Neo-Nazis comfortably adopted this situation and exploited it to the full. All this of course Pfeiffer knew only too well; however, the sight of this underground missile base was a far cry from the Neo-Nazi elements he'd had to deal with as a Polizei officer in the past.

Its destruction was paramount if the world as he knew it was to survive. His thoughts were disturbed as Perzinski called to Larousse for cover. They made their move as Larousse threw everything he and his team had against the small pockets of resistance determined to prevent their gaining entry behind the control room.

Perzinski slid the last few meters along the concrete floor whilst holding on to his helmet and his wound. He tapped Larousse on the back, saying, 'Well done, Larousse! We'd never have found that God damn hole in the ground if it hadn't been for you.'

'It's not me you should be thanking, it's Cameron here, he's the one who got up there and opened both the platform and the door to the tunnel for us. He's a bloody hero, I'll say. My daughter, where is she? Robert said he saw her on a monitor not so long ago, is she okay?'

'She's okay, bud. I sent her back to that doctor's place with a couple of my men. Oh! And before I forget, I've sent your guy Gerrard back to the tunnel mouth, he took a tumble down that damn mountain when he saw our train. He won't give up though.'

'I tried persuading him to go with your daughter to von Rauch's, he refused. Anyway, I sent your daughter back with two of my guys as soon as I saw the platform drop, I knew it would get pretty damn hot down here. Hey, she's some gal, that daughter of yours, I hope you're proud of her. I would be if she were mine,' said Perzinski, grinning slightly.

'Some gal! I'll give her "some gal" when I get my hands on her. She could have got herself killed and not for the first time in these bloody shambles.'

'Listen, Larousse,' interrupted Perzinski. 'Your daughter was the one who knew where to start looking in that tunnel, she recognised this cufflink she gave to our friend Cameron here. We found it lying on the track. If she hadn't been there, I doubt we would have realised its significance.' Perzinski passed Robert the cufflink.

Larousse reached into his inside left breast pocket and produced the other. 'Here Robert, you deserve to have these returned, it was quick thinking on your part, those cufflinks have played a major part in our locating this bloody cavern.'

'Thanks, Monsieur Larousse, Commander. It was all I could think of at the time but don't you think we should be doing something about destroying this bloody place, rather than chatting about a pair of cufflinks; there's only eight minutes to the deadline.'

Robert took the cufflinks and placed them in his pocket as the others took heed to what he said and discussed the situation.

'Where's Pfeiffer? Is he okay?' asked Larousse.

'I've got him setting up a communications link with the railway control through their signal and telegraph system, we must inform the others of the position before well, just in case. Well hell Larousse, you know the score.'

'Before the Air Force out there reduces this mountain to a mole hill, you mean?'

'Like I said. You know the score.'

***

Stoltz, Oefner and Wittenberg had by now scurried down a narrow tunnel winding its way down the short distance towards the railway tunnel where the entrance was concealed in one of the drainage overflow tanks in the tunnel floor. A few meters before the chamber, several sets of civilian and military clothing were packed into wooden chests recessed into the wall. Stoltz opened one of them, saying.

'Come, change into these, with a little luck we'll pass as NATO troops, there's bound to be a military presence at the entrance. Axel and I shall pose as injured officers, neither of us speak English without an accent. Wittenberg, you speak good English; if they question us, think of something quick.'

'You are in no position to command me, Herr General,' said Wittenberg with indignation.

'Perhaps you are correct, Max but if you want to get out of this alive, I suggest you keep your resentment for another time. Well, are you with us or not?' demanded Stoltz.

'Yes alright, I'll go along with it, so long as you don't expect me to follow any more of your orders, Herr Stoltz.'

'Understood Max. I understand your denunciation and I apologise for our intention to leave you behind with the others. So, may I suggest once we are safely out of here, we are on our own; Axel and I have our plans, you can go your own way, does that suit you, Max?'

Max agreed and the three stripped off their outer Nazi garments and removed the NATO uniforms from the chests. Stoltz advised them to upturn one end of each wooden chest were placed below was the current issue NATO pistol with belt and holster.

Max studied the uniform he was to wear and noted it was also the current NATO issue, Stoltz sensed Max had realised the uniform and weapon was not something put away from some time ago and informed him he had placed them there only four weeks hence as a contingency measure.

'Insurance Max, that is all. I hoped it would never come to this but you must plan for the unexpected. The dream has failed, for now, Max, let us face the facts.

Even if they manage to send out the signal to launch the missiles and even if the target is destroyed, the Oberammergau Base will be destroyed with it. There is no escape for our Kammeraden and there's no point dying in there along with them.'

'We've tried to change the world for the last time, you and I and Axel here, we've all given it all we had to give. I for one have no intention of drowning with the sinking ship, there are others like us out there, let them taste the glory of what will one day be the Fourth Reich.'

Max reluctantly nodded in agreement and slipped into the uniform. Stoltz and Oefner daubed plentiful amounts of theatrical blood upon their heads and bandaged themselves up to portray injured men. Yet more props from the contingency chest.

A few moments later, Stoltz operated the door leading into the chamber and offered Oefner first place. Oefner stepped inside and the door revolved around the casement sealing him against the ingress of water from the drainage tank as it propelled its way upward and through.

He operated the internal control, which was luminously marked and raised himself up into the tunnel refuge where Oefner exited then returned the chamber below. Max insisted he follow next as he did not trust Oefner or Stoltz to return the chamber for him.

Once all three were out, Stoltz returned the chamber probably for the last time he surmised. He glanced up and down the tunnel checking for any troop presence.

'All clear,' Stoltz whispered. 'Come, this way,' he said as he cautiously leaned out into the tunnel.

'You first Axel, then you Max. I'll be right behind you. I must seal the door from the inside.'

The two men stepped out onto the tracks and stood hard against the wall as Stoltz stepped back inside to arm a self-destruct device designed to reduce the Oberammergau Base to ashes. He timed the device to blow shortly after 03.00 hrs, just enough time for them to be well away from the tunnel, it also granted enough time for the missile codes to be fully transmitted to the satellite in order to arm and fire the donor missiles and from there, reach their prescribed targets at 03.00 hrs thus giving his incarcerated Kammeraden a taste of glory in their hours of martyrdom to the Reich. Stoltz remained confident the control room would remain impenetrable to attack for some time.

Stoltz, whilst still somewhat anxious, stepped out of the canister, in doing so he dropped a package which fouled the door operation as it rotated around. He operated the control for it to return underwater to lock in position and scurried to join the two others slightly ahead of him; being in a hurry, he failed to notice the problem, saying.

'Walk confidently Max, while Axel and I pretend to hold on to you for support. And don't look back.'

In the distance behind them, two of Perzinski's troops were escorting Katriana out to safety as requested, they could see the shadow of the three men in the distance ahead but paid little heed. Naturally, they assumed two wounded members of the assault team were being assisted to safety.

Passing Stoltz's escape route, Katriana noticed a faint glow permeating from below the grid of the drainage tank and tugged at one of the troops.

'Look! What's that?' she said, pointing. The soldier stopped.

'Hey Brad, look at this, looks like some kind a'. 'Well to be honest, I don't know what the hell it is. Looks like a light shining down here.'

The three of them cautiously looked down into the gloom, they could see a cylindrical chamber protruding slightly upward from the ground inside the recessed refuge. A faint glow was emanating from within casting a dull beam of light through the constantly rippling water as the percolation from the mountains continued to trickle in.

One of the soldiers moved into the refuge and lay on the ground, trying to open the door to the chamber fully but the door pressure was too great, he managed to reach in and press the luminous button marked with an arrow pointing upward, the canister released from the base of the tank and proceeded to rise. The soldier eased himself out of the refuge, grabbing his rifle and joined his colleague and Katriana.

'What the hell is it, Brad, Ma'am?' he asked.

'I'll soon find out!' said Katriana as she pulled at the door but the mechanism still held it firm.

She looked at the luminous arrows, simply points on a compass, north, south, east and west. She concluded they must be up, down, open and close.

'Could your rifle reach the buttons, do you think?' asked Katriana.

'I'll give it a try, Ma'am.'

The soldier just managed to get the angle and distance and just as he was about to press, Katriana called out.

'Wait. Press the open button.'

'Yes, Ma'am,' the soldier replied a little sarcastically as that was exactly as he'd intended.

'Stand back both of you, just in case,' the soldier advised. 'In case of what?' She replied, then realised what he meant.

Katriana gave him an apologetic smile as he pressed the open button gingerly. The chamber door rotated open and Katriana was first to enter. She took a good look around and saw a package on the floor. She reached down to pick it up when Brad called out.

'No Ma'am, it could be booby-trapped.' Katriana stepped out as Brad reached down, he quickly concluded it looked suspiciously like a NATO issue automatic rifle clip. He double checked then lifted it up.

'What the heck is this doing here?' Brad said as he showed it to his colleague. Whilst they were both examining it, Katriana stepped into the chamber and closed the door. In complete silence, the chamber slowly descended until it reached the bottom. The two soldiers began to panic. 'Where's she gone, for Christ's sake?' One exclaimed. 'We'll be in the shit now, for sure,' said the other.

The two men stared into the depths of the tank. They could see nothing, the cylinder had completely vanished, the safety grilling on top resting precisely between the others as the chamber descended, the top plate of the chamber itself acting as a simple panel affixed to the base of the tank. The soldier who was already wet jumped in again and felt the bottom of the tank all around, he came up for air.

'Christ! I know it's there but I can't find it.'

He crouched down and felt the base again, as he did so he felt his right leg rise. He placed his other leg on the upwardly moving panel and stepped off onto the grid as it came level. They awaited the canister to stop, whereupon Katriana stepped out at ground level. Opening the door partially, she shouted hysterically. 'They're going to blow the place up! My Papa and Robert are in there! We must get to them, come on!' She returned below before they could restrain her then sent the chamber back for the soldiers. One decided to accompany her, the other decided to run and inform an officer.

He thought it best to head to the northern portal where he knew contact could be made quicker than returning to the assault area. Brad, the dry one, lowered himself down into the tunnel.

'Are you sure they're going to blow the place, Ma'am?'

'Yes, of course! Look!' She pointed to a small switchboard on the wall, with the strong clear cover sealed and displaying a red light, below which was a specially designed key switch whereby the intricate barrel assembly once activated was completely removed, rendering it tamper proof.

'What does it mean, Ma'am? Bewaffnet and Entwaffnen.'

Katriana looked at the two words on the box again, one at twelve o'clock the other at slightly after three.

'It says armed and disarmed and the switch is pointing to armed, they're going to blow the place up, I'm telling you! We must stop it, my Papa and Robert are in there somewhere, we must stop it.'

'Yeah, okay Ma'am, come on!'

They ran a few meters before Brad caught sight of the partially open wooden chest in the recess. It wasn't the chest that caught his eye. It was the end of a sleeve from a tunic, which was hanging over the edge. He stopped so suddenly his feet lost grip as he slid and fell to the ground.

'What's the matter?' urged Katriana, desperate to reach her father and Robert.

Brad threw the lid to the chest back to find three Nazi uniforms bundled in on top of several sets of civilian clothes and one NATO officer's uniform.

'Shit!' he exclaimed. 'It looks like three Nazis have made a run for it.'

'Let them! We've wasted enough time, our men in there are going to be blown up any minute!' yelled Katriana as she tugged at the soldier.

Brad made a quick decision. 'Okay Ma'am, let's go!'

Katriana and Brad ran along the narrow tunnel, one behind the other as fast as they possibly could, before long they could see a door in the distance. The soldier slowed down and approached it with caution. He operated the door release button and stood back against the wall, rifle at the ready.

The door opened into a dark confined space where chinks of light could be seen filtering through the floor in places. He gestured Katriana to follow him, they headed for the brightest light and he found it was a roof panel to a lower room, he cautiously uncovered it and took a look below, it was some sort of office but no one was around.

The light filtering upward illuminated a sliding alloy ladder affixed to the wall in front of them, he slid it down and cautiously descended through the gap then assisted Katriana down. Both of them eased their way to the door. He turned the handle gently to avoid making any noise, even though gunfire and explosions could be heard in the distance, which would have muffled the sound of the lock turning but Brad was taking no chances.

Once released, he slammed the door back and jumped forward into a corridor, still no one. Their luck was holding for the moment. Both rushed along the corridor towards the sound of the gunfire. Passing a room where the door was ajar, Brad saw a collection of armaments.

'Quick Ma'am, grab some of these! We may need them.'

Katriana picked up a couple of pistols, Brad placed them back, saying. 'Can you shoot, Ma'am?'

'Not brilliantly.'

'Then take this.' Brad handed her an automatic rifle and several clips of ammunition.

'You can't miss with this, Ma'am.'

Katriana stuffed the clips behind her belt. Brad looked at her thinking of the film Annie get your gun, he said aloud, 'No shit Annie, eat your heart out, baby!'

Katriana realised the significance and forced a smile. Brad realised it was not the time to crack jokes.

'Are you ready for this, Ma'am?' he asked.

'Ready as I'll ever be. Come on, let's go!' she said with determination. Brad had collected several weapons, grenades and a rocket launcher and slung what he couldn't carry in his hands over his shoulder, they proceeded towards the increasing sound of gunfire yet again. Katriana, stiff in her resolve to help her father and Robert. Brad doing what he'd been trained for.

The other soldier who ran to warn the others saw the figures of the three men ahead, silhouetted against the tunnel portal in the distance. The soldier, immediately recognising them as officers by their caps, called out.

'Sir! Sir!'

The three men stopped and turned around slowly. The tunnel portal was about 500 meters in the distance. The young soldier continued forward to the officers. Struggling for breath, he said.

'Sir. Sir, there's an entrance back there with a tunnel and some kind a' detonating device on the wall and it's armed, it's gonna blow this here mountain at any time Sir, we've got to stop it, Sir.'

'Is that so, Private? We'll have to see what we can do about it then shan't we,' replied Max Wittenberg. 'Kill him,' he said callously.

The soldier caught unawares reacted too late and was shot as usual between the eyes by Oefner using his silencer attached pistol. The three Nazis bundled the dead soldier into one of the refuges and continued their masquerade towards the tunnel portal.

***

In the base itself, the NATO troops had overcome the Nazi guard completely and were almost ready to breach the entrance to the complex behind the control room. They were still throwing everything they had at the control room itself with little effect.

Larousse and Perzinski were maintaining the assault on the entrance whilst within a lull, they came to realise someone was mounting an attack from the rear of the doors. Perzinski called to all commanders to verify if anyone had breached the base from another position, the reply was negative and all groups were accounted for.

'It doesn't make sense, who'd be trying to get through from behind there,' commented Perzinski.

'Listen! Gunfire! Whoever it is, he's on our side,' Malhotra said as they listened to the sustained gunfire and grenade explosions emanating from behind the door. Eventually, in fact it was less than two minutes, the door began to give way to the pounding they had received from both directions.

As they did so, Perzinski's men charged the opening to find a dozen or so Nazi guards dead on the floor behind and Katriana and a NATO private, standing there to welcome them.

'Larousse! Christ! Over here!' shouted Perzinski. Larousse dashed over. 'What is it?' He said, fearing something was far from right. As he came into line with the door, he saw his daughter appear in the doorway before him, brandishing an automatic rifle. She was in tatters. He was aghast.

'What in heaven's name are you doing here, Katriana? How the bloody hell did you get in there?' She ignored the questions and came straight to the point.

'They're going to blow the place up, papa! Come on, get out of here now. Where's Robert?'

'How do you know that? They're all trapped up there. We have control on the ground.'

'Papa! Some of them, we think three, have escaped and set a timer switch to "armed" in the tunnel we found. It's set to go off, I'm telling you! Come on, there's no time left!'

Larousse looked dumbfounded. He looked at the soldier.

'It's true, Sir. We found a tunnel leading into a drainage tank, someone's got out and set this place to blow.'

Perzinski chipped in. 'Told you she was some gal, eh.' Larousse ignored the comment.

'Okay. André, Carl, there's no more you can do here, there's no time to waste. You both take my daughter back down the tunnel leading to the old building, it must be the shortest route out of here. Perzinski, we must immobilise this control room before 03.00hrs Then make a run for it ourselves.'

Larousse took a quick look around. In an exasperated tone and without consideration for his daughter's presence, he shouted.

'Where the fuck's Cameron?'

'Yes, Papa! Where is Robert?' pleaded Katriana as she too looked around the vast cavern.

During the short lull prior to Katriana's arrival, Robert had busied himself investigating a group of cables leading from below the control room floor, which had been exposed by the sheer firepower unleashed at the rock beneath. He had climbed through a tight gap where the armoured cables were seen to disappear.

Once his body had squeezed through a tight channel perhaps three or four meters long, grazing himself in places he'd rather not have in the process, he dropped vertically to the floor some three or four meters below.

The room he fell into was in darkness, bar for the shaft of light penetrating through from the gap above. In the distance, he could vaguely make out some sort of metal framework protruding out from the wall. Something was operating in a corner, an engine of some sort, what was it? Why was it?

In the half-light now as Robert's eyes had become accustomed to the gloom, he moved to the source of the sound. It was at a time like this he wished he'd smoked, if so, he may have had a lighter or a box of matches to hand but no, he'd have to make do.

The smell within the room soon registered with Robert, it was the smell which emanate from electrical apparatus affected by the current flow through the contacts and windings, etc. He cautiously felt his way around the walls for fear he may touch a live contact.

He could feel what appeared to be electrical control boxes all-round the walls, he concluded he was within a switch-room or similar. Robert knew time was of the essence. He found the softly vibrating machine, there was a fixed cage preventing his reaching it though.

From what he could make out, he concluded it was a generator, only a small one, not capable of sustaining the power needed for the whole base, simply a back-up provision, lighting perhaps. He continued to feel his way around, with luck he found a light switch. He turned the contact, closing his eyes in the process in case it could be a trap. Luckily for all, it was just a light switch.

The room now illuminated; he could see he was indeed within the Main Electrical Switch Room complete with sub-station supplying the base with its electricity needs. The engine he'd heard rumbling away was behind a locked metal cage alongside a much larger version, which was idle.

The small machine was an integral portable type of transportable generator unit, the sort of machine contractors use when working on site. Robert thought little of it for the time being as he focussed his intentions to cutting all the main electrical circuits within the base, which he hoped would render the control room circuits redundant.

Robert pulled each and every lever downward, cutting the power to the circuit it controlled. One by one, groups of light fittings suspended from the roof within the cavern blanked out. The lights in the corridors blanked out, everything went dark. This alerted Larousse to the fact that this could be Robert's doing.

Larousse at that moment was dragging his daughter away and ordering André and Carl to get her out while he returned to help Robert. Perzinski and a team of six meanwhile, had worked their way up to the doors leading to the control room. They mounted an unbelievable assault on the doors with anti-tank missiles, grenades and armour piercing shells; everything they had but still the doors remained closed. Battered but closed.

***

Inside, the Nazi hierarchy under emergency battery powered lighting were watching with bated breath the timer as it calmly marked the minutes, seconds, tenths of seconds and hundredths of seconds without the merest hint of a malfunction. Four minutes, thirty seconds left.

They were in jubilant mood considering their predicament, for regardless of the outcome of the long-awaited test, they would surely now perish within the confines of the Oberammergau Donor Missile Base.

General Conrad Braun called for silence.

'Herr Kammeraden. In slightly over four minutes, the missiles will be launched against their targets and the targets ultimately destroyed. The world will know the Fourth Reich has begun. We shall undoubtedly not live to see the glory of our Fourth Reich! But! We have many followers far beyond the confines of this cavern, this country and this continent even.'

'Younger men, men capable of taking the new Fourth Reich to glory. To die here is an honour. We must be remembered. No! We will be remembered by our people as martyrs to the cause. Our retribution against the Allies a success. I give you The Fourth Reich!'

They all swallowed a shot of Schnapps from the lead crystal glasses provided for such an occasion and toasted The Fourth Reich. All that is, bar one. The young man from the carriage who stood up to Braun on the journey to the base.

'Herr Braun!' he bellowed at the top of his voice to draw attention.

'I warned you, you incompetent, power lusting egoistic bloody fool. I am one of those breeds of younger men you talk of. And yes, remember, I warned you to call it off. But no! Oh no! You had to play the martyr, you and those like you here, all in your sixties, seventies and eighties! What was it? The Final Solution! Eh?' screamed the young man, enraged at his predicament.

Braun pulled his father's service Luger from its pouch and aimed it between the man's eyes. The Kammeraden spread out from behind the target.

'I forewarned you aboard the carriage, your insolence will not be tolerated.'

'That's right! Shoot me. Shoot one of your own like you did in nineteen forty-five, you murdering bastard you.'

The man fell to the floor with a thud, he'd been shot directly between the eyes. The others remained silent, too afraid to challenge Braun. They knew their death was inevitable but please, not from the barrel of a German gun. The control room took on an eerie silence as their attention returned to the timer.

***

Katriana had broken away from Carl and André who couldn't find it in themselves to handle her as she indeed needed to be and had run back into the cavern and was screaming Robert's name, hoping and praying he would answer. As she reached her father, with Carl and André just shrugging a gesture he just sighed and shook his head.

No one knew where Robert had gone.

Pfeiffer had remained back in the rail tunnel, ensuring contact had been maintained directly with the Railway's Traffic Control. He verified the position with the signal and telegraph operative who had made the appropriate connections to the telecommunication cables in the tunnel and was in direct contact with the Railway Control Centre awaiting instructions. They advised him there had been no further rail activity along the line.

'It's almost 03.00 hrs, Sir. They're asking what the position is. They have gunships circling overhead awaiting orders.'

'Tell them to hold on! Give them a few more minutes. They must, tell them,' pleaded Pfeiffer.

Robert had shut everything down in the switch-room bringing the cavern into bleak darkness. All went deathly quiet as the gloom descended, it was then Larousse saw the shaft of light penetrate through under the control room.

'There!' he pointed.

'Look, the light! That's where Robert is, it's got to be Cameron,' he said, still pointing up at the source.

'Robert! Robert! Is that you in there?' shouted Katriana as loud as she possibly could as she jumped up and down with total disregard to the condition of her feet.

Robert heard her faintly. 'Yes, it's me sweetheart! Is your father with you?'

'Yes, Robert. Hurry.'

'Is it over?' he asked.

'No! No, it's not! We must get out! It's set to blow up! Come on, Robert!' She screeched. 'Hurry, hurry!'

Robert replied he was coming but he knew he couldn't, not until the job was done. Katriana stood nervously fidgeting at the base of the wall, awaiting Robert's appearance for what seemed like a lifetime but there was no sign of him. She called for her father amid tears of anguish. She had to get Robert out at any cost.

The troops had now replaced the eerie smoke and dust ridden darkness with bright beams of light from their portable equipment.

Robert was still studying the circuitry within the switch-room. He was still investigating the power source to close it down; he knew the small generator was of no value to the machinery housed within the base. There was a much larger marine derived diesel engine and generator standing idle, this would be the power supply for the machinery if there was an interruption to the main source, he concluded. There had to be another source, he had to find it.

Katriana called to him telling him again, the base was about to be destroyed any minute. It mattered not now, he had to stop the madness of it all, he was able to do so if only he could see how to. He shouted for her to go, then suddenly the wall to one side of him began caving in, the result of the bombardment Perzinski was maintaining against the control room from above.

Then he saw it. The whole picture became clear to him in a flash. Cables burrowing their way towards the railway tunnel. The power came from the railway's overhead power supply, it had to. There was something in the region of 25,000 volts in those power lines that would be the reason for the sub-station.

The high voltage was transformed in the sub-station and that was behind the caged area also. The supply had to be cut but he was trapped, he hadn't thought about it but he couldn't get out, the roof was too high, the door was closed and locked from the outside.

Frantically, he began tossing the debris which had fallen in against the wall, it wasn't enough, he couldn't get the height. What could he do? He looked at his watch 02.55.20. -21. 22. 23. 24. Robert concentrated. Yes! Eureka!

He ran the few short feet to the switch controlling the overhead lighting and switching the lever on and off he rattled out, Cameron Acknowledge. Cameron Acknowledge. Cameron Acknowledge! In Morse code.

André understood the message the second time, he pulled an air horn from his equipment and ran over to Larousse.

'François! It's Cameron! He's signalling for you to acknowledge.'

'Do it, man!' Larousse snapped unintentionally.

André blasted the horn in acknowledgment.

Robert signalled. "Cut overhead power in rail tunnel now!"

André translated the message, though Larousse had already understood. He radioed to Pfeiffer at the platform.

'Pfeiffer, come in! Pfeiffer.'

'Pfeiffer here.'

'Have the railway control cut all overhead power now! No arguments! Now!' Pfeiffer gave the order.

The whole area stood still, afraid to move. Almost everyone looked at their watch. It was slowly reaching 02.57. The tension was unbearable. By 02.57 and ten seconds, the power to the base was cut. The threat seemingly over for the outside world but not for them. They still had the threat of the self-destruction to contend with.

And Robert was trapped. Perzinski ordered his men out. Larousse ordered his men out also and to take his daughter with them. Carrying her in any manner if need be.

Katriana protested violently as she kicked and struggled in André and Carl's arms. Everyone ran for the railway tunnel; the other tunnels were too small to handle the exodus of men in volume. As they did so, they were oblivious to the fact that Robert had encountered yet another problem. A major problem, in fact!

The main generator had cut in automatically when the power supply was interrupted. It mattered not what switches he pressed; the machine kept running. He resorted to brute force and pounded the copper fuel supply pipe, which was clipped to the wall with a jagged piece of severed steel displaced from the dislodged control room support frame until it flattened and eventually burst open spraying a jet of diesel fuel over him and the general area.

He bashed at it until no more fuel could flow through to the engine. The regular rhythm of the powerful engine began to falter, Robert pulled and bashed and pulled and bashed, until finally, it ground to a halt as the pipe was fully severed. He sat down aside the generator, holding his head in his hands and thanking the Lord above. He looked at his watch again, it was 02.57 and 40 seconds.

In the control room, which was badly bruised but not quite out of commission, Braun and his Kammeraden watched the innocent little timer tick away the final few seconds to glory. And glory it would have been if it had not been for Robert sitting amid the dust, filth and diesel fuel he was now drenched in and looking at the other little innocent piece of equipment, the little generator still rumbling away in front of him.

He looked again at the supply pipe bringing the fuel to the innocent machine. He traced it to a vastly oversized tank suspended above, too vast for a machine which he previously assumed would be used in an emergency.

It hit him!

This could be the machine providing the power for the missile control unit! A separate low voltage supply! Electronics don't need high voltage, this was a failsafe precaution, there was no time to re-evaluate, it worked once and it should by the grace of God work again.

He reached down and picked up the same piece of steel and bashed at the supply pipe as close to the machine as possible in order to prevent as little of the precious drops of fuel reaching the innocent machine.

The hierarchy were in jubilant mood as the clock turned over. 02.57 55. 02.57 56 02.57 57. 02.57 58. 02.57 59. 02.58 00. 02.58. 01 02.58 02. It had stopped.

Braun could not believe it; in his anxiety, he thumped the clock face in a determined effort to re-start it. The emotions and the disbelief inside the control room was only matched by the sheer alleviation felt by Robert. He sat back in the dark and held his ears, just in case.

From behind him came the end of a rope, which had been fired through a small cavity by Sub-Lieutenant Malhotra, Robert fumbled in the gloom then grabbed onto it, tied it around his waist and gave it a tug. He was pulled up and through the cavity at speed, by Malhotra and Chambers.

His face, chest, arms and legs grazed along the rocky points protruding from all directions. It mattered not, at least he had a chance of survival now. He was dragged straight out of the wall as Larousse caught him in his arms. He shouted out.

'I have cut all the power.'

Larousse shouted to Perzinski to advise the NATO commanders the threat was neutralised and to withdraw the air assault on the Oberammergau Base. Perzinski passed on the message to his superiors.

'Come on, Robert! This place is about to blow!' shouted Larousse and Perzinski, as they all ran for the railway tunnel, which was the closest to Perzinski.

Robert followed Larousse at speed towards the platform when just short of them arriving, a series of explosions threw them off their feet bringing down rock above in the process. Perzinski looked horrified as he saw the gap close whilst awaiting Larousse's team. What could he do now?

'The old tunnel,' shouted Robert. The group turned quickly and ran in the general direction. Another explosion by the entrance sealed it off, all around them explosions began erupting. It was no good. There was no way out. Another massive explosion rocked the foundation of the control room, it began to fall from its mountings dragging the metal framework, which had protruded into the solid rock face with it.

'Look! The control room,' Robert shouted as he pulled Larousse back.

The tremendous explosions erupting throughout the cavern eventually caused the structure to weaken. The whole control room structure fell forward and down to the cavern floor, rolling over and tossing both men and machinery about inside.

It settled upturned on the cavern floor. A massive fireball burst through the hitherto impenetrable structure, ripping the end section clean off and sending it hurtling across the cavern.

'We've had it, Monsieur Larousse! We're trapped.'

'Never say die, Robert. Katriana got in from behind there somewhere, we must find it. Come on!'

Both shielded themselves as they ran towards the burning wreck of the control room and the breached entrance beyond. Passing close by the torn off end of the Nazi stronghold, Robert looked in, he could see to the rear a fire still raging working its way through the plastics and consumables readily to hand. He could see the partially charred bodies of the Nazi warlords thrown about into heaps soon to be cremated in their own tomb.

'What about them?' asked Robert.

'They've had their day, let them rot in it,' replied Larousse as he glanced in. He turned away then swiftly turned his stare back.

'What is it, Monsieur Larousse?'

'Those look like blueprints, perhaps they're the missile system designs. I'll have to get hold of them, our people in Whitehall will be very interested in those.' Another explosion rained boulders down from above, followed by one inside the remains of the control room, which threw them to the floor. They had no hope of getting hold of the plans, the whole place was crumbling down around them, they only had time to head for an unknown entrance somewhere behind in the labyrinth of corridors.

Robert caught sight of two small sections of material broken off the face of the control room. One large enough to shield himself, the other a small fragment.

He placed the small fragment in his pocket and shielded himself against the heat with the large section, then dashed over, picked up the plans and stuffed them down his trousers. He looked in at the bodies scattered about.

'What about that bastard Max, I don't see him in there. Or the General.'

'Never mind them. What's that for? A souvenir,' criticised Larousse as he pointed to the bulge in his pocket.

Whilst they were running, Robert replied.

'Not exactly Monsieur Larousse, I couldn't give a damn about a souvenir. It's the material, what in God's name is it? Just look at it, after what we've thrown at it, it should be wrecked, mangled, yet it's still intact. I'm going to have this analysed if we get through this.'

'Christ, Cameron! You're certainly not the fool I took you for a week ago. In fact, I'll go as far as to say you're one of the finest men I've ever met,' said Larousse meaningfully, breathlessly.

They shook hands as they continued running in search of the concealed entrance.

Whilst searching the corridors amid fire, water and debris being lashed down upon them, they could hear someone calling out. They ran in the direction of the voice. It was Carl, he had gone back for them when Katriana told him her father hadn't been told the location of the tunnel.

The four men ran like the wind down the narrow tunnel to the chamber. Larousse entered first and stepped out to be greeted by his daughter and André.

'I'm sorry François, this is as far as she would go.'

'It's okay, André.' He looked at his daughter. 'My precious, are you alright?'

'Yes, I'm okay papa, are you? Is Robert with you? Is he alright?' she said, crying floods of tears and holding on to her father tightly.

'He's just fine. Robert's going to be okay, my precious,' he replied as he caressed her gently.

The canister returned and Robert stepped out slightly bruised but far from beaten. Katriana released her father's hold and rushed to him.

'Oh, Robert! Robert! You're alive. God, you're alive! I love you, Robert. I love you so very much.' She threw her arms around him, he reciprocated. They stood kissing until Carl, Malhotra and Chambers surfaced from the tunnel.

All held each other as if some kind of invisible bond had been formed between them. They would surely remember this moment for a very long time.

Chapter Fifteen

The five strong group were making their way along the railway tunnel as swiftly northward as Katriana's progress would allow, giving the fact she was still barefooted. Katriana was concentrating on her every step, ensuring she stepped centrally on each railway sleeper, one by one, or occasionally two if she felt able to reach.

Her intentions were simple, the soles of her feet were already injured quite significantly from her exploits since her escape and the thought that a greater and unnecessary pain would certainly be inflicted should she stray from the sleepers to the jagged stone ballast was enough to exercise caution.

Her progress, however, was hindering the group's evacuation markedly as the explosions reverberating through the tunnel were reaching a crescendo, causing the rock around them to weaken in places, permitting sections to dislodge and crash down from above.

Katriana was being assisted and guided in the poor light provided by André's battery-powered lamp, both by her father and Robert; suddenly, a rather large section of rock crashed to the floor only inches in front of them, the three of them stumbled over and fell to the ground. Carl took the initiative, he assisted Katriana to her feet and promptly stooped down and raised her to his shoulder, shouting out, 'Monsieur Larousse Sir, I'll carry your daughter, we must hurry.'

Larousse agreed. This was no time for modesty.

André took the lead with the lamp and quickly they gained a fair distance between them and the sound of now diminutive explosions from behind. Stepping sprightly still, rather than running, they could now see the tunnel portal silhouetted against the night sky quite clearly. With only five hundred or so meters to go, they could congratulate each other knowing at least they had made it to safety.

Just then, as André cast the beam from his lamp sideways as he ran, he noticed a figure bundled up in a refuge. He ran over, calling out. 'François! There's a soldier over here!'

André lifted the soldier's head up gently, he blanched at the sight before him, he knew this was no death from the recent conflict but a calculated cold-blooded execution, the bullet having passed through directly between the eyes. André turned around to look at Larousse.

'He's dead,' he announced breathlessly as he fought against his gorge rising. André turned the soldier's head away as he continued, 'This is no ordinary casualty François, he's been murdered!'

Carl lowered Katriana to her feet to see what had happened. Larousse gestured to his daughter to stay put and dashed over. It mattered not, Katriana had seen the soldier's face.

'Papa! He's one of the two soldiers taking me to Doctor von Rauch's when we stumbled on that chamber thing. One of those escaped Nazis killed him?'

Larousse had no need to think. He knew.

'My God, Katriana, if you had still been with him, you could have been killed! Jesus Almighty, I've been such a bloody fool.'

Larousse sprung up and hugged his daughter as an impassioned sense of guilt came over him, knowing just how susceptible a position he'd brought her to. He was clearly perplexed at the notion. It had been so close. He felt so belittled to think, yet again, he'd led her into such potential danger. He could do no more than apologise profusely for so doing.

Katriana reached up, kissed her father and told him she loved him very much but it was as much her decision and she knew the risks. He was not to blame. Carl picked up the body of the soldier.

'I'll carry him out Sir, if that's okay with you, mademoiselle?'

'Of course, Carl,' Larousse said remorsefully. Katriana nodded tearfully.

The small group continued wearily on in the dark as the sound of explosions still erupted from behind them. They all agreed that there would be little chance of the Fourth Reich using the Oberammergau tunnel as a base again.

Reaching the tunnel portal, all hell had broken out in Oberammergau with the arrival of the military in force. Telephone lines and roads were jammed by citizens giving bizarre reports ranging from earth tremors felt, to explosions, sound of guns firing and smoke belching out from the tunnel vents and portals.

The Polizei, Emergency Services and other authorities had cordoned off the approaches and were awaiting both information and orders before proceeding. The helicopter gunships, which had been circling overhead had moved off but not away completely, their sound could still be heard in the distance.

As Larousse and the others reached the tunnel portal, they were confronted by a group of officials surrounded by armed officers from both the military and the local Polizei. The countenance visible in their faces was portentous. The leading official blurted a demand in German.

Larousse replied, 'Sprechen Sie Englisch.' He was in no mood for translations.

'Who is in charge here?' demanded the official, obviously exasperated at the situation. 'What in heaven's name is going on?'

'Don't tell me you don't know!' said Larousse.

'I've been given two versions to date. First, I've been told this was a NATO exercise which has gone wrong by one of your NATO officers who was helping two wounded colleagues. He said an ammunition train had derailed and crashed in the tunnel.'

'And second, these troops here tell me you're flushing out a Nazi base of some sort. Now I know which one I believe, and I want to know why a train of that description is passing through this country into a dead-end tunnel without clearance from our authorities!'

Larousse disregarded the official's request completely. He demanded, 'What officers? Where are they?'

He instinctively knew they could only be the Nazis who had used the tunnel to escape and now he knew there were three of them.

'The officers passed through about ten or fifteen minutes ago, two of them were injured.'

'Describe them.'

'What?'

'I said describe them, you idiot!'

'How dare you Herr—' the official was cut short by Larousse who was furious with his incompetence and that of the military on guard.

'Listen you bungling idiots, you've just let three Nazi bastards get away scot free, while we've been almost blown to bits down there preventing bloody World War Three! Now tell me what the fuck they look like.'

Larousse suddenly realised there was no sign of Gerrard.

'Nazis?' said the bemused official.

'Yes! Bloody Nazis. Bloody "Reichsbürger" bastards. Look, have you seen one of my men? He was positioned at the tunnel mouth to advise the troops of our position. Haven't you lot been told anything?'

'No, nothing! But those three NATO officers you're calling Nazis told us there was another man in need of medical attention at the entrance, he was unconscious. He's been taken to hospital along with the injured officers.'

'Don't tell me?' Larousse said, incongruous at the thought. 'You didn't put him with those other three, did you?'

'Of course. We had no reason not to. The two injured officers in one ambulance and the other man together with the uninjured officer in the other. They're on their way to Murnau right now!'

'Christ almighty! Does it ever end!' Larousse bellowed.

The expostulations continued for a few moments longer. Larousse then demanded action, both to save Gerrard and to capture the three Nazis. The beleaguered official stood with a vacuous looking expression, his mouth agape at the allegations. In protestation, he challenged Larousse to prove the source of such allegations.

Larousse pointed to the still figure of the dead soldier in Carl's arms, remarking on how he'd been shot directly between the eyes and told him if that wasn't enough, to take a walk down the tunnel and he would see for himself that what he regarded as allegations, were in fact the truth.

The official held his stance and demanded Larousse and his team remain under guard until he could verify their allegations. Larousse and the others were livid. They'd risked their lives to prevent a catastrophe only to be detained by an armed guard themselves.

Larousse attempted yet again to inculcate their position, all to no avail. The official was awaiting his orders from a higher authority before making any decisions.

Larousse suggested while they wait perhaps, he could be so kind as to describe the men who passed through posing as injured. A few moments later, he eventually began to describe the three men, starting with the one who was assisting the others.

Following a brief outline, both Katriana and Robert announced simultaneously that it was Max he was describing, the man who had lured them into the trap.

'Now, do you believe us?' asked Larousse.

A few moments later, Perzinski, Pfeiffer, along with Marcel and several truckloads of troops descended on the already chaotic situation. Perzinski soon took control of the situation, his authority in matters of military security in the region undenied. He confirmed the fact the Nazis had indeed made yet another attempt at world domination but the threat was passed.

He himself could not understand why the local authorities had not been given any warning. The official could do no more than apologise for the inconvenience whilst maintaining his department's innocence in the matter. Larousse simply shook his head in disgust.

Perzinski told Larousse his two naval officers had remained with the troops to attend a de-briefing and that he'd signalled the "All Clear" coded message, which would be relayed to all nations via the Admiralty. He congratulated them on a mission well accomplished, Pfeiffer included.

'Hold back the congratulations a while longer,' said Larousse. Perzinski and Pfeiffer listened with imperceptibility to Larousse detail the recent events.

'Before we get too excited Leo, we've got three Nazis heading for the hospital in Murnau together with my man, Gerrard. Courtesy of our friend here,' he acrimoniously advised.

Perzinski grimaced at the thought. He pulled Larousse to one side.

'We'll have to go after them, we've no choice. They may have the missile system designs with them. In a matter of a few short months, whatever, the bastards could have similar built and operational again.'

'Don't you think I'm aware of that possibility, Leo. For Christ's sake, I know it's not over but my daughter, Robert, André and the others, they've been through enough. God, it's small wonder they made it this far without being killed. As for the drawings, Cameron salvaged a few but of course there may be more, we'll never know.'

Perzinski agreed to their position without hesitation and suggested they all withdraw from further involvement; Larousse was relieved and thanked him but insisted he continue to finish what he started. It was agreed between the two of them.

Several vehicles had been made available from the forces who had taken up position on the outskirts to take the troops back to base. As the troops, authorities and locals alike congregated around the hastily erected check point to discuss the events, Doctor von Rauch arrived. Larousse vouched for him and he was led through.

He offered immediate medical assistance to the injured members of the team, the gentlemen allowing Katriana to have her feet attended to first. After which, he offered Larousse and his team refreshments and accommodation as a gesture of friendship and gratitude. Larousse would have been willing to renege the offer but thought of his daughter and her condition, plus his mind was on Gerrard.

He thanked him and ensured the local officials had been satisfied their involvement was authorised before they all said their goodbyes and farewells and proceeded with the doctor to his home, leaving the locals and the military to tidy up the mess. It was agreed to make use of the story of an ammunition train accident due to a signalling error, at least for the time being.

Heidi had prepared rooms for them all and offered them the use of the bathrooms to shower or bathe, advising there was ample hot water for everyone. But everyone was too exhausted to contemplate anything other than sleep. The doctor checked the dressings again before they retired.

Heidi showed them upstairs. André, Carl and Marcel were given rooms to the right of the corridor whilst Larousse was offered the main guest bedroom, Katriana and Robert adjoining rooms on either side.

Katriana looked cautiously at her father while holding onto Robert's arm tightly, her eyes casting a loving glance towards Robert momentarily. Her father sensed her mood but felt awkward with the situation, he knew she wanted so much to be with Robert but his principles forbid the thought of it.

Not here. Not now. Not in these circumstances. He no longer thought of her as his little girl. He couldn't after what she'd just been through. She was a woman now and he knew it but still, his heart couldn't let go. His principles unyielding. If they truly loved each other, they would wait.

He stepped over to her and lifted her chin with his forefinger, with a slight wince and a blink of the eyes, he transmitted his disapproval for the moment. She understood and bid Robert good night without any fuss. Robert was in no mood to challenge; he wanted her as much as she'd wanted him but there would be time. Plenty of time. The right time.

He also bid them all goodnight and retired to his appointed room.

Less than half an hour later the sound of a vehicle was heard slowly approaching up the path leading to the doctor's residence. With the events of the day, Larousse was confident everyone would be earning a well-deserved sleep in no time at all. He'd arranged with Perzinski to collect him, from which both of them accompanied by Pfeiffer and a team of volunteers would proceed to Murnau and the hospital.

The sound of the vehicle and voices whispering in the garden below had disturbed Katriana, she hadn't fallen asleep as expected, she was too alert from the ordeal, her mind attempting to come to terms with, after all, what was a remarkable series of events. Events from which she had so nearly come to grief over. And of course, there was Robert, he'd been through far worse, poor soul.

She couldn't stand the intrigue any longer, throwing the covers back she slipped off the bed and crept over to the window, she was wearing the rather unappealing night-dress Heidi had loaned her, although she was grateful for the thought, she hoped she'd never be seen wearing such as a matter of choice.

And worse still, she hoped Robert would never see her in such attire. She quietly crossed the floor, aware of the creaking floorboards and ensuring she did not announce her movements. Looking out, she could see her father still dressed in the camouflage combat clothing, talking with Perzinski and two other soldiers.

She looked to the street in the distance where she was sure it was Pfeiffer standing by another vehicle, an army vehicle. She wondered to herself what was happening. Was it over or not? She had to know, had to find out for sure.

Katriana opened the wardrobe door and selected some ladies' trousers from the rail and a warm sweater from a shelf. The fit was loose, she assessed as she inspected herself in the mirror to find she was somewhat pleased with the results.

She finished dressing and painfully slipped on a pair of shoes over the bandaging and proceeded quietly downstairs, she took an overcoat from the hall stand then eased her way out of the house through the patio doors in the study to the garden. Creeping around to the corner, she crouched down and listened intently to the conversation between her father and Perzinski.

'Well, what do you suggest, Larousse?'

'Look Leo, Gerrard's been with me for more years than I care to remember, I don't care what it takes, I have to go to Murnau and find him. He put his life on the line when I gave him the choice last week and again earlier in the tunnel, so now I intend returning the favour, that is, if he's reached the hospital and I say if, because those three Nazis were most probably faking the injuries for all we know but let's assume he has and they weren't, then with any luck Gerrard will be there and they'll be in the vicinity. I mean, they would be stupid to try anything before they were far enough away and what better escape than a pretence journey in an ambulance.'

'Okay. I agree. I've organised the chopper for the three of us and a few guys, we'll get there pretty soon.'

'Right Leo, there's no time to waste, I'll go and ask Doctor von Rauch to keep an eye on the others and to say nothing about where we're going, just give me a moment.'

Larousse returned inside to the sitting room where von Rauch awaited the news. He told him of the plan and asked him to take care of things until he returned. The doctor agreed and wished him good luck. Katriana decided she had no intention of leaving her father to deal with this alone, in any case she could identify Max, he couldn't. Slipping back into the study, she scribbled a note:

"Gone to help Papa, he's gone after Max. Please forgive me darling, I love you".

She knew there was no possibility of her accompanying him, so therefore she would have to make her own transport arrangements. Slipping out into the garden, she waited until her father and the others had gone and heard the doctor lock the front door.

Creeping along the side of the building, she reached the Range Rover which to her joy was unlocked with the keys in the ignition. Opening the door quietly, she ensured before starting there was adequate fuel registering on the gauge, this was not the time to run out of petrol.

Satisfied with the reading at half full, she turned the ignition key and the engine roared into life. Immediately, she selected first gear and sped off down the path to the gateway thence onward to Murnau.

Von Rauch had of course heard the unmistakable sound of the powerful V8 engine start-up and the tyres of the Range Rover churn up the loose gravel on the path. He dashed out only to see the taillights disappear as the vehicle turned out from the gates.

Not knowing who had taken the vehicle he ran upstairs first to André's room, knowing him to be Larousse's second in command. He knocked frantically but not noisily on the door to gain his attention, calling out his name in a low voice. André rose and opened the door gently, wondering what could possibly be wrong now.

'Von Rauch! What's happening?' he asked, still a little exhausted. 'Someone's taken the Range Rover; I don't know who.'

'It'll be François, he'll have to double check everything's okay and I know him only too well.'

'It's not Herr Larousse. He's gone to Murnau to find your other man.' André cut in. 'I told you; he's got to ensure everything's okay.'

'No! No, you do not understand. Three Nazis escaped I'm told and they've gone to Murnau together with your man in two ambulances. Herr Larousse had all of you withdrawn from the operation, for your own safety you understand but he had to go with the NATO officer and a few others to find them. He insisted.'

'Christ! Who the devil's gone after him? Is it Carl or Marcel? Or is it, Cameron?'

'I don't know.'

'You check Cameron's room; I'll check on Carl and Marcel.'

Carl had heard the whispering in the corridor and rose to find out the reason. He was told of the events and within a few moments, everyone was milling around the corridor, querying the problem. No one had thought of it until Robert asked where Katriana was?

Heidi offered to check her room. She opened the door and looked in; Katriana had placed the pillows lengthways under the covers in the time-honoured fashion to avoid detection.

'She's asleep,' said Heidi. 'Poor thing's exhausted I've no doubt,' she muttered, then offered them all some coffee, knowing no one would sleep this night.

Von Rauch had no option other than to tell of Larousse's plans to reach Gerrard and find the three escaped Nazis into the bargain. Robert inculcated the fact that only he, Katriana and Marcel could identify any of the Nazis, more so him for he had seen most if not all of them, it was incongruous for Larousse to have gone alone with no idea who he was looking for.

The discussion continued downstairs to the extent of excess verbiage by all concerned. No decision or plan of action had been resolved before Heidi arrived with the tray of coffee. She poured each cup, politely inquiring if sugar or milk was required, among obsequious proposals from Larousse's crew whether to follow him to Murnau or not. Robert, however, suddenly halted proceeding by announcing.

'Hold on! If we're all here, who took the bloody Range Rover? I mean that's what started all this.'

'It'll have been Perzinski or Pfeiffer or someone.'

'No. Not them, they went with Herr Larousse I'm sure, I'm sure of it,' said the doctor.

'Heidi, will you fetch my route map of the region and the street map of Murnau, please. If these gentlemen do decide to go, they will need some idea of the roads. They are both in the study.' Heidi acknowledged; von Rauch added. 'What am I saying, of course you know where they are. Heidi keeps things in good order for me, I can be untidy, you understand.'

Less than a minute later, Heidi's screeching was heard as she dashed through from the study to the drawing room in hysteria.

'Herr Artz! Es ist schrecklich! Die Frauline!'

'What's happened?' shouted almost everyone.

'Heidi! Bitte! Bitte!' the doctor called as he rushed over to calm her. 'What has happened, Heidi?'

Heidi was breathless with shock. She managed to convey the message by producing the note left on the desk by Katriana.

'It's a note!' Von Rauch read it aloud.

"Gone to help Papa, he's gone after Max. Please forgive me darling, I love you".

'Katriana!' shouted Robert. 'But she's upstairs!' he exclaimed as he leaped over a chair, rushing to check on her. She was gone, of course.

Everyone had followed him up, Heidi was still in a state of shock and trying to explain how she could have seen her if she was not there. Robert showed her the pillows laid out under the covers; Heidi began to cry. Von Rauch comforted her.

'Doctor. We will need your car,' stated Robert bluntly. 'Are you all with me?' he added.

Before he could look at each of them individually, all three announced confirmations. The doctor provided them with his BMW 535se and the maps. He reluctantly offered the only weapon he had, an old revolver which had been locked away in the bottom drawer of his desk for many years.

He pointed out the authorities would not take kindly to someone carrying a weapon and suggested they avoid attracting attention to themselves. They were grateful for the advice but more so the revolver, for it was now the only weapon they had as all others had been collected by the troops once the Oberammergau assault was over.

Carl looked on ominously as he mentioned the fact his pistol had been secluded within the Range Rover. This was an oversight, he admitted but under the circumstances, he had simply forgotten his prime duty to protect Larousse's daughter.

André lightened his anguish by being supportive and understanding. Before long, the four men were tearing along the road towards Murnau as dawn was about to break.

***

Stoltz and the others had planned to use the ambulances as far as the outskirts of Murnau, having taken control shortly after leaving Oberammergau. Oefner overpowered the paramedic who began giving attention to Stoltz's faked wounds and ordered the other to drive on as normal.

Max was in a similar position; he had the two paramedics under gunpoint and refused them permission to attend to their patient.

Gerrard meanwhile was sinking fast; he had suffered badly at the hands of Oefner and Wittenberg who had beaten him senseless rather than shoot him for fear even a silenced shot may be heard. Gerrard had sensed there was something wrong when he challenged the three officers to show their identities.

He thought at the time how did they get out but it was too late, Wittenberg had done the trick of removing a concealed gun from below his cap whilst Gerrard was glancing at the I.D. cards. From which his rifle was taken from him and he was beaten until unconscious.

When the three Nazis came upon the checkpoint, Max used him as bait, telling the officials there was another man in need of urgent medical attention. They had brought him out of the tunnel in the hope the ambulances were standing-by. The local officials and the troops were none the wiser to the plot and placed Gerrard in the ambulance with them.

Wittenberg had kept an eye on Gerrard, the paramedics and the road, until the outskirts of Murnau could be seen. He ordered the driver to take a side road and stop out of sight from the main road, the ambulance behind followed suit. Wittenberg taped the hands of the two paramedics behind their back, then told them to get out.

As they nervously stepped out of the ambulance, Oefner approached and with a single shot to each between the eyes, he killed them both as he had already done so to the two paramedics in the rear ambulance, one of whom was a woman.

Wittenberg was enraged, he began expostulating to Stoltz who concluded the actions were valid for they had to eliminate any witnesses. Wittenberg demanded they separate here and now as he did not wish to be party to any further murders. Stoltz agreed and wished him good luck.

Max stepped away from them both, walking sensibly backwards, he no longer trusted the General or his lap dog, he made his way cautiously into the woods and the relative safety of cover it provided. Stoltz and Oefner discussed their next move together and luckily for Gerrard, forgot all about him.

They walked off in another direction under the watchful eye of Max who was wary of any double-cross being conspired between them to finish him off also. Satisfied they were on another course to his intended, he set off in search of suitable clothing, the NATO officer's attire whilst impressive was obviously impractical giving the circumstances.

A few moments later, the sound of a helicopter was heard overhead. Max took cover in the bushes though the trees offered plentiful. He listened to hear if it was simply passing or circling; it was circling. They must have spotted the bright markings of the two ambulances in the road. They were on to them. He knew it for sure.

Casting aside the officer's tunic, he darted through the woods as the sound of the helicopter faded, he reached the outlying village of Gratenaschau where he posed as a jogger taking a very early morning work-out.

The outfit of camouflage trousers, boots and vest proved quite acceptable to the few early morning locals, bidding him "Grüß Gott!" or "Guten Morgen!" as they passed. He acknowledged accordingly.

Stoltz and Oefner were not fairing so well, Stoltz was in no condition to jog anywhere and therefore made slow progress through the woods in the direction of Walchensee. When the woods came to a sudden end, they were trapped. They couldn't risk crossing the open fields with the helicopter hovering above. They waited patiently for it to land.

The helicopter had found a place to put down as close as possible to the two seemingly abandoned ambulances. Radio communication between Murnau hospital, the authorities and Perzinski's helicopter had been made and the hospital had already dispatched further ambulances backed by armed Polizei.

It was no longer solely a military operation, the authorities had to be involved now and involved they were. Larousse and the others split up and cautiously approached the two ambulances from all sides, there was no sign of movement.

On closing in, two of Perzinski's men radioed that they could see two blood-stained motionless bodies lying on the verge beside one of the ambulances and that they appeared to be the paramedic crew from what they were wearing. Pfeiffer only moments later was appalled at the sight of the lifeless figure of one paramedic.

Her head slumped out of what was once the side window and surrounded by the remains of shattered glass and blood running down the outside of the door, forming a pool below. A nauseating feeling overcame him and he was forced to relieve himself there and then.

He'd seen the results of many a murder and many a gruesome sight, nevertheless, this was beyond his grasp of reality. The whole situation simply sickened him. Overcoming his condition, he joined the others who had assessed the situation as safe and had moved forward to render any assistance possible.

Larousse jumped into the back of the rearmost ambulance to find it empty then dashed the few meters to the forward vehicle where he found Gerrard still lying lifeless on the stretcher. There was no medical equipment attached to monitor his condition nor to feed his body any medication, the first thing any paramedic would do under the circumstances.

This told him the paramedics were challenged from the outset to follow the Nazis' commands. But Gerrard? Was he dead or alive? Had he been murdered along with the four others? Larousse checked his pulse, then his eyes for dilation. The pulse was very weak, his eyes partially dilated. He was alive but only just.

Perzinski radioed their position; the ambulances were only a few minutes away. Larousse told Gerrard to hang on and that all was well, the base destroyed and the threat passed. He was talking to him but could he hear him? Gerrard remained unconscious.

The ambulances arrived and the paramedics rushed into action. Their professionalism was unquestionable, considering the sight they beheld. Four of their own colleagues murdered in cold blood whilst carrying out their duties. But Gerrard was for the moment their prime concern, he was still alive, barely alive but alive. Larousse was quick to clarify that Gerrard was one of them and not part of the Nazis' scheme.

In a quick decision, it was considered unnecessary to air-lift Gerrard to Murnau as it was only minutes in the ambulance where he could receive continuous attention on the way. Gerrard was rushed off in the helicopter whilst the bodies of the four paramedics were taken in the two ambulances.

Officers from the Polizei cordoned off the area and closed the road to traffic, pending forensic examination. Larousse and the others though were permitted to scour the area in the hope the Nazis' had left some sort of clue to their direction of escape.

Murnau and surrounding area was put on high alert for the escaped Nazis' and Polizei patrols were extremely evident throughout as the townspeople began rising and venturing into the streets. Television and radio broadcasts were hurriedly compiled to warn people to be on their guard against "Three escaped prisoners dressed in military style clothing and regarded as dangerous. If seen, to contact the Polizei immediately and not to approach them alone as they may be armed".

***

Katriana by this time had reached the turn off leading to the murder scene, she'd passed it before noticing the helicopter standing-by in an adjacent field. Slapping on the brakes, the Range Rover quickly slid to a halt, she selected reverse gear and almost regardless of what may be approaching from behind, she reversed under full throttle until reaching the turn off.

The Range Rover tyres screeching into the tarmac alerted the Polizei guarding the area. The policeman stood in the middle of the road and signalled the vehicle to halt. Katriana slammed on the brakes as she leaned out the window shouting.

'My father! Is he in there?'

'Who are you?' The officer replied in broken English.

'Frauline Larousse! My father is Herr François Larousse. Please! Is he in there? He's with the NATO Commander.'

'One moment, Frauline.' The officer radioed to the mobile command centre. 'Is there a Herr Larousse with you, Sir?'

'Yes, why?'

'Frauline Larousse is here, she demands to speak to him.'

'Very well. One moment.'

The police commander shouted for Larousse to join him. 'You have a daughter, Herr Larousse?'

'Yes?' said Larousse apprehensively. 'She is at the checkpoint.'

'Impossible! She's at von Rauch's asleep.'

'May I suggest you go down there and see for yourself?'

Larousse did so and got the shock of his life when he saw her pacing back and forth along the taped off perimeter.

'What in heaven's name are you doing here, Katriana!'

'Papa! Papa. You don't know what he looks like, Max I mean. I can identify him, Papa.'

It suddenly struck her something must be terribly wrong to have the area cordoned off, effectively sealing off the road altogether.

'Papa! What has happened? Are they trapped in there? What's going on?'

'Best you don't know, my dear, it's a bit nasty, I'm afraid.'

'Gerrard! Is he alright?'

'He's been taken to hospital, he's not so good to be honest, my dear. But what I want to know is what possessed you to follow me. Had I wanted anyone for identification purposes, I would have asked Robert, he's seen them all, for God's sake. You're very foolish coming out here like this and you know it!'

'I don't care, Papa. I'm not going to let that Nazi, Max, get away with it.'

'You may have no choice my dear, they're well and truly gone from here now.'

As he concluded, the roar of yet another vehicle approaching at speed could be heard in the distance.

'What in heaven's name is happening now?' said Larousse as he looked over his daughter's shoulder towards the oncoming vehicle. Skidding to a halt, all four doors opened simultaneously and Robert, André, Carl and Marcel jumped out.

'My God, Katriana! What the hell do you think you're playing at?' scolded Robert, most annoyed at her actions.

'I'm sorry, Robert but I knew you wouldn't let me go if I asked you.'

'Too bloody right I wouldn't.'

'Now there speaks a sensible man, Katriana. You should listen to him if you won't listen to me,' Larousse said surprisingly.

His daughter retaliated by saying this was getting them nowhere and that they should be deciding what to do next instead of arguing between themselves.

Larousse concurred and agreed they had a much better chance of finding them by working together. He called for Perzinski and Pfeiffer to join them in the search, leaving the authorities to their own methods of investigation.

Perzinski, having had contact with higher authority, reluctantly reneged due to his official NATO involvement, this was no longer solely a military objective and his objective had been achieved. He was now under orders to hand the matter over to the local authorities.

Pfeiffer also pulled out, knowing he was already in serious difficulty regarding his position. He would not be looked upon kindly by the authorities in Murnau, some of whom he now could not trust. Larousse reflected on the situation and thought it best for all concerned to end it here.

He knew his continued involvement could bring about further danger to his daughter, his comrades and of course, Robert Cameron whom he'd now come to admire.

He announced his official withdrawal to all present and suggested they return to Doctor von Rauch's until he organised transport to Marseille. Katriana asked outright if he were attempting to trick her again, he told her not to worry, it was over. They were going home.

She kissed her father on the cheeks and asked. 'And Robert?'

'Oh, he's coming with us my dear, we'll have to introduce him to your mama. I'm sure she'll be pleased. He's a fine man and that's the truth.' Larousse offered his hand in genuine friendship. Robert gripped it and both men shook and embraced each other with equal admiration.

'Thank you, Monsieur Larousse, I'll treasure those words after what we've been through together, eh.'

Larousse smiled, adding, 'François; Robert, please call me François.'

Both shook hands again as Katriana rushed in to hug them both, crying out. 'Papa, Robert, I love you both so, so, much.' She sobbed on her father's shoulder then turned to Robert and kissed him, a passionate kiss. Larousse showed no malice, in fact quite the opposite, he looked positively pleased.

The parties boarded the two vehicles, turned them around and headed back towards Oberammergau. When they reached Doctor von Rauch's, he was awaiting their arrival on the doorstep, eager to hear the outcome of the blunder at the tunnel. Larousse informed him of the situation, the knowledge of which appalled him.

Four more innocent lives taken at the hands of the Nazis. He offered them their room again but no one wanted to sleep. The group made use of his hospitality and bathed or showered to rid themselves of the filth they'd accumulated over the past twenty-four hours.

No doubt they wished the filth of the Nazis would wash off as easily. Von Rauch attended to Katriana's injured feet yet again as they had started bleeding once more. He also checked on the others whose injuries he'd dressed previously.

Heidi had decided with a friend in the town who owned a clothing shop to provide fresh clothing for all and the lady in question had arrived with a selection for them to peruse. Larousse was overwhelmed at the doctor's generosity when he refused to be reimbursed for the cost.

He asked if both he and Heidi would care to spend some time with him and his wife in Marseille. Von Rauch agreed it was a possibility and thanked him for his offer.

Meanwhile, Heidi had prepared and cooked a delicious hot breakfast for everyone whilst they were cleaning themselves up and dressing. The atmosphere around the large dining table eased the tensions of the previous day and night and everyone seemed at ease regarding the situation excepting Gerrard's condition, of which everyone had due concern.

By 09.00 hrs, breakfast was over and everyone was eager to return to normality. Larousse contacted Perzinski at the NATO Base to ensure all matters had been taken care of. Perzinski assured him everything was in order and that he should submit his report to the Admiralty as soon as possible. Larousse advised he would investigate it when he returned to Marseille and not before.

He asked Perzinski to take care of the Range Rover, which would be parked at von Rauch's and to pass on his regards to Pfeiffer and tell him to call him sometime over the next few days. He then had a few last words in private to thank von Rauch and Heidi for their kindness and assistance.

Perzinski had planned for the six of them to be picked up and flown by helicopter to the NATO Base at Böblingen and from there by private charter plane to Marseille, Larousse though, thought it only right to look in on Gerrard before leaving.

He knew he was in good hands and that the doctors would do their utmost for him. He simply felt the urge to see him even if he was unconscious. It was his duty as his employer and as a friend.

At around 11.45 hrs. the helicopter collected them from what was still a town in a state of shock. The local townspeople could be seen milling around the military perimeter, trying to come to terms with what had happened. A terrible accident remained the media story for now.

Larousse and his team could be justifiably proud of their efforts as they gazed down from above as smoke continued to billow out from the tunnel mouths and the mountain itself in places. The threat was over, sanity had returned to the Tirol Mountains, and all was at peace.

Gerrard would pull through his ordeal, the doctors assured Larousse. Everyone was elated at the news especially as Gerrard opened his eyes at the stroke of three o'clock in the afternoon. He had been unconscious for a full twelve hours.

He looked at Larousse and the team and a tear ran down his face when he saw that all of them had made it safely through the ordeal albeit battered and bruised.

'It's going to be alright Gerrard, we did it, we stopped them,' Larousse told him.

He moved his hand to hold Larousse. Larousse grasped it tightly and said, 'You hurry and get yourself fit Gerrard, I need you back at the chateau.'

Katriana leaned over and kissed him on the cheeks. Gerrard smiled and nodded off again.

The party returned to the helicopter and took off towards the NATO base for transfer to the private jet awaiting them. Whilst they were in the air, the pilot called for Larousse over the speaker. Larousse went forward for a few moments then returned.

'I have some news all of you may be interested in,' he said casually. 'Well, Papa? What?'

'The Polizei have found one of the escaped Nazis dead and another has been shot dead trying to evade arrest.'

Calls of who? What happened? And where? Reeled out from all present. 'All I know is that the Polizei cornered the two of them in a barn on the outskirts of a village called "Walchensee". One of them took a cyanide capsule, the other attempted to shoot it out.'

'Who were they?' asked Robert.

'The Polizei named them as Heinrich Stoltz and Axel Oefner. Oefner was the one who was shot.'

After the cheers subsided, Robert and Katriana looked at each other, Katriana then looked over to Marcel. He said, 'Two down, one to go.'

'Yes Papa, what about the one called Max?'

'Perhaps one day my dear, who knows. He's well on his way by now, that's for sure,' answered Larousse as he rose and headed to the galley section.

'I hope I bump into him again,' said Robert with vehemence.

'God! I hope you don't, Robert,' Katriana replied instantly as she grabbed his hand.

'Let's hope none of us do! Eh! Come now, let's celebrate what we've achieved, I think we deserve it,' called Larousse as he popped a bottle of champagne, which had been provided by Perzinski.

The team filled their glasses and drank to the future. Katriana looked longingly at Robert and he to her. Larousse saw the love in their eyes.

'Go on, man! Kiss the girl, for God's sake!'

Robert took the initiative; he clasped Katriana in his arms and gave her a long and passionate embrace. Larousse knew his daughter was in good hands. His little girl was no longer a little girl. He was happy for her and happy for Robert.

His memories of his other love came rushing back, that of his wife Claire-Louise, whom he'd all but abandoned in the past ten years or so because of his frantic business life taking precedence. It would change, he vowed. It would change this instant.

Robert whilst sitting holding Katriana throughout the whole journey, suddenly cried out.

'Shit! Oh sorry, I've just remembered.'

'Remembered what, Robert?' shouted Larousse, wondering.

'The Official bloody Receiver! I was supposed to be at his office at ten o'clock sharp last Tuesday!'

Everyone laughed out aloud, thinking of the irony of it all. Larousse advised Robert he would sort the matter out, saying, 'I owe you that at least.' The laughter continued a few moments longer as the pilot advised they were approaching the airfield.

***

The plane touched down at a military airfield close to Marseille. Arrangements had been made for their transport to the chateau. The two cars drew up outside the impressive frontage. Pascal was on hand to perform his duties.

'I trust you had a pleasant voyage Sir, Mademoiselle.'

Katriana began to laugh aloud as she stepped out of the car, assisted by Robert. She limped over to Pascal; her feet tender from the bruising and lacerations.

'If only you knew, Pascal.' She laughed.

Her mother had glanced out of the window as the two cars drew up. Seeing her husband alight had her wondering because he was back from the Bahamas so soon. Seeing her daughter limping and being assisted by a rather handsome stranger to whom she was clinging to with affection had her curious.

She waited no longer; she dashed out from the chateau and down the steps. Dressed in a knee length two-piece navy suit, Claire-Louise looked a picture of beauty and elegance to Larousse as she approached. He hadn't noticed the concern in her eye though.

'François! What has happened? Katriana, my dear, my baby! Your feet! What has happened to you?' She asked with concern as she knelt to look at her daughter's bandaged feet.

'I'm alright mama, honestly, I am. There's someone I want you to meet mama,' Katriana said as she held Robert close to her.

Madame Larousse stood up and looked directly at Robert with a kindly expression.

Katriana's mother was no fool, she'd seen the glint in her daughter's eye. She knew this stranger was more than a passing fancy. She could also see the glint in his as he'd attended to her daughter from the car. She offered Robert her right hand. Robert took it and kissed it.

'Madame Larousse. My name is Robert Cameron. It's a pleasure to meet you,' he announced nervously.

'Bien-venu, Robert. May I call you Robert?'

'But of course, Madame,' replied Robert, a little surprised.

She reached up, placed her hands on Robert's shoulders, drew him forward and give him a true French welcome by kissing him on both cheeks.

'Please, Robert. No more Madame, please my name is Claire-Louise, you are very welcome to my home.'

'I told you, Robert. Remember?' shouted out Larousse.

Robert looked over at Larousse who was standing to one side, smiling a cheery smile.

'Remember what, François?' Replied Robert, bemused. Larousse joined the threesome.

'I told you the welcome would be more pleasant than that of before. Eh!' Robert smiled a knowledgeable smile as he understood the meaning.

Larousse also welcomed Robert in the true French tradition. The welcomes and introductions over; Claire-Louise took Katriana's arm as they headed for the chateau. She whispered to her daughter.

'Do tell your mama, dear, where did you meet him? He's gorgeous, you lucky girl you.'

Katriana giggled as she clung onto her mama's arm as she danced up the steps like a love-struck little girl. Her mama knew she had found her true love.

'It's a long story, mama. A long story.'

The End

Epilogue

It soon seemed indeed officially the end for Robert, Katriana and her father, François as they returned to normal life. Gerrard had also returned to the château after release from hospital with instructions to take things easy. Larousse ensured he followed doctor's orders.

Didier was enjoying the Ascension Islands aboard the luxury yacht whilst awaiting his orders, Larousse advised him to make haste for Marseille and return to the château. Chambers and Malhotra returned to normal duty with the Royal Navy and were to be honoured for their bravery.

An update also came through regarding Katriana's late boyfriend, Dieter Schaffer, the report showed he had complained to the university he had been attending, citing a worrying anomaly with some of the electronic equipment's description on the African Envoy IV cargo manifest, after inspection he had stated to an customs official it was described as being a simple computer server unit but appeared more likely a high-tech communications and satellite control system more powerful than he had ever encountered.

The university told him they would confer with the customs office and two days later, he was found to have suffered his fatal accident at Hamburg Docks. The Polizei had concluded it was just that, an accident. This, Larousse was informed, was now being looked into again by Interpol as an independent body.

Larousse was pleased to inform Katriana that Dieter was indeed an innocent victim most probably of the Reichsbürger plot. She was relieved and asked her father to make recompense to his family, he naturally agreed.

Pfeiffer is considering his position with the German Polizei. Prior to any decision, he visited Herr Mayr and asked if he could arrange to provide the old man with a carriage of some description as the original had no doubt been destroyed in the base.

Mayr agreed to do what he could but made no promises. Larousse was informed by Perzinski of Pfeiffer's situation and had offered him a position as part of his security section, he is considering the offer.

In the subsequent months, the contents of the numerous filing cabinets, boxes of paperwork salvaged from the tunnel plus the blueprints Robert had salvaged were being scrutinised by the German Polizei Anti-Terrorist Division, British MI6, The Pentagon and Interpol.

In a shock event on Wednesday, 7 December 2022, German Polizei and other officials stormed several addresses in a coordinated search and arrested 22 suspected "Reichsbürger" supporters across the country on suspicion of plotting the Federal government's overthrow.

Alleged members included a descendant of German royalty and former member of Germany's lower house of parliament, The Bundestag, plus all manner of high-ranking German citizens including Polizei and military figures; this investigation was ongoing, said German prosecutors and many local media reports.

***

As was the search for Max Wittenberg!

***

One positive outcome from those events in October 2022 was the fact Robert and Katriana remain together and remain truly in love, both François and Claire-Louise are delighted for them both.

Robert together with Larousse's contacts are having the properties of his souvenir piece of "super-steel" currently being investigated by NASA!

***

Robert still does not like flying!

***

The serene mood may change however as Max Wittenberg may soon be on the witch-hunt.!

***